Judy Budnitz

was born in 1973 and grew up in Atlanta, Georgia. She attended Harvard University, was a fellow at the Provincetown Fine Arts Work Center, and received an MFA in creative writing from New York University in 1998. As well as *If I Told You Once*, which was shortlisted for the Orange Prize, she is also the author of *Flying Leap*, an acclaimed collection of short stories which was a *New York Times* Notable Book of the Year. *Flying Leap* is also now available from Flamingo in paperback.

Further reviews overleaf

'Absorbing, bewitching… An incredibly enjoyable read.' *Big Issue*

'In her bold first novel… Budnitz's story unfolds with the edifying, cocoon-like mystery of a tale from the Brothers Grimm… A powerful telling of the immigrant experience.' *Los Angeles Times*

'Folk tale, fable, and contemporary novel, *If I Told You Once* is a splendid example of what can happen when all of these elements come together in perfect harmony. What can and does happen, in fact, is a wonderfully rendered work of fiction by a talented writer. More than this, however, Judy Budnitz's debut novel affords the reader that rare ability to become transported into the world she has created – a priceless gift from author to reader.'
San Diego Union-Tribune

'Part dark fairy tale, part weird family history, *If I Told You Once* is altogether strange, inventive and ethereal.' *Washington Times*

'At the heart of Judy Budnitz's startlingly imaginative first novel lies the power of stories – the stories we hear, the stories we tell ourselves, the stories we recount to our children and hope they will pass on to theirs. *If I Told You Once* is built out of stories and driven by their ability to bind, enthrall, and occasionally sever generations within a single family.' *San Francisco Chronicle*

Also by Judy Budnitz:

FLYING LEAP

07463K

This book is to be returned on or before the last date stamped below.		
10/07 - 9 MAR 2009		

WITHDRAWN 31/5/21

Flamingo
An Imprint of HarperCollinsPublishers

Flamingo
An imprint of HarperCollinsPublishers
77–85 Fulham Palace Road,
Hammersmith, London W6 8JB

Flamingo is a registered trade mark of
HarperCollins Publishers Limited

www.**fire**and**water**.com

Published by Flamingo 2001
1 3 5 7 9 8 6 4 2

First published in Great Britain by
Flamingo 2000

First published in the USA by Picador USA 1999

Copyright © Judy Budnitz 1999

Judy Budnitz asserts the moral right to be
identified as the author of this work

Photograph of Judy Budnitz by © Victor Buhler

ISBN 0 00 655184 X

Set in Goudy

Printed and bound in Great Britain by
Clays Ltd, St Ives plc

For my grandparents,

Samuel and Phyllis Robbins

and

Max and Rose Budnitz

If I Told You Once

Ilana

My family had lived in the same village for as long as anyone could remember. It was a place that lay buried in snow for nine months out of the year followed by three months of mud. It was the most desolate spot on earth and my family did not even realize it, because for generations they never ventured more than forty kilometers from the place. They were stubborn people.

It was a place where someone had forgotten to add the color: low gray clouds, crooked houses of weather-beaten wood, coils of smoke rising up from cookstoves and rubbish heaps. All the wives of the village cut from the same dull cloth to make clothes for their families. We ate gray bread. The men made a fermented liquor so colorless it was invisible, nothing but a raging headache stoppered in a jar.

People were simpler then. They kept their desires within reach. They had few possessions: a goat, a half-dozen chickens, a brass teapot, a cat so ugly it could kill mice merely by looking at them.

That was enough. After days cutting wood in the black forest with ice clogging their nostrils, the smell of a goat was a welcome thing.

In a place like that, the color of an egg yolk was something of a miracle.

My people were a clutching, clinging people. They had to be.

What little they had, someone was always trying to snatch away.

I was born in violent times.

I am told I was a breach birth. My mother was in labor for more than thirty hours. I was her first child. All through her labor a winter storm ripped shingles from the roof. My father wanted to go for the midwife, but the violence of the storm kept him in. He could hear the evil spirits in the wind waiting to trick him, lead him in endless circles in the snow. People had been known to freeze to death just meters from their homes after getting lost on their way to the out-house. My father paced in an agony of frustration.

In those times childbirth was the realm of midwives and women-friends. Men were forbidden to witness it, they were bad luck; they were kept out of the birthing room, often out of the house altogether. My mother writhed and moaned on the bed while my father stumped from window to window, caged and frantic. The house had only one room. He crouched in corners, tried to make himself invisible.

As the storm grew worse, so did my mother's pains. My father put his fingers in his ears but could not bear it any longer. He went to the bedside and found my mother thrashing and screeching like one possessed, her long hair pasted to her face in sweaty scribbles. He knelt and rolled his sleeves, he put his blunt hands tentatively on her belly; he nudged and prodded, thinking he could shift the little body into position the way he did with unborn lambs. He tried to look only at the tight belly, not at my mother's hectic face, her fingers tearing at his shirt, the pulpy strangeness between her legs. He pushed. Something burst with a wet pop. The bed was suddenly soaked with hot blood and my mother screamed with renewed vigor.

Just then there came a knock at the door.

The midwife! my father thought with relief, and flung the door open.

Two heavy figures filled the doorway and half a dozen more dark-ened the snow behind them. The men were shapeless in snow-stiffened clothes, their faces wrapped against the wind. But my father knew them immediately and his heart froze. He knew by their fur hats, the knives in their belts, their rank smell of raw meat and stolen horses. They were the bandits who haunted the black forests and roadways. They attacked indiscriminately, rich and poor alike.

The bandit leader slouched in the doorway as snow swirled past him into the room. He held out his hands, stepped closer to my father, smiled at him through his face-wraps.

Greetings, neighbor, he said, we wondered if you might extend your hospitality to such weary travelers as ourselves.

My father stood out of the wind, in the shadow cast by the door.

The bandit leader pulled his knife from its sheath, casually wiped it on his sleeve, and said: You wouldn't turn anyone away on a night like this, would you? That would be too cruel, wouldn't it?

He cocked his head; his ferrety eyes sought out my father's. His band crowded closer. Their smell swept into the room like a foul breath.

Then my father stepped full into the light. He stood drenched in sweat, shirt torn, his beard standing up on his face in wild tufts, eyes bulging, and his arms wet to the elbows with blood. My mother's squeals flew about him in a fury, a windstorm of shrieks and venom.

He held his hands out to them. Gentlemen, he said softly, as soon as I finish killing my wife, I will be glad to oblige you.

They looked at the blood, his crazed eyes, the scratches my mother's nails had left on his chest. But it was my mother's wrenching, inhuman cries that drove them back out into the storm.

I was born soon after, I slid out feet first and blue, the umbilical cord looped around my throat. Later people said it was an evil omen and I was destined for the gallows. My father caught me up, a slimy horrible thing, and shook me frantically like a defective toy until I screamed in indignation.

My mother, who had more right than anyone to call me an evil omen, instead declared that I was a lucky child, twice blessed and twice stubborn, destined to make my own way in the world.

Later she would go on to bear eight more children. At the start of her labors my father would walk seven kilometers into the forest and cut wood for hours, until my mother sent me to tell him it was safe to come home.

They loved each other very much, my parents. But love was different then. People didn't talk about it, didn't even think of the word, but it was there in every mouthful of food they shared. It was a simple thing, certain, it needed no discussion. Certain as blowing out a candle. Do you need to discuss whether the room will be dark?

My father was an enormous bearish man, hairy and dark, with a beard that enveloped half his face and seemed to trap more food than reached his mouth. People used to say that if my father got lost in the woods, he could survive two months or more with his beard to sustain him. My mother was small, less than half his size. She wore endless skirts and petticoats that billowed around her and made her seem as wide as she was tall. The skirts disguised her figure so completely that she looked the same whether she was nine months pregnant or not at all.

My growing-up years were a dark time. The bandits lurked in the woods. The timber wolves came down from the north. They mated for life and hunted in pairs; they were the size of calves, with ice-blue eyes. They were temperamental as children. Sometimes they came right into our yards, playing like puppies; other times they could snap a man's leg in their jaws with no provocation. They were not pack wolves; they cared only for their mates and pups. In times of hunger she-wolves had been known to eat the pups of other wolves to gain the strength to nurse their own.

And there were bands of soldiers, too, who raided the villages periodically. They were more unpredictable than the wolves: they might demand livestock, or liquor, they might set homes ablaze for the sake of warming their hands, to melt the frost off their spurs. They took the young men off for the army, dragged them away in carts as the mothers ran alongside screaming good-byes to their sons and heaping curses on the soldiers. Such men were never heard from again.

Sometimes the bandits attacked the soldiers and stole their military boots and jackets for themselves. Sometimes the soldiers wore shaggy fur cloaks to keep out the cold. Sometimes the wolves walked on their hind legs like men.

In the dark they were indistinguishable from one another.

Once a week during the long winters people crowded into the village meetinghouse to pray. We were not particularly fervent; we came for the change of scene. People said that being trapped in one room with the same family members for months on end could drive a person mad.

People liked to tell of one couple who lived in the village before I was born. The two were newlyweds, and they decided to avoid the weekly services and live out the winter with no one but each other. They spent the entire cold season sitting side by side on the same bench before the fire. They stayed there so long they grew together, flesh to flesh. Like rolls running together in the oven, their skins melted and became one. When the spring came, they could not fit themselves through the door. People who peeked through their windows saw a single broad, monstrous figure scuttling madly about the room, sideways like a crab, the two faces cleaved cheek to cheek, the hands grabbing at bits of food and stuffing them indeterminately in either mouth, the hair of both heads grown together in an impenetrable mass.

All the men and women of the village came together. They broke down the wall of the little house, dragged the couple into the street. Eleven men and an ax were required to pry the two apart. There was blood in the snow and screaming. When the man found himself free he spun himself around three times and staggered off into the forest, bloody and torn down his left side. He was never seen again.

The woman stayed in the village. Her screams eventually faded to a constant low muttering, but she was never again whole. Her right arm and leg atrophied; she hobbled on a crutch. People took pity on her, they brought her firewood and rags. She dug clay from a corner of her yard and made soup from it. When I was a child I saw her often, wandering the forest or the village streets, singing and gathering stones, checking over her shoulder every few paces as if expecting someone. She was harmless, and some said holy.

When I was three my mother gave birth to my brother Ari.

He arrived in a snowstorm, as I did. The women say he crept from the womb unaided, took air without crying. They looked at the two bony knobs on his forehead, the wiry hair on his legs, and said he was a changeling, a goblin child. The women drew back from the bed, covering their mouths with their hands and pulling their skirts tight about them. They feared the changeling spirit would corrupt their bodies as well. The midwife, who was past child-bearing age, wrapped the baby tightly and volunteered to carry him deep into the woods and leave him there. This was the practice in such cases, so that in the night the forest imps could take the child underground to his rightful home.

But my mother frowned and held the baby's head to her breast. Stroking the thick dark hair, she said she would do the chore herself. She could not be dissuaded; as soon as the storm slackened she left me in the care of my father. Weak and bowlegged from her labor, she waddled into the forest.

My mother returned two days later, with the child asleep in her shawl. She was pale and resolute and my father did not question her. He held her in complete awe. Also he was glad to relinquish his responsibilities. My father could kill timber wolves with a wooden club or face down outlaws, but the cries of a three-year-old child drove him to distraction.

People said Ari seemed unchanged by the excursion, except that he had grown three teeth. My mother never offered an explanation but resumed her work and nursed the child without a word. No one dared confront her; she was known throughout the village for her fierceness. Rumors spread that she had marched into the forest and demanded an audience with the goblin king himself, then haggled with him relentlessly, as if he were a shopkeeper, until he agreed to exchange the goblin child for an identical human one.

Ari was quick to crawl but slow to walk. As he grew he loved to watch dancing and the fall of my father's ax. He loved hair—he liked to pluck out bits of my father's beard or the hair on his arms. Ari early developed a taste for raw meat. He infuriated my mother by sneaking raw scraps from the storeroom, and trying to sink his teeth into chickens before they had stopped twitching.

I grew up slowly. In that place many things grew slowly, the cold caused plants and people alike to shrink, contract, conserve their energy. My brother Ari soon grew taller than me, but his size was a liability; he was constantly hungry and cried through the night. My mother nursed him until the third child was born, and then she put him to sleep with me. At first I let him suck on my fingers, for comfort, but I soon discovered the sharpness of his teeth. He gnawed in his sleep. So I went down to the river and found smooth stones for him to suck, and he liked that. I gave him stones that I thought were too large for him to choke on, but I would sometimes wake up late at night and hear him crunching and swallowing them, his baby face smooth and serene.

As Ari grew older his forehead lost some of its knobbiness; he had my father's strength and black hair. He was quick in his movements, but slow in speech. When people spoke to him, when he demanded explanations, I was the one to help him. He seemed to understand the words better in my voice.

My parents were constantly on the lookout for the soldiers who tried for years to catch my father and force him into the army. He was older than the usual conscripts, but famous for his strength. My parents knew that if he were taken away it was likely he would never return. Whenever soldiers came into the village searching for him, he would have liked to meet them with his fists, but my mother subjected him to her methods instead. She hid him: under the eaves, in a feather bed, in a rain barrel, once in her own voluminous skirts. When the soldiers came to call that day they found her placidly sewing beside the fire. After they left my father rolled from beneath her skirts gasping for air. He was flushed and embarrassed by his proximity to her legs; he fled the house, shamefaced. In those days people were intimate only at night, in darkness, under the covers and in the strictest privacy.

So my father evaded conscription year after year, and my mother produced more children, at yearly intervals. Practiced at labor, she learned to predict the time of birth and would lie darning stockings, peeling potatoes, until the last possible moment. My father had to add on to the house to make room for the children. He built us a

7

kind of shed in the backyard, as if we were livestock. We slept on hay.

My mother taught me to knit and crochet, she taught me her knowledge of roots and herbs: plants for sickness, for cleansing, for visions. Ari was my constant companion. He was monstrously strong for his age, but thoughtless; he crashed into walls, tumbled down wells. Wherever he went in the village I had to accompany him to keep him from damaging our neighbors' property. When I saw him reaching out to touch geese or lambs I had to grab him by the ear and pull him away. Soon he grew so large that when I did this he could jerk me off my feet by shaking his head.

People in the village whispered that he had a tail like an ox rolled up inside his trousers. I had seen no such tail when he was a baby; but then perhaps it sprouted when he entered adolescence, which began early in him. The villagers' gossip did not affect him, but when my mother scolded he buried his head in her skirts and howled.

He often went on rampages in the forest. We did not know what he did there; he would disappear for hours and return with his hair full of burrs, his clothes in shreds, a brown crust on his lips, peaceful.

Only once did I lose my temper with him. It was one evening as I sat mending his padded jacket for the tenth time in as many days. The fire was low, and I pricked my finger again and again, and the hay padding was full of the small creatures my brother liked to collect, they rustled and squeaked horribly. Finally I flung the jacket at him, as he squatted humming in his usual corner, and cried: What is *wrong* with you? Have you no sense at all? Why can't you act like other people?

He hugged the jacket to him, rocked back and forth on his heels humming in the back of his throat and staring glassy-eyed into the fire. My mother looked up sharply from the child she was nursing and said: There's nothing wrong with him, he's perfect, he belongs here. The look on her face, as she stroked Ari's hair and held the child to her breast, made me feel I was the strange one.

· · ·

When I was twelve my father killed a she-wolf and my mother sewed the hide into a cape for me. The wolf's head made the hood, with the ears still intact; the front legs draped my shoulders, the tail dragged on the ground. It was a heavy, coarse thing with a rank smell, but it was warm.

That winter my mother sent me out often to gather the medicinal plants that grew under the snow. She could not go herself, she was expecting her fifth child and could not bend. So I put on the fur hood and spent hours in the woods. The trees there were dark skinned, broad limbed; even without their leaves they blocked the sunlight so that the forest was dim even at noon. The air was always deathly still except for the hush and slide of shifting snow, the trees moaning softly in the wind.

Each time I went I pushed deeper into the forest. I kept my ears pricked for the muffled crunch of footsteps in the snow. I hung a drawstring bag around my neck, crawled on my knees, and dug through the snow with my bare hands to find the plants my mother requested. My fingers grew red while my back and arms ran with sweat. I dug, warmed my hands in my armpits, dug again.

One afternoon as I knelt resting with my hands inside my blouse I heard a branch snap. It was early yet, but the light in the forest was like dusk, the snow glowed intensely blue. I had the sense of trees crowding around on all sides as if watching.

Ho there, young lady, said a voice.

I glanced around, pushed back my hood, and looked up. I saw dangling boots. A man sat perched on a branch high above my head. I wanted to run, but my knees were locked from kneeling in the cold so long, and I couldn't move.

He said: It's a lovely day, isn't it? and smiled.

I stared. I knew he was a bandit, I could tell by his clothes, and the soft leather boots that came to his knees. The people in my village swaddled themselves against the cold, they wrapped themselves in layers of wool and burlap. But this man was dressed in clothes that cleaved to his body, tight trousers and short jacket, leaving his arms and legs free. He lounged there loose limbed and catlike.

You've been quite busy, haven't you? he said.

I managed to stand up. Now I could see his face more clearly. It was a clean-shaven, sharp-featured face, blotched red and white from the cold. He smiled; there was something strained in the smile, in the way the sore-chapped lips stretched back from the teeth. His eyes were extraordinarily bright and piercing, I had never seen anything like them, little chips of ice in his face; even from that distance I could feel them drilling at me. His hair lay over his brow in long heavy tangles.

He looked so foreign to me; I had seen so few young men in my life. In my village adolescent boys were forced into the army the moment they began to lose their boyish figures, and the older men were like my father: bearded and barrel-chested with hair in their noses.

He tossed his head like a horse to shake the hair from his face. I saw the hunting knife in its sheath slung across his chest. I longed to run, my throat ached with it; but I could not look away from him, I was painfully fascinated by him, as by a mad dog, so that I was afraid to turn my back on him even to run away.

What have you got there, young lady? he said. His voice was the strangest thing of all, as if what he said was not at all what he meant. My knees creaked. I showed him the dirt-colored mushroom in my palm.

Give it here, he said. I gave it a toss; he swung out and caught it. I looked at him in that moment, stretched against the sky. I saw the straining cords of his throat, the delicate underside of jawbone.

I thought: he should wear a scarf, he will catch cold.

He held the mushroom between thumb and forefinger, inspected it with disgust.

What's it for? he asked.

I could feel myself flushing.

Speak up he said, what will happen to me if I eat it?

It is for easing your birthing pains, I whispered.

He barked a short laugh, then said, I'll keep it, since you found it near my tree. It's my favorite tree, you see, because it has a face like my old granny. Do you see her nose, where that branch is broken off, and these two knotholes are eyes, and the rotted hollow down below just like her pruned-up mouth. Come closer and look. Come closer, I said.

I had never thought about things in such a way before, but suddenly when he described the face I could see it, as if something hidden had been swiftly revealed by his words, and I realized with a kind of sickening jolt that there was more than one way of seeing the world.

Since you gave me this, I should give *you* something in trade, he said. He slipped his hand into his shirt, pulled something out, and dropped it carelessly in the snow.

I should not have picked it up, but I did. It was shaped like an egg, but covered in stones that glittered like fire and ice, and shiny metal etched with tiny curling designs like lace. It glowed there in my cupped hands. I had never seen such colors before in my life.

Look inside, he said.

I peered into the peephole at the small end of the egg and saw a walled city with turnip-shaped towers, a garden, a sparkling frozen fountain, a domed sky full of stars.

Oh, I said. I raised it to my eye again. Such green, such gold, such unearthly blue. When I looked up at him once more the outside world had gone dull.

You like it, do you? he said. He was cleaning his nails with a knife as long as his forearm.

I nodded. His eyes moved in his face like insects.

Aren't you a pretty girl? he said.

No, I said. I was not being insolent. I did not understand what he meant. In my village we knew only big and small, strong and weak, alive and dead. Any further distinctions were unnecessary.

Ha, he said. The pink tongue curled around his teeth.

Suddenly he straightened and slid the knife in its sheath. He reached into his shirt for the mushroom and with one smooth movement threw it far into the trees, so far I could not hear it land.

Look at that, he said. I seem to have lost your mushroom.

I saw the muscles tensing up beneath his trousers; the branch creaked a warning.

I suppose, he said, to be fair, you ought to give me something else.

I saw him preparing to leap. I spun and ran.

I staggered wildly, panting, limping on my stiff knees; I ran in a nightmare, the air thick as water, the afternoon light dying moment by moment. My breath crashed so loud in my ears I could hear nothing; I stumbled, fell, gathered up an armful of skirts and flailed on. I glanced over my shoulder expecting to see him just behind me, laughing with his little pointed teeth.

But he was not. I was light enough to run on the hard upper crust of snow, but the man had broken through it with his leap. I could see him far in the distance, wallowing and thrashing waist-deep in soft snow. Faintly I could hear his curses.

I ran home breathless, dragging my heavy soaked clothes. My mother looked at my slick face and asked what was the matter. I told her about the man in the forest, the tree like a face, his leap from the sky.

I did not tell her about the egg.

The egg! I should have flung it away when I ran, but I had been too frightened to think. So I kept it in my pocket, told no one; it was my first secret.

My mother knit her brow. She warned me not to tell my father. His solution would be to go bellowing off to the bandits' camp in the woods, swinging his fists, cursing and brawling until they cut him to pieces.

She told me she would take care of it and said nothing further. Late that night I heard a stirring in the house. I crept to the window and saw her in the moonlight, waddling heavily toward the dark trees.

A week later she told me to go back to the forest to finish gathering the plants she needed. Her time was near. I did not want to go, I looked at her pleadingly, but she brushed me away and told me it was all right.

So I dressed as before and trudged back to the forest. The sky was dark and lowering, thick clouds scurried across the sky as if fleeing something just over the horizon. I jumped at every noise; darkness seemed to tease at the corners of my eyes. I did not want to go there, and yet I went there, I was drawn back to the same place I had been before, drawn by a kind of dread and a dreadful curiosity.

I approached the familiar tree. I saw a dark shape in the snow at its base and hesitated. It did not move. An abrupt hush fell over the woods, no wind stirred. I paused in my tracks and then a horrible cawing rose up all around me as hundreds of black crows launched themselves from the surrounding trees and took to the air. There were hundreds of them, flapping in their clumsy way like black rags jerked aloft on strings, beaks open with their harsh croaking. I felt droppings splatter on my cheek. I knew crows liked to travel alone or in pairs, they were not flocking birds.

Their cries faded away. I reached the tree and there, in a trampled place beneath its branches, lay my bandit. I knelt beside him. His throat was torn open. The blood had frozen before it dried; bright red smears colored the snow. I could study him closely now. His eyes were open and congealing; the irises were green, they looked crystallized, faceted, hard as glass. The skin on his face was smooth. I could not have said how old he was.

His hair fell back from his brow as if he had tossed his head back a moment before. His body lay stretched out loosely, as if he were napping, but all was cold and hard. His lip turned up; he seemed to be smiling. I could not be sure that he was dead. In that winter country the cold slowed the dying just as it slowed the living.

I learned later that my mother had gone to the forest at night carrying the scent glands from the she-wolf my father had killed; she had used them to leave wolf scent on all the trees in the area. This drew the she-wolf's grieving mate, he came following the smell and seeking her; and as he nosed about whimpering like a child at the roots of trees, smelling her scent and unable to find her, he must have looked in the uncertain dusky light like something he was not.

Perhaps to someone sitting in the trees above, he might have looked like a girl, kneeling, dressed in fur. Perhaps he had looked like me.

Imagine him jumping down.

The man and the wolf must both have been disappointed to see each other.

I sat a long time in the snow, looking at the face, holding the sparkling cold hand of a man preserved in ice; and for the first time I saw that I was not of that country, I did not have my mother's fierceness in me, I did not have that fierceness of love that had kept my family alive for generations in that harsh place. It was a blind devotion, a vicious bloody animal love, and I wanted no part of it; for the first time I knew that I would leave.

I feared my mother, who pushed out child after child with her athletic loins, and seemed to grow stronger with each one, and clung to her children more tightly with each passing year. I grew in secret. I waited.

There were three of them.

They were always there, in the village where I grew up. With their milky eyes and incessant hissing, their hands tugging at invisible strings and weaving them all together.

Three old women.

They sat in a row on a single bench in the center of the village. Three women with the same face. People said they were sisters, or mother and daughters, cousins, no one knew for sure. In winter they huddled in their shawls with snow up to their knees. In summer the flies hung back from them at a respectful distance.

They had the same face, skin delicate with age, soft and threatening to tear like wet paper. The same face three times over, same violet-colored eyes sunk in purple-veined pouches of skin. People said if you watched closely you'd see them blink and breathe in unison. The pulses beating together in their temples.

In their hair insects wove their cocoons and greasy silk tents.

They had the same face but different mouths. One woman had an overabundance of teeth, two rows of them, overlapping each other like shingles. Another had no teeth at all, and a mouth that seemed to lead nowhere, a shallow wet impression in her face. The third had only one tooth. It was three inches long and pointed, a long yellow tusk, protruding from the corner of her mouth like a crafty cigar.

They worked as they jabbered. They sewed in unison, as if one brain led their six hands. One would unspool the thread, the second would measure it, the third would cut it. Or they would knit, weaving their way inward from three different directions, meeting in the middle to make sweaters designed for hunchbacks or armless giants. They could pluck a chicken in a matter of seconds, their hands swarming over the limp body like ants.

We had forgotten their names and were embarrassed to ask. They never moved from their bench. Their debris—the feathers, the ends of thread, the wads of phlegm they coughed up and spat into bits of paper, the crusts of bread—piled up around them year after year. Some said they were the grandmothers, or great-grandmothers or great-aunts, of everyone in the village. No one could remember. Their faces were indistinct with age, their features had run together like melted wax; no eyebrows, noses flattened and ridgeless, earlobes stretched long.

Talking, gossiping. Day and night.

Their voices were identical, and shrill, birds scolding. They interrupted and spoke over each other, a sharp irritating music, almost in harmony. Sometimes sweet and wet, mixed with harshness, like the sound of a mother crooning a lullaby to her child and bickering with her husband between verses.

They were telling each other stories, those three. Telling each other everything that had ever happened since time began.

We did not like to go near them. But still we could feel their eyes, hear their hissing and know they were speaking of us. The words they said would sound familiar, as if they had been eavesdropping on our dreams.

They recounted their version of history for anyone who would listen. We did not like to listen. We tried to ignore them, or drown them out. They spoke of things too terrible to bear. Like a mother who needs to forget the pain of childbirth so that she can go on to bear more children, the people I lived among needed to forget so they could go on.

The three women wove together threads of dark brown and red-gold and black; they were the hairs of everyone in the village, people said. We all felt the tug. We felt it when hesitating at a crossroads, we would feel a pressure on our scalps, and then later we would blame our decisions, good or bad, on the three women whom we thought of as witches or saints but were careful to never dignify with a spoken name.

I dreamt of them sometimes, and woke with my hands pressed to my ears.

There came a time when they began to speak, more vehemently than before, about a darkness rising up, a dark tide turning and coming to wash over us. Of atrocities beyond our comprehension, bodies piled high as haystacks, blood flowing like rivers through the streets, fire that would roll across the earth, blotting out the sun and making everything black. They spoke urgently of these things, gesturing, their spit flying in our faces.

But we ignored them, we told ourselves the darkness they spoke of was merely the next nightfall, or their own encroaching senility and approaching deaths which we secretly hoped for, to be rid of them. They're mad, we said. Don't listen, we told each other.

And it happened that it all came to pass, everything, just as they had said, with biblical accuracy. By then I had left the village, I had sought to escape their wagging tongues, the tugging of their crabbed fingers, the gossip they told of a future that was written, sealed, inescapable. As irrevocable as the past.

I told you so, they must have said when everything did come to pass. When the walls came down and the fire burst forth and the people raised their hands above their heads in supplication and swayed like a field of wheat in the wind.

I was not there to hear their voices ring out yet I heard the words anyway, those words followed me long afterward like a shadow, a slug trail, a mocking school yard chant: I told you so I told you so I told you so.

My mother taught me everything she knew, and for a long time I thought it was all I would ever need to know.

I sometimes saw the mother-love in her face, that animal fierceness, when she gathered my brothers and sisters to her, crushing them against her belly as if she wanted to swallow them whole. I saw it in her when they fell ill with fevers, when they were late coming home and she scanned the darkening forest for them, calling their names like a holy summons.

I saw it when Ari came to her and lay his head in her lap, his legs folded beneath him like a dog's, nuzzling against her. She could trace his wanderings by the scars on his back. I saw how she wanted to fold her wings over him, conceal him, though he was bigger than she was.

That smell of his when he came back from the woods. The crust beneath his long yellow nails. He was unnatural.

I knew better than to say anything more about it in front of my mother.

Our neighbors came complaining of him, of animals he had fondled and stroked so roughly they collapsed. My mother looked at them and said: He's only a child, he knows not what he does.

Some of the neighbors gave up when they saw my mother's stubborn chin. But others persisted, pounding on our door every evening, demanding restitution. One called: Send your son over to pull my plow, seeing as how he killed my donkey. My mother ignored them, though their pounding made the bowls of soup jump on the table. Nails popped from the walls.

Those neighbors who persisted woke up several mornings later to find their beds infested with fat white worms, worms that burrowed into the crevices of their bodies as if seeking warmth. The worms bored into the flesh of their legs and bellies, as if they were corpses, leaving oozing tunnels to mark their progress.

They stopped bothering us; I suppose they decided to take their complaints elsewhere.

My mother instructed me to watch when she next gave birth. The cold room gradually grew hot as a furnace from the heat of her body and the windows steamed up. It was strange to see her lying down, splayed out like an overturned beetle. Her hair escaped her braid, it clung to her face and the bedclothes and wrapped itself around my hands as I wiped the sweat on her face.

She glared at me. I can wipe my own face, she said. I don't need you *here*, I need you *there*, to see what I can't.

I did not want to, but I lifted her skirt; she had not even undressed, she had stopped her sweeping only moments before. Her breath gusted through the room, lifted the hair from my damp forehead.

I saw her legs which I had never seen before and they looked just like mine, thin with knobby knees, fine dark hairs. Then I looked between her legs, and that was a sight.

It was something swollen, juicy, turned inside out. I thought I saw the scar, the place where her flesh had torn when I was born and then grown together again. I felt guilty for the damage I had done her. She was straining at the seams. I could see already the bulge of a skull, mottled white, a tracing of veins under skin, pushing outward larger and larger like a boil about to burst.

Remember, remember, this is what it is like, I told myself over and over, and I saw my mother's hand tighten into a fist, heard her breath catch and crackle in her throat, and then the head came out, followed by the anticlimactic scrawny body, soft limp arms and legs, smeared with blood and white scum, and I took it, and shook it, and it screamed, and my mother sighed.

It was another girl.

My mother was up and at the stove within hours, feeding the other children, smiling at my father, her breasts hanging heavy and leaking dampness on her dress.

I said I would never have children. Said it to myself.

Soon after that, red wetness bloomed for the first time like poppies in my underclothes.

I was terrified, I did not know what it meant; I thought of my mother giving birth, the blood, the bulbous baby's head nudging its way out of her body. The smell of blood, her smell and mine, was the same.

I thought of a baby coming out of me, a small one, perhaps the size of a rat, or a sparrow. Somehow I was certain it would be dark, hairy like Ari, with a wrinkled ancient face and tiny needle-sharp teeth. It would have whiskers, claws; it would gnaw disappointedly at my nipples which still lay flat on my chest, it would cling to me like a monkey. I imagined it crying, that abrasive baby-cry that cannot be ignored, but I also heard it berating me, in a deep petulant voice like the voices of our neighbors complaining. Can't a man get a decent meal around here? it would say, pinching my breast with pygmy fingers.

I could already feel the thing moving inside me, shifting and cramping in my lower belly. How did it get there? I did not want it. I refused. I bent, clamped my legs together. I would not let it out. I would hold it inside me until it smothered. No one would know.

I folded myself small, I thought I was invisible, but my mother saw me crouched against the wall and asked what my trouble was.

I'm going to have a baby, I told her.

Her eyes widened, her lips drew back from her teeth. She said: How do you know? Did you meet someone else in the forest?

I told her about the little man I could feel trying to scratch his way out. I told her about the blood dripping. Just like yours, I said.

I see, she said.

She did not laugh at me. She explained to me what it was and why, and then she told me how to make a child, and how to unmake a child right after it has been made, and how to keep from making a child in the first place.

I was not as stupid as you must think. For years I had watched animals do it. But for some reason I had thought people were different from animals.

I don't know how I could have thought so. Look at my mother.

Look at Ari. Look at my father, toiling in endless circles like the ox hitched to the millstone.

But then I thought of the dead man in the woods, the man made of ice, his skin blue and white, his delicate features and shattered eyes. He was different, I thought; and inside his egg I thought I saw a picture of life more refined, more considered, a world where people had found a way to distinguish themselves from animals, a difference far beyond a two-legged stance or a knack for forks and spoons.

I wanted to find my way there.

My grandmother and grandfather lived in a one-room house within sight of ours. I did not know how old my grandmother was. She did not know herself.

She and my grandfather were so accustomed to each other that a single word or gesture between them carried the meaning of whole conversations. They had shared a pillow for so long they had begun to look alike. They even seemed to have exchanged some of their aspects. My grandfather's hair was long and white and hung in ringlets like a schoolgirl's. My grandmother had once had hair like that. Now it was nearly gone, it covered her head in a thin soft down and she had a man's thick strong hands.

Their trade was the preparation of leather, and it seemed the chemicals they used to preserve the animal hides had worked to preserve their skin as well.

My grandmother had taught my mother her knowledge of herbs. Sometimes they went gathering together. My grandmother always walked first and my mother followed behind her, placing her feet in the prints my grandmother had made in the snow. When I went with them I walked behind my mother, stepping in the footprints that my grandmother had made and my mother had deepened.

I remember that my grandfather had a high ridged nose, narrow and red. My grandmother always washed his feet for him, every evening before they went to sleep. His circulation was so slow that he could no longer feel it, but she performed the nightly ritual anyway. It had become a habit.

My grandfather died suddenly one day in spring, simply froze up at the table, spoon in midair, soup dripping from his chin. Wipe your mouth, my grandmother told him sharply. It was the first complete sentence she had spoken to him in twenty years.

What, do you mean to say you don't like it? my grandmother asked when he did not move.

After all these years? Too salty? she asked. Why didn't you tell me, she said and the tears began to trickle down her face and that was how we discovered them hours later, salty soup and tears dripping down their faces and plinking back in their bowls with a sound like rain.

My mother brought my grandmother to live in the house with us. Our house did not seem to agree with her; she spent her time running around the kitchen and yard barefoot in her nightgown, hurling stones and insults at imaginary foes. She's grieving, she misses your grandfather, my mother told me. She's ill, my mother said. But I had seen my grandmother lift my father's ax and hack chunks out of the walls of our house. She did not seem sick at all, she was stronger than ever.

My father tried to keep her shut in the house, for her own protection. She scampered about the rafters and kept company with the rooster. She told the rooster long garbled stories as she stroked his red drooping comb. Stories of how she had been forced to marry at the age of nine; stories of her nineteen children and the deaths of eleven of them.

That's not true, is it? She's making it up, isn't she? I asked my mother.

How would you know? my mother sniffed. Were you there?

My grandmother became afraid of the floor and would not leave her perch in the rafters. My mother tossed food up to her. My grandmother hoarded bread and kept the rooster tucked beneath her arm, sometimes vanishing for days at a time in dark places under the eaves.

One evening she unexpectedly descended, went to the door, and released the rooster. He misses his flock, she announced and watched him strutting and preening in the yard for a long while before she joined us at the table. She perched on a chair and I saw that her toes had grown as long and grasping as a monkey's.

She looked at me then, seized my fist in her own, and said: You don't believe me now, but one day you will. You'll see. You'll see what it's like.

I pretended I did not know what she meant, though I did. Apparently she had missed nothing from her perch above our heads. I tried to talk of other things and drown her out.

She spoke calmly and lucidly all evening and helped scrape the dishes, and afterward she stretched out on the table to sleep, declaring that a hard bed was best for an old back.

I slept with my hands over my ears that night to shut out her snores.

The next morning we woke to find that she had barricaded herself into a corner of the room. She had taken her cache of bread, stale, weeks old, hard as stone, and stacked the loaves up like bricks all around her.

We could hear her within, the tiniest of breaths.

We tried to dismantle her cairn, chipped away at the hard gray bread for hours.

By the time we reached her she was no longer breathing, just a curled-up mass of arms and legs, a dry husk. Clutched in her lap we found the rooster, his claws clenched in her nightgown, one red eye frozen and empty.

It was a winter years later when I made my decision. I must have been about sixteen then, I think, about your age. My mother and I were wringing wet clothes, hanging them out to dry in the cold air, my mother hugely pregnant as usual. Snow gritty as dust stung our faces. I saw her pause, sniff her fingers, then inhale deeply. She looked around wildly and ran. She had smelled the gunpowder stink of approaching soldiers.

We followed, my brothers and sisters and I. We were all so occupied with helping our mother hide our father that we neglected Ari.

We forgot Ari, so the first thing the soldiers saw when they entered the village was my brother tearing a live sheep apart with his bare hands, not for sport but simply out of his rough love.

The soldiers on their recruiting mission had heard rumors of a boy with impossible brutelike strength, and they had searched far and wide for him. Though nothing was said about it we knew it was our disgruntled, worm-racked neighbors who must have told them where to find him.

The soldier captain watched Ari rip the sheep piece from piece, till it was nothing but bloody meat, and then Ari laid the pieces out, carefully lined them up. He was trying to put the animal back together, licking his fingers and crooning, cramming the limbs back into their sockets, breathing into the nostrils, trying to divine the clockwork that made it all move and bleat.

The captain watched, and his eyes gleamed; he clapped his hands, one of which was made of wood. His company of soldiers circled, and they wrapped my brother in iron chains which on his massive wrists and throat looked like flimsy jewelry, and they loaded him bawling into a cart to take him away to hone his special skills for the grand art of war, or so they said, and they tossed the chunks of sheep in after him, hoping to quiet him.

My mother ran from the house and chased after the departing cart, flinging curses at the soldiers, heaping them tenfold on their heads. The soldiers leaned down and jeered at her, with her swollen belly and waddling run. She spat at them, and one leaned down and dealt her such a blow that she fell in the mud and went into premature labor, right there in the street, before the eyes of all the men in the village.

For a single man to witness a birth was bad luck; for all the village men to witness it was such a bad omen that all the ensuing trouble that later befell the village was heaped on my mother; everyone said she was to blame for all that happened after and the village women never spoke to her again.

When all these things happened I knew it was time to leave.

· · ·

Once upon a time, on a night when the houses lay buried to the eaves in snowdrifts and bits of ice danced on the wind, I left my village intending never to return.

Earlier that evening I had gone to bed in the back room with my brothers and sisters as usual. The others sighed and slept. I felt the warmth leave my fingers and feet.

I listened to my parents in their room. The bed frame creaked as my father sank down on it. I could picture him, his feet hanging off the end of the frame, head tipped back and the coarse beard sticking straight up.

Light seeped through the crack beneath their door. My mother was awake, I pictured her finishing some mending or nursing the latest child. She kept her hair covered during the day, and at night she put it in a single tight braid that reached past her waist in a thick, vicious-looking rope.

I listened to the sounds of the other room, my ears yearning toward the door: the whisper of candle flame, the creak of her chair, the chilling click of teeth as she bit off the thread. I hoarded the warm patch I had made in the sheets.

A strip of moonlight slanted through the window. I could see arms, fingers, ears: my younger brothers and sisters, sleeping in a heap like puppies. Some sucked their fingers as they slept; some sucked each other's fingers. I could not distinguish between them in the dimness.

Ari had been my dear one, my favorite. He had absorbed my attentions, and now he was gone. I missed his rank warmth. When he was restless in the night I used to stroke his head, his hair so thick I could not see his scalp when I parted the hair with my fingers. He always slept with his eyes half open, the whites glowing and shifting like iridescent fish. His back made a graceful curve as he lay on his side, he clenched his teeth in what might have been a smile; in the dark you could not see how the thick hair grew down low on his neck, ending in a point between his shoulder blades. He roamed in his dreams, legs twitching like a sleeping dog's. In the mornings when I drew the sheets back to air them I often found dry leaves, night crawlers, double-tailed insects waving their feelers in the sudden light.

I wondered where he slept now.

The wind thrashed around the house, the boards creaked; I heard the softest of breaths as my mother blew out the candle. One of my brothers cried out in his sleep: *Look out—the fire!* and then subsided. My father let out a businesslike grunt as he hoisted himself over my mother and began the task of creating yet another child. There came a sound I never heard from my mother during the day: a cooing, like mourning doves. The dim light from the window grew even softer; it began to snow.

It was falling thickly and steadily. It was the sort of snow that could hide a person's tracks completely in a matter of hours.

It was time to leave.

I dressed in underclothes, flannel petticoats, skirts, jackets, woolen stockings. My mother had knitted the stockings so tightly they could almost stand up by themselves. Last I put on the boots, which would have fit half the people in the village. The local cobbler made boots in only two sizes, for the sake of convenience.

I wrapped my head in a shawl. My brothers and sisters were quiet, their faces blissful in sleep. They lay in a tangle of curves and bulges, whorled shapes, like vines in the garden patch. I suppose they looked like me, their hair, their eyes, but I had never bothered to notice. For too long I had thought of them only as annoyances that asked impossible questions and demanded breakfast.

I dug beneath my mattress and pulled out my secret, the egg I had kept warm under my body for years. It was still as deep and glittering as ever, with the city inside: the pointed towers, the starry sky, the carriages pulled by white horses with feathered headdresses, footmen with velvet trousers and mustaches like wings. I thought I saw them move. Perhaps it was my breath.

I left by the window and set out, the air prickling my face, the snow swirling around, white clouds against a darker sky. I tried to step lightly, but my footsteps crunched rudely in the snow, like cows chewing.

I did not look back.

It was the only home I had ever known. I could feel it behind me, hunched and glowering, its shoulders frosted with snow.

I felt a cold breath on the back of my neck, a sharp twinge that ran down my spine. I tried to run, but like a dream my steps seemed to grow even slower as my heart raced.

I knew my mother was watching from the window.

Standing with her arms folded beneath her breasts, chin out, her braid swaying pendulously behind her. She was at the window, or perhaps she was in the yard, heedless and barefoot in the snow, her eyes raising the hairs on the back of my neck.

I could feel her drawing me to her; like a spider she was sending out her threads, I could feel their tug in the small of my back. They drew tauter with every step I took. I knew if I paused, those threads would tighten, they would snap me back, I would be pulled home gliding so smoothly over the snow like an errant sled.

Oh, how she pulled at my hair. My scalp smarted.

I knew she was rolling up her sleeves, stretching out her arms; she was pursing her lips kisslike to draw in such a breath that my clothes streamed out behind me; she was undulating her fingers in the entrancing way she used to hypnotize the chickens before she chopped off their heads.

I kept walking, I knew not to look back. My mother had taught me nearly everything she knew, so I knew what she was up to, I was wise enough not to look at her face.

And yet if she had called out my name then, I think I would have gone running back to bury my face in her lap. The warmth of her body through her clothes, a smell like fields of wheat. Her voice could do that.

But she did not call out. Perhaps she was too proud for that.

I forged on, forcing stiff marionette knees. Her eyes nipped at the backs of my legs so that I stepped faster, and faster. I glanced over my shoulder and saw that the village looked no bigger than the magic city inside my egg, and my mother was too small to be seen.

I was free of my mother at last. The threads snapped. I had beaten her. My body was my own; I felt something melt inside me, a hot jelly, sliding loose and shifting downward, pulsing. It was a frightening feeling, not unpleasant.

To the east, a faint glow paled and spread; the bare trees were thrown into stark black silhouettes against the paling sky. And I was very, very cold.

I tramped for hours as the snowfall abated. My nose and lips were numb, they were blunt stupid things stuck to my face; I wished I could knock them off the way you knock icicles from the eaves.

I thought of my mother. I supposed she had cursed me, cursed me the way I had seen her curse soldiers: with words too dangerous to utter aloud, so that she had to draw their shapes with her fingers in the air, with her own face carefully averted. The venom of her curses was so powerful it could sometimes rebound and scald her, like drops of boiling oil bouncing off the pan.

The thought of my mother's curses brought on a stitch in my side and a blurry, sticky cloud in my right eye.

I had no idea where I was going, I only knew I was lengthening the distance between myself and home. Between myself and a life like my mother's, a path worn deep in the dirt, a path packed so hard no grass could ever grow there, much less flowers.

I had never been outside my village, but I knew there were places that were different. I had glimpsed them in the egg, and in the words of the bandit in the woods. I thought of him, my bandit, with his sharp face and strange talk. I saw him lying in the snow, sunk deep as if in a feather mattress, his throat necklaced with blood and the marks of wolf's teeth.

After I had found him so, I went home and burned my wolf hood. It made an awful stink. My mother watched but said nothing.

I would never have to feel her eyes again.

The thought should have made me happy.

I walked on. Once I heard an ax biting into wood, echoing through the trees. It reminded me of my father. From the sound alone I could judge the weight of the ax. I hurried on.

Twilight was falling, swiftly creeping up behind me.

I told myself I would keep traveling until I found a city, a place like the one I had seen in the egg. I would give myself a new name, walk among a different sort of people. I wanted to walk slowly in gardens, carelessly snapping twigs off branches as I passed, tossing pebbles in a fountain, watching the surface of the water break apart and, quivering, come together again to show me my face. That seemed the most perfect kind of luxury.

I stuck my hands in my jacket pockets. They should have been empty. I had brought nothing.

And yet I drew from my pockets several chunks of bread, some large leathery mushrooms, a carved wooden comb.

Gifts from my mother. She must have known all along.

In another pocket I found a pouch filled with my mother's favorite herbs, the ones without names, dried and tied in bundles. There were plants like miniature trees, like tangled pubic hair, seaweed, bird feathers, crumpled paper. The smells rose up from the bag and fought each other.

My egg was knotted in my petticoat.

How stupid of me to think I could leave home without my mother knowing. She had known I would leave before I did. She had allowed me to leave. Perhaps she had watched, and tugged at me with her eyes merely to test my resolve. It seemed no matter how I tried to escape, I was still entangled in my mother's plans.

I saw her braid swinging.

I saw her figure plowing smoothly through the snow before me, as if she had cart wheels beneath her skirts instead of legs.

I walked for five days.

On the evening of the fifth day I saw smoke in the distance. As I came closer I came upon a village, not unlike the one I had left. I wanted to go to one of those houses, ask for a place to sleep. But

I couldn't; they were too familiar. I had the sensation that which-ever house I called at my mother would open the door. She'd fill the doorway, dusted with flour, sleeves rolled, arms folded, children clinging constantly to her skirts as if they'd been sewn there as ornaments.

So I skirted the village as night fell. I smelled bread baking.

How ugly the trees were now. Behind me the lights of the village glowed like warm embers.

Then, like a granted wish, I came abruptly to a clearing in the woods, and a small house with a peaked roof and smoke curling from two chimneys. A stone path led to the door, and I found myself knocking on it before I'd had a chance to think.

I could hear rustling inside, the crackle of fire. The doorstep on which I stood was worn, and the spot on the door where I'd rapped my knuckles was a silky smooth depression in the wood, as if count-less hands had knocked before me.

Yes? said a voice and the door opened slightly. I stared into eyes that were a disturbing yellow, lashless and unblinking.

She looked me up and down. The eyebrows rose in crafty peaks.

Are you in trouble? she asked sharply. She wore shoes tipped with iron.

I nodded.

Well then, she said briskly, come inside, though you should have known to come to the back door.

The room inside was small and familiar. Wooden chairs, a low bed, a stone floor. Bunches of herbs hung drying near the fire. A piece of knitting lay interrupted on a chair.

She helped me remove my clothes. What I had at first thought was a hat perched on her head was in fact a dense mass of silvery gray braids wound together, a huge round loaf of hair. Her hands were spotted with age.

She hung my clothes on a chair to dry and said: Why don't you sit and warm yourself for a minute? I opened my mouth to speak but she clicked her tongue at me and turned away.

There was a smell in the air, musty, faintly sickishly sweet; I could not place it. On shelves nearby stood stoppered jars and bottles of the sort people used for pickles and preserves. I looked closer and saw stored there twisted roots suspended in brine, the pale floating bodies of frogs, the milky globes of cows' eyes, and jars and jars of a viscous liquid, reddish brown, with a dry crust on top.

A kettle stood on the hearth, and two mugs. Had she been expecting me? No, the mugs had been recently used; dregs of tea clung to the insides.

I heard the woman scrubbing her hands vigorously in a tub of water. Did you happen to bring anything to give me? she asked, peering over her shoulder.

I shrugged, shook my head.

Ah, they never do, she said to herself. She turned then and came toward me. I quickly backed away. Are you ready, then? she said. Her bared arms were terribly thin.

Don't be changing your mind now, after you came all this way, she said. Hop up on the chair now, there you go. Her voice was firm; she grasped my arm and I found myself standing on the chair. Strands of my hair hung before my eyes like the bars of a cage.

She looked up at me with those yellow eyes, she put a hand on my thigh to still its trembling. The smell in the room was strange and terrible, a sweet rottenness; I could taste it.

My tongue seemed to have gone to sleep.

I saw that she held in her hand a bit of metal, like a piece of twisted wire.

Lift your skirts dearie, she said, you know it has to be done.

Her voice carried such command that I automatically gathered my skirts in my hands; I had lifted them nearly to my knees before I came to my senses and pushed her away and tumbled off the chair.

Hush, hush, she said and reached out to me, but I scuttled away from her on all fours. Hush, she said as I tried to explain myself at the top of my voice.

I quieted when the woman put away her horrible wire. She did not seem amused by the misunderstanding, but she gave me a bowl of soup and said I could sleep in the shed. I asked for her name; she told me to call her Baba.

That night as I lay in the shed, warming myself beside Baba's yellow-eyed goat, I wondered about this strange woman. I thought about the house, how it had appeared as I approached with the stone path and the two chimneys. I realized there must be a second room, a second fireplace I had not seen.

I woke thinking of Ari, and found the goat nibbling my hair.

I thought I would move on that morning, but Baba came to me with a cool assessing look and said she could give me work if I cared to stay on for a few days. She had wood that needed splitting, and there were errands I could do for her since she did not like to go down to the village. In return she offered me a place to sleep.

I accepted, though I did not like or trust her. In the daylight her eyes took on a thick muddy color, like pus.

I did not like to admit to myself that I had left my mother only to find another. A grim substitute. I tried not to think about it.

So I spent days chopping. My father had taught me how to swing an ax. I worked myself into a rhythm and Baba stood by the back fence, watching.

She needed a great deal of wood; it seemed she kept both fireplaces burning much of the time. By now I had noticed the door that led to the room I had never seen. Although Baba entered it several times a day, she never invited me in. She sometimes emerged with dirty dishes, stale bed linen. I sometimes heard her voice through the wall, mingled with another's.

From the village gossip I learned that Baba was the local herb woman, both midwife and doctor. There were whispers that she was a witch: some swore they had seen her flying through the air in a bucket; others insisted her house could raise itself up and walk about, on a pair of giant chicken legs.

And they whispered about the girls from neighboring villages who came to Baba secretly in the night, hoping she could save them from disgrace with that piece of wire that made me think of a rabbit snare.

One day a girl my own age beckoned me aside and told me something more, about the men of the village going to Baba in the dark hour before dawn, but her breath was so heavy in my ear that I could not understand what she said, and when I asked her to repeat it she blushed deeply and ran away.

In the evenings, sometimes, Baba combed my hair. I did not like the way she gathered my hairs from the comb, so carefully, then balled them and slipped them in her pocket.

I did not like her much.

During the day I saw sick villagers come to her door for ointments and tonics. Sometimes at night there would come a knock at the door to the shed where I slept, and I would find a pale nervous girl shivering outside. I'd bring the girl through the connecting passage to the main room, to Baba, who would immediately send me back to bed. I sometimes lay awake listening for the cries, the sobs, and Baba's stern, soothing tones. In the mornings the floor would be scrubbed and clean.

Also at night came the older women worn out by childbirth. Baba gave them herbs to toughen their wombs, keep a new child from taking root. These women seemed more ashamed than the girls; they bowed their heads and gulped, these women who had borne ten or twelve children and felt guilty for calling a halt to it.

I watched all these things and stored them away.

One day in the village I heard rumors of a soldiers training camp nearby. The people spoke of a new recruit, a monstrous man of unnatural size and animal appetites, who ate flesh raw, wrestled bulls to the ground, and howled at the moon. The army officers hoped to train him, he would make a marvelous killing machine. The officers were having difficulty teaching him, he seemed not to understand their words and would sit moaning and scratching for hours. When provoked he went on rampages. People said he had already killed two men during one of his panics. But the officers would not give up, they would break him like a wild horse if necessary.

As I heard the story, my heart leaped up, then dropped like a stone.

It was Ari. I was sure of it. I would find him if I could, and take him with me wherever I went. It seemed an easy plan, in my head.

I did not like the way people spoke of him. He was not the monster they made him out to be. The things they said were true and not true at the same time.

Soon after, I was awakened late in the night by footsteps. The house was full of the heavy bumbling sounds of men. Their smell, manure and iron, reached my nostrils. I opened the door that connected the shed to the main room of the house, and peered in.

More than a dozen men from the village crowded the room. Baba stood among them, yellow eyes unblinking. No one spoke. Each man handed her something: a bag of sugar, silver coins, a basket of eggs. The men seemed restless, shifting their feet, with sweat standing out on their faces and necks. When Baba had received all the gifts she went to the door of the secret room, unlocked it, and led the men inside.

About fifteen minutes later they emerged. They seemed even more agitated than before and did not want to leave. But Baba herded them out and locked the door behind her. The men filed out into the snow.

On subsequent nights I awoke more and more often, to hear the shuffling of heavy feet and to witness the silent ceremony of gifts and visits to the secret room.

The next time I passed through the village I overheard the men talking in the blacksmith's shop. They were talking in hushed tones of a love sickness, they spoke of going to Baba's house to get the cure. It was a dangerous addiction, they said.

One of these men passed me later in the street. He was black haired and red skinned; he gave me a mocking smile, touched his cap, and went on his way.

I recognized him. He was one of Baba's nighttime guests; his wife had borne him fourteen children and had recently come to Baba for an herb to stop a fifteenth.

I chopped wood and great horny calluses rose up on my hands.

One morning Baba was called away early to assist at a premature birth. When I was sure she had gone I began exploring her shelves, peering in boxes, holding jars up to the light. I heard a faint tune; at first I assumed it was something in my own head. But it did not go away, it went on and on and grew faintly annoying.

It was coming from the secret room.

It was the same voice I had heard many times before. But today it was clearer than ever.

I turned to look and nearly dropped the bottle I was holding. She had forgotten to lock the door, it was slightly ajar.

I put the bottle back on a shelf and walked toward the door as softly as I could, which was not soft at all, considering my cloddish shoes.

I pushed at the door and stepped inside.

The room was swathed in lace, yards and yards of it, the sort Baba spent hours knitting in the evenings. It draped the walls, hung in festoons from the ceiling. A fire burned brightly in a stone fireplace. The room was so warm I felt the sweat pop out on my face.

An enormous bed filled most of the room, a high bed covered in more lace, finely woven shawls, and quilts. And on this bed lounged such a girl as I had never seen before.

She lay sprawled in a loose robe, regarding me with unconcerned green eyes. She had the softest, whitest flesh I had ever seen; her face, her throat, her hands were smooth and unblemished. Her robe had fallen open in the front; I could see one of her breasts, a pale perfect mound. It looked like something rich and creamy you could eat with a spoon. Most extraordinary of all was her hair: somewhere between red and gold, it hung loose from her head, cascaded over the pillows, her shoulders, lay on the floor in a thick shining carpet. I was nearly stepping on it.

That rotten sweet smell was even stronger here.

Her face was pale and flowerlike; the cheeks were two spots of pink that I suspected were painted on. I gaped. She did not seem human; I wondered if she was something Baba had created: carved out of soap, baked in the oven, cultivated in the dark like a mushroom.

Close the door, cow-eyes, there's a draft, she said. Her voice was that annoying singsong that had faintly haunted the house since I arrived.

I closed the door and stepped closer. I knelt beside her and studied her. I could not resist poking her arm; her flesh was as cushiony as it looked. It was flesh that had never worked or sweated under the sun. I poked her again. I fingered a thick handful of hair. She was a fascinating plaything. She lay there limply, regarding me indifferently.

Baba said there was a girl here, but she did not want you to see me, she said.

Why? I said, watching the hair slide and shimmer like water.

She said in her grating voice: I hate it here, I'm going mad in this room.

How long have you been here?

More than two years, I think. I'm not sure.

Why don't you leave then? I said.

At that she raised herself up and began tossing aside the blankets that covered her lower body. Her legs entranced me: smooth, white, hairless. And then I saw that she had no feet.

How . . .

She leaned back and sighed. She told me how a man had gotten her into trouble, a married man her father's age who pushed her down in the forest without a word and held her there. She had been in trouble and had heard Baba could help her out of it.

She said: I used to live in a village far away, I had to walk all night to get here, it was terribly cold and by the time I arrived my feet were frostbitten. Baba got rid of the baby, and I hardly felt it, for the pain in my feet. I got terribly sick and she took care of me for weeks, and when I came out of the fever I found myself here, in this room, and Baba told me my feet had turned black and fallen off, she hadn't been able to save them from the frostbite. I couldn't go home, after the trouble with the man, so she has kept me here, all this time.

Your hair, I said. Has it always been like this?

No, she said, it's Baba's doing, she rubs a horrible green paste into my scalp every night, and then it grows like weeds.

I said: Those men, why do they come here at night?

She laughed shrilly and said: They like to look. All they do is stand around and stare, with their mouths hanging open and their hands in their pockets. They stink, and they say the stupidest things.

Do they touch you?

Baba won't let them, she has told them I am some kind of ridiculous fairy creature, and if they touch me I'll shrivel up and turn to dust.

And they believe that?

Men are foolish, she said, they believe what they want to believe.

They only look?

Yes, Baba tells them that what they feel is an illness that requires a cure. Whether they believe that or not, they keep coming back. And bringing friends.

Do you like it? I whispered.

She said scornfully: Men are like cattle, easily led.

I fingered her hair. She let me. I wondered if Baba did the same thing.

When you leave Baba, will you take me with you? she said suddenly. I'll go mad if I stay here much longer.

Her eyes traveled over my face. I felt myself flushing. I was conscious as never before of the sallowness of my skin, the narrowness of my face, the pink birthmark at the corner of my lips like a dribble of wine.

She said her name was Anya.

During the following days I visited her room often.

How I hated her whining voice.

But her body was a white smooth thing that I wanted to swallow whole. Even the blunt stubs of her legs were beautiful to me, there was something so naked and helpless about them. I split wood into smaller and smaller pieces and let the sweat run down my face to burn my eyes.

Baba watched us both and smiled.

The men continued their secret visits. As the winter dragged on they came more and more often, red eyed, distracted; they could not really see me, or Baba. They saw only the milky smooth skin, the red-gold hair that grew over the floor and climbed the walls like ivy. They looked and wiped their mouths.

Anya said scornful things to them, yet she seemed to luxuriate beneath their gazes like a cat being stroked. She kept her legs discreetly covered.

The men began coming every night. There were more than two dozen of them now. They shuffled into Anya's room in shifts for their precious minutes. They began to come earlier in the night, some even came at dusk and lurked among the trees waiting for Baba to admit them. These men were burly with bushy beards like my father. But there was a desperation about them that made them slack mouthed and helpless. They seemed not to understand it themselves; I saw them shaking their heads over nothing, clucking their tongues.

Now when I went down to the village I heard muttering among the women. They had noticed the change in their husbands. They knew their men were visiting Baba's house late at night, but none of them knew about the footless girl hidden there. Some women suspected Baba was offering herself to the men. That old hag? Impossible. How could they? the women asked each other. No man would touch her, they reassured themselves. But there were a few who said: She has bewitched them all.

Night after night they came.

On a night when the men were more frantic than ever, one of them refused to leave Anya's room when his allotted time was up. Baba spoke sharply; he ignored her. She tugged his arm, but he brushed her away and swiftly knelt by the bedside, reaching out to touch Anya's face as she recoiled in disgust.

Baba cried out angrily; the other men reluctantly dragged their friend from the room. Baba herded the men onto the doorstep, told them never to return, and turned the lock after them.

She watched from the window as they wandered back to the

village, hanging their heads, sullen in the moonlight. Go to sleep, she told me. She went into Anya's room and locked the door behind her. I lay awake thinking of her brown spotted hands touching Anya's white ones.

The days that followed were queer silent ones.

One evening I heard the wail of a rising wind. The trees moaned and scraped against each other. A storm was brewing. I heard footsteps, glimpsed a dark figure darting among the trunks. I whirled about.

A branch snapped and I saw one of the village men approaching, his eyes cold and thoughtless. I ran to the house and he lurched behind me. Men were emerging from the wood on all sides, swaying and staggering up to the doorstep.

I slipped into the house from behind and barred the back door. I saw Baba standing in the front doorway, facing the men gathered there. Their bodies were dark and indistinct, their eyes glowing, like wandering spirits. They were demanding entrance, bellowing and snorting.

I saw Baba refusing, saw her hands brushing them away. The men's faces fell. Like spiteful schoolboys they kicked each other, spat, began hurling small stones that flew past Baba and tocked on the floor.

Then a stone the size of a fist struck her on the temple and she fell back. I caught her under the arms and pulled her into the house. Her heavy head lay against my shoulder. The men looked shocked, suddenly ashamed, and they backed away, melting into the trees. I barred the door behind them.

I dragged Baba to the bed. There was no blood, but her breathing was shallow and a greenish bruise was rapidly forming over her temple.

In a matter of hours the bruise had deepened and spread over her entire face, as if her head were a rotten melon. In the dark hour before dawn her breathing stopped.

I wiped her mouth, pressed her lids shut. I held her head, touched the dense loaf of hair. I realized with a shock that it was not a mass of braids, or a knotted bun. Her gray hair was only the outer covering of a hard bony knob—an outgrowth of the skull itself. It was some sort of malignancy, some evil tumor, and most likely the blow had broken some membrane, freed the evil juices to seep through her head. Already her face was unrecognizable.

I watched the body settle and shrink, the skin drawing more tightly over the bones. Her body became a dry, light, tidy thing, almost childlike. She looked quite peaceful. Except for the violently discolored face.

I took the key from her pocket and went to Anya's room. I told her Baba was gone and we made plans to leave.

But the men were back, circling the house like wild dogs.

Night fell. We heard them, they were running, circling, howling at the moon. We saw their eyes glowing green as they raised their heads, flaring their nostrils, scenting the wind.

They can smell you, I told Anya.

Don't let them in, she said.

They circled, scratching at the walls, pounding at the door, wailing and chewing their lips.

Maybe if they could just come in and see you, they'd go home satisfied, I said.

No they wouldn't, she said.

They waited all through the next day. They pressed their faces against the window, their eyes red and wild, their beards matted and sticky. They licked the glass.

Soon they would begin tearing the walls down.

I thought of my mother, felt my eyes darting and jumping like hers.

I went to Anya and said: I have a plan.

I helped her dress. Then I put my arms around her and tried to lift her from the bed. She was not much taller than me. But her body was impossibly heavy and limp. Her flesh was so soft in my arms, like a down mattress; I thought that if I slit her white skin, she'd spill out feathers. My knees buckled; I saw sparks, and I collapsed on the floor with her warm, flaccid, bedridden body on top of me.

Your hair, I panted.

Her abundant hair accounted for at least part of the weight. It was many meters long, and tangled and twined around the sheets, the bed frame, the oceans of lace that surrounded her like a cocoon.

I tried to free her hair, to gather it up like an armful of wheat. She lay uselessly on the floor as I tried to bind it up. Massy and bright, it slid from my fingers. I tripped over it, it was caught in my teeth.

It has to go, I said.

She screamed in protest as I went looking for scissors. She thrashed on the floor like a beached mermaid. Her hair resisted me; soon the scissors were blunted. The cries of the men outside made me frantic.

It has to be done, I said.

I fetched the ax from the shed and stood above her, her hair pinned beneath my feet; I raised the ax above my head, and as she cursed and her sideways face contorted in anger I let it fall. Again and again I chopped through the lush growth, severing it from its roots.

I caught my breath and smiled. Anya continued to heap her curses on me, even as she ran her fingers through her cropped hair savoring the new weightless freedom of her head and neck.

I lifted Anya, propped her outside the back door. Then I went to Baba's bed, wrapped her brittle body in a sheet, and carried it into Anya's room. I covered it in lace, arranged the armfuls of Anya's red-gold hair around the head as if it grew there.

I blew out the candles. Moonlight from the one narrow window fell across Baba's face.

The men had gathered again at the front door; they smashed their fists against it. The whole house shook. Their voices rose in unison.

I opened the door. The faces, thirty or more, filled the doorway, a single creature with many heads and countless hands. They reeked of musk and sweat and foul saliva held too long in the mouth.

Do you want to see her? I said.

They closed their mouths and nodded; I held the door open and they tramped past me. Heedlessly they stumbled into Anya's room, pressing around the bed, all of them packing in at once.

I locked the bedroom door behind them.

Then I went outside, hoisted Anya across my back, and staggered out into the snow.

Soon we heard the screams, the blows, the breaking of glass, the splintering of wood. I tried to hasten my steps.

I had nearly reached the trees when I heard the crash of the door being broken down. Men were pouring from the house. Anya gripped my ear. I longed to fling her down in the snow and run, but she was so heavy I was rooted to the spot.

But the men did not come after us, though my tracks were clearly visible in the snow.

They were brawling with each other, hurling accusations, trampling the snow, staining the clearing with blood, beating each other with their fists. Each was accusing the other of touching the fairy-girl, as they had been warned not to do. Each blamed the others for turning their dream-woman into a rotting bag of bones and dust.

All of them held skeins of red-gold hair wrapped around their fists, or balled in their mouths.

I set out again, with Anya bouncing on my back like a sack of grain. Far away, down in the village, I saw a line of lights steadily approaching. It was the women of the village, who had finally decided to take matters into their own hands. They came carrying torches and kitchen knives, some with babies bound to their breasts. They were coming to burn out the witch, break her enchantments and end her filthy practices, and bring their husbands home.

I could hear them singing.

I walked for hours in the dark.

Near dawn I let Anya slide from my shoulder. Her skin was blotchy from the cold, her lips blue, her patchy hair disheveled. Looking at her flabby face, her piggish black nostrils, I remembered the strange desire I had once felt for her and wondered when exactly I had left it behind.

She rubbed her hands, glared at me.

I cleared a space in the snow, gathered dry sticks, lit a match. We huddled together, our breaths making clouds.

41

I heard a footstep and my heart froze.

A huge shape darted from among the trees, paused in the early-morning light, and squatted before our fire.

Anya gasped.

I smiled.

Ari picked at his teeth and watched us warily, crouching on his heels. He had grown a great deal in the months since I had seen him. He was broad shouldered, bulky, shaggy as a bear. His beard had begun, though he was still a child. Some clumsy past attempts at shaving had left scabs on his face. But his eyes were the same, and the curve of his spine graceful as a horse's neck.

Oh Ari, I said. I went to him and cradled his head in my arms, stroking the stiff hair. He looked up at me, sighed, and curled his lip in the grimace that was as close as he came to a smile.

My brother, I told Anya. He can carry you, I said.

Ari's lips were chapped and bleeding, and he licked at them hungrily. Did you escape? I asked him. Although it was obvious, from the coarse uniform he wore. The cheap army-issue boots were falling to pieces.

I tried to hold his hands. He shook me away as he always did. Then I noticed the leg iron, rusted with dried blood, on his left ankle.

Anya was watching us, fascination and disgust on her face.

I knew the soldiers would be looking for him. I had to bring him to a safe place. I knew we should have started walking right then. Ari could have taken Anya off my back. We might have gone a good distance before night.

But I fell asleep, my head pillowed on my arms.

Sometime later I struggled out of sleep to see Ari and Anya staring at each other across the fire. Ari looked at her with a kind of wide-eyed wonder, the way he looked at a new animal he had never seen before. His mouth worked; his fingers plucked at each other nervously. He ducked his head, then looked back at her and laughed. His laugh was a harsh sound, like choking.

Anya was pleased by his attention, I could tell. I could see the familiar, languid, lazy expression creep over her face. Ari held her eyes and eased slowly, fluidly closer.

Anya smiled. And then she ever so slightly loosened her coat, showed him a patch of white skin at her throat.

Ari reached out slowly to touch a stray bit of hair. She laughed nervously. And then Ari grunted, leaped, pounced. Suddenly she was splayed out in the snow. Ari had his mouth at her throat and was tearing insistently at her clothes, twisting her head this way and that, pressing and tugging at her limbs, sniffing in her ears and eyes.

He was just a child. He was only trying to see how she worked.

Anya screamed.

She screamed and screamed and would not stop screaming, not when I pulled Ari away from her, not when I slapped her face, not when the company of soldiers in their ugly brown uniforms came running stiffly through the trees, barking orders to each other and surrounding my brother with their guns.

They had been tracking my brother for two days; they had recently lost his trail but Anya's voice led them back.

I stood and watched as my brother was taken away. The officer of the company stood beside me and barked orders. He wore tall shiny boots and carried a riding crop which he flicked impatiently against his leg. Between orders he ground his teeth; I could hear the rasp and squeak.

He sent one of his subordinates to fetch a horse and bring Anya back to the army camp. The other officers will be very glad to make her acquaintance, he said. I told him about her feet; he shrugged and said she would not need them.

I could not look at her as she was taken away. Her screams still echoed in my head. That gaping mouth.

Now I stood alone with the officer. I was not afraid of him. I could see his viciousness, it was something I understood. I had seen it before.

You should give up on my brother, I told him. He will never learn.

I'm not yet convinced of that, he said.

He's too old, I said, he has been the way he is for too long for you to change him.

There are ways, he said.

What if there were others just like him? I said. Other ones, as big as him, and as strong, but young enough to teach the way you want.

What are you saying?

We have younger brothers, I told him. Take one of them, take all three of them, train them, and give up on Ari.

The officer chewed over the idea. I heard his teeth clicking.

What is the name of your village? he asked finally.

My village was too small to have a name.

So he said I would have to show him. He hoisted me up behind him on his horse, and we rode, to the jangling of bit and spurs, over hills and through forests, and I clung to his belt and felt immense hatred for the layer of red, bristly flesh that bulged over the collar of his uniform.

I did not know what would happen next. My younger brothers were not at all like Ari; they were ordinary, big headed, knobby kneed little boys with runny noses. I did not want to give them up to this officer. In my desperation I had been thinking only of my mother. I thought somehow that if I brought this man back to my mother, she would find a way to make everything all right. This man's viciousness was no match for my mother's.

As we jolted and galloped over hard-packed snow, I thought of her and wanted to crawl into her lap. She had managed to bring me home after all.

I knew she would smell us coming, with her nose for soldiers. I thought of her eyes snapping, skirts whirling as she formulated plans.

My mother.

We rode until we came to a place that I knew so well, I knew the shape of the hills and the bend in the river. I felt a pang as I thought of home.

We crossed the last rise, emerged from the trees.

The village was gone.

It was a black scar in the snow.

We rode slowly down the only street. The houses were blackened skeletons, still smoking. A bloated cow lay in the road, legs in the air. Dogs, cats, goats lay in frozen twisted shapes in the gutters, daubed with red.

The smoke made black smudges in the sky.

I saw blotches and blooms of blood flowering on walls. I saw a boy's cap in the road, cupping something dark and gelatinous.

I saw a familiar skirt. I saw a fork, a spoon. I saw a pair of severed feet, lined up as neatly as shoes beside a doorway.

I thought of Anya and how she could use them, and I heard myself laughing.

I pressed my face against the officer's sour back so I would not see any more.

We are too late, the officer said musingly. He was riding slowly, looking about.

Such a pity, he said, such a waste.

I thought I heard a softness in his voice.

To think—three more just like your brother, he said. That would have been amazing. Our company would have been the best in the division.

He clucked his tongue at the horse as it shied at a child's dress blowing on the wind.

I held myself stiffly away from him all the way back to the army camp.

I told myself that my mother had escaped, of course she had, she must have scented the impending disaster, certainly at this very moment she and my father were hiding in the woods with my brothers and sisters gathered around, roasting potatoes over a fire, my mother a whirlwind of activity and foresight.

I still felt hope, I did, I held my chin like my mother always did. I told myself I would be brave like her, and resourceful, and I would do what I had to do to save them all.

I ought to skip the next part of the story, you are too young to hear it.

But I won't.

When we returned to the soldiers' camp, the officer offered me another bargain, a trade. Your brother's release in exchange for the pleasure of your company, he said.

Just a little while, he said. It won't take long.

We stood in the mud, among tents and milling horses and the jangle of harnesses and spurs. A subordinate came to take the officer's horse; as it was led away I saw that its legs were still flecked with the soot and debris that had once been my village.

I looked at the officer whose eyes were set too close together, pinching his nose. Hair in his nostrils. I thought of my mother, her power over men, men meaning my father, the way my father jumped to do her bidding and cowered from her though she was half his size. And I thought of Anya, who could make men act like fools or grunting animals simply by rolling her eyes at them.

I knew I was stronger than Anya. I had carried her on my back, I had dragged her through the snow. She was weak, I thought, and stupid, and not even whole, and yet she had driven a townful of men to madness.

If she had that sort of power, I reasoned, then surely I did too. I looked at the officer, who was tapping his riding crop against his boots, flicking away flecks of mud, admiring them.

I thought: surely I can get the better of him.

I thought: I will drive him mad, he will do whatever I say. Because that is what women do to men.

I thought: that is what Anya did, and I am far better than her, look at my two perfect feet. Cold but lovely.

That was my reasoning. I thought it sound at the time.

I nodded and the officer took me by the arm, not companionably, he grasped me near the armpit and jerked me toward the inn where the officers had their rooms.

And in that room, which was low ceilinged and too warm, I saw how his body drooped without the stiff uniform, saw the flabby ring of flesh at his waist that matched the one on his neck. And he laid his hands on me, hands that looked like disease, with their knobby joints and yellow nails. He began pulling off my clothes and I wanted to change my mind but the door was locked and it was already too late, I was backed into a corner behind the bed, a high bed with an iron frame made of bars like a prison cell.

He pulled off my clothes, layer after layer, and it took a long time, and I was aware suddenly of how my clothes reeked of goat and ash and the tart sweat of panic, and I was momentarily ashamed. But he kept pulling and tugging and did not notice, hardly seemed to see me at all, I was a service, less to him than his horse or the subordinate who had taken it away.

It was all happening too fast; I was not having the expected effect on him but it was too late, he snapped a cord and the last of my clothing fell and pooled at my feet. I felt as if he had gone too far, as if he had gone beyond my clothes and stripped off a layer of skin, my body felt raw and sensitive all over like a fresh cut, a hangnail.

This was the moment when he was supposed to grovel at my feet, look up at me with worshipful eyes like the men in Anya's room. Instead he muttered something about chicken bones and boosted me onto the bed.

He threw himself upon me, and I undid my hair and let it fall all around so at least he would not see my face as he did what he did. He puffed and groaned and breathed his sour breath into me, and dug out the deep places in my body and scraped and chafed against them so long I thought I would develop calluses before he was done, and as he did this I looked up at the ceiling at a crack in the plaster that seemed to be branching and spreading even as I watched it, like the crack in an egg as the chick begins to peck its way out into a harsh new world.

When he was finished he lost no time in getting back into his trousers. He put on his tunic, polished his boots with a cloth and then put them on, gazing down at them fondly. He was brisk, efficient, on his way to a fine dinner, no doubt.

I asked him when I would see my brother.

He laughed into the mirror. He was smoothing his mustache with oil.

You'll never see your brother again, he said.

You promised, I said.

If you want a promise kept you should get it in writing, he said.

Your brother's no better than a horse, he added, if they can't train him they'll take him out back and shoot him.

I leaped from the bed, landed on his back, sank my teeth into his neck. I could not inflict much, his flesh was leathery tough meat, my teeth could not pierce it.

He smashed the handle of his pistol down on my fingers and I fell from him. He raised his foot to kick, but the polished perfection of the boot made him reconsider. He did not want to soil it, after all.

He stepped around me, put on his coat, paused at the door. I expect you to leave here before nightfall, he said. And he added: Rinse the sheets before you leave. There's water in the basin.

He opened the door, paused, and said in a fatherly tone: You should be careful in the forest at night. There are timber wolves, they are unpredictable.

Then he was gone.

I stood a long time before the mirror; it was black speckled, rippled with age, looking into it was like looking into a deep pool that sucked up most light and only gave a little back as reflection. But I could see enough. I saw how my bones stuck out like scaffolding, and the skin was sallow and rough. The officer had left bruises shaped like fingerprints all over my shoulders. There was nothing in my face that could tempt or intrigue; my hair was long but it looked only like hair, not like precious metals or sunsets or fires. Worthless merchandise.

How foolish of me to bargain with this.

How foolish to think I could move mountains just by being a woman.

I stood looking at the girl in the mirror who held her breasts in her hands and cried. Stupid girl, I thought.

I had never seen my mother cry.

Outside the sky was crowded with clouds dark as smoke, or smoke thick as clouds.

I washed and dressed and went to the stables and stole a horse because although I may have been ignorant of men, I understood animals and knew how to win their complicity. I ached between my legs and each step the horse took sent a jolt of pain a little farther up, a little deeper in.

My brother was nowhere to be seen.

So I rode away from that ugly place.

Those three old women who used to plague my village told me a story once.

I was a child then, their ancient faces frightened me.

I did not want to listen to them. I turned my face away and pretended that I was very busy thinking of other things, the way *you* do sometimes. But their words bored in.

The story went like this:

There once lived in the village a girl who was so spirited, so lighthearted her feet barely touched the ground. Her mother had to sew stones into the hems of her daughter's skirts, knot clothes irons and horseshoes into her hair to prevent a strong wind from blowing her away. But the girl was irrepressible, she could run fast as a deer and all day long she flitted through the village, her bright sharp voice spangling the air around her.

Everyone in the village knew her. As a small child she had been inquisitive, appearing unexpectedly at people's elbows to ask them questions. She pestered the blacksmith at his anvil, dodging the sparks; she floated through the clouds of flour at the baker's, dug through the cobbler's greasy leather. She might show up in any house, at any time of day or night, regardless of locks or manners. She would simply *be* there suddenly, an extra face at the dinner table. You might see her nose pressed against your window, feel her breath on your neck as you squatted on a stool milking into the bucket between your feet.

As she grew older she became taller but lost none of her lightness. Her mother often kept her inside now to work. But when she could get away she wandered through the village as before, stopping where she pleased. The villagers were used to her now; some anticipated her questions and answered them, while others good-naturedly ignored her.

She had a vitality they could not understand. They looked at her and thought she was happy, but in a way that made no sense to them.

She took to wandering the fields and forests, singing to herself, sticking weeds and flowers alike in her hair. The villagers saw her from afar; some liked to romanticize her, saying that her singing brought birds and butterflies flocking to her, perching on her shoulders and joining their voices to hers. Others said she had a low, rough voice, couldn't sing a note, she just wandered aimlessly, dragging a stick over the ground, shamelessly idle while everyone else gathered vegetables.

But they all agreed, later, that this was when the forest spirit first saw her.

She was walking among the trees, her light feet barely rustling the dry leaves, when she reached a clearing and came face-to-face with one of the spirits. He had yellow eyes, antlers sprouting from his forehead, thick legs ending in huge hairy hooves. He wore a white shirt and a soldier's braid-trimmed jacket above, and nothing at all below.

He was spitting through his teeth; as the wet drops fell they pattered like rain, and where they touched the ground the grass withered and died in rust-colored patches.

The girl paused and stared.

The spirit smiled lecherously and unrolled a tongue that reached to his waist.

The girl saw that he was balding, and that his nails were bitten to the quick like a nervous child's.

She was afraid then, for she had heard the old people in the village speaking of imps and spirits, of the forest, of the river, of stone, and of the hearth. They said young spirits were harmless, stupid; it was only the older spirits who were clever and malicious.

But this spirit did nothing, merely looked her up and down, and then trotted back into the trees. The two tiny wings that grew from his shoulder blades flapped feebly as he went.

She ran home, and thought no more about the incident, except now and then, when she seemed to feel someone watching her, or when she saw a reflection not her own in the distorting bowl of a spoon.

It was months later that she heard a beat drawing her to the woods, a regular pounding that matched her own heart. She followed the sound, gliding among the trees, and came upon a young man, his shoulders nearly as broad as two men put together. He was splitting wood, in a regular rhythm, using an ax that matched his girth.

She watched as he worked, his back and shoulders so graceful yet so heavy. She saw in him a solidity that matched her lightness, and for once she could not think of a question to ask.

She returned again and again to watch him at his work. He was so practiced in his movements that he could stare back at her, lining up the chunks and letting the ax fall without ever looking.

Watching him she felt as she did when she saw the moon clearly reflected in a pool of water, or rain dimpling the surface of a river, or a young sapling sprouting from the rot of a decaying stump. It was a sense of symmetry and completeness.

She made her feelings known, without a word.

The young man came to the village to speak with her father.

The girl's parents were pleased with his request. They had assumed no one would want to marry their daughter; she was flighty, an indifferent worker, and they had expected her to remain a light but troublesome burden the rest of their lives. The father was happy enough with her suitor, and the two laid plans and conditions and sealed it all with a firm handshake, both men testing the other's grip.

During the months and weeks before the wedding the girl became lighter than ever. She was not permitted to be alone with her prospective husband, so she watched him from a distance, savoring the musical sway of his body. She drifted through the woods, rose to the level of the treetops, and watched him from above. She swooped and tumbled in the sky, dove to earth and rose again, climbing the air as if it were a staircase. At night she darted batlike against a backdrop of stars, all the while humming her tuneless nothings or clucking her tongue like a falling ax.

The villagers saw her skimming the treetops and muttered: Silly girl, she'll break her neck.

And: She should be home helping her mother.

While she flew carelessly above, trouble came to the village down below. First it was flies, thick dark clouds of them. They settled everywhere, attacking with their stinging bites, feasting on anything left uncovered, burrowing into the hides of animals to lay their eggs.

And then the yard behind the girl's home began to collect water from an unknown source. The ground became sodden, the garden plants rotted, the earth sank. Within days the yard had become a swamp, and lugubrious black frogs had taken up residence. They moved lazily, their skins as slimy-black as oil. White clusters of their eggs made a scum on the surface.

Thick clouds lumbered in, clogging the sky. For a week day was as dark as night.

These were bad omens, and the villagers eyed each other suspiciously, wondering who was to blame.

A week before the wedding, the girl woke in the night to find her window open, a sour breeze licking at her forehead. And then she saw the close-bitten fingers on the sill, two yellow eyes glowing in the dark, and a long pink tongue unrolling and creeping along the floor.

The tongue reached the foot of her bed, lifted the sheet, and burrowed underneath. She felt the rough tip as it nudged its way up her legs, creeping upward to help itself to the thing she was saving for her future husband. She tried to scream, slapped at it with her hands, leaped up in bed. She snatched up a hairbrush and struck again and again, but the pink worm seemed to be everywhere, writhing and soiling the sheets. So she shot upward, toward the ceiling, and fluttered there mothlike, seeking an escape.

The spirit let out a roar with his tender tongue. He sprang into the room, filled with a jealous rage. He had hoped to lure her into the spirit world with him, he had brought her a crown of hemlock and mistletoe, a wedding veil of spiderwebs.

Now he snatched at her as she bobbed just out of reach. She sought an exit but the window had disappeared, as if it were a wound that had healed; the door was gone and even the cracks between the floorboards had sealed themselves. The walls drew in closer, and closer, and closer, the spirit nibbled greedily at his fingers, and she covered her eyes and screamed and screamed, and the spirit leaped up and dove into her body.

If he could not have her himself, he would prevent anyone else from having her.

Now the girl wandered through the village day and night, her eyes glazed, her face strangely slack. She did not float, she staggered and crashed into fences, she clawed at windows, plucked at her own hair. She spun like a top, her skirts rising to her waist, her hair hanging loose, streaming behind her, a dark streak. She sank her teeth into her own arm, and drank.

The voice that came from her was not her own. It was deep, hoarse, a man's voice, it came from deep within her and flowed out her mouth, spilled out over her unmoving lips.

She wallowed in mud. She rent her clothes.

Wherever she went, dogs, cats, children fled. But she was followed by chickens, a flock of them, all watching her with their pink eyes and dodging her drunken feet. Wherever she stepped, worms rose from the ground and the chickens pecked at them greedily.

The villagers recognized the signs. They barred their doors. The girl beat at their walls, calling and cursing in her harsh voice.

Her betrothed tried to restrain her and she turned on him savagely, clawing his face to the bone with her fingernails. He stumbled away, blinded by blood. Forever afterward he wore a beard, to hide the scars.

When it began to rain, the girl looked up, slaver coating her chin. She limped to the village meetinghouse to take shelter. The villagers watched from their windows; her father crept out and barred the door behind her.

The villagers met in the street, rain soaking their clothes, to decide what to do. Many had seen girls possessed by dybbuks before, but they were divided as to the identity of this invader. The future husband was quick to suggest forest spirits; he feared they were revenging themselves on him for killing so many trees.

Other villagers thought the dybbuk was the spirit of a girl who had died ten years earlier, three days before her own wedding day. Such spirits were jealous of living girls who would soon know the pleasures of marriage. These spirits were childish and petty, more lonely than malicious. They could be coaxed out of their victim's bodies with gifts, white dresses, music, cake.

Some said the girl had been strange from the start, there was no helping her.

The villagers listened as the hoarse, choking voice rose up inside the meetinghouse. They heard pounding, crashes; they saw a tortured silhouette flashing past the windows.

They knew they would have to act quickly, or the girl would be lost to the human world forever. But they could not agree on the method: some said fire, some said prayer, some suggested a drink of lye, others wanted to sweep out her insides as one might a clogged chimney. As the rain poured down the villagers armed themselves with hoes and paring knives and prayer books. They straightened their shoulders, prepared for battle.

As they approached the door, they heard again the hoarse guttural voice, raised in anger. It bawled and faded, gibbering, arguing with itself; it rose into hysteria, and exploded. The windows glowed orange, the rain falling on the roof hissed and boiled. A section of the roof blew apart, showering shingles and sparks. A dark and howling shadow swirled up into the sky and disappeared.

Inside, the room was filled with smoke and the smell of goat. The villagers found the girl crouched on the floor, her clothes charred and her face sooty. But she stretched her arms out to them, gave them a familiar smile.

She had forced the dybbuk out of her body herself.

She had drawn in her sides and forced him out with one violent breath, as she had seen the blacksmith force air from his bellows. She had rolled and kneaded him out, as she had seen the baker knead the air bubbles out of his dough. She had plucked him from her body, as she had seen her future husband pull free his blade from a stubborn block of wood.

All the things she knew she used, to return to herself.

Everyone could see the dybbuk was gone. The proof was in the small bloody spot, the size of a pinprick, on the smallest toe of her right foot.

But afterward she was not the same.

She had lost her lightness. Her body now clung to the earth like anyone else's. She felt a new strength, but also the kind of tiredness she had never known before: the longing to lie down and stay there, as close to the earth as possible, the desire to close her eyes and sink down, down, down.

Before she had known only lightness. And then she had known the claustrophobia, the smothering feeling of the alien spirit cramming itself into her body. And with the trespasser gone, she came to know earthly heaviness, the ties that anchored her to people and places and things that needed to be done.

She felt the heaviness when she looked at her parents' weary faces, and when she looked into the face of her future husband and saw the scars her own fingernails had left, and a lingering fear that never went away.

She could still recall the lightness. But it required some effort.

Some villagers said that for years afterward she bore traces of the dark spirit that had inhabited her. She saw things no one else could see.

On her wedding night, her new husband drove himself into her, just as he drove his ax into logs; and her thighs fell open, like the cleft wood that fell apart from his ax in two clean white halves; and she felt a heaviness that had nothing to do with her husband's weight on her belly. It was a new kind of happiness, a contentment, filling her like bricks, anchoring her, laying its foundations and rising up like a fortress to the sky.

And when she became pregnant she felt more secure than ever before, as if the baby anchored her.

People used to say that girl was my mother.

That was what the three old women told me.

It was only a story they liked to tell.

I rode back to my village for the second time, or to the place it had been. Perhaps it would still be there, perhaps I had led the officer to the wrong spot. Perhaps the earlier visit had been a bad dream.

I reached the place that I recognized from the shape of the hills and the narrow frozen river. The village was gone, there was only a burnt scar in the snow. Peaceful now; smoke no longer rose from the ruins.

For a long time I sifted the ashes through my fingers. I wanted to find evidence, a bowl, a pipe, a needle, a ring. Any proof that would show that people had been here.

But I found nothing. The place was picked clean, as if vultures and maggots had swept through and done their work and left.

Not a bone, not a shoelace. Only charred bricks and ashes.

As if no one had ever been there.

I spent the night there, picking up stones from the riverbank, and because there were no graves to place them on I laid them where houses had once stood.

I thought I heard the voices of the three women who had been a more permanent part of the village than the houses, I thought I heard their hisses on the wind and their keening, mourning the dead.

My hands were frozen, the fingernails a lovely blue.

Soon, I thought, the forest will stretch out its arms and spread over this place and it will be as if this clearing had never been here.

However far I had traveled, I always found myself in a forest, and in a disturbing way it seemed to be the *same* forest, as if I had not gotten anywhere but had only been walking in circles. That forest trailed me, fastened to my heels like my own shadow.

I tried to recall how the village had once looked, but already my memory had faded. I looked around that empty place and I began to wonder if it had ever really been there at all. Perhaps the village had only existed in my head, the way the miniature city existed inside my treasured egg.

Could a thing exist without witnesses? Without proof?

It occurred to me that there was not much difference between a real thing that existed in memory, and something that was born in the mind from the start.

The sky was now the pale expectant color that preceded sunrise. Where was the horse? I looked around and heard it scream.

I saw it in the distance, rearing and frothing. Three skinny scarecrow figures sat jammed together on the saddle. They raised their arms and shrieked, in terror or delight, as the horse reared again, panicking. Three sets of bony heels stuck out from the sides of the animal, kicked against it impatiently. It began to run, and the women clutched each other with their tattered shawls and long unbound skeins of hair streaming out behind them. I thought I could almost see their cries trailing in the cold air like ragged banners.

I thought I could even see the red of their mouths, but it must have been the first red light of the rising sun.

I knew I would not catch up to them. Yet I walked after the shrinking shape, black against the sun. They veered, and now they were driving directly toward it as if the sun were a tunnel they could enter.

I came to the top of a rise of earth and looked down, and there in a hollow on the other side of the hill I found all the proof I could have wanted.

They were stacked in a mound, piled high as a haystack, all of them, and frozen in a way that was familiar. Some were in pieces, most were not; all had the whitest skin. They were cold and hard as statues, fuzzed with frost, saliva frozen in the corners of their mouths. The blood on them was beaded red and smeared purple and crusted, clotted black.

I saw the mass of backflung heads, angled this way and that as if in conversation, and the feet laid together, some shod, some bare.

I could not have moved any of the bodies even if I had wanted to, they were all frozen together in one solid mass.

How can I explain how peaceful they looked, their eyes unblinking, perfectly silent as the sun rose and the soft light touched their faces.

Too silent.

My mother, my father. Lying side by side.

I don't want to hear a sound out of you, I ordered them. Not a peep.

No one stirred.

Don't move, don't even breathe, I told them. Play dead.

I crouched near them and said: They'll never find you now. They're stupid that way. As long as you all stay quiet like this, they'll never find you.

They obliged.

You're safe here, I said, as long as you stay here and don't ever move and don't ever breathe, you'll always be safe, do you understand?

They did.

I turned my back then and started walking and did not look back. I had the proof I needed, there was no more reason to stay. Solid proof that you can touch, that you can see—that's all the proof you need to believe in something. Sometimes it is too much.

I came to a town ten times larger than the village where I grew up. The streets were paved with stones and lit by lamps at night. The people spoke differently here. I saw women with stuffed birds and fruit on their hats, and children dressed in white like angels.

I found work here with a woman who lived in a house on a cliff high above the town.

She was very tall, with red hair in crinkly waves and a white immobile face like a mask. Her eyebrows were arched so high they must have been painted on; there was a beauty mark, like brown velvet, absolutely round, perfectly centered on one cheek.

She said she liked me because I did not talk much.

When I first came to her she showed me around the vast drafty house.

Come meet my husbands, she said and led me down a long gallery.

Aren't they beautiful? she said with a wave of her hand. All of them dead so young. Sad, isn't it?

A row of framed portraits hung on the wall; I counted seven. Heads and shoulders, nearly life-size. They all had puffed-out chests and a kind of barnyard cockiness, in spite of their elaborate clothes and carefully manicured hair and beards. They all had eyes that met yours, that seemed to follow you as you moved.

I never wanted to marry so often, she was saying, but what could I do? They kept dying. Unlucky in love, I am.

I spent my days lighting candles, cutting the pages of books. I mended her shoes, dozens and dozens of them, high heeled and jewel toed, and I went to the roof to feed the pigeons, but most of my work revolved around hers, for she was a painter. Her hands were always smeared with colors; the portraits of her husbands she had painted herself.

She taught me to mix her paints and clean the brushes and to cut wood into frames, though she stretched the canvas on them herself.

She sometimes spent hours looking at a stone or a piece of cloth with the sun shining on it.

I learned that she was a well-respected artist, much in demand to paint portraits of the aristocracy. She traveled to far places for commissions.

I liked to watch her work, the way she could give a picture such depth that the canvas seemed merely a portal to a deep and distant world. Yet I didn't trust it, it was all trickery, wasn't it? It fooled the eyes. And the paintings were lies, they showed you a moment that was gone. Those husbands, who looked so hearty and red cheeked in their portraits, were all dead. It seemed a cruel deception.

Of course I did not say so.

One day she told me she wanted to paint me.

Just for practice, she said, just to keep my hand in tune.

No, I said. I pointed to a blank canvas and said: I don't want to be caught there.

Are you afraid I'll capture your soul? she laughed. Is that another one of your superstitions? When are you people going to come out of the dark?

She said: I'll give you a dress, you can pretend to be someone else, you won't even recognize yourself when it's finished.

So I agreed, and she brought out a dress and for a moment I was thrilled. I pictured myself all sweeping skirts and dancing grace and icy grandeur. Like her.

She held it against me and I saw that it was all a sham, it was not a dress, only the front of a dress, to be draped conveniently across any posing sitter. It was unlined, unfinished inside, embroidery unraveling, threads dangling. She made me sit on a small gilt chair, and turned my face, and pinned up my hair with ornaments that even to my untrained eye looked false, with the greasy iridescence of oil on water.

But she was satisfied, she went to her easel and ordered me not to move and to fix my eyes on the distant doorway.

She was many days at it and when she was finished she showed it to me. I took one long look and did not look again.

I can see from your face that I've done well, she laughed. You look exactly like the portrait right now.

Looking at the portrait was not like looking in a mirror, for a mirror was only surface. The portrait showed me from the inside: she had captured the tension in my jaw from clenching my teeth, and that shameful pink drool—the birthmark at the corner of my mouth, and the hairs of my eyebrows all in disarray, and the eyes. The eyes were both fearful and calculating, the eyes of an animal deciding whether to flee or attack.

I had not known I looked like that.

My face made the fine clothes look all the more ridiculous.

Soon after she told me she had been commissioned to paint a countess. She asked me to look after her house while she was gone.

Don't think I'm getting fond of you, she said. We understand each other, that's all.

She looked at me shrewdly, then sent me down to the stables to summon a coachman I had not known existed. Perhaps it was a trick of the light, but as I entered the stalls I thought I saw the coachman with his head in the manger, licking up oats alongside the horses.

Back in the studio I packed up her brushes. I heard her step and turned. She stood in the doorway in trousers and boots and a greatcoat that fell to her knees. Her face, which had always seemed painted on, now looked to be sketched in with rougher charcoal strokes. How broad her shoulders looked. Perhaps the coat was padded. She had a mustache and beard painted on.

Don't look so disturbed, she said. I get many more commissions this way.

She took the box from me and left. I heard her boots echoing a long time. I watched from the window as the carriage rolled down the long winding road to the town, and then beyond.

I wondered which of her clothes were the charade.

The house was even larger than I'd thought. There were many locked doors.

I went down to the town, to the marketplace. I heard people gossiping about her: her wealth, her isolation, the husbands who went with her to the dark house on the hill and never returned. She loves them to death, wears them out, they said, her body is unnatural. Bluebeard, the men called her, and made obscene gestures.

The men never come out alive, people said.

She eats them up, they said.

Cuts off their things and eats them with a vodka cream sauce.

They pointed to the house, whispered as if she would overhear them.

I kept the fires burning to keep the chill out.

She was gone many weeks and returned with a new husband.

He was young and fresh and gallant, with pale hair like flax and gaudy clothes. He held himself proudly, though he was slightly shorter than her. He rubbed his hands together and looked about at rugs and lamps and the rooms so long you could not see the end of them, and there was a bit of greed in him, you could see it in his mouth.

She was dressed in her long clinging gowns again, her hair loose, her face perfect. He put his arm around her waist, caressed her neck. Over his head she gave me her shrewd look.

That night they were loud and vigorous in her bedroom.

The next day when I was alone with her in her studio I asked how she had found him, when she'd been dressed as a man.

She said: Some men like an adventurous woman. Besides, she said, nodding toward the bedroom, he is a third son and will inherit nothing.

She painted his portrait but kept it in her studio.

In a short time she announced she had been offered another commission. She could not take her husband with her. I have to preserve my reputation, she told him.

She handed him a ring of keys and told him he could enter any room in the house but one.

I trust you completely, she told him. Please honor my request.

He nodded but he was not paying attention; he had his hands on her breasts.

Then she left and we were alone in the house, he and I. We seldom spoke and he spent his days riding a black horse through the fields, hacking at the bushes with his sword and shouting like a child.

There was a night when he fell asleep in a chair in the library, a book open across his lap, and I slipped the keys from his jacket pocket.

She had never forbidden *me* from entering the room.

I found it, high in one of the towers at the top of a spiraling staircase. I had only a candle, it threw my shadow wild-haired on the walls. I fit the key to the lock; the door swung open. I stepped inside, cringing, expecting to spring some hideous trap but too curious to stop. All was silent, the room was empty save a bed, and on the bed lay a woman. It was a young woman, pale and beautiful and stretched out on her back, arms extended as if awaiting an embrace.

I thought suddenly of Baba's house, and wondered if *all* unusual women kept young girls hidden away in secret rooms. As if they were trying to cling to a younger version of themselves.

I breathed on the woman's face, I touched her arm. She was cool, didn't move. I jostled her. She was not real at all; she was made of soft wax or clay and her skin, I saw now, had a hard waxy sheen. I could see that her mouth led nowhere, there was nothing beneath her eyelids. I punched her stomach, my fist drove right through her.

From a distance, though, she had been convincing. Lifelike. A work of art.

I pulled the sheets away to see more. I saw a flash of steel and quickly jumped away. There, set between the legs, were jagged metal jaws, like a monstrous bear trap.

I snatched my candle, raced away from the strange thing. Locked the door, crept down the stairs.

I considered keeping the keys, to avoid any possible accidents.

But when the husband cornered me the next day, asked me if I'd seen the keys, accused me of stealing them in his loud pompous voice, I handed them over.

There was no need to worry, I reasoned. If he kept his promise to my painter, and stayed away from the room, then there was nothing to fear. And even if he *did* break her trust, and make his way to the secret room, I was sure he would not be so foolish to mistake a waxen girl for a real one.

And even if he *did*, I thought, he would not be so unfaithful to his wife as to do the thing that men seemed always intent on doing.

This was my reasoning. I did not think he would come to any harm.

Although it was true I did not like the gleam of ownership in his eye, or the way he shouted and spit in my face and called me a country cow.

I did not think he would do anything foolish, but the very next night I was awakened by a metallic snap, followed by the most unbearable screams I had ever heard. I ran to the tower room, pounded on the door but it had locked behind him. I could hear him gasping, I shouted to him to throw the keys underneath the door, but there was no room for them to slip through even if he had.

This is unpleasant to hear, I know. It sounds like the kind of story people tell children to frighten them into good behavior.

But that's not why I am telling it to you.

I am telling you because it is what happened. It is the truth. No other reason.

Dawn broke and pink light seeped into the studio where I stood, and then I heard a horse's footsteps far away but coming closer. It was the painter, returning as if she had known all that had happened.

She strode in, still in her man's clothes, looking windswept and happy. She gave me a list of errands as long as her arm and sent me to town. She had forgotten that I did not know how to read, but I knew enough to stay away from the house until nightfall.

When I returned all was quiet. She greeted me serenely, and in answer to my look she said: He failed the test, you see. It's a pity, it's impossible to find a man who can remain faithful these days.

She touched my shoulder with a hand that was sticky, smeared as usual. You should not feel responsible, she said. It was his own fault, he should not have gone poking into forbidden places.

He broke my trust, she said, and then she hung his portrait on the wall beside the others. I could not look at it.

I stayed with her a while longer. I loved to watch her paint but could not look her in the face. She went away again and returned with her ninth husband. When I saw him I knew I would have to leave because he was a soft mild man who walked with a limp. He looked at her with worshipful eyes and touched her gently and he helped me light the lamps in the evenings. I could not bear the thought of him ending up with his head hung on the wall with all the others.

So when she announced she was leaving, and handed him the key ring, I stole the keys from his pocket while he slept and went to the tower room and set off the trap with my candle and then I locked the door and threw the keys down a well for good measure.

Then I left. I did not want to be there when she returned to find only a candle snapped in half, instead of the disappointment she anticipated. She would know I was responsible and I could not guess what she would do.

I knew the new husband was not completely safe; I knew she could easily give him another set of keys and again disappear and let him succumb to curiosity and temptation. But I hoped he would not. Perhaps he would pass her grisly test and win her trust and they would live happily together and he would teach her gentleness and they would fill that great house with children and leave that waxen doll to rot in her tower.

So I left.

I did not like the thought of the portrait she had done of me, I had wanted to destroy it, but she had hidden it away somewhere. I did not like to think of her keeping my face.

But she had paid me well for my time with her and the money jangled inside my dress. I had heard people talking of a place, far away and across an ocean, where people stayed young forever and there was room to breathe and everything was hopeful and new and run by machines. They said the streets were paved with gold. I wanted to go there.

The streets of gold, I knew that was just a story. But the rest rang true.

I passed through villages and larger towns and as I traveled farther from home I noticed changes. The lengths of men's beards. The sound of their voices. More iron and steel, coal instead of wood, engines and machines that moved and steamed of their own accord as if they were alive.

These things amazed me, but as I traveled farther and wonders piled on wonders, I began to anticipate them and ceased to be amazed. I think if I had seen men walking up the sides of buildings like spiders or flying through the air with dragonfly wings I would not have been surprised.

When I walked through these towns I heard people speak of a Great War and when I asked where this war was they laughed and called me a yokel. They asked where I had been hiding all this time, and stared at my hair which had never been cut and now fell past my knees, and they laughed at my wooden-soled shoes. I ran away but heard them shouting after me: The war's over, little fool, and there will never be another.

I kept going, for this was not the place I was looking for. These people, for all their fine clothes, were as violent as all the others. Their faces were greasy and lewd. I saw a man beating a yellow horse that would not move because the cart behind it was too heavy, piled to the sky with cast-off furniture. The man beat and beat it, cursing til he ran out of breath and still the horse would not move. He beat until the horse sank to its knees, pink foam running from its nose, and only then did he stop to wipe his brow. And then the top-heavy cart tipped and a clattering shower of broken chairs and legless tables rained down upon him and buried him utterly and no one passing by on their daily business paused to help him. Or the horse.

The towns were full of glittering surfaces and engines of convenience, but in the surrounding fields nothing had changed. On the country roads I passed women bent like harps, with burdens on their backs twice as large as themselves and babies strapped to their breasts. And at night I saw harpies circling in the sky just as they had over my village. Harpies had the bodies of hawks and the heads of women, and sometimes they borrowed the faces of the dead to frighten passersby. Once I thought I saw one wearing my mother's face like a mask, and I quickly looked away.

By now my hair reached my heels and was tangled with twigs and colored thread. Sometime earlier I had spent the night in a stable among the horses, and in the morning I found that some local boys had tied bells in my hair while I slept. Tiny bells the size of thimbles that jangled faintly when I shook my head. I found many of the bells and pulled them from my hair, but there were some I could never find though I searched through my hair strand by strand. So I made music now when I walked, though it was a cheap tinkling sort, and people thought I was a gypsy.

I came to a new town one evening. The people on the streets took no notice of me as they went hurrying past, their faces bright and expectant. Children darted among their elders; women carried babies cradled in their arms or slung over their shoulders, or balanced on their hips. They were all streaming in the same direction, so I followed.

They were heading toward the large meetinghouse in the center of the town, and I realized they were going to pray together.

There were three old women collecting money at the entrance. I thought they were beggars and gave each a coin before I went in and sat with the others. Rows of benches filled the room, it became closely packed, the air warm as breath, and noisy as the people jabbered to one another and babies cried. I had never been to a prayer service like this, where men and women sat together.

The room grew dim, and the flow of voices ceased as all the people looked to the brightly lit platform at the front of the room. In the hush a man leaped on to the platform, followed by another, and they began speaking in loud strident voices.

More people joined them on the platform, men and women too, and they all seemed excited and wrought up about one thing or another, and they clasped their hands and wept. I was shocked, for they were speaking of very private personal matters, but doing so in such loud voices that everyone in the room could hear. And the people sitting around me, instead of politely turning aside and pretending not to notice, were watching intently and drinking in every word. I felt I was eavesdropping; it seemed wrong.

The people on the platform ignored us even when we laughed or gasped; they were too intent on their own troubles. They seemed detached from us, in their own brightly lit little world, and yet at the same time they seemed more real, more intensely alive than anyone I had ever seen. Their faces betrayed every thought, their bodies were eloquent with suffering.

I wondered when the praying would start.

There was one man in particular who held my attention. He paced the platform, clutching at his hair, he seemed tormented by inner demons. I gathered that he was grieving for his dead father.

His suffering made sense to me. After a particularly long rant, with much arm waving and foot stamping, he paused and his eyes swept the room. I could have sworn he looked at me for a moment. His eyes were the most unnatural blue.

Much later I discovered there were tears on my face. Around me babies squalled and sucked loudly at their mothers' breasts, men lit their pipes, restless children crawled between the benches and butted against people's knees, but all I saw was the brightly lit platform and the young man's exquisite agony and I wanted so badly to comfort him that I could barely sit still.

Something holy was happening here.

Time must have passed; the faces around me were slick with sweat, the air was hazy with smoke, babies lay sleeping, their faces slack. But the action on the platform continued, seemed to be building to its breaking point. I could not understand all they were saying, but I felt the tension increasing like threads being gathered up and drawn tight. The platform was crowded now, voices raised shrilly, and then there was an expectant hush, and I saw the flash of long knives.

It was some kind of ceremonial killing, I realized. A sacrifice.

The man with the blue eyes, my poor man who had already suffered so much, now had sweat running down his temples and his eyes rolled upward, the veins leaped out of his throat; he knew he was going to die, I saw, it was inevitable, he was giving himself up to the ritual.

Those seated around me leaned forward eagerly.

What grisly ritual was this?

There was a great flurry of action then, a confusion of cries and limbs and blows, the knives dove like hawks and I saw my man fall and suddenly great gouts of blood spurted everywhere. Help him, someone. I leaped out of my seat, I went flailing toward him, he was lying on the boards covered in blood, but all around me hands snatched at me and pushed me back down.

I can't see, muttered voices behind me.

We missed the best part, they said.

Surely, I thought, these were the most barbaric people I had ever known.

And then I was even more horrified for they rose from their seats, clapping and shouting their approval. Even the children had the bloodlust; the boys were whistling, standing on benches to see better.

I was surrounded by madmen.

Feeling ill, I stood on my toes so I could see the platform over the sea of shoulders and shawl-bound heads. And I gasped for I saw the man with the brilliant eyes rise up, his clothes all spattered with blood, and he smiled and faced the crowd and bowed his thanks. He had risen from the dead, and yet he smiled as if it were all a game. I stood amazed, but no one else seemed to acknowledge the miracle, it was mine alone.

Then I was frightened. I realized the crowd pushing around me would be disappointed. They had been cheated out of their sacrifice; now they would demand that he be killed again.

But they only roared their approval, and I looked around and saw tears on the faces of some of the women; they had been as engrossed as I, their babies draped forgotten over their arms.

Then the other people on the stage came forward and bowed their heads, and I saw the tension run out of their bodies, they sagged and their faces relaxed and lost their sharpness, and suddenly they looked as ordinary as the people around me.

I had to have it explained to me that they were actors, that it was an entertainment, that it was all fancy words and foil swords and chicken's blood.

I understood this and felt foolish, but a part of me refused to understand, a part of me clung to the sight of him opening his eyes, rising to his knees and standing and mocking death with a smile and I knew it had been something miraculous.

People poured out the doors and into the night. The sky had cleared and the stars were sharp and piercing and seemed close enough to touch. Women walked homeward pressed closer to their husbands than before; small boys made swordplay with sticks.

I paced in circles that night, wearing a path deep in the snow, and in the morning I watched the actors packing up their wagons. They were a traveling theater company, and were on their way to the next town.

I happened to see the young man, black hair falling over his forehead as he washed the blood from his clothes. He looked smaller than he had seemed on stage, but the color of his eyes had not changed. He hung the clothes from the back of one of the wagons to dry, then rubbed his hands together, flexed his fingers. He opened a black case and drew out an instrument; I later learned it was a violin.

He tucked it beneath his chin and began to play. The other actors shouted and whistled at him; and three women, they were the three beggar-women who had collected money at the doors the night before, they began to snap their fingers, and they straightened up against the humps in their spines and lifted their skirts high above their bony knees and laughing wildly they began to whirl and dance.

Then all was ready, wagons piled high and horses puffing in the cold. The actors climbed in and they set out, passing a bottle of liquor around and talking loudly. The young man jumped up onto the back of the last wagon without ceasing his playing for a moment.

The music trailed after them a long time.

And after the music faded, the wagon tracks were clear in the snow to show where they had been.

I followed after.

Only because they were heading in the same direction as me.

No other reason.

I walked as quickly as I could. Only because of the cold.

When they stopped in the next town I did too, and that night I sat in a crowded hot room that reeked of wet wool and watched their performance. I thought the luster would be gone now that I knew it was all artifice. But instead it was better than before. The young man raved and tore at his hair and I could not take my eyes off him. He was familiar, he touched something deep in me. This time I followed the story more closely, I saw how he was alone and suspicious in a world that conspired against him, how he argued with the queen his mother and cast longing looks at a lady with a thick curtain of golden hair and fluttering hands. I felt a guilty satisfaction when she died.

And at the end, when the stage erupted in noise and confusion and he fell amid flashing swords in a most graceful death, I gasped in shock though I had been expecting it all along. For agonizing moments he lay there, unmoving, and I thought this time, surely, he will not get up. He will not get up. I tried to accustom myself to the thought. It was unbearable.

But he did rise, and smile, and it was more miraculous than before.

I clapped and clapped, but it was not enough.

Afterward I walked outside and looked at the stars. My cheeks were wet again and I could not understand why I felt so happy and so sad at the same time.

People passed me on the way to their houses, eyes thoughtful and faces slack.

Women balanced babies on their hips in that universal posture. I had seen it a thousand times, but tonight it seemed noble and beautiful.

Little boys, jousting with sticks. Some things were the same everywhere.

I felt a touch on my arm.

You must have liked it very much to see it twice, he said.

Yes, I said.

Here he was. I could not stop looking at him, it was almost unbearable to have him so close, like staring at a very bright light. The blue eyes were calm, quizzical; he worked his eyebrows up and down until I laughed. He looked so young to me, I was accustomed to seeing men with beards. I looked at his jaw, the cords standing out on his neck.

His black hair hung long in his face and around his ears, his features were sharp and pale from the cold. His clothes were still gaudy with blood from the performance.

I like to watch you come back to life, I said.

He smiled.

I could do it again if you like, he said. As many times as you want.

He clutched his heart and collapsed at my feet.

And as he lay there in the snow, spattered with blood, his head tipped back, I saw that he was like the bandit I had met in the woods, years ago, who was perhaps even now lying there buried in the snow with teeth marks on his throat like a ruby necklace.

Hey there, hey now, he said jumping up. Why are you crying now? he said. I'm all right, see?

He took my hands. His were impossibly warm.

I was looking away, trying to shake my hair forward to hide my face. I felt safe in the thicket, it was dark.

He pushed my hair back. The bells tinkled faintly.

He grasped my hands again and held them to his chest. I almost jerked them away in surprise for I could feel his heart thumping so strongly it felt like a bird trapped beneath the cloth of his shirt.

Snow was falling, again. I could see the black forest, beyond the town, creeping subtly closer.

Where are you from? he asked.

I did not know how to answer that.

Have you been in school? he asked.

From the way he asked I thought *school* was the name of a town. I shook my head.

I tried then to tell him the places I had been. It took a long time. Snow clung to his black hair and gave his jacket white epaulettes. It buried our feet. He waited until I was finished.

I think you have been to school, after all, he said finally. It sounds more difficult than the usual kind.

He took my arm then, and we went to the rooms where the actors were sleeping for the night. It was too cold to remove our clothes and I slept with my head tucked beneath his chin, where he had rested his violin. I could feel his heart beating through his shirt.

The next morning I woke with a start and sat up. I looked at the white vulnerable curve of his neck, his hand cupped beside his face. I did not like to see him with his eyes closed, so still. I touched him and felt the slow thud of his heart and was reassured.

He opened his eyes then, saw my hands pressed against his chest, and he reached up and pressed his against mine. He smiled. Then the actors came shouting and pounding the walls: it was time to leave.

We rode in the back of the last wagon, lurching and jerking from side to side, our legs dangling. He cradled the violin against his belly, plucking tiny tunes from it with his fingers. His hands were as callused as mine, but in different places.

His name was Shmuel.

He asked me where I was headed. I told him about the place across the ocean, the golden gates, the wide avenues and long warm days and the machines that swept and polished the streets of gold every day.

His eyebrows jumped. He laughed and said, yes, those are good stories, I love those stories.

They're not just stories, I said. Are they?

He said nothing.

It *is* possible to go there, isn't it?

Oh, yes, he said. I'm going there myself. My sister and I. We are going quite soon, in fact, and we will find work there and set up a home and send for our parents as soon as we can.

My heart leaped up, though I could not say why.

Where are you sailing from? he asked, and then spoke of a port city I had never heard of.

Yes, I'll leave from there too, I said.

Have you booked a passage yet? he asked curiously.

No.

Do you have money?

Oh yes, I said.

Do you have papers? he said.

Papers?

Identification papers, he said, you can't go without them.

I'll get some, I said vaguely.

He opened his mouth, but said no more, and we rocked together with the motion of the wagon, it was like waves on a stormy sea.

Night after night, in town after town, I watched the play. Night after night I waited in dread, gasping and then sighing as he died and came back to life. After each performance it was a relief to see his smile, his crooked teeth, touch his warm skin and feel the blood thrumming through him.

Every night he rubbed his thumbs under my eyes, wiping away tears.

He could not understand it.

He said: How can this frighten you? This show is child's play compared to all the things you've seen.

How could I explain.

We slept in side by side, or back to back as I had with Ari long ago. Until the night when he laid his head on my chest and tentatively slipped his hand under my skirt. Then I laughed so hard his head rode up and down on my breast, because I knew I was wearing such a multitude of clothing, so many layers of skirts and petticoats and underclothes that it was a maze down there and he would never find his way.

I pushed his head away and stood up, and he thought I was angry but I only wanted to help him. I began to strip it all off, as I had one time before but this time there was no shame in it and I could not do it fast enough. He stared amazed as the rough woolen clothes began to pile up on the floor. The mound rose as high as the bed and still I was struggling with buttons and clasps.

Finally I was free of it all, I could feel my hair brushing against my back and legs, and I felt wondrously light. Air touched me everywhere like a bath. Goose bumps raised up all over my skin but I was not cold, simply alert at every pore. I knelt beside him again and took his hand.

My God but you're a tiny thing, he said. I would have never guessed. You must carry your own weight in clothing.

I was cold, I said.

He undressed then, and I saw that his body was as finely made

74

and tightly strung as his violin; when I touched him in one place he vibrated elsewhere. I fingered the bones of his back, one by one, and as he pressed hard against me I looked into his ear as if I had never seen one before and it was perfect, whorled and many-chambered like some sea creature.

That night I felt something I had never felt before, a pulsing warmth that began low but soon swelled and swelled until it filled me entirely and crowded out all other feeling, and finally when it could not swell anymore it popped like a bubble and died back down and I felt again his hands on my back.

I thought then about the people I had seen, men and women both, and the strange things that women had driven men to do, and that men had driven women to do, all in the name of desire, and for the first time I began to understand it a bit.

Afterward when he lay beside me breathing slow and even (his eyes were closed, so I could not bear to look at him) I glanced down and saw that I was sprinkled with hair. Dark curly hairs from his chest that had stuck to my chest and belly. They looked as if they had taken root there, a new field in springtime, as if he had planted a part of himself in me and it was growing.

He raised his head then, and looked too, and smiled and said: Be fruitful and multiply.

Then he slept.

In the night I heard a trio of voices, screeching like owls and lisping like babies, and I covered my ears with my hands to block out the sound. I was afraid Shmuel would hear them but he slept deeply, with a smile on his lips.

In daylight he said: You must get the papers. You must book a passage. You have to come with us when we sail.

I said I would. I said I needed to leave him for a while, there were things I needed to do before I went so far away. I said I would meet him later, in the port city he had spoken of.

He said he would come with me. I said I had to go alone.

He did not like that, and slept that night with two handfuls of my hair wrapped around his fists.

But you see I had to try once again to find Ari. He was all that was left of my family, I wanted to bring him with me. If he was alive. And I could not bring Shmuel to search for Ari. Strangers frightened Ari, there was no knowing what he would do.

So I parted ways with the acting company the next morning. I stood by the road as their wagons creaked away and Shmuel sat in the last one angry and disheveled with dark shadows around his eyes. When he saw me watching he stretched out on his back, stiff as a corpse, contorted his face and closed his eyes and didn't move.

That still had the power to disturb me, and I was a moment away from running after them when he broke the pose and sat up and waved to me, and pointed to his eyes as his way of warning me not to cry.

I walked into the forest which grew close on either side of the road.

It was the same forest I had known all along. I crunched along, calling Ari's name over and over. My voice knocked against the trees, it rode along the wind.

I knew he would hear me.

You see, the forest was like a body of water. My voice was a pebble thrown in a pool, sending ripples outward. Wherever Ari was in the forest, my voice would reach him and he would be able to find me.

You think this makes no sense. But that is only because you have never been in a forest like this.

I knew he was among trees somewhere. The forest was his home. He could not survive anywhere else.

I walked and I called his name for three days, and on the evening of the third day I heard a crashing in the underbrush and a hoarse animal grunting that was dear to me.

He was approaching. My summons must have reached him.

I sat very still and waited. I did not want to startle him. I wondered suddenly if he knew what had happened to our parents, our brothers and sisters.

He burst into the clearing then and even I who had known him and slept beside him for years was surprised. He had grown enormously in the time since I had seen him, and he stood squinting in the light from the fire, pausing on bent knees as if prepared to spring. The bones of his face had thickened, and an uneven beard grew on his chin and neck. Shaggy gray hair covered his shoulders and upper back. The worst were his feet, they were bare, gray and blue and dead looking, so damaged by frostbite they were solid as hooves.

His brows were ferocious now, a thick line across his forehead.

But his eyes were the same as they had always been. He knew me, his eyes softened as he studied me intently. I saw a sadness there.

I suppose I had changed a great deal as well.

I beckoned to him then, so I could scratch his head the way I used to. He stepped closer to my fire, and I saw that he had not given up his liking for raw meat—he cradled several large wet chunks in his arms. His mouth was smeared.

Then his smell struck me, massive and musky like a bear's.

He knelt beside me and obediently bowed his head. I began to scratch; his hair was now stiff as bristles, and as I scratched I stirred up all manner of things which burrowed in deeper. He closed his eyes contentedly.

I began to plan how I would coax Ari onto a ship (I had never seen one myself but I could imagine it), and how I would keep him quiet and fed during a long journey. It would be difficult, but it could be done. If I could explain it to him. If I could make him understand. See how quiet he was now, how serene.

Think how happy he would be in a new land, how free.

Then I happened to look down and I saw what he held in his arms. There was a large haunch, torn and bloody on one end, but it was not from any animal I knew. It still wore the remains of a trouser leg.

I sank down beside Ari and watched him. He tore into the meat, chewing contentedly. My stomach knotted suddenly, for I recognized that leg, that shiny shiny black boot. A boot still so well polished that I could see my face reflected darkly while Ari sank his teeth in the other end.

I saw among the pieces of flesh scraps of a uniform, even medals, and if I had any doubts they were quelled when I spotted the riding crop, broken in half and tangled in the debris.

I crouched a long time by the fire as Ari finished his meal. My insides fought among themselves; my gorge rose in revulsion, and yet my spirit rejoiced in sweet revenge and my heart ached with a tenacious love.

I remembered a thick bulge of flesh above a uniform collar.

Remembered how rough it was. How coarse and thick, that skin.

Even Ari seemed to be having trouble biting through the leathery flesh.

I did not know what to do.

Ari was finished, he tossed bones over his shoulder and sucked his fingers then lay down with his head against my thigh. Such a heavy head.

How could I take him with me? How could I lead him through a city, shut him up in a ship? Shmuel had told me that the promised land was gated and guarded, and you were only allowed to pass through the gates if you had the correct papers. If you did not you would be sent back.

How could I say to the guard at the gate: No, I don't have any identification papers, but I *do* have my brother here, and he has a taste for men in uniform.

I could not take him out of the forest. The forest was his home, he could not exist outside it.

I stayed with him through the night, watching him twitch and snarl in his dreams. I remembered him as a baby, how I had held him on my hip.

In the morning when the first light broke through the trees, sending long shadows across his face, Ari arose and staggered to his feet. He gave me a long last glance, as if he understood, and then lumbered into the woods.

I heard him crashing and grunting for a long time. Then I heard nothing.

I did not admit to myself then, and do not like to admit now, that I was ashamed of him.

There was Shmuel, you see. I did not want him to think my family were monsters.

I traveled day and night and made my way to the city on the coast.

The air grew warmer the farther I went. I removed layers of clothing and rather than carry them I left them on the wayside.

In the fields the brown earth showed through the snow. The roads ran with mud.

Spring was coming. I was entering a new place and new season at the same time. Or perhaps it was always spring here. The way it was always winter where I had been.

I was feeling hopeful, you see.

Now and then I took the egg from my pocket and held it to my eye. It felt always warm, as if there were something alive within; and the scene inside sparkled and grew sharper in focus every time I looked. That miniature magical city was the one I was traveling toward; I knew I would find it in the land across the sea.

I was getting closer to it with every step. That was why the scene inside the egg grew clearer, more detailed. I could see curtains in the tiny windows, fish in the lake, I could see leaves on the trees, and dragonflies.

Making footprints in mud was not the same as footprints in snow.

I saw men plowing in the fields. I saw women bent double under great loads of dry branches; they looked like dead trees with legs, creeping along.

I thought of Shmuel, and wondered how I was going to conjure up some papers, and wondered what his sister would think of me.

It was past midnight when I spotted the city in the distance.

I reached it near dawn. I walked in its streets, among the tightly packed buildings. Steep shingled roofs, crooked chimneys, narrow staircases that led nowhere. I could hear my heart beating because the place was so utterly silent.

Not a single shutter creaking on its hinges.

Dust lay in the streets, so thick I left footprints in it.

A rustling made me jump. Only a scrap of paper blowing down the street. I saw a face but it was mine, reflected in a shop window.

My footsteps echoed.

I saw a wagon without wheels, propped on bricks. Broken shoes here and there in the streets. The great bells in the bell tower had no clappers.

No garbage in the gutters except smashed clocks and spools of thread all unwound. A wooden toy dog with a red tongue.

It doesn't matter, I said. As long as the ship is here.

I tried a door, it would not budge.

Maybe I was too late.

Shmuel, I said. And I started to run.

Down one street, up another. The dust so thick it muffled my steps. The gutters full of wooden spoons and combs with broken teeth.

I saw stronger light ahead. I thought it must be the docks, the sea, light reflecting off the water.

Would they be waiting? Or was I too late?

I thought I could hear the water, now.

Buildings blocking me at every turn. The sun getting ever higher in the sky. It's a trial; if I can't navigate a few city blocks, why should I be allowed to go halfway around the world?

Then I was running toward the brightness, the street straight and empty. I left the gloom of the buildings and plunged into the open air. My feet now were pounding on the wooden boards of the docks, louder than my heart.

Racing to the edge, seeing nothing but the end of the dock, a mad dash to reach it before I took another breath. And going so fast I nearly went over, and caught myself at the last moment.

I looked down. And down. And down.

Head spinning. Feet kicking out over endless empty space.

Such a vast terrible sky.

My love. How could you leave without me?

I had never seen such a limitless sky. So empty, not a cloud in it. And yet the light was tainted, soured, like the light during an eclipse.

The end.

I looked down, and the dry updraft blew in my eyes but I looked again because I could not believe it; looked down, and down and down at the dry ocean bed hundreds of meters below.

For there was no water.

Only an endless deep canyon. The dock I stood on jutted out over the emptiness like an unfinished bridge. I could not see the end of it, the horizon was a dusty haze. I could not take it all in.

You would need eyes on either side of your head, like a fish, to see it all.

Looking down I saw the ships, far below on the canyon's floor, listing and broken like fallen birds, tattered sails still hung from some of the masts. Their hulls were pointed toward the horizon, as if they might still sail away. But great holes had been torn in their sides and the wooden innards spilled out.

Skeletons, some of them.

Dust.

I glanced back, at the long wooden dock leading to the dark city clinging to the side of the cliff.

Shmuel, I said.

If I had seen birds flying over it, that at least would have given me hope.

No birds.

You could not imagine crossing such a void. There was not even a crossing cloud to hitch your fancy to.

The dock swayed beneath my feet. It rested on impossibly long spindly pylons, like spider's legs, sunk in the ocean bed far below. I saw now how rickety it was, hastily knocked together as if by children. I looked between my feet and saw the old boards bending and giving beneath my weight, nails tearing through the wood like it was flesh.

The dock sagged, and below, the pylons were slowly kneeling.

I ran then, feet pounding, and the dock softly collapsed behind me and fell into the abyss below. The canyon was so deep, and the dust so thick, that I did not hear the pieces when they struck the ocean floor.

When I reached solid ground and turned back, there was nothing left.

I ran then, in a blind panic. I thought I would be trapped in that hateful place forever. The promises I had heard about the land across the sea were all lies. False hopes and an eggshell full of misread visions. A mirage on the horizon.

The land I had seen so clearly existed only in my head.

I ran, bells jangling in my hair, my eyes nearly closed, until a farmer driving a wagon full of hay drew up even with me. He offered me a ride but I flailed on, unheeding.

He rode beside me, staring. Finally with a decisive grunt he leaned from the seat and his massive arm came swinging down like a scythe, and back up, and I found myself facedown in the hay.

I must have slept.

When I woke I opened my eyes to a riot of color, to the frenzy and noise at the heart of a city. The narrow streets were crowded, masses of people moving about, their voices rising in a babbling wave. I had never seen so many people in one place, so many faces, all different, peering over the sides of the wagon. The gutters here were crammed with refuse, rotting vegetables. Buildings rose on either side, confining the din, and women leaned shouting from windows, and I could not keep my eyes on any one thing, there was too much to see as the wagon kept jerking forward.

I smelled bread baking, and smoke; I smelled fish, I smelled spices and garbage. Pale-faced boys ran by, whacking each other with sticks and shouting. Dirty water rained down on the street from dishpans, a girl drew on a wall with chalk, flies buzzed, and nearby a horse raised its tail and released a golden load.

What relief.

I jumped from the wagon at its next pause and my knees ached. I wandered through the marketplace, and merchants thrust potatoes and carrots under my nose. Long underwear and stockings fluttered in the breeze. Through these streets I walked for hours, circling, and then I looked up and saw that I was near an open space, an expanse of air and light.

And as I made my way toward the light I smelled salt, and fish, and saw gulls circling, heard their cries and the shouts of sailors and the slap of water, and the creaking and rubbing of the boats against the dock. And then I could feel the very ground beneath my feet thrumming from the pounding of the water.

I stepped out finally to where I could see the harbor, and I could see the sea stretching out into the distance. Nothing can prepare you for that. It was a vast shining plain, a sparkling desert, it was the sky made corporeal.

Far on the horizon the sea met the sky in a thin blue line. I had never seen anything so perfect.

The ships were enormous, hulking, they were not the graceful winged things I had expected. The docks were swarming with activity, men loading and unloading goods, running about and shouting. I walked among them dodging elbows and great splashes of water. I saw people walking up the gangway of one of the ships and I ran to watch.

People were calling out to one another, waving, crying, holding children tightly by the wrist. I saw no familiar faces. I watched the ship fill, scanned the crowds packed on the decks. I shouted, but my voice drowned in the others.

I watched as it set out over the shining waters. The sun had laid down a golden path for it to follow.

I had not expected everything to be so big. There were so many people, too many, always in motion, always changing; how could two ever find each other?

I thought of wolves in the forest, marking the trees with their scent.

I waited three days by the harbor. I walked up and down the many docks, watching the sailors and the rats. I sat on coiled rope as thick as my arm. I watched people streaming past, coming and going with their luggage and plans. Every time I looked at the water, at the horizon line, my heart leaped up.

And then on the fourth day I saw a face I knew.

He was so far away down the dock I could have blotted him out with my thumb.

He turned and saw me and his eyes widened; and then he was nearly knocked flat by a flood of flopping silver fish that poured from one of the fishing boats next to him.

He came running, slipping, his boots covered in fish scales.

Here was his face now, what a shock to see it again, black hair standing up on his head. I had to touch that face, it was hot and damp with sweat and his eyes were red. The pulse pounded visibly in the side of his throat.

He was puffing too hard to speak.

His familiar smell. How tall he was. I had carried his image in my head so long I'd forgotten how he was in life. How tall, and how long his hands were, hard calluses on the fingertips. His head blocked the sun, he blotted out everything, the rest of the world shrank.

I've been here looking for you for two weeks, he said.

This is the right place then?

Yes. Of course.

Then I must have gone to the wrong place at first. I must have gotten lost, I said.

He said: But earlier you told me you knew this place, you knew exactly where to go.

I said nothing. I did not want him to know how ignorant I was. I had my face against his jacket, a button digging into my eye.

You should not have gone off by yourself, he said, it's a miracle we found each other.

I could feel his voice buzzing in his chest.

I found your clothes scattered all along the road, he said, I was afraid to think what had happened to you.

He put his hands on my shoulders then, held me at arm's length.

Did you get the right papers? he said. Did you buy a ticket, like I told you?

I looked at his eyes. I was thinking: they are bluer than the sea. But then the sea is not blue at all, is it?

You didn't, did you? he said.

His eyes hardened then, more metal than blue. He turned, took my hand and pulled me along. He hurried me back to the city streets while behind us the ships rained forth boxes and barrels and bales of foreign things, and sailors swung from the rigging like monkeys.

We stopped in a square, before a bronze statue of a short fat man in ruffled clothes. Pigeons clung to his head and shoulders. He stood in droppings.

Listen here, Shmuel said. Do you want to come with me, or not?

More than anything.

Yes, I said.

Then why didn't you get the papers like you told me you would?

I whispered: I don't know how.

He sighed. That's what I thought, he said.

I waited.

Look here, he said finally. I have my sister's papers, here, and her ticket, already bought. But she can't go now. Why don't you come in her place?

Why can't she come? I said.

She's . . . she's ill, he said. She'll be all right, but she can't make the journey now.

What kind of sickness?

He said: I don't know. I don't know. But she can come later, with my parents. . . . I'll write to them. I'll send them the money. When I write to them they'll understand . . .

When did she get sick?

I don't know! She's sick! It doesn't matter! All that matters is that her papers are here, and you are here, and you're coming with me. Yes?

I looked at him. His jaw was clenched, he grabbed at his hair. It was not at all like the graceful distress he suffered on the stage.

I said: Can I do that? Isn't it a lie? Isn't it wrong?

Wrong? he said. That depends on what laws you're going by.

I said: I'm coming. But your sister—

My sister! Here, take this, he cried and pressed the envelope to my chest and let go; I caught it before it fell. They're yours now, he said, you're my sister now. How does it feel?

He caught my arm, and whirled me around in a desperate gaiety. How does it feel to be my sister, he said.

I was looking only at his mouth now, his teeth so fine and white, shining like smooth stones in moonlight; stones laid down in a path I would follow anywhere, whether deeper into the forest or all the way home.

Again and again I tried to tell him about the city of dust, the grounded ships like wounded birds.

You must have imagined it, he said. You must have been dreaming.

I said: No. Impossible.

There is no such place, he said.

I insisted. I don't know why. In that city my worst fears had been realized, they had sprung to life all around me. In my frantic dash through those dusty streets I had hoped and prayed that it *was* all a dream.

But it had not been. My throat was still sore, I still found pockets of dust in my clothes. The terrible empty sky was not something I could have imagined on my own.

Now that I had left it behind I should have been able to forget it. But I couldn't.

I did not want to.

I felt I had been granted a reprieve.

I did not want to forget this gratitude. Did not want to get fat on my good fortune, complacent as a cow.

We sailed on one of the enormous dark ships we had seen in the harbor. It was utterly crammed with people, hardly a breath of air between. An entire village packed like summer vegetables preserved for storage.

As the ship pulled away from the dock I stood on the deck, pressed against the railing so tightly I could not raise my arms.

I heard a hoarse cry and a splash as the ship slid out to the open sea. Heads turned, people pointed and shouted incomprehensibly. Behind us by the docks I saw arms thrashing, water churned to white. Above or below or in spite of the noise, the ship's engines, gulls' cries, waves, voices all around, through it all I heard the swimmer's grunts.

Familiar, perhaps. I could not be sure.

I thought I saw a massive dark head, slick dark hair.

The figure was growing smaller every second; I would never know for sure.

I turned away.

Shmuel standing behind me said: Look, someone's trying to race the boat.

I stared out to sea.

Guess he didn't want to pay for a ticket, Shmuel said. He was waiting for me to laugh. When I did not he said: Not out there, back *there*. He raised his arm beside my cheek and pointed to the white foamy spot in the water, tiny now.

I didn't want to look.

Shmuel said: Didn't you see him? A great tall fellow, he comes running down the docks, knocking people down, he saw the ship leaving and jumped right in. You can still see him, barely, he's not swimming back. He's following us out to sea.

I can't look, I said, it's making me ill.

So I turned my back as the land slipped away, I took no final ceremonial look as the continent where I had been born slipped out of sight. Shmuel watched, and waved for the both of us but I turned my back and looked only at him, at the frayed collar of his shirt and the underside of his jaw.

I did not want to see that spot of white in the water, that last reminder of what I was leaving behind.

I did not get ill on that voyage though most of the passengers did.

I found the rocking motion of the ship soothing. It was like a child's cradle, an old woman's rocking chair. Rhythmic and endless.

Shmuel did not fare so well. Sitting together in our tiny berth I watched his face turn ashen, then greenish. I brought him water and did what I could. We were traveling as brother and sister, and we were never alone, so I could not do many of the things I wanted.

One early morning he sat up and said abruptly: My sister was not sick.

What?

My sister. I lied. She was never sick, she was ready to make the trip, but when I went home to collect her, I took her papers and left without telling anyone in the middle of the night.

Why? Why did you do that?

He took my face in his hands, roughly. I felt the calluses on his fingertips all up and down my temples.

Why do you think? he said.

He turned his head to the wall then, and closed his eyes.

I went out on deck, which I did as often as possible to check our progress. No one else came out, the wind was fierce and cold and during choppy weather showers of spray rained down. But I liked to go out, and get my bearings as the wind pushed me back against the door.

Every day looked the same: no land to be seen behind us, and none before.

Only the same gray flatness, with our ship in the exact middle.

After a week of this I said: I think I should tell the captain. We're not moving. The ship is stuck.

Shmuel laughed and stroked my hair. The room was so clamorous you could not hear the bells. Day and night there were loud voices, laughter, babies crying, sounds of love, sounds of retching. Men gambled and smoked their pipes and the haze rose to the low ceiling and curled in corners.

He spoke again of his family, saying: I'll write to them as soon as we arrive and explain. I'll work like a dog, I'll raise the money and send it and arrange for them all to come. Where we're going the people love music and they love to throw their money away, there are theaters, dancing-places, I'll play in the streets if I have to.

Will your parents be angry? I said.

He laughed bitterly. What do you think?

He mentioned them again and again, sometimes even in his sleep. This was the only way, he begged in the night, it had to be done, there was no other way.

So you see we both had ghosts from the old world following us to the new one.

Happiness touched by guilt.

We held each other as the ship rolled and dipped.

We tried to hold each other as a brother and sister would. That was difficult.

I was impatient all through the long hours. I wanted to learn English. Shmuel tried to teach me a few words. But all the words he knew came from songs and love poems, so they were of little use. Later I could use them in the bedroom, that was the first place I became fluent. In our new bedroom I recited the words to him over and over until he cried *yes, yes, that's it, that's perfect, oh yes* and the floorboards shook.

But on the ship the most powerful words he taught me were *yes* and *no* and *thank you* and *America the Beautiful*.

By the time we arrived Shmuel was a skeleton with a ruffian's hair.

There were no great golden gates to welcome us.

Instead there were endless rooms, hordes of people as confused as us clutching their possessions and trying to shape their mouths around questions.

There were long lines in which we waited endlessly, only to be told to wait in other lines. People assigned numbers to us, pinned paper tags to us as if we were animals or packages.

I was inspected by a doctor who peered into my eyes and mouth and was mystified by the jingling in my hair. He said he had never in his life seen anything like my feet.

I took this to be a compliment.

An inspector spent an hour shaking Shmuel's violin, peering inside, holding it up to the light. He thought there might be something smuggled inside.

Nothing but music, Shmuel said.

Later we stood before two inspectors who peered at our papers through thick glasses.

You do not look twenty-seven years old, one said to me suspiciously.

She's kept her youth well, hasn't she? Shmuel said.

The other inspector said: Is she really your sister?

Of course. Unless my parents have been lying to me all these years, Shmuel said and worked his eyebrows up and down.

I did not think it was a time for joking, but the inspectors only glared and waved us on.

We spent four days waiting in lines. We were given new papers, with strange new names written on them.

And then we were taken outside and set free.

The apartment was two narrow rooms in a tall crooked building on a street that was crowded day and night. There were only two windows, each the width of a single pane of glass. But every afternoon the sunlight fell through those windows and lay in golden liquid bars on the floor. I loved it, I wanted to sweep it up and save it for another day.

The sounds of the city crept in everywhere, street traffic and horns and the cries of vendors and children, and a deep subterranean rumbling that seemed to arise from the cobblestones.

The stairs were impossibly steep, you had to lift your knees to your chin to climb them; they moaned and reeked of garbage. At first I felt uneasy living so high off the ground, but I grew accustomed to it quickly, as I did to so many things.

Everyone in the building had come here from elsewhere, like us.

Many spoke a language that was familiar to us, and the cooking smells that wafted in the alleyways smelled of home. I saw women who wore their skirts as I did.

And then there were those others who spoke in fantastic tongues, who had eyes and skin like I had never seen before.

Where are the Americans? Which ones are they? I asked Shmuel every day.

And every day he said: Look around you.

The city was far too vast to see all at once. I had to concentrate on one corner at a time. The street where we lived, the neighborhood around it, occupied me for years. The shops and bicycles and men on stoops and women calling in the night. Stray cats that screeched like children, children who bit and scratched like cats. Bread baking. Blood from the butcher shop running red in the street. Ash bins and organ grinders and laundry strung high across the street. Buildings like ours full of apartments, each window wearing a different set of curtains, each window pouring forth different music, a different conversation.

In the summers we slept outside on the fire escape. The black struts and beams were like tree branches against the sky. They cut the sunset into pieces so that it looked like a stained glass window.

No one knew us when we moved there; we lived as man and wife and no one questioned it. Why should they?

Later, when we had settled and Shmuel was working, he told me he wanted to get married. Officially.

But how? There was the matter of our identification papers which declared us brother and sister. How would we get around that?

They might send me back, I said.

He said: Don't be ridiculous. Then: Don't you *want* to marry me?

More than anything.

Yes, I said. That was all I could say.

He knelt right there in the kitchen and pulled me closer and buried his face in my dress. Marry me, he said. My hands were covered with flour. I looked down at his dark tousled hair.

I said: All our neighbors already think we're married. What will they think if they see us getting married again?

They'll think we're mad, he said and lifted me up, spun. My head grazed the ceiling.

I gasped: If we say we're married, then we are. We don't need papers. Saying so makes it real. We don't need to do any more than that.

I had my floury hands on his head now to keep from falling.

He was waltzing us around in the narrow space between stove

and table. Up, down, up, like a stormy sea. He knocked over a chair. I was laughing too hard to breathe. Our neighbor below knocked at her ceiling with a broom for the tenth time that day and shouted for us to be quiet.

We're married, I said, it's done.

He stopped his spinning and let me slip suddenly so that we were face-to-face. But what will we do when we have children? he said.

I guess we'll just *have* them, I said. And enjoy having them. And have more.

Yes, he said.

I looked at him and saw that his hair was dusted with flour from my hands so that it looked gray. This is how he will look as an old man, I thought.

To see him as an old man. That was all I wanted anymore.

Those years all blur together.

That golden light everywhere.

There was a roundness, a fullness to things.

I forgot the egg, it lay deep in a drawer. I did not need to look inside it to see happiness.

It is only with bad times that you remember every detail.

Those good years do not make for good stories. You are bored already, I can tell. You like to hear about the friction between people, the heat. It's the harsh words and rough edges that snag your attention.

Shmuel found work in the theaters. He accompanied musicals, vaudeville acts, ballets, anything he could find. He learned the music quickly, practiced in the apartment in the afternoons before heading out to the shows. He had no proper suit; I had to piece one together from cheap cloth thin as paper. From a distance you could not tell the difference. We covered his brown boots with black paint.

These theaters were gaudy as palaces, everything gold, red plush seats, fat cherubs holding up the stage, heavy velvet curtains. I did not like them; the finery was false, the gilt paint I could chip off with a fingernail and beneath was plaster. The red plush of the seats was worn thin in the shape of people's hindquarters. And I could not see Shmuel, he sat in the pit and I could not pick out the sounds he made from the rest.

I liked to go to the tiny theater in our neighborhood where plays were performed in the old language. Shmuel acted in these when he could. The closely packed benches, the heat, the crying babies and smell of wet wool, all so familiar. The man I knew became a stranger then, he was a king and a pauper and an angry father and once, in an emergency, a vain stepsister in paper curls and a purple gown. I saw him sing and dance and weep, I watched him take a woman in his arms and speak words of love. I saw him die, over and over. I knew it was a play, it was all artifice and tricks, and yet I thought there was something real in it, something more pure and true than the life outside on the street.

I slept with my ear to his chest at night.

He grew a mustache. He still looked like a boy to me.

He still left his curly dark hairs scattered on my belly after he had lain against me. Whenever he noticed this, my belly like a field sprouting in spring, he would say as he had before: Be fruitful and multiply.

He liked to say that.

And soon I was. And soon we did.

My belly swelled and my skirts grew tight. I hitched the waist-bands higher and higher to accommodate the ballooning, until the day I realized I was wearing a skirt with the waistband just beneath my breasts, the hem barely reaching my knees.

I made adjustments then but still my body expanded like dough rising. I recalled my mother's indiscernible pregnancies, and I could not understand it.

I thought of my mother when my back ached and my feet swelled.

I remembered the time I had seen her give birth. I remembered it too clearly; I wished I had forgotten that. It was one of the many memories I wished I could pluck out.

At least I would not have to watch it this time, I would have my eyes on the ceiling above my bed.

My belly was enormous. I had to stay in the apartment, I could not manage the stairs.

It was summer, and I had never known heat like this. Drops of sweat crept over my skin like insects. I was baking bread, the kitchen was like a furnace. I had knotted up my hair but half of it had escaped and lay plastered to my face and neck.

I could not imagine a world of snow.

Strange how we adapt so quickly to a new climate, and the old becomes a dream.

Earlier in the pregnancy I had thought of my mother's punctual certainty, the way she laid down her work and headed for the bedroom moments before birth. How had she known? I had worried that I wouldn't know when my time was about to come. An idle fear.

When the time came I knew, I have never been more sure of anything in my life.

I was lowering myself to the bed when Shmuel came home. He rushed to my side.

I screamed at him to get out.

I'm going to stay right here with you, he said. I'll hold your hand.

Get out, get out, it's bad luck, I cried.

That's an old wives' tale, he said, stroking my head unconcernedly. When are you going to give up those old superstitions? You're living in the dark.

You can't stay here, I said. We'll be cursed.

Can you prove that? he laughed.

My mother giving birth in the street. Frozen bodies piled up like cordwood, the village a black scar in the snow.

To him I said: No.

I'll help, he said and went to the stove to boil water. He did not know what to do with it, only remembered from his own childhood that boiling water always accompanied a birth.

He boiled pots and pots of it, lined them up on the floor beside the bed.

Get out, I said when he staggered in with the laundry tub filled with hot water.

He shook his head.

Out, I screamed and hurled one of the pots at him. Steaming water splashed the floor and the pot clattered against the wall beside his head. He stared.

Out, I said again and heaved another pot. This one glanced off his knee. He let out a bark of pain then pressed his lips together. Why couldn't he see that I was trying to save his life?

I picked up a third pot and then dropped it with a cry because the contractions had begun.

I said: I'm not having it until you leave, I swear. I'll hold it in.

He looked at me, and for a moment I saw an expression on his face that reminded me of my father.

I'm going to find the doctor, he said, I'll send in one of the neighbor women.

He backed away and I heard his running feet on the stairs.

I was glad when he was gone. I could scream as much as I liked without frightening him. Screaming felt very fine. My lungs felt strong. The floor was awash in hot water; the uneven floorboards sent the water rolling to one corner of the room.

The neighbors both above and below were knocking with their brooms.

My belly had a life of its own. It bubbled and boiled. It was a sackful of puppies.

Things were shifting, sliding around. Things were not lining up correctly.

You see, there were two of them. I should have guessed before now.

There were two of them, and each was fighting with the other to be the first out of my womb.

The struggle went on a long time, and as no doctor appeared and no Shmuel either I saw no reason to stop screaming, since it seemed to clear my head. Water rolled from one corner to another, as if the entire building were swaying. As long as I kept up the noise, my neighbors up and down kept up their knocking, and I watched a hairline crack appear and grow in the ceiling plaster above my bed.

As the afternoon passed the sun fell through the windows and lay across my belly, and I thought it turned my skin translucent, I was sure I saw two heads within and the tiny raised fists.

Incredible pressure then and my hipbones creaking in protest. I felt their heads. Side by side, they were trying to butt their way out of my body. Simultaneously.

Such pain then that I thought it could not go on. It could not go on. It was not possible.

But it did. For quite a while.

I am telling you these things just as my mother told me when I was your age. I can see that it repulses you, just as it did me. You are making a sour-lemon face. But I am telling you for your own good.

I watched the crack widen and branch out across the ceiling, like something about to hatch.

The two heads battled for entrance to the channel. They were at a stalemate.

Suddenly there was enormous pain and then relief, as the first shot out of my body with the second on his heels. The two of them were lying in a stew of juices between my legs, and chunks of plaster began raining from the ceiling, and just then there were drumming footsteps and Shmuel burst into the apartment with the midwife from a nearby neighborhood.

She had dark skin and a deep voice that was like music though she spoke too quickly for me to follow. But her hands were wise and capable, they smacked the babies and made them squall and then cleaned them with brisk efficiency. She laid cool hands on me, and did what she could with the soaked, plaster-strewn bed.

Lord, she said.

She bundled the babies in blankets and laid them both in Shmuel's arms. He stood amazed and terrified as first one and then the other began to cry.

I took them then, and my arms were full.

In all the confusion no one had seen which was born first.

They were black-haired boys, and we named one Eliahu after Shmuel's grandfather, and we named the other Wolf, which was my father's name.

One named for animals, one named for prophets.

One for the body, one for the spirit.

They were identical in appearance but opposites in everything else. They had entered the world wrestling each other and never stopped.

When one cried, the other cried louder.

Whomever I nursed first would drink all the milk and leave nothing for his brother.

Time passes quickly when you are watching children grow up.

While I'd been pregnant I'd pictured myself doing my work with my future child propped on my hip, as my mother had done, as women have always done. But I had not planned on there being two of them. I did my best to hold them both, one on either hip, a balancing act. By the time I mastered this trick they had grown too big for me to manage.

It seemed Eli and Wolf went from sitting to crawling in the time it took to blink, went from crawling to walking before I could catch my breath. I turned my head for a moment and when I looked back I found them in short pants and button shoes, shouting and dueling with sticks.

They were fierce, my boys. They had thick black hair at birth; it fell out the next day and grew back even thicker, hair like a crow's wing. They had dark eyes like mine and Shmuel's sharp features. How quickly they grew. I would piece together a shirt for one of them, and by the time I finished sewing it he would have outgrown it. Great hairy wrists sticking out of the sleeves. Brand-new jackets, straining at the shoulders. I grew accustomed to the sound of ripping cloth.

How they ate. They devoured everything like wildfire. I did what I could, but it seemed they were always hungry. There were many evenings when I had not prepared enough, and Wolf and Eli prowled about scraping the bottoms of pans and licking their fingers to trap the last crumbs, and casting dissatisfied glances all around, and Shmuel would joke that he feared for his life. Don't bother with me, boys, I'm all bones, he would say.

They grew so quickly. Sometimes in the night I would hear them moaning because of the growing pains in their arms and legs, their growling stomachs. First one would shoot up, then the other. It was as if they were racing, to see who would be the first to bump his head against the sun.

Shmuel could not understand it. He was a slight man, narrowly built. Me, I had stopped growing early. And here we had two sons who towered over us. Shmuel often said: Where in the world did they come from?

I thought of my family, my father and brother. It all made sense to me.

Shmuel said: It's because we're in America. Everything is bigger here.

Then he said: We should have another child.

He said this often.

From the beginning he played his violin for the boys and they would listen enraptured. He played theater music, waltzes and dance tunes, and when he played fast jigs and reels the boys danced for him, jumping up and down imitating the organ grinder's monkey with their caps held out for coins. Even when they grew much older, and forceful in their opinions and impatient with everything, the music still had the power to tame them.

They adored their father.

Partly, I think, because they saw him so little. He had to work so hard then. Every moment he was home was an occasion.

I want a house full of little monkeys, he said.

The boys were still small then.

Another time, apropos of nothing: Are you ready yet?

And later he said nothing, simply asked with his eyebrows.

At night we shared our bed as we always had, and his body seemed to grow more beautiful to me as time passed and the years polished his bones. We were happy with each other, and regular in our habits; night after night he emptied himself and then half jokingly addressed my belly, imploring it to be fruitful and multiply. So he could not understand why I did not conceive.

I knew why. My mother had taught me well.

I did not want another child.

You see, I did not want to have to share my attentions.

I wanted to give all I had to my sons. I did not want to divide my love among a horde of children so that each got only a splinter. I did not want a houseful, a shoeful of children, children whose needs would overwhelm me, whose names I would forget.

I wanted to know my children. I did not want a faceless litter.

I tried to explain this to Shmuel.

Let's just have *one*, then, he said. One more won't make a difference.

Shmuel's eyes were unfaded, still that startling blue. I had hoped our sons would inherit them, but no.

Just one more, he said. Eli and Wolf should have a sister.

He said nothing more, and I knew he was thinking of his own.

A month after our arrival in this city, and every month thereafter, Shmuel had written to his parents and sister. He had sent them money regularly, had begged them in the letters to come join us. He offered to arrange everything if they would give their consent.

For a year they did not answer his letters.

He continued to write, and to send money though there were times when we could have used it.

Eventually he received a note from his sister. In two blunt sentences she informed him that she had married a local man, and that her parents wanted to live near her rather than with their irresponsible former son in an unknown land.

At the bottom of the page she had added as an afterthought that she was expecting her first child.

Shmuel read me the letter and then never mentioned it again. But he continued to send money to his parents, and perhaps also wrote to them, and in his sleep he argued with them endlessly.

We had photographs made of our boys, uncomfortable and scowling in their best clothes. I had seen photographs in the newspapers, but never seen photos of people I knew, never held them in my hands like this. Shmuel took them all from me and sent them to his parents.

There was no forest here, no snow like that all-encompassing snow.

There were no journeys to be made.

We never left the city. This city was all of America to us.

We began to accumulate things: cast-off furniture from our neighbors. A radio that almost worked sometimes. Shmuel saved for years to buy a violin, all golden wood and graceful curves and smooth varnish, though he still cherished the old one and played it sometimes so it would not feel left out.

My hair. I trimmed it. You could still hear the bells, now and then. Though that part of my hair should have grown out long ago.

I grew herbs in little pots that I lined up on the windowsill.

In the summer evenings women gathered on stoops and fire escapes to gossip. I never thought to join them, but their voices were comforting; I remembered my village and the women talking over fences, whispered confidences.

Shmuel and Eli and Wolf were my whole world then, and it was all I wanted. I still looked at my sons sometimes with awe and wonder; to think that I made these amazing creatures, they came out of my body. Look how they run and jump and think for themselves. Never mind that their faces were dirty.

My boys had made the city their playground. They ran with other boys in packs, shouted and fought and stole rides on the streetcars. Nine years old and they were smoking cigarettes and picking fights with boys twice their size. Shmuel forbade them to do these things, but I knew they did them anyway and I was secretly proud.

I wanted my boys to be ready.

Ready for what?

Anything.

They spoke one language in the streets and another to their parents and did not think it strange. I was trying to learn but slipped back into the old language when the new one failed me.

Watch me, watch this! Wolf said as he balanced on the railing of the fire escape, and then hung by his knees, six stories above the street.

I applauded.

My daredevil.

No, watch *this*, Eli said. He stood on his head till his face turned a rich mahogany color, legs pedaling.

Very good, I told him.

He had always been the more cerebral of the two.

I could hug Wolf, briefly, perhaps kiss his brow before he ducked. Wolf liked to be touched. Eli was more aloof in that way. I could hug him only at bedtime, lights off. Both were stiff and manly in their father's presence, brushed off my caresses. Out in the streets I was not allowed to hold their hands.

I would have smothered them if they had let me.

But I was also proud of their pride, their uplifted chins and boxer's stances.

At home they argued incessantly, pummeled each other. But on the streets they were inseparable, they were each other's staunchest defenders.

They were like that from the start. When they were a few weeks old Eli began choking, turning blue in the middle of the night, and Wolf screamed and screamed until I woke and came running to help. By the next morning Eli had recovered and his brother was kicking him in the head.

I was so happy then.

Perhaps the contentment made me less vigilant. Perhaps I let down my guard.

Perhaps I was careless with my mother's preventive medicine.

Whatever the reason, I discovered I was pregnant.

The boys were nine years old then.

I did not want it.

I could have gotten rid of it, but I did not.

I did not want to have the baby, but I wanted to be able to tell Shmuel and see his face light up.

So I did, and Shmuel, who had given up hope, was beside himself with joy. I had never before seen tears in his eyes. He brought out his violin, tucked it under his chin, but was too overcome to play.

I wished there was a way to give him the pleasure of the good news without actually giving birth.

But there was not, so I had to proceed with a pregnancy I did not want.

I did it for him. It seemed a small thing to do, in exchange for his happiness.

I would have done much greater things.

My belly swelled.

My boys. I knew I would be distracted, I would neglect them, they would despise me.

But all through the pregnancy they went blithely about their business, did not seem to care that I had less time for them. In fact they seemed happier with their increased freedom, they roamed farther afield, came home smiling with slingshots and black eyes and enormous appetites.

This pregnancy was so easy compared to the last. The unborn baby so docile I wondered if it was dead.

My feet swelled again, and I craved foods I could not name.

I went to the marketplace in the Chinese neighborhood and passed among the stalls staring in wonder at fantastic fish, bright orange ducks, skeins of noodles, seaweed and mushrooms in nightmare shapes, incense and sandals, searching for something to satisfy the craving.

The streets were loud with voices and I could not understand a word. I was used to that, I had felt it before.

I was studying the painted kites shaped like fish and dragons, wondering how much they would cost and how my sons would love them, when I heard my name spoken, felt a hand on my arm.

The voice was soft but in that place full of foreign tongues my name pierced like a scream. The hand on my arm was a pure ungodly white. Like snow.

I turned and saw a woman with a face as pale as the hand, her head bound tightly in a scarf though I saw strands of red-gold hair escaping and blowing across her face.

She pressed close, peered at my mouth. I smelled her breath. She would have pressed closer but my belly stopped her.

Anya, I said.

Snow and trees and men baying like hounds in the night. Here it was again.

I stood there surrounded by Chinese matrons and vegetable stalls and the heat and stink and traffic of a summer afternoon, but I was not there at all.

Anya. Her face had sagged, her flesh grown heavy. She looked human now, no longer the ethereal creature trapped in a room of lace like a butterfly in a spider's web.

The last time I had seen her was when the soldiers had carried her away. To press her into service, they said. She had not looked back; her stumpy legs had bounced against the horse's shoulder.

I looked down.

She followed my gaze.

Yes, I bought these, she said, lifting her skirt to show me.

They're not perfect, I'm no dancer, she said and showed me her cane.

But I wanted to be able to buy pretty shoes, you see.

I could not meet her eyes. I looked at her hair and remembered how I had hacked at it with the ax.

I'm glad to see you still alive, I said.

Yes, she said, I'm alive and I'm here. Double happiness, as the Chinese say.

Her voice was harsh, the color of her clothes a bit too bright. I could not look at her without squinting. She wore rings on every finger.

You are doing all right, I see, she said and touched my belly.

A chill ran through me. I thought I had left my home behind me forever, traveled over land and over sea, beyond the barrier of papers and visas that was higher than any gate. I thought I had escaped that place. And now a piece of the past had caught up with me, was breathing my air, was touching my future child.

You've found yourself a man, she said. Good for you. I never would have thought . . .

I looked at her fully then and saw that she had a shrewdness she had not had before. She had learned something, and it had hardened her. I looked again at her clothes, at the sweat running down between her breasts, and I saw that she was a woman who used men for business. I saw she had nothing but contempt for them, sought only to profit from them and break them. Beneath her sagging beauty she still had the power I had once envied, the power to manipulate men.

It was something I no longer wanted.

I remembered how she screamed, how she brought violence and despair down upon us when she screamed.

I was suddenly afraid she would do it again.

Just behind Anya I saw a Chinese man gutting a huge fish with one quick stroke. The intestines burst forth inevitably, uncontrollably, there was no way to hold them in.

I must be getting home, I said.

She read my face and stepped back, turned to hobble away.

I tried to help you, back there, I said.

She said: I know you did. And now I can offer you my help. If you want it. There are things I can do for you, you only need ask.

She smiled and touched my arm, said: You know, inside we are not so different, you and I.

How could she say that?

She had disappeared in the crowd.

I had lost my appetite. My belly felt cold at the spot where she had touched it. The child inside shifted restlessly.

This time when the labor began I was certain Shmuel would respect my wishes to stay away. But instead he removed all furniture and knickknacks from my reach, summoned a doctor, and knelt beside me through the whole process.

I wanted to die from the shame of it.

Not one but *two* men bearing witness.

A bad omen. I kept telling them what evil luck would befall us now.

They laughed at me. Come out of the dark, the doctor said.

The birth was swift and easy.

A healthy baby girl, the doctor said. Do you call this a bad omen?

He held her up by her heels and she bawled.

Get him out of the apartment, I said.

Shmuel saw the doctor out, and when he came back I said: You have killed us all.

I wanted to weep.

He thumped his chest and smiled.

I held the baby and she spat at me. Her thin hair, her beaky nose, her hands curled like claws. She seemed tainted to me, the past had touched her and dirtied her somehow. She was not pure and new like my sons.

She was wrinkled and bitter, born old.

Later I put her to my breast and she bit down hard with sharp gums.

Shmuel put his arms around me. Me and her both.

A daughter, just like we wanted, he said and his face shone with happiness.

I tried to smile with him but I felt uneasy.

I told myself I would love our daughter for his sake. This was what he wanted, and he was what I wanted. It was an exchange. I would balance it out this way.

Then I felt nauseous, because I was thinking the way Anya would, I was thinking of people as pawns, to be moved about and toyed with. The last time I had reasoned this way was the night I offered an officer my company in exchange for my brother.

My body clenched then, I gagged and vomited up bile and blood, and Shmuel swept the baby out of my arms just in time, and I felt stinging pain on my cheeks from the tears, tears that burned they were so salty.

We named the child Sashie, after my mother.

She never liked to ride on my hip. She did not fit there properly, somehow. She preferred her cradle, or her father's shoulder.

My boys were men now.

In body at least, and their minds were catching up fast.

We still lived crammed in the same apartment; Eli and Wolf filled one room, Shmuel and I slept with the stove and the kitchen table, and for Sashie there was the hidden closet we had made into a bedroom for her. We had heaved in a mattress that was too big on all sides and climbed the walls. She plastered every surface with photographs of film actors and actresses, and spent hours in her room stargazing.

She kept the door shut. A sulky girl.

In the mornings and evenings the apartment was loud with my sons' clumsy bulk, their boots the size of wheelbarrows, the banged elbows and slammed doors. Their deep voices, berating each other and teasing their sister.

Shmuel had bought them razors that they cherished, and all three shaved together in the mornings, clustered around the bit of mirror, the black-flecked blobs of lather raining down.

Wolf had found work on scaffoldings and cranes, building the skyscrapers of the city. Eli worked down on the docks, loading and unloading and repairing the ships.

One loved the sea, one loved the sky.

One wanted hot tea in the evenings, the other craved cold milk.

I could not understand why people called them identical twins. They did not look at all identical to me. Even from a great distance I could tell them apart; the very shapes of their bodies as they moved were different. They curved distinctly like two different letters of the alphabet.

I was finally learning to read, you see. But slowly.

They were so close, those two, they had a rough bawdy friendship but it ran deep.

They began to notice women now, and women began to notice them.

In the evenings they combed their hair carefully and went out. There was an urgency about them then, a heady impatience and a lightness in their feet as they clattered down the stairs to the street.

Wolf and Eli no longer did stunts to impress me. Their minds were on other things.

I was glad. It was the natural way of things.

At first I worried. About the women. Because of the power men and women have over each other, the way desire can drive people to ruin their lives, break down the bonds of family. A woman, I thought, might be the one thing that could turn this inseparable pair against each other.

My sons had always been so competitive, you see.

I feared what they might do to each other if they desired the same thing.

But I soon discovered I had no reason to worry, because their tastes were so different. Wolf adored older women, the motherly ones who were sedate and sturdy and radiated wisdom and smelled like yeast and butter, the ones who would hold him against their large bosoms and kiss him on the forehead rather than the mouth. Eli chased the younger girls, the shrill flighty ones whose eyes were never still, whose hands clutched everywhere at once, who sheltered beneath his great arm like birds from a storm.

I kept forgetting about Sashie. She lived in the shadow of her brothers.

She was a strange girl, tall for her age and angular with limp hair that she brushed for hours. From an early age she liked to play at make-believe, at creating worlds of her own to live in. She sat in her room calling herself a princess in a tower, a queen on a throne.

And even when she was not playing, she tended to invent her own version of events around her, twisting the truth to her liking.

For example there was a long period when she was convinced that her hair was naturally blond, and that it was merely dirt, or some trickery of her mother's, that made it look black. She would wash and wash her hair, then rub it violently dry, checking the towel to see if the blackness was rubbing off as she tried to return her hair to its original state, the blond curls of her cinema idols.

Her brothers watched her quizzically night after night, scrubbing and rubbing her head, whisking the towel fast as a shoe-shine boy. When I told them what Sashie thought she was doing, they laughed uproariously and she fled to her room red-faced and ashamed for she worshipped her brothers.

They had laughed, but afterward she was angry only at me.

She did not give up the hair notion for a long time; she stopped her obsessive washing but told herself the blackness would eventually grow out, and she inspected the roots of her hair carefully using two mirrors, searching for a hint of gold.

It was something I could not understand, the way she refused to see the truth that was right in front of her eyes, how she lied to herself without knowing she did.

All this time, all these years Shmuel had continued to write to his parents. Sometimes he lingered over the letters late into the night, head propped in his hand. He still sent them money. They never answered.

He received the odd letter, now and then, from his friends in the theater company; they passed along news. From them he heard that his parents were still living in the same house, the house where Shmuel had been born and his father too. He heard that his sister now had seven children who labored in their father's bakery.

The thought of his nieces and nephews plagued Shmuel; he wrote to his sister begging her to send some of her children to us to raise here. He wrote: Your children have no future over there. Surely you can see that.

Later he wrote: I will pay their passages. We could adopt them. They can have a life here that you cannot even imagine. At least ask the older ones. Let them decide for themselves.

His sister never responded.

I thought of these phantom children, dusted with flour and white as ghosts. They stood around our bed at night.

He continued to write to his family, more and more often as we heard the rumors of what was happening over there, the whispered rumblings of the dark tide rising up and threatening to wash over everything.

The newspapers droned of war with their tiny print and blurred photos of a man in a mustache with his arm outstretched. Newspapers were a reliable source of the truth, apparently. Shmuel and Eli and Wolf read them and argued far into the night.

Me, I did not trust printed words.

Along with the papers there were the rumors we heard, the letters, and the words of frightened travelers who had managed to slip away and sail across the ocean. They came here in their shabby coats, moved in with relatives and disliked to go outside. They shunned daylight.

These people with their haunted eyes, casting suspicious glances everywhere, they tried to tell us things but could not find the words. There was no language excessive enough to describe what they had seen. No words wide or deep enough to hold it. Stories so fantastic, so sweeping in their atrocities that no one could believe them.

No one wanted to believe them. Our neighbors, and even Eli and Wolf, said: They must be mad, these people, seasick and frightened, spewing nightmares and visions. These stories cannot be true, they are fairy tales told to frighten children.

That is what people said.

But I have seen many things. I know that anything is possible.

These stories the new arrivals told, they were too hideous for anyone to have made them up. No mind could twist itself like that.

I have told stories that no one believed. Stories I know in my heart to be true.

Shmuel voiced no opinion, but his eyes were sunk deep, lost in shadows, the color muted. His hands shook, the skin worn thin and transparent over his knuckles like trouser fabric worn through at the knees.

I wanted to hold him, those tensed shoulders. I wanted to comfort him in bed in the dark of night.

But lately he did not sleep at all, he sat up through the night at the kitchen table, writing letters to his parents and sister, beseeching them, begging them to save themselves, come over before it was too late. He wrote: You don't have to forgive me. Come for your own sake, the sake of the children.

He sent the letters though he despaired of their ever arriving. He sent money. And more money. More than we could spare.

In the night sometimes he looked up from his writing and I felt his eyes travel over my body and shy away from my face. There was an anger in his look that I had never seen before, an accusation. *You made me do this. See what you drove me to do.*

His sister's identification papers, they hung between us like a shroud.

I will say for him that he never raised his hand in anger, never spoke a word of blame to me. But there was a cloud over our relations.

We both thought of home now. I thought of Ari as I had not in years.

Our life here seemed false and hollow, suddenly. Our children with their vigorous health and appetites were a mockery of something.

More refugees crept into our neighborhood. One moved in with the elderly couple who lived two floors below us. She was a young woman, the wife of their nephew. Or so she claimed.

The old couple had not seen their nephew since he was a child. But they took her in.

They were too stunned to object.

You see, she came to their door in the middle of the night, she came pounding and crying out until the entire building was aroused. We all came out in our nightclothes, barefoot, complaining, stood squinting in the hall, on the stairs. Her appearance shocked us all to silence.

We could see that she was young, perhaps not yet twenty; her body was starved but still had the pliancy of youth. Her skin unravaged. And yet her short-cropped hair was stark white.

She spun about and regarded us all. Her eyes were the most frightening thing: the pupils shrunk to pinpricks, utterly cold uncomprehending eyes, unmoving as if they had frozen in a moment of unspeakable horror.

She turned to the old couple then and told them that her husband, their nephew, was dead.

They swiftly took her in their arms, pulled her into their apartment and shut the door. The rest of us slowly drifted back to our beds, to uneasy dreams.

But over the next few days many of us returned to that apartment, to listen to this woman's tales as she sat dwarfed by an overstuffed chair.

She spoke of hunger and cold and disease, and these were things we could all understand. The confinement she spoke of, the sudden violence—we all had known that. But she also spoke of a world where logic had gone awry, where babies were taken from mothers, husbands separated from wives, gold teeth drawn from living mouths, bodies piled up like haystacks, hay made into soup, people given numbers because names were an indulgence. A place where great fires burned constantly, black smoke filled the sky yet everyone was dying from the cold. A place of dogs and casual bullets meeting the backs of heads, everything as arbitrary as the made-up rules in a child's game.

Telling us, she laughed at the absurdity of it.

Her pupils never dilated, not even in dim light, as if they were holding something in; they were the eyes of an animal that feels the cold shadow on its back and looks up to see the hawk coming down.

Impossible, my neighbors whispered.

Madness, they said.

She spoke on and on of these unspeakable things, gasping, babbling, letting out barks of laughter and choking on her breath. She could not get the words out fast enough, an endless stream; she watched us, her hectic eyes jumping from face to face.

She inhaled endless slices of bread and cups of tea, seemingly without pausing in her speech. She loaded her tea with sugar, she piled it on bread, she ate it from a spoon, her eyes rolling in a kind of holy ecstasy. She licked her fingers, she could not eat enough sugar.

She's mad, people said. Her mind is gone.

She looked it, with her fingers in her mouth and sweet dribble on her chin. But even then you could see the beauty in her features, the grace of her thin arms inside the cheap dress. Her beauty clashed strangely with the ugliness etched in her eyes, with the raised scars on her neck and on her scalp beneath the white hair. Like fungus growth on a ripe fruit.

She would not tell us how she escaped from such a place.

When we asked she said only: I pretended I was dead. It was not difficult.

She ignored our questions, shook her head violently when we began the litany of names: have you seen . . . did you know . . . what happened to . . . have you heard of . . .

She droned on and on, shrilly, her hand going from sugar bowl to mouth, again and again the touch of grainy fingers to her tongue like a benediction, and she closed her eyes in bliss.

One by one the neighbors stopped coming to see her. This mad girl whose stories they did not believe, or did not want to believe.

As if to acknowledge these things would make them real; whereas denying them would somehow hold them back, keep them confined to the space inside the girl's head.

She had brought the darkness close, brought it into our lives and living rooms and set it loose. People thought she was to blame somehow.

This mad girl stuffing herself with sugar like a child, this girl who would not sleep for fear of her dreams.

I sat with her long after the others had turned away. I watched her pluck at her dress.

Within weeks her teeth rotted away, and then her face was more jarring than ever, with the white hair and blue gums of an old woman, and the lips and cheekbones and eyelashes of a young one.

She ate up her aunt and uncle's sugar ration.

Although they doubted more and more that they really were her aunt and uncle. To doubt her was to believe their nephew was still alive.

When I spoke to the reluctant aunt on the stairs, she said softly: If only she had some proof. Something to prove those stories. I would believe her then. How can we be sure? She doesn't even have a wedding ring.

I hid my hands when she said that.

I watched her trudge down the stairs.

Couldn't they see, the proof was right there, in the girl's flesh, in those eyes, in that hair gone white from shock. What more proof did they need?

That evening I sent Eli to their apartment bearing the last of our sugar.

He stayed there several hours and was silent when he returned.

The next evening both he and Wolf went down and sat with the mad girl as she lisped through her gums, her tongue thick and coated with sugar.

They returned again and again. They were fascinated by her decaying beauty.

They listened to her stories night after night. They sat on either side of her without speaking. They did not know what to believe. The things she spoke of were beyond their imagination.

Like the aunt they too said: If only there were some proof. If only we could be sure.

In spite of this they were both falling in love with her, for she combined the aspects they both desired. For Wolf she was an older woman, with her white hair and weary knowledge of the world; for Eli she was a sugar-fed child, lost and helpless.

I had thought that if the two of them ever pursued the same woman they would be driven against each other, would punch and pummel each other as they had when they were boys.

But no, this love had brought them closer together. They puzzled together over the mystery of her. They stood quiet, respectful in the face of this thing they could not understand. They would never touch her. Their love for her was a protective, chivalrous love.

They wanted to be heroes, I think, they wanted to place themselves between her and the dark thing that threatened her. But they could not understand what that thing was. They did not believe her description of the beast.

One night after they had been with her for several hours, I heard their raised voices, heard their feet pounding up the stairs.

They burst into the kitchen and faced us, Wolf with his hair standing on end, Eli pressing his eyes with his fingers. They could not stand still, they rocked and paced.

We have to leave, Eli said.

Now. Tomorrow, Wolf said.

We've decided, they said.

I asked: Are you in trouble?

I thought of the girl, her bones and pointed breasts, and wondered if I had misread their feelings after all.

No trouble, Wolf said.

They began sorting their clothes, making plans.

You see, they had their proof finally. That night the girl had pushed back her sleeve and showed them the evidence. It was written on her flesh, just as I had thought.

A girl showed them her arm and it was all the proof they needed.

They enlisted in the army the next day.

I had known this time would come, but it happened sooner than I thought.

Shmuel had told me to expect it. He had warned me they would be drafted sooner or later.

Enlisting this way made them feel more decisive, more in control of their destinies.

I watched their broad backs as they folded shirts on the bed. I was inarticulate with grief.

I wanted to warn them.

I longed to say: Don't go back there. Don't go. You have no idea what it's like there.

I touched their shoulders, but they brushed me aside. They were excited, they were boys leaving home for the first time.

If you go to that dark place, you will never come back to me.

What's happening? Sashie said. Where are they going?

I ignored her. Shmuel told her the news and she began to weep.

Don't you know that you can cross the ocean only once?

Make the journey more than that and you're tempting fate.

Will you miss your boys? Wolf said, grinning.

More than anything.

Yes, I said.

Don't go into the forest. You will never come out again.

We'll write to you, Eli said.

Sashie, silly girl, was hugging one then the other, dragging down their necks.

How can I make you understand? There is no logic over there. Natural laws do not apply. Trees walk on human legs, houses walk on chicken feet, villages and oceans disappear without a trace.

I should have told you these things before. Now it is too late.

Why so quiet, mother? Eli said.

She's wondering what she'll do with her time, now that she won't have to cook twelve hours a day, Wolf laughed.

This is the last time I will ever see you.

Bring warm socks, I said, it's so cold there.

Wolf said: Is that all you can say?

Eli said: That's her idea of giving us her blessing.

They went to their father then, and bowed their heads. He put a hand on each of their crowns and recited a prayer.

I embraced each of them then, they bent and I hugged their necks tightly with my cheek against their ears. I wanted to whisper something wise and final to each of them, but I could think of nothing to say. No words wide enough.

We'll take care of each other, Eli said.

Wolf promised: I won't go anywhere without him.

Eli said: Likewise.

Framed in the doorway they were strong shining men, their hair grown too long over their collars, their teeth chipped from childhood fights and accidents.

I hope you remember the fierceness of your boyhood.

You will need it where you are going.

I remember fierceness.

What, no tears, mother? Wolf teased.

Then Eli: Don't you love us?

More than anything.

Wolf said: She's waiting until we leave.

Yes, I won't do it, I won't cry until you leave. I swear. I'll hold it in.

Wolf bowed and Eli gave a clumsy salute. Then they turned and jostled each other good-naturedly, both pushing to be the first one out the door.

I watched their backs. They clattered down the stairs, racing, neck-and-neck. I wanted to tell them there was nothing at the finish but death and a lonely place. But they raced on, just as they had once battled in my womb, both wanting to be the first out in the new world, the first to draw breath.

Eli and Wolf were at a training camp at first, and they sent letters regularly. Reading was still a struggle for me, so Shmuel read the letters aloud, or Sashie did.

The letters were cheerful and chatty but I did not trust them. I did not trust words on paper. Anyone could put words on paper, how could I be sure my sons had written this?

I knew other people trusted printed words; they thought once words were written down and embedded in paper they could not change, they preserved a moment. But I knew better. Words in print are slippery. They can conceal things, they can lie.

I thought of those identification papers I still had which declared I was Shmuel's sister.

Anything that can be manipulated so easily is worthless.

Shmuel and I had never told our children that we were not married. How could we tell them they were illegitimate? They did not need to know.

As for myself I did not care. We were married in spirit, words did not make it more or less so.

But I think Shmuel, even after all these years, Shmuel still longed for a document, our union sanctified through official words on paper.

And Sashie loved her brothers' letters, she took them to her brothers' room which was now hers, and she read and reread them, sniffed them, tasted them, and squirreled them away. She papered the walls with clippings and photographs.

116

When I heard that my sons had been shipped overseas, I knew they were truly gone. I wore black, I tied my hair with black cord, I covered the mirrors, I refrained from washing.

Mother, what are you doing? Sashie cried.

And Shmuel echoed: What are you doing? Do you *want* our sons dead? You're inviting bad luck, mourning people who are still alive.

Funny that he should speak of bad luck, he who had mocked my precautions all these years.

I knew I would never see them again. I recalled Sashie's birth, and how Shmuel and the doctor saw what they should not have seen. A tradition had been violated, and these were the consequences.

For the two men who had watched, I had lost my two sons. An even trade.

I grieved for them for weeks, sat up rocking in bed through the night. I studied the few photographs I had of Wolf and Eli, though I did not trust even photos to show me the truth.

Shmuel grew thin and bent, his eyes were cloudy. One evening he seized my shoulders and shook me till my head rattled, shouting: Why are you doing this? Thousands of people are dying, being killed every day! How dare you sit here grieving for two that are still alive!

It's desecration, he said more softly.

Another time he said: Why are you inviting the worst? Parents should not have to mourn the deaths of their children. It goes against the natural order of things.

Hastily scrawled letters arrived from overseas. Shmuel and Sashie rejoiced in them. I did not believe the charade for a minute.

Shmuel wrote faithfully to them both. One night he said: In their letters Eli and Wolf have asked after the woman downstairs. What should I tell them?

I did not know what to say.

You see, the week before she had hung herself. Some said she had done it because she was grieving for her dead husband; others said she did it simply because she was mad, and that was what the insane did, they killed themselves, it seemed to be the one thing they were good at.

People gossiped, puzzled over her identity.

We would never eat sugar in the same way again.

What should I tell them about her? Shmuel asked a second time. How should I put it?

It doesn't matter, I said.

He sighed. He said: I'll tell them she's peaceful now. I'll say that she no longer has nightmares. I'll say that her hair is still white. That is all they need to know.

He bent again over the paper.

Lies again! Lies written down on paper! Even Shmuel used words for lies and dissembling. How could he possibly trust them?

Sashie wrote too, laboring for weeks over a single note to her brothers. It needs to be perfect, she said.

Shmuel played his violin for weddings, funerals, whatever work he could find.

I hardly went outside. When I did the sky was invariably low and gray; the tangles of pipes and fire escapes clinging to all the buildings reminded me more and more of twisted black trees. I tied a scarf around my head to shut out as much as possible.

I sat in the apartment watching night fall and dawn break, over and over like a tedious dream. I dug the ornamented egg, now dull and tarnished, out of a drawer and peered through the eyehole. The scene inside was dim and far away, mist covered the magic lake and the swans had their heads tucked under their wings. I thought I saw two new figures, black haired, leaning from the highest tower.

Days and weeks went by, and I hardly noticed my daughter.

Sashie, I called to her one day.

She came out of her room and said, Please, I want to be called Shirley now.

Why? I said.

She twisted a lock of hair around her finger and said: I hate the name Sashie.

It was my mother's name, I said. Have I ever told you about my mother?

No, she said.

I knew I had, but she must not have been listening.

She blurted: Sashie is so old-fashioned. I'm American, mother, I want an American-sounding name. Call me Shirley.

I said: You can't change your name. It's written on your birth certificate, you can't change it. And you can't ever get away from where you're from. Your past stays with you, you can't make it go away by dressing up in a fancy name and pretending to be someone else. Remember that.

But I wasn't born in the old country, I was born right here, she protested.

You can't ever escape your family, no matter how you try, I said.

She glared at me darkly from beneath her brows, and twisted her hair tighter, and for the first time I saw how much she resembled me. It was like looking into a fairy-tale mirror that gave me back my youth.

She turned then with her shoulders high and tense and stalked back to her room.

I could not understand her at all. And I suddenly looked around me, at my life, as I had not in years. It had taken a shape I could never have imagined beforehand.

I thought how strange it is, the way the shape of your life grows up around you unbidden, like weeds. In the beginning you do not intend to live any particular way, you think you are living freely, are hardly aware of the subtle choices you are making. But as the years pass your life slowly closes in around you, hardening like a shell, crowding you from all sides, hemming you in with furniture and debts and habits, forcing you into narrower and narrower channels until suddenly you find you have no choices any longer and can only continue in the same direction until the end.

I thought too about love, the different kinds of love. There were people you loved by choice, plunging into it recklessly, headfirst, swallowing it whole, giving in to it without a thought.

And then there were the people you loved by default.

· · ·

A man came knocking, with a shabby suitcase and an exaggerated face like a sad clown.

I called for Shmuel, and when he came to the door he and the stranger embraced without a word.

This man was one of the actors from Shmuel's company long ago, and he sat in the kitchen and I made him tea. I remembered him faintly; the women's roles often fell to him because he was very thin and thus could be swept up in the arms of the hero without too much trouble. I remembered him in a golden wig and false bosom, I remembered his gentle laugh.

Now his cheeks were sunken in, his skin yellow, there were hard sores crusted on those lips that most of his comrades, at one time or another, had been obligated to kiss. Deep creases radiated from his eyes; his hair was falling out, pale strands drifting down to his shoulders. He had just arrived in this country.

How did you get out? Shmuel said.

The actor's face darkened, he started to speak then noticed Sashie listening. He said: I stowed away in a barrel of pickles.

He reached behind his ear and produced a pickle. He reached into his mouth and pulled out another and handed them both to Sashie. He drew pickles from his armpit and nose and pocket, he took off his shoe and found one there. He gave them all to Sashie and kept producing them until her hands were overflowing.

His face never brightened though Sashie giggled and even Shmuel's mouth relaxed. He was remembering their days of traveling together.

Then the actor rose, and drew Shmuel aside, and told him the news about his family. Shmuel sagged, and his actor friend held him and I held him but he was too heavy for us all.

His parents, his sister and brother-in-law and seven children, all gone. Swept away.

He did not speak for the rest of the day and that night in bed he did not weep, there were no tears, but he groaned and swore and beat his fists against the wall and the mattress.

I thought he would hurt himself, I caught his arms and pushed him down flat and held him there, I put my ear to his chest and heard his heart thundering frantically as if wild horses were trapped within.

I felt his hands then, he touched me as he had not for a long time; and we became reacquainted with each other and took comfort in it.

We both wore black now, though he said my unnecessary grief was a mockery of his.

He spoke less and less as the days wore on and he was losing his hearing as well. It had begun the day he heard the news, and every day the noise of the world grew softer and softer.

The news of his family had hurt him so badly it seemed he could not bear to hear any more.

It's like the world is buried in snow, he said abruptly one morning. Everything is hushed.

It was one of his last speeches.

He could no longer work, since he could not hear the other musicians, could not hear himself, could not tell if he was off-key.

He squinted as if that would improve his hearing.

I do not think he particularly missed voices, footsteps, traffic, wind. He could have lived without them. But the loss of his music was a terrible blow.

For weeks he stayed in the apartment, sawing away relentlessly at his violin though he could not hear the notes. As if there was a single magical note that would restore his hearing if he could only find it. Finally he put the instrument aside in frustration.

He missed the music so much. Music was the greatest truth to him.

He would not eat, missed his mouth with the spoon, lost his balance crossing the room. It was as if the deafness had dulled his other senses.

He could not speak, his voice was an awkward squawk now. When he needed to communicate he wrote messages on scraps of paper. I struggled to read them, had to ask Sashie for help. I felt like a fool.

But he did not really want to talk. Neither out loud nor on paper.

Some feelings are too broad for words. There are some stories that defy telling.

We understood each other without speech as people do when they have been together for so long.

His hair grew lushly, he hid his face in the thicket. He went about with his face twisted, teeth bared like a madman's.

I remember the day his scowl lifted.

It was the afternoon that he stood at the window, curtain pulled aside, watching the first snowfall of the season. The flakes fell swiftly, softly, the street below was already blanketed in white. He smiled at me then and held out his arms and I knew he wanted to share this thing, so we could be together in the same white muffled silence.

We stood close in the cold white light from the window, and it fell on us like the softest snow, it lay pale on Shmuel's head and on the tops of his shoulders. And I looked at his eyes, the blue so vivid, and at his teeth shining like a path of stones glowing in moonlight that would lead me through the forest to safety.

And though we were indoors I pictured the snow piling up around us, burying our feet, muffling every step. We waded through the snow to the bed and sat among the white sheets. Shmuel unbound my hair then, and let it fall, and took it up in both his hands and shook it beside his ear. He smiled as if he could hear the bells.

I had not heard them for years. I did not hear them now.

Or perhaps I did.

He lay down then and closed his eyes. I looked at his black hair spread over the pillow, at his nostrils, his eyelashes, his brows. His eyebrows jumped and waggled at me; he was teasing me, he knew I was staring. I lay down beside him and tucked my head beneath his chin and slept.

In the morning he was cold.

It was because of all that snow, piled up around us.

Don't you know how dangerous it is to fall asleep in the snow?

I waited for him to open his eyes but he did not.

I knew he was teasing me, it was always like this, I would watch his face and wait and wait until I could hardly bear it, until I thought I would go mad or burst into tears, and then at the very last moment he would open his eyes, and smile, and laugh.

So I waited beside him.

I waited a long time. He knew how impatient I was, he was testing me. This time I would prove my faithfulness, I would not let him outlast me. I promised I would not move from that spot until he opened his eyes.

I waited. This was a good joke. In a moment he would sit up and we would laugh and laugh.

Sashie

When my father died my mother could not believe it.

She sat by his bedside for two days, holding his hand. She would not allow anyone to remove the body.

He'll be getting up any minute now, she said. In a moment he'll open his eyes.

I was only a child then and even I understood that he was gone.

He's an actor, she insisted. He's only acting.

That blood on his shirt, it's only chicken's blood, she told me though his clothes were clean. She said: They hid rubber bladders filled with chicken's blood in their costumes. So that when they got pricked during the sword fights the blood spurted out like that. It was only a trick, you see.

Any second now he'll stand up and take his bow.

Your father, you know how he likes to tease.

Another one of his jokes.

She repeated these things and would not be convinced until the doctor came, and even *he* could not convince her until he let her listen to my father's chest with the stethoscope.

Ah no, she said then. No.

I will say in her defense that my father *did* always look more vivid, more alive than other people somehow. Even in death. I remember his eyebrows were poised, his lips pursed as if he were about to say something. His hair on the pillow still black and unruly. He still had a sharp-featured boy's face; the lines and creases on his cheeks were incongruous, as if he had drawn them on with his stage makeup for a joke.

The apartment was so empty in those days.

With my father dead, my brothers far away, it seemed like the rest of the world had broken off and drifted, leaving us alone. We had only each other.

There was not much to say.

We circled each other like suspicious dogs.

My mother wrapped herself in black, she sat for hours cradling my father's violin. Not the beautiful golden one he had bought here, but the old squeak-box he'd brought over from the old country. She enveloped herself in a cloud of grief, and it was as if she had removed herself to an unreachable place, far away.

I admit we had never been close.

I treasured the letters from my brothers more than ever. Those letters were far more eloquent company than my mother, though they arrived infrequently and were brief and sloppy.

My brothers were fighting in Europe. Somewhere over there. Even they could not say where exactly. Wolf and Eli both complained bitterly over the fact that they were not together, in the same company. Brothers were always separated, as a rule, but mine had never been apart before and it affected them. Each wrote, in their separate letters, that he did not feel like a complete person without his brother.

Eli wrote: I'm forgetting what I look like without him around. I need to see his ugly mug.

Wolf wrote: I talk to him like he's here. I hear gunfire and I shout, Eli, look out! The guys think I'm nuts.

They missed each other, I think, almost as much as they missed me.

I knew they missed me, though their letters were addressed to my parents.

Wolf wrote: I know mother can't read this, so you must tell her I love her.

Eli wrote: Knowing her, she won't believe it.

Wolf wrote: Tell it to her anyway.

I *did* read the letters to her, or at least I tried. But as soon as she saw the thin envelopes she would push me away.

Don't you care about them? I said. Don't you want to hear what they have to say?

They're dead, she said, you know that.

I said: How can they be dead if they're sending us letters?

Lies, all lies, she said. How can you be so foolish? How can you be so easily duped?

She was the foolish one. *She* was the one who mourned my father and my brothers equally, treated their memories exactly the same. As if my brothers really were dead, or as if my father really were not.

She was secretive, always tinkering in the kitchen, lighting candles and brewing herbs into tea. I did not like to go out in the street with her, she did not look like other women. She wore her skirts long, dragging on the ground, no brassiere or girdle. Thick woolen stockings all year round. It was as if she had never left the old country at all.

Even the women in our neighborhood, who were her age and came from the same place, had taken to plucking their eyebrows, trimming their hair, wearing modern clothes that were only a few years behind the fashions.

My mother did not care, or did not notice, she kept to herself. She held photos of my brothers in her hands, staring at them for hours. The few clothes they had left behind she sniffed and smoothed and folded over and over. She ran her fingers across the dark marks on the wall where Eli had kicked his heels; it had been his favorite spot to stand on his head. The marks rose up the wall, marking his growth with the years.

The way she spoke of them as dead, it was almost as if she wanted it to happen. As if she were trying to kill them.

She seemed to wallow in her sorrow, as if she almost enjoyed it.

When I wrote to my brothers I wrote: Dear William. And: Dear Edward.

These names suited them better, I thought.

Every time they wrote they asked about the madwoman from downstairs, the one with the white hair who had been found hanging behind a door with her tongue out.

I did not like the way they asked about her.

They never asked about me in their letters.

They asked if she was healthy, if her hair was still white, if she had stopped pulling at her dress the way she used to, pulling as if it choked her.

It was *inappropriate* for them to ask.

That was a word I had recently learned.

I wrote to them saying that it had turned out her missing husband was not dead after all, he had reappeared and taken her away with him to a house in the countryside. I wrote that she had gotten fat from all that sugar.

When my father died I wondered how to tell them.

I asked my mother and she said: You don't need to tell Wolf and Eli. They already know, they are with their father, the three of them are all together now.

She was no help at all.

In the end I could not bear to tell them either. In the end I wrote simply: Father has a cold. He loves you. Mother misses you terribly.

It was all true, in a way.

This time when the news came it was in the shape of an official-looking letter.

Two letters, actually, that arrived on the same day.

My brothers were both dead.

I wanted to scream but could get no air.

I told my mother.

But I know that, she said. I've been telling you, all this time.

She was calm, resigned. She had accepted it long ago.

She held me as I cried and I felt how hard and strong her shoulders were, beneath her rough clothes.

The letters were identical, typed with a fancy seal at the bottom. The writer praised Eli and Wolf highly, said they had been killed in action, had died courageously while fighting for God and freedom and justice for all.

I read the letters to my mother.

But I know all that, she said. I don't need a letter to tell me.

To her they were trash. But I treasured those letters. They meant something to me.

My brothers had died hundreds of miles apart, on different battlefields, on the same day.

It was not until the war was over that we got the other letters.

One came from a man named Jimmy, somewhere in the Midwest. He had been a buddy of Wolf's, he wrote, and had been near him when he died. He described how in the thick of fighting, Wolf had suddenly jerked and cried out and clutched his side, and a little blood had dribbled from his mouth.

Yet he had not been hit, there was not a mark on him. Some strange thing, Jimmy wrote, a near miss, a phantom bullet maybe.

Jimmy wrote: Odd things happen in a war, incredible things. Things you would not believe if I told you.

He recalled the look that had come over Wolf's face then, a look of despair, as if he had just lost the one person he loved in the world and no longer wanted to go on living. Wolf had let out a great yell then and dashed out into the open with his mouth gaping wide, and he killed several of the enemy before being torn by bullets, and even then he kept running forward, running impossibly on shredded legs, surging forward with his arms outstretched as if to embrace them.

Wolf had been a swell guy, Jimmy wrote. The best.

The second letter came from a Nicholas in New England, a comrade of Eli's.

The strange thing was that his letter's tale was nearly identical to Jimmy's. He wrote: It's like this. We're in some thick stuff. All of a sudden bam Eli gets knocked clean off his feet. Goes down. We think he's a goner. But then he gets up. Not a scratch. He's laughing, feels lucky I guess, but then he gets this thinking look on his face. Like he's realized something. His face just breaks like a plate dropped on the floor. My brother's dead, he says. Then he lets out this whoop and breaks cover and goes running right at them like a mad dog. Gets all ripped up then.

Neither Jimmy nor Nicholas could tell me the exact times of their deaths.

I read both letters to my mother.

Usually she was loudly scornful of letters, didn't trust a word. But this time she sat musing, her face dreamy, after I'd finished.

We never knew which was the oldest, she said finally. You see, there was such confusion when they were born, they both fought so hard to be first, and no one saw when it happened. Always racing, those two. One always right on the heels of the other. They could never leave each other behind. They bore each other up.

I remember, I said.

I remembered a time years before. The one time I went with my mother to watch my father perform.

It was something she had always done alone. She had never invited us children to go along. Not inviting my brothers I could understand, they were wild, rambunctious, always causing havoc with slingshots and wolf whistles.

But I could not fathom her reasons for excluding me.

I knew how to behave in public.

I think I knew how to behave better than she did.

Something mysterious happened during her evenings out; she would come home with her eyes alight, shaking her hair out of its tight braids, and when my father arrived later they would be unusually tender with one another.

She never told me the plots of the plays. Or what part my father played. Or even the titles.

Of course her exclusion of me made me all the more eager to go.

So I cornered her one evening as she was slipping out, and I begged to go with her.

You won't like it, she said, you won't understand it.

Oh *please*, I said. I had never been to a theater but I had heard they were like palaces, filled with chandeliers; the seats were red velvet like the insides of jewel boxes and the ushers wore white gloves. At the end people threw roses and stood and shouted Encore! I wanted to sit in the balcony, I had never even seen a balcony but I imagined sitting in one and looking down would be the absolute height of elegance.

I wheedled, and my mother gave in because she was already late and an argument would delay her even more. I snatched my coat and followed her out into the dark of an early winter evening.

To my surprise she headed downtown, rather than northward where all the big theaters were located.

Aren't you going the wrong way? I said.

She did not answer.

I tagged behind her. My mother could walk faster than anyone I knew. She could walk more swiftly than my brothers could run. I had never seen her legs; sometimes I wondered if she had wheels and a little steam engine beneath her long skirts.

She waited for me in a doorway, then led me inside and down some narrow stairs.

I smelled snuff, mildew, wet wool.

This was a theater?

We were in a low-ceilinged basement room, impossibly packed already with women in head scarves, men with untrimmed beards. It was uncomfortably warm, people's faces were already slick with sweat, they were like oily sardines in a can. The noise was overwhelming: a hundred tongues wagging in the language of the old country. The harsh gutturals filled the air with saliva.

I knew a word here or there, of course, for my parents still spoke that language at times, usually moments when they forgot themselves, when they were excited or angry.

I knew the words but I felt like a foreigner, I honestly felt like an explorer in some distant land standing among the natives. I was conscious suddenly of the few inches of leg that showed between my hem and high shoes, and I blushed.

No one noticed. They were too engaged in their conversations, their gesticulations. I saw women nursing babies, right there in the open.

We found seats near the back and I was pressed in on all sides by scratchy wool cloth and damp arms and the smells of cabbage and yellowed prayer books.

The play began and the audience did not cease their gossip but simply lowered their voices a notch. Consequently the actors had to raise their voices, practically scream.

Not that I understood much of what they said. The lines were in the old language.

I could follow it easily enough, because it was the worst kind of melodrama, the sort of predictable story everyone knows, with people contorting their faces like clowns, bawling at the tops of their lungs, gnashing their teeth. Everything was played at full tilt, top volume. True love, utter hatred. The simplest hand gestures originated in the shoulder, so that they became athletic feats.

The story had all the usual ingredients: innocent love, hopeful promises, ill-fated seduction; all followed by betrayal, sword fights, murders, impassioned speeches, and endless moaning death scenes.

All that excessive emotion, it was embarrassing to watch. They seemed so naked, the actors, with the emotions spilling out of them sloppy and embarrassing as vomit, loud as a belch. Pure uninhibited feeling, raw as a wound.

The people in the audience all around me were leaning forward, thoroughly engrossed. The action on the stage elicited laughs and gasps, and sniffling perfectly on cue. The people in the audience spoke loudly, and often, they commented on the action, they spoke directly to the characters on stage as if they were old friends, offering them advice or insults.

I saw my father on the stage but hardly recognized him. My dignified father had the role of the fool, a dim-witted and drunken lout. He staggered and rolled about the stage, eyes unfocused, trousers unfastened. When the lovers' romantic declarations grew tedious he burst in with bawdy songs, he relieved tense moments with a smirk or hiccough.

The audience loved him, they laughed till they wept.

I did not want to laugh like the rest of them, it did not seem proper.

But I did, I couldn't help it.

As the tension escalated and the audience leaned even closer, the pale anguished hero seemed on the verge of collapse but the audience's hot breath buoyed him up, it was all that kept him on his feet.

And later, after the hero had died an anguished writhing death, he returned as a ghost and drifted across the stage and his feet seemed not to touch the boards. He truly levitated, for a minute or more, I saw the empty space beneath his feet. Then the villainous rival appeared and our hero flew across the stage and landed on the man's back and seized his ears and twisted his head completely around. The audience gasped at the flight, and gasped louder at the loud cracking sounds the villain's neck made. Red gouts of blood bloomed on his costume, and then the vengeful ghost twisted his head completely off and dropped it with a dull thud on the stage, where the eyes continued to blink and the mouth still issued protests.

I must have dozed off. I must have imagined that part.

I grew tired of straining my neck to see the stage so I watched my mother instead.

Her hands were clasped, her scarf had slipped unnoticed from her head and lay on the floor behind her. She had her gaze fixed on the stage, not just on my father but on all of it, all the gaudy spectacle.

There were tears glittering at the inner corners of her eyes.

I saw that the play meant something to her, in spite of the chintzy costumes and overblown speeches. It spoke to her somehow; these drunks and witches, and princes and scholars and bankers' daughters were all real to her, more than real, they were larger than life.

She liked it, I think, because they acted out the things she felt inside but did not know how to express.

I did not see the ending of the play, did not even know if it was happy or sad. I was too busy watching my mother.

The room exploded with clapping and suddenly I was surrounded by bellies and back pockets because the audience had risen all together. The actors bowed again and again and my father got the biggest laugh when he bowed too low and fell drunkenly off the stage.

My mother and I stood outside in the street watching the people walking home arm in arm. The cold night air felt clean and good. My father came outside to join us for a moment. He put his arms around my mother, wiped her cheeks with his thumbs. Now he looked like my father again, the drunken glaze was gone from his eyes, he stood erect and graceful.

Was I that bad? he said.

Wonderful, my mother said, rubbing her eyes.

Still wonderful the twelfth time? he laughed. She had her hands on his chest.

Did you like it, Sashie? he said.

Yes, I said.

He left us then and went back inside to remove his costume and prepare the room for its daytime role as a classroom.

I walked home with my mother and she was silent, lost in her thoughts.

In a way, I think, the play was what was real to her and daily life was a pale charade.

My mother did not ask me to come again.

I would not have wanted to go anyway. It had made me uncomfortable to sit next to her in the audience. My mother was a private person, she usually kept her thoughts to herself. But during the play I had seen her face unfold like a flower, had seen her thoughts splashed plainly across her face.

It was a private moment for her. I felt I had been intruding, to sit and stare.

It was too much, just to sit there next to her was too much, my thigh touching hers.

Too much, too hot, too close.

I did not want to get too close to her.

I would not want her to see me naked and exposed with my heart splayed out, as I had seen her in the dark of the theater.

I was only a child then but I could sense what my mother was like; she was capable of anything if provoked, she was like a wild animal, fury-driven and ferocious.

I knew, somehow, that she could tear me to pieces if I let down my guard for a moment.

I did not want to get too close.

I dreamt a dream night after night that began like my favorite fairy tale and then turned sour.

The dream always began somewhere dark and close, like a forgotten drawer. There was soft slippery dust that clung to my lips and clothes and when I came out into the light I could not brush it away.

Then the dream was like a film set, with bright lights and director's chairs, scaffolding, and cameras. I knew I was meant to play the princess, it was written in the script—but no one would believe me. They all laughed, they could not see past the gray film on my face and my dirty dress. You're no princess, they said. There was a black coating on my hair but I could see out of the corners of my eyes that it was golden underneath, if they would only look.

Then my mother came toward me in satin hoopskirts with her face like a painted doll's, and she did not walk, she rolled, as if she had wheels instead of legs. And behind her came my brothers, with ribbons in their hair, in pink and lavender dresses that strained across their chests and left their hairy calves and feet all exposed. When they saw me they pointed and laughed behind their hands, and simpered like evil stepsisters.

And then I realized what the story was, what their roles were and what mine was, and I felt relieved because the good parts of the story, the fairy godmother and the balls and gowns and glass slippers and handsome princes, were still to come. My mother handed me a broom and I swept diligently at the ashes on the floor and a thousand bright lights shone on us and many people, directors and assistants and technicians, seemed to be watching from the shadows. I swept and swept and my mother watched with her arms folded and I thought that the sooner I finished the task the sooner I would be dancing in the arms of the charming prince at the ball.

But the dust refused to behave, it rose up and stuck to my skin. I looked at my arm and it was covered with a gray linty fur that I could not scratch off. My brothers laughed and rolled in the dust, kicking up their legs so that I could see the enormous lace knickers they wore underneath.

The dust was coating my tongue now, crowding my eyes, I could not blink it away. I looked down and saw that I was entirely black and white and shades of gray like a newspaper photo though my brothers in their dresses were so gaudy colored they hurt my eyes. The cameramen pointed their camera at us and it was shaped like a cannon.

Then the fairy godmother appeared in a ball of light, and waved her wand and said in her flutey voice that her name was Glinda, good witch of the north, and she looked at me *so* kindly and seemed *so* familiar. But she was swept away by a horde of dwarves before I could remember where I had seen her before.

Where was my ball gown? And my dancing slippers and pumpkin coach?

It did not matter because we seemed to have skipped over that part of the story, and were already near the end. Here came the prince with the telltale slipper on a silken pillow. It was bright red with a low heel, covered in rubies with a bow on the toe. The prince's face was bare and featureless as a plate but he had the most beautiful hair, a blond scroll of it like the jack of hearts in a deck of cards.

He knelt and I was glad that this silly charade would soon be over. All I had to do was put on the slipper and then everyone would know who I really was, the dust and rags would fall away and a royal crown would sprout from my head.

How could we have not seen how beautiful she was before, how could we have been so blind, the film directors and the prince and even my mother would say.

Printed on the label inside the shoe were the familiar blond boy and his dog, winking and beckoning me.

I drove my toes into the shoe's mouth.

My foot would not go in.

There must be some mistake, I said.

The prince raised the flat blank front of his head to me, but he was no longer dressed like a prince. He was in a dirty soldier's uniform and I realized he had no face because it had been blasted clean off in battle. He held his lost face, spread out on the pillow he held in his hands. An inverted mask, eyes like hard-boiled eggs and teeth laid out in a grin, a web of blood vessels holding it all together.

My brothers' dresses had turned into uniforms, and my brothers now lay facedown and unmoving in the dust.

And now soldiers began raining from far above, they fell all around and their parachutes refused to open so when the men landed they collapsed, folded up like accordions with cracking snapping sounds. My mother wheeled about trying to catch them before they touched down; she held her skirt out in front of her to bag them, as if they were falling apples.

Pull the red cord, she called to the ones in the air but they did not seem to hear.

I tried again to jam my foot into the shoe but it would not go.

My foot bulged horribly all around, like a fat neck in a too-tight collar.

I somehow knew that if I could just get that shoe on my foot, everything would be all right.

I pushed and pushed as the men fell heavily all around, grunting as they landed.

My fat foot. The stubborn shoe.

I found a knife in my hand.

I sawed at my toe, hacked at my heel. Blood spurted, though I felt nothing. The little nubs of flesh fell in the dust. I tried my foot in the shoe and saw I would need to hew a strip off the side.

I tried again and the shoe finally fit, though it pinched sharply. I stood, I stamped, I clicked my heels together but the rain would not stop and my brothers did not rise.

I tried to turn them over, first one then the other, but they were stuck to the ground like scabs and would not budge. Men were piling up everywhere, arms and legs and limp useless parachutes spilling out too late and puffing up like blisters, and I drove my foot farther and farther into that shoe trying to make everything right.

The blood welled up.

I always woke with my left foot wedged between the bedpost and the wall.

The movie stars smiled comfortingly down at me. Trapped inside the black-and-white photographs, pinned to the wall, but they shifted and blinked and smiled all the same.

A trick of the light.

The first time I had the dream I told my mother about it. She listened, nodded sagely. I thought she would have some insight, an interpretation. But she said only: You should clean under your bed more often, maybe. And not eat fruit before bed.

The next time I had the dream I did not tell her. Nor the next time, nor the next.

The shoe never fit, no matter how hard I pressed.

In the dream I thrust my foot in, again and again, kicking my foot against the wall, night after night. I would kick and then wake to hear my mother calling from the other side of the wall: What's that knocking? What is it? Is that you?

And before I could answer, she would always say: Shmuel? Is that you?

Lying in the dark, coming out of the dream, listening to her voice on the other side of the wall.

Hearing her say: You're so late.

But I've been waiting up for you, she would say.

I would draw my sore foot back under the covers, try to catch my breath.

Be quiet, she would say then. Quietly, Shmuel. Don't wake Sashie. If she hears you she'll have bad dreams.

She'd say that and then I'd lie awake till morning.

My mother spoke often of my brothers. I listened to her stories and said nothing, but it bothered me that she was so wrong about them. She had missed so many things about Wolf and Eli, had never really seen them clearly. I knew them much better than she did, so it bothered me to hear her speak so authoritatively.

She could not see their flaws. I suppose she was blinded by her love, a fierce instinctive kind of love like what a mother animal feels for her young.

I did not correct her, I let her babble on. She was wrong about them. But then, she got a lot of things wrong.

The apartment seemed so empty with my brothers and father gone.

Echoes lingered, like week-old food smells caught in the curtains. I thought I heard their heavy footsteps, their laughter, my father practicing wedding music on his violin.

The emptiness, the silence did not go away as months and then years passed.

I tried to fix up the place, decorate, but the apartment resisted me, the very walls were stubborn. The pictures I tried to hang slid down the greasy wallpaper and fell on their faces.

My father and brother were the ones who had brought life and color into the rooms. Now all was dull and faded. I could hardly bear it. When I looked around I wanted to scream at the bareness, the peeling paint. The only break in the grayness was my mother sitting there in her mourning black.

With no men in the house, there was nothing to do. No one to please.

I went to school. I met some girls.

I grew, I suppose.

The months and years passed like a monotonous dream, like stitching an endless seam.

There is nothing worth telling about those years.

What is there to tell about a mother, a daughter?

My mother's life had stopped when her husband died.

I've figured out that interesting things happen only when men are around.

Men make life interesting. Men make things happen.

Everybody knows that. All the songs say so.

My mother took in laundry and repaired shoes to make ends meet.

I was waiting, waiting, in those years, I did not know what for, but I expected it any moment to come and knock at the door.

Ilana

I knew I should not have let them take him away like that.

I knew he would come back to me if I waited long enough.

He came at night, his teeth glowing in the moonlight. I would hear his footsteps first, tapping on the floorboards, and then see his shadow thrown huge and wavering against the wall and climbing halfway across the ceiling.

He came and sat at the edge of the bed and I spoke to him though I knew it was useless. He had lost his hearing, after all.

I could never see him as clearly as I would have liked, and he never stayed long. I thought it was because we had never been made man and wife in law, as he had wanted.

I thought that if I had a marriage contract I would have more of a claim on him, could make him stay with me.

His parents and his sister were always snatching him back to the other side.

There were icicles in his mustache.

He only stayed long enough to remind me of his absence. Like the twinge of pain when you put your tongue in the tender hole where a tooth had been.

He left an imprint of his body on the white sheets, like a snow angel.

In the mornings it was gone.

Perhaps if we had had more children he would be more inclined to stay.

In the mornings I looked at the face of my daughter, at the mark between her brows already deep from frowning. She washed her hands, over and over as if to rid herself of something.

I did not want her to repeat my mistakes, I wanted to tell her to get the official papers when the time came with her name and his side by side, to get rings and promises, and to have children to seal the bond so that her husband would never have reason to go away.

But she stood at the sink and when I drew near she raised one shoulder as if blocking a blow. She rubbed her hands under the cold water, a muscle twitching in her jaw. She scrubbed and scrubbed at some stubborn stain that only she could see.

Sashie

It's time I went and found a nice husband for you, my mother said.

Oh, *no*, mother, you really don't need to do that, I said. I had just walked in the door, red faced and gasping from the stairs.

It's time, Sashie, she said.

Call me *Shirley*, I told her for the hundredth time.

I knew she wouldn't.

It was autumn, chilly out. My mother was busy with the week's laundry; she was using a wooden paddle to stir the clothes in an iron pot on the stove. The steam billowed up around her, damp wisps of hair clung to her face. Clotheslines stretched across the kitchen, some already slung low with sodden clothes. I had to push them aside to make my way across the room.

Tell me what you want and we'll find it, she said.

It's too soon for me to think about *that*, I said.

Tomorrow then, my mother said without looking up.

I was eighteen now. I was taking courses in shorthand and typing and stenography. I had considered finding an apartment of my own, living the life of a single girl, but I felt I could not leave my mother alone. She was no longer young. She had no one left; I knew she needed me.

Also I admit I couldn't afford to live alone.

And there was a part of me that didn't want to leave her to her own devices. I didn't want to let her out of my sight, not for a minute. Who knew what she could get up to once my back was turned? I thought of my brothers, their faces were hazy but I remembered how she had not wanted them to leave home. And when they did, they had died in a faraway place just as she had known they would. It had been all her fault somehow.

I did not want to go away and have the same thing happen to me.

She had killed my brothers, practically.

She talked to ghosts.

Don't you want to get married? she said.

Of course, I told her, but not right this minute.

I had never discussed marriage with my mother before, although I did notice men. That fall they seemed particularly vibrant, in their bright ties and crisp shirts like birds in mating season. I saw them filling the streets of the city, walking briskly with their shoes polished and their hair sleeked back. I made a game of picking out my favorites as I stood waiting for buses.

I certainly did not want my mother's help. I knew her feelings about thrift and practicality. I suspected her idea of a perfect man was one who would work steadily for sixty years without a break, wear the same suit of clothes day after day.

I respected my mother but she had no sense of refinement, no *delicacy*. When I accompanied her to the marketplace, I was always shocked by her feinting and thrusting, her swift grabs at dead fish and plucked chickens, her fierce haggling over carrots and cabbage. She liked to stand nose-to-nose with the shopkeepers, jabbing them in the chest with their own produce, until they threw up their hands and gave in.

She seldom spoke of my father anymore.

Now my mother hoisted the wet clothes from the pot with a grunt and loaded them into the wringer.

Tomorrow we'll go, she said.

I can't, after my classes I'm going shopping with Tessie and Marianne, I said quickly.

My mother worked the handle. The clothes twisted in agonized postures, tighter, tighter; water dribbled out.

Then Sunday, she said through her teeth. Sunday evening we'll go, no excuses.

I saw one of my dresses pass through the wringer, its sleeves flapping in protest.

All right then, I said. Go where?

You'll see, she told me.

The following afternoon, as I walked the streets gazing in shop windows with Tessie and Marianne, I wondered what my mother had in mind. I walked between the two of them, we linked arms and stepped in unison. I was so preoccupied I think I would have stepped in front of a streetcar if it weren't for them.

My mother had only seen my friends once, from a distance, but she disliked them. Those girls, they're nothing but leeches, she often said. All soft and hungry, sucking the life out of everyone around them. Girls like that, they'll let their husbands waste away, they'll lock their children in closets to keep the house clean. You should be careful or they'll get you too, Sashie.

Shirley, I'd remind her. And she'd say: Remember, a leech's bite numbs you at first, so you don't even notice it until it's stuffed itself with your blood.

As I walked with my friends, I could not help recalling my mother's words. She had a knack for doing that: casually painting unappetizing pictures that affixed themselves like halos to everything I held dear. It was true that Tessie and Marianne were unusually plump and healthy looking. They both had long graceful legs, they filled out their dresses generously, they had no corners. Marianne wore her blond hair in a permanent wave; she had a large flat face, rather shovel-like, but still quite pretty. Tessie had auburn hair and freckles which she covered with thick pasty makeup. She talked a great deal, with much waving of hands, and had a sense of style I greatly admired: her jewelry, her scarf flung over her shoulder just so, her hats decked with dried flowers, false fruit, stuffed birds.

We strolled along looking at the splendidly dressed mannequins, with their aloof faces and pointed toes. Every now and then I caught a glimpse of our reflection in glass, two pale swans with a dark shadow between. I had grown to be slight and wiry and dark haired like my mother. My mother called me skin and bones; I called it svelte. I also had her probing eyes, although I could not use them as she did. My mother could intimidate young men into giving her their subway seats or drive away salesmen without a word, merely with a glance. I did not. Still, when I studied myself in the mirror and saw my mother's eyes staring back, I felt a twinge of power, the potential in me.

But I did not want to be like my mother.

I did not want to be a force of nature. I wanted to be a *lady*.

So I avoided my mother's ways, her pugilist stance, her out-thrust chin. I'd paced with books on my head for years, practiced enunciation with a pencil between my teeth. I bought high-heeled shoes; I loved that nice clatter on hard floors. The tap-tap of shoes, a pair of gloves, a precise tight-lipped smile with no vulgar teeth showing: these were the hallmarks of a lady.

Shirley, for God's sake, said Tessie.

Where's your head? That cab nearly flattened you, said Marianne.

You ought not moon about like that. Those fellows thought you were staring at *them*, Tessie said.

I did not know which fellows she meant; the streets were full of men, in groups, in pairs, in suits, in shirtsleeves, leaning against walls with cigarettes. Some touched their caps when we passed, others touched the front of their trousers and smirked.

The wind whipped our skirts. Tessie's gossip whirled about in a flurry of shrill words, like dry leaves.

The men turned up their collars, cupped matches like secrets between hand and mouth.

We stopped at a drugstore soda fountain. The sudden warmth indoors made me breathless. Tessie and Marianne hoisted themselves up on the only empty stools, their hips overflowing. I stood, my elbow on the counter, and watched as they sucked up their sodas. Ravenously they pulled at the straws, their cheeks drawing in, their mouths so red.

Tessie bought some candy in a white paper sack and the two of them dug into it. They daintily licked their fingers.

Shirley? Tessie said, offering the bag.

No thank you, I said. Bad for my complexion, I said.

You should try drinking a glass of milk in the morning, with a raw egg mixed in, Marianne offered. That should clear those spots right up.

Mmm, I said. I'd been avoiding sweets merely to maintain my figure; my skin didn't *need* improvement.

How's your new fellow? Marianne asked Tessie.

Ah, that oaf, Tessie said. Took me skating last weekend, told me he was a pro. Helps me on with the skates, offers to hold my hand. And then the minute we're on the ice there he goes, crashed out, knocking people down like ninepins.

No! How embarrassing!

For *him*, yes. *I* pretended I didn't know him.

You didn't!

And wouldn't you know, he gets up, falls right back down again with his trousers completely split up the back.

How terrible!

But it turned out quite well. I met this fascinating man; when I told him I was alone he bought me coffee and walked me home. He was a charming skater and he could speak French. And *he* at least could keep his trousers in one piece.

Marianne and I digested this.

But men are all the same, they're all fools, Tessie said, sinking her teeth into butterscotch.

She'd had more experience than us, we could not argue.

They're all fools, Tessie went on, they go from their mothers to their wives, and if they have any time in between, they don't know what to do with themselves. It's single men who cause all the trouble in the world. Look at wars, tavern brawls, tramps—they're all single men. If men stay alone too long they start touching their private parts, more and more, until they fall off. Then they turn into criminals, or lunatics, or artists.

You've got it all figured out, Marianne said admiringly.

Though I knew it was not what Tessie had meant, I found myself picturing a man's private parts propped before an easel holding a paintbrush.

You'll see, girls, Tessie said wisely and patted our hands.

I thought of my brothers, their broad-shouldered hulking presence throughout my childhood. I recalled their massive shoes, sour socks, the mess of beard stubble and soap scum they left in the sink. Tessie made men sound as flimsy as a handkerchief, to be folded neatly or soiled according to whim; but when I thought of my brothers I thought of glaciers making their massive, inexorable progress, permanently reshaping the landscape as they passed.

Oh, shy little Shirley, Tessie said. One day you'll find a man.

She never said such things to Marianne. But then, Marianne was blond.

I'm not shy, I said automatically.

Marianne snorted. Daintily.

Tessie sighed and slouched, resting her bosom softly on the counter. Her breath in my face was heavy with chocolate and cinnamon. She settled her hips more comfortably on the stool, and a passing stock boy turned his head and stared and stumbled, his load of cotton balls and white stationery spraying everywhere.

Are you ready? my mother said on Sunday evening.

Yes, I said.

I knew she was. My mother had her own rules of propriety. Her hair was strained back from her face, braided, looped and knotted and tucked away. *Not a hair out of place* was her mantra. She was superstitious about such things: if she noticed stray hairs or eyelashes on her clothes she'd put them in her pocket. She carefully collected her fingernail clippings, burned them in the stove and made me do the same. She had a good figure for a woman her age but refused to flatter it; she wore drab, baggy clothes. Fine clothes, she said, tempt the evil spirits. By this I assume she meant pickpockets. She never carried a purse, kept the apartment keys on a chain at her wrist, her money stuffed down her dress.

As for me, I wore my rust-colored wool dress, new stockings, hat and gloves and the cameo pin. I had bought the pin because Tessie had one like it. When my mother first saw it she asked: Who is that a picture of? When I said I didn't know, she asked: Why do you want to wear some stranger's picture?

My mother wore no jewelry, she did not care about such things, she preferred to collect bits of hair, crushed insects, a ticket stub from ten years ago squirreled away in her pockets.

We walked through the darkening streets. The sidewalks were crowded with men and women, with gangs of children having a last lark before they were called home.

If you saw us then, strolling arm in arm, talking companionably, you would have thought us the best of friends; you would be surprised when I told you we were not.

Oh, we talked, but only of the most mundane things. My mother is not an articulate woman.

She spoke of recipes, of clothes she had mended for me, of pipes she had repaired that day; she had an uncanny knowledge of plumbing. How did you know what to do? I asked, and she shrugged, saying: Have you ever seen the inside of a cow? Next to that, the sink is nothing.

She spoke of the sick people she had visited with her herbal remedies: patients too poor for doctors, or too superstitious, or else they were illegal immigrants who distrusted everyone who did not speak their language. She grew the herbs herself, in pots on our windowsills; they were twisted, skeletal ugly little plants, and she kept their names and uses to herself.

I knew a good daughter was supposed to take her mother's arm on the street, to help her over the curbs and puddles, to support her feeble steps. Not so with *my* mother. When I took her arm, she ended up dragging me, my hand clamped beneath her elbow, my feet hardly touching the ground. She led me through a neighborhood I hated, with the tenements and narrow streets, foreign cooking smells and babies' cries pouring from the windows.

We turned onto a quieter street.

Ah, here we are, she said.

We paused before an apartment building of weathered brick. At street level was a butcher shop, brightly lit. We could see the red-and-white marbled meat in the glass cases, resting on soaked paper, and the ropes of sausage, all different thicknesses, hung on hooks. Behind the cases stood a heavy, jowly man in a stained apron, his arms folded and resting on his protruding stomach. He watched us through the window, tiny eyes sunk deep in his face.

A smell of blood, of spices, of mopped floors hovered in the air.

Hung on the wall of the shop facing the cases were photographs, framed and glassed in, photographs of smiling girls in wedding gowns. Even from the window I could see that they must have been his daughters or nieces, they had his embedded eyes, his thick shape. I could see the girls' meaty pink faces, flushed from excitement or the tightness of their dresses, their fat fingers choking the stems of flowers. No grooms, only the red-faced girls in their identical dresses, lined up like a row of merchandise.

The butcher glared.

146

My mother tugged me away from the display window. My breath had clouded the glass.

What are we doing here? I asked.

This way, she said and steered me to the stairs that led to the apartments above.

On the second floor the hallway was narrow, high ceilinged and dark. The paneled walls glistened with varnish, or perhaps condensation. Water dripped and echoed somewhere. I could not see the end of the hall.

My mother rapped at one of the doors. We heard shuffling feet; the door opened and a large red-haired woman ushered us in.

The apartment was close and cluttered; everything seemed out of scale, and awry, as if a dollhouse had exploded. Claw-footed chairs crowded around a coffee table buried under telephone directories and loaded ashtrays. Bookshelves were crammed with trinkets, encrusted teacups, a fishbowl filled with murky scum, photograph albums. Doilies covered every surface. Drapes hid the windows and much of the walls. Great fuzzy piles of knitting covered the sofa and lay in corners like a slowly encroaching moss, like cobwebs or dust balls run amok.

A radio played soft music. There was a smell, both sweet and faintly unpleasant, like food left out too long. The red-haired woman took my coat from my shoulders. She was my mother's age, with perfectly white, flawless skin; it was soft and sagging with age, but still striking. Her hair was a strident, metallic color that did not match her skin, a botched dye job. She had green eyes, eyebrows painted on in dramatic sweeps, a round, ample body; she wobbled on her feet as if her shoes were too small.

I knew immediately that this woman and my mother were old acquaintances; they stood silently, giving each other long assessing looks; understanding passed between them in the tightening of a mouth, a tug at a sleeve.

The woman turned to me, took my hand between her hot, damp palms. Come in, sit down, she said and her accent was like my mother's; they were from the same place. I'm Annabelle, she said; I saw my mother flinch at the name.

147

This is *Sashie*, my mother said firmly.

Shirley, I corrected, nodding and smiling.

Annabelle gave me an understanding look.

She hobbled stiffly to the chairs, adjusting cushions, tsking softly in her throat as puffs of dust rose up. She tinkled and rattled as she moved, she wore several strings of beads, and two pairs of glasses on chains around her neck, as well as a third pair hooked in the bosom of her dress.

We sat.

Your mother tells me you're looking for a man, Annabelle said briskly.

Ah, well, not— I began. Annabelle and my mother both leaned forward intently. And then it all became clear: the photograph albums, the cardboard boxes brimming with letters and pictures, stacked everywhere.

I don't need a matchmaker, I said sharply.

She blinked her eyes innocently: Oh, but I'm not—

I snapped: My mother didn't tell me why we were coming here. I'm sorry to waste your time— I rose, thinking: *calmly*, Shirley, a lady never loses her temper.

Annabelle raised her hands. She said: I'm hardly a matchmaker, Shirley dear.

She's not, Sashie, that's not why we're here, my mother told me.

I don't need this, I'm perfectly capable of meeting a man myself; in fact, I *have*; in fact, I've met *several*! I said.

Of course you have, Annabelle said soothingly. Of course you don't need a matchmaker. A lovely, talented girl like you? Hardly! She smiled ingratiatingly and said: Look at you! Beautiful! Boyfriends right and left!

Careful, Shirley. Under no circumstances does a lady slap someone in the face, no matter how much she wants to.

I said this to myself and very slowly sank into my seat.

Annabelle leaned forward and clasped my hands. Her breath smelled of cigarettes and dinner, pickled beets and boiled cabbage. She said: There are plenty of men in the world for you, too many, it makes it difficult to find exactly the right one. I'm going to help you with that.

How?

You'll see, she said and smiled. Shirley, she said, the world is full of fine men, handsome men, but you can't go out and have them as easy as picking flowers. You find a man, you have to *wait*, you have to let him *notice* you, wait for him to ask. Men get to choose first; a girl can say only yes or no. You can't approach a man yourself, not if you're a lady, and I know that you are. Men are dull witted, it takes time, there are always complications. I'm going to save you time, save you the trouble; here *you'll* be the one to choose, you'll get to take home exactly the one you want.

Really?

She nodded.

My mother said: I don't want you wasting your time, chasing this one and that one. Find the right one now, spare yourself and me the trouble.

I looked from one to the other. So you're *not* going to show my picture to a bunch of middle-aged men and their mothers, and ask them what they think? I asked Annabelle.

She laughed.

And you're *not* going to show me a bunch of men's photos, men hiding their bald heads under hats, their fat stomachs behind car doors, themselves ten years ago? You're not going to read me their lists of requirements?

Hardly, she said.

No letters? No chaperoned meetings?

She laughed again. I own this building, she said as if that explained everything.

She stood with a clink and a clatter, my mother stood, I stood, and we all filed out of the apartment.

I followed Annabelle's stiff hobbling gait down the hall. In a dark corner she stopped, removed a ring of keys from her pocket, and unlocked a door no wider than a single board.

My mother and I followed her up a narrow, grimy staircase and down a narrower passage. At first I heard nothing but the soft fall of dust, the skittering of mice. I noticed smells of soap, of sweat, of bedclothes, and the sounds of living, oblivious behind the walls.

As my eyes adjusted to the dimness I saw that the building had been remodeled at some point; the original rooms had been divided into smaller apartments with flimsy thin walls, and the passage we stood in had been carelessly left over. I followed Annabelle, my right hand brushing cold brick, the left plywood. The newer walls were so thin they faintly glowed with light, and seemed to quiver with noise and breath like the tight head of a drum.

Hush, someone said.

I bumped into Annabelle's soft back. She had paused before a splinter of light, a peephole in the wall. She peered in, the light slicing across the green glass of her iris. She moved aside, beckoned to me. When I hesitated, she seized my head in her impatient hands and forced it to the opening.

Oh, I said. I saw a man, a small drab man sitting on one chair with his feet up on another, his shoes off, wearing trousers over long underwear and eating beans out of a can with a fork.

His socks were all holes, his suspenders hung around his hips, the ends of his straggly mustache fell in his mouth, he chewed beans with a kind of abstracted concentration, his throat working. How he ate those beans, grinding them to mash, his mouth going round and round, as if they were the most important thing in the world!

Oh no, I said.

We shuffled on. Annabelle beckoned me to another peephole, and I bent to look.

I smelled sweat. Then a glistening figure hopped into view, disappeared, hopped in again. He was stripped to the waist, wearing an athlete's tight short pants, his hands held in fists. He was boxing with himself, dancing lightly on his toes, circling, ducking, hooking and jabbing at the air.

The sweat dripped from his face, he grunted like an animal, he blotted his face with a towel. The hair spread in an irregular pattern over his chest and stomach and in two fugitive tufts on his shoulders.

His apartment was bare, only a narrow iron bed and a chair. A long mirror stood propped against the wall. The man abandoned his invisible opponent, bounced to the mirror, punched the air twice, then stopped and looked at himself. He looked a long time, flexing his muscles, looking deeply, lovingly.

No.

In the next room I saw a man still in the vest and tie he had worn to his work. He sat at a table reading a newspaper, pushing up his glasses with an index finger. Every few moments something he read seemed to anger him so much that he slammed the paper down and swore incoherently. Then he would pick up the paper and resume his reading. Sometimes he grew so incensed that he leaped up from his chair and raged about the room, muttering and spitting and shoving the furniture about. Eventually he would quiet down and pick up the paper again, only to be offended anew.

We moved on.

Men are at their truest when they are alone, Annabelle said.

We paused at other apartments. Annabelle took a kind of vicious, condescending interest in the men; she looked and smacked her lips, nearly sneered. My mother seemed indifferent; an uninterested zoo visitor.

We climbed another narrow flight of stairs and peeped into a new series of apartments.

I lingered for a long time at some of the rooms. Annabelle and my mother did not try to rush me.

I saw a man with a beautiful face, lovely blue eyes and blond curls like an angel, but his body was a broken puppet's, he was staggering and drunk, the bottle still in his hand, his shirt twisted nearly backward. As I watched he turned toward me, he seemed to meet my eyes, he stumbled forward, clasped his hands, rolled up his eyes in a pious and holy expression. And then as I watched he bent double and began to vomit.

I saw a man I thought I liked, he seemed sober and industrious, he sat hunched over a desk with papers spread all about him. His brow was deeply furrowed, his fingers ink stained and his lips too, from nibbling the pen.

Perhaps he was a poet, a composer. Perhaps he was a genius in need of affection.

But then I heard him mutter numbers, costs. He was merely doing accounts. Then I saw the thinness of the shirt where it stretched over his shoulders, worn nearly transparent. I saw his too-long hair hanging over his collar, his worn-down shoes, the meanness of his possessions and the careless clutter all around him.

I could never care for a man who cared so little for himself.

I saw one man who seemed more alive than the rest. He was shirtless, his arms sinewy and strong. His eyes were wild, he grinned with white square teeth. Then he spoke, he was laughing, he had a beautiful laugh. There was music in the room, and candles. I saw a handsome camel-hair overcoat hung over a chair. I wanted to know his name.

I saw him crouching over the bed at the far side of the room, he was talking and cooing, stroking, I thought perhaps there was a dog on the bed. A cat.

Then I heard soft feminine laughter.

Annabelle pulled me along, whispering apologies.

I looked in on every little cell. One room was exquisitely decorated, Oriental rugs on the floor, red leather armchairs, stuffed game birds, a grandfather clock looming in a corner. But the resident was short and fat and triple chinned, pompous and monocled; he strained the seams of his fine clothes. And beneath the veneer there was a whiff of vulgarity: he moved his lips as he laboriously read the paper; he drank his port and belched and chomped a cigar; with those finely manicured hands he scratched himself in ways a gentleman should not.

I watched men eating, reading, sleeping, polishing their shoes with earnest attention. I saw men studying comic books as solemnly as they would the Bible; I saw a swaybacked, pear-shaped young fellow practicing his walk with a book balanced on his head and I had to look away. I saw a man playing the trumpet, and my heart went out to him, a musician, a creative soul. But the sounds he made were terrible, and his neighbors on all sides banged on the walls and shouted at him, and he cursed back at them with a self-righteous anger that was ugly to see.

I saw a man sitting hunched on the edge of the bed in his underwear, looking at a magazine held two inches from his face, his other arm working like a piston.

I saw a man on his knees, eyes closed, a rosary in his hands.

I saw a man cleaning a disassembled gun.

I saw a man tentatively removing his hairpiece, then rubbing ointment into the angry rash it had left on his scalp.

I saw a man carefully lining up rows of pills in a rainbow of colors, dozens of them in neat regiments. I saw him pour himself a tall glass of water. He had a long horse face, pale lank hair lying across his forehead.

We climbed more stairs, I browsed through more men's lives; they were as wide-eyed and oblivious as fish in an aquarium.

This will never work, I whispered finally. How can I possibly find—

But Annabelle hushed me and nudged me to the last flight of stairs. Top floor, I keep the best ones up here, she said.

I wanted to go home, I was exhausted.

And then I saw him.

He was so handsome, so full of life. His face was a healthy color, his hair thick and dark. As I watched he combed it back and smoothed it until it shone like patent leather. His face was square and sharp cornered, the eyebrows were active little punctuation marks. He was a big man, broad shouldered, but light on his feet as he walked from closet to dresser to mirror. He wore a lovely gray suit that fit him perfectly. I watched as he stood before the mirror knotting his tie. He fixed it once, scowled at it, undid it and tied it again twice more.

He did not stop until it was perfect.

He tied his shoes, whistling. Whistling! How can you not like a man who whistles?

The apartment was tidy. Unlike the other apartments which smelled of sweat or medicine or lingering food, his apartment smelled impersonal. Like a coat closet, it smelled of leather, wool, rubber boots.

There were small photographs hung on the walls, propped on the dresser. The sepia-toned cardboard kind, of the sort my mother kept.

Probably his parents came from over there as well. We had that in common.

He stood before the mirror smoothing his shirt. He stuck out his chin, studying one profile then the other. I did not think him vain. He acted like a man with a fine new car: not vain, simply justifiably proud. He looked strong. He looked as if he had a healthy appetite. He moved with dancing steps.

He reminded me of my brothers, he was like a refined, chiseled version of them. Perhaps if you skinned one of my brothers like a bear, if you peeled off the heavy thick skin, you would find a clean-shaven, well-groomed fellow like this inside.

He fixed a carnation in his buttonhole. Wearing a flower in November! The audacity!

He put on an overcoat and paused for a final inspection before the mirror. I realized with a sudden sinking feeling that of course he was about to go out to meet a woman.

I sighed but could not stop looking at him until he left the room, still whistling. How dear the back of his head looked; the nape of his neck, the backs of his ears were boyish looking and vulnerable. I felt a gush of concern for him, I imagined him cornered in a dark alley, thugs pounding on that sweet unsuspecting neck with a crowbar, mussing the perfectly smooth hair.

Seen enough? Annabelle said.

I nodded. We made our slow way down to Annabelle's apartment. She hobbled more stiffly than before on her tiny useless feet. They made me think of stories I had read about Chinese girls whose feet had been bound since birth.

We sat again in the crowded apartment as Annabelle lit a cigarette for herself. She was puffing and haggard from all the walking, but her voice was more intense than before.

So, which one? The last one, isn't it?

Yes, the last one.

Hmmm, she said. Ten-B. Good. His name is Joe. Steady job. Parents are dead so they won't get in your way. He's a good one, Shirley, I promise you. Built to last.

He looked like he was getting ready for a date, I said tensely.

Annabelle waved her hands. Pay it no mind, he's all yours, she said.

I looked at my mother. Her face was thoughtful, undecided, the way she looked when she tasted a soup in progress.

What now? How will I meet him?

I'll send him over to your home for dinner. Next Sunday? Some night this week. Thursday? Wednesday? The sooner the better.

I don't understand. He's never even seen me. What will you tell him?

Ah, Annabelle said and brought her face close to mine, smoke drifting from her nostrils. You see, Shirley, some men are bad with money. Most of the men here are behind on their rent, and some owe me for other favors as well, they have debts. I've been very generous with them. And if they are disagreeable, I have a special arrangement with the butcher downstairs.

She cocked her head, shared a glance with my mother. My tenants, she said, are always willing to return a favor. They're always glad to oblige. Especially if it means sharing a meal and some sparkling conversation with a beautiful girl like yourself.

I'm not—

You want to get to know him, don't you, Shirley? This is your chance. It's as good as done. Your Joe will be delivered to your doorstep promptly on Wednesday evening. That I can promise. After that it's up to you and your mother.

My mother nodded, her lips pursed.

My head was whirling. Joe. His name was Joe. I could not stop thinking of the smooth black hair, the long legs in the trousers, the flat plane of his cheek, the lines around the mouth. Just like the movie star men in the curling magazine photos on my bedroom walls.

Like a new toy in a shop window, and I was six years old again.

Shirley, just wait; when you see him again he'll seem even more wonderful than before, Annabelle said. Men are at their truest when they're alone, but they're at their very *best* when they're with a beautiful woman.

She turned to my mother. It's true, isn't it?

My mother nodded, then said: We must be going now.

And as I had known earlier, without words, that my mother and Annabelle were old acquaintances, I now saw with equal clarity that they were not friends.

Stay a bit, Annabelle said. I have soup on the stove we could have.

No. We'll go, my mother said.

Shirley, ah, *Sashie* should really have some, she needs it, Annabelle said.

They exchanged glances.

My mother sat back down. So did I. I felt weak, giddy. Normally I hated beet soup but now I drank down a sweet, spicy, bright red bowlful with shreds of beet hovering at the lightless bottom like seaweed.

I set down the bowl, my mouth on fire. I felt very strange. My mother and Annabelle sat watching me; they had decided not to have any after all.

My mother and I put on our coats. Annabelle clasped my hands and wished me luck. My mother thanked her tersely, then handed her a packet of dried herbs. Annabelle gave her a dark stoppered jar which my mother hid in the depths of her coat pocket.

Words passed between them: the gutturals of the old language. How rude of them to exclude me, I thought, but I was too light-headed to really care.

As we walked home that night my feet wobbled drunkenly beneath me; to walk a straight line seemed an impossible thing so my mother loosened her grip and let me weave all over the street. The cold made the stars seem brighter than usual, closer; I thought I could hear them, a buzzing like fluorescent lights.

Are you sure this is what you want? she said.

Positively.

Good, she said.

Is this how you found my father? I asked, feeling bold.

The entire city went quiet, waiting for the answer.

Your father was the finest man on earth, my mother said shortly. When they made him they broke the mold.

The grim set of my mother's mouth, the glitter in her eye made me want to take her words literally. How angry she looked; she seemed to think that if someone had not broken the mold, she could have used it to cast a second version of my father, in bronze or iron or some stronger stuff more lasting than the first.

In my mother's world, on my mother's terms, such things were possible.

My fiancé is coming over for dinner tonight, I told Tessie and Marianne.

Shirley! You sly thing! When did this happen?

Since when do you have a fiancé?

Who is he? Can we meet him?

How could you keep it from us?

My God, Shirley, are you pregnant?

All this time, we thought you were such a shy little mouse—

Afraid of men—

What color is his hair?

When did he propose?

When is the wedding?

What is his name?

For heaven's sake, Shirley, how can you be so calm?

Can we please come by tonight and get a peek at him?

I knew it was unwise to tell them before everything was settled. But I couldn't resist.

I went home early that afternoon to set my hair. My mother bustled about the kitchen, among boiling pots and clouds of steam, with her sleeves rolled and her hair plastered to her face. It would have seemed like laundry day if not for the vigorous smells and the sheen of grease.

Why does he have to come here? I said. Why can't he and I go to a restaurant alone? How can I get to know him with *you* here?

How can *I* get to know him otherwise? she said.

I had no answer for that. I went to my room. The night before my mother had soaked my hair in one of her evil-smelling herb solutions. Today it was strange and downy and full of static electricity. I put my hair in curlers, I varnished my nails. I had bought a girdle for the first time. I put it on underneath my dress; I could hardly breathe but I was pleased with my reflection: for the first time in my life I had a figure.

I applied makeup carefully, as Tessie had taught me. I put a drop of vanilla behind each ear. My mother disapproved of perfume.

How strange I felt, then. As if my heart and throat and stomach had got shuffled up. As if a helium balloon were inflating inside my chest, pressing on my rib cage. I could not sit still.

It must have been the girdle.

He arrived punctually at seven.

I opened the door and there he stood, flowers in his arms and a smile on his face. Our eyes met for the first time. His were blue! I had never noticed before! He took my hand; his was cool and smooth; he smelled of lime aftershave lotion.

Oh his eyes! His manners! Impeccable!

Even my mother seemed charmed. He kissed her hand. She dropped him an old-world curtsey. He sniffed the air appreciatively.

I took his coat, went to hang it. I trod on it by mistake, stumbled into a wall. I don't think he noticed. It was so long, his coat. How tall he was.

Of course the conversation was awkward. How could it not be? He thought we were strangers, he and I. He spoke of his late parents, his job in insurance. Insurance! How dependable, how respectable that sounded! He had a lovely laugh; whenever the conversation lagged he turned on his laugh and kept it going, kept unrolling and unrolling it like a never-ending carpet, until I thought of something else to say.

We sat down to eat. My mother lit candles. Everything was going so well. I looked across the table at him, the candlelight making his eyes dark and velvety, his skin golden. I felt I was glowing; I caught my reflection in a spoon and hardly recognized myself.

How sophisticated I felt, so poised and glamorous. He would never guess that it was the first time I had ever dined with a man.

Of course nothing had been said about love or marriage. But do these things really need to be said? I could feel a bubble of happiness swelling in my chest, ready to burst. His hands! The hair on his knuckles! Cuff links! I wanted him to whistle again.

I felt something new as I looked at him: a feeling of certainty, like bricks being stacked up, mortar slapped in between. A solid, definite feeling. Foundations laid, a future, a firm base. I felt sure of something, for the first time in my life.

My mother brought in the soup. Borscht again. We drank; it set our mouths on fire, stained our lips red. My head began to spin. The borscht seemed thick, meaty; it made me feel carnivorous and wild. I found myself looking at the fleshy parts of his body: his earlobes, the pads of his fingers, the tender morsel of his chin.

Joe looked at me, his eyes were dancing. I offered to help my mother; she pushed me down in my seat. She poured wine and brought out plates and serving platters.

She filled Joe's plate first, set it before him and paused, serving spoon uplifted.

Well Joe, she said firmly, so when are you marrying my daughter?

Joe started, his face froze. Then he started to laugh, or he tried to, he could not seem to get his laugh engine running this time.

I'm afraid I don't—

When are you marrying Sashie? my mother repeated.

He attempted the laugh again; it sputtered and died. You misunderstand, he said.

I don't think so, she said.

Annabelle asked me to come here, and I was glad to, but I didn't realize—he said and looked at me. We've only just met, he added apologetically.

My mother waved her hand dismissively.

But you see—I'm in no position to—I have these debts, you see, I can't possibly. I have no inheritance—a fondness for gambling—nothing serious, of course. But my hands are tied. And then I already have a young lady friend—

My stomach went cold. The brick wall crumbled.

Your daughter's a lovely girl, but—it's ridiculous—

His face blurred, my eyes grew hot. I couldn't be crying.

My mother fixed her fierce gaze upon him. He writhed under her stare. In his embarrassment, he turned to his plate. He shoved a forkful in his mouth, then another, and another. Sweat broke out on his face. I saw a flush spread over his neck.

How handsome he looked even then.

Rather than meet our eyes, he kept eating, even as the beads of sweat became a sheen. I heard pops, snaps, as he splintered bones between his strong white teeth. His face turned redder and redder and shaded to mahogany; his eyes bulged. My mother must have had a heavy hand with the spices.

Tears were bubbling in the corners of his eyes, as if his very head were boiling.

He moaned without pausing in his chewing, so the sound came out of his nose. I could see blue and purple veins in his temples, like rivers and roads, the map of his self.

And then he began to choke. His wheezing breath stopped abruptly; all we could hear was a clicking in his throat. He looked at us now, eyes rolling, one hand to his throat, his mouth gaping like a fish's. He looked at my mother, then at me, his feet kicking and stamping beneath the table.

A dribble of food ran from his mouth and made a black stain on his shirt. Oh, his clean shirt!

He slammed his fists on the table. The silverware danced.

My mother watched him calmly. She sipped her wine and dabbed her mouth daintily. She twisted her napkin, tighter, tighter, between her fingers. Her lips were red stained from wine and beets. Then she moved the bottle of wine closer to her, so Joe would not knock it over with his flailing.

He stared at her imploringly, stretched out his arms. She lifted her chin in a questioning way. He turned to me. I stared, fascinated. His face was filled with such desperate longing, such desire.

He collapsed in the chair, his eyes began to glaze.

My mother said: Sashie, help him.

I ran to his side, I stood behind his chair. I wrapped my arms around him and squeezed beneath his ribs, as I had been taught. How broad his chest was. I could barely reach. It did no good. Limp and heavy as sandbags, his body tumbled to the floor.

My mother tossed her napkin aside and drank her wine.

I took his head in my lap (how heavy it was! I had never held a man's head before). I wiped his mouth, loosened his tie. I parted his pretty lips, reached deep down his throat, and plucked out a tiny fish bone, curved and translucent as a fingernail clipping.

I placed the bone on the table, stroked his hair, put my lips to his and breathed into him (my first kiss! how romantic it all was!). He flopped about like a beached fish. I saw his eyes snap into focus, saw them fill with wonder.

Wonder at being alive, wonder at being in love, wonder at lying in my arms.

He clutched at me, sucked greedily at the air.

Everything was decided right then, without words.

I thought I saw my mother reach over to take the fish bone and slip it into her pocket. But I must have imagined it in the confusion.

I was in love, after all. People in love can never be trusted.

Joe told me later that when he had opened his eyes and seen my face hovering over him, he thought I was an angel. You had light shining all around you like a halo, he said, and a holy look on your face. I thought I was dead, in heaven, I've never seen anything so beautiful.

After that first dinner, Joe came to see me nearly every day. I don't know what it is, he said, but I can't seem to stay away from you.

My *angel*, he called me.

Silly Joe.

Each time he came my mother made him drink one of her herbal teas to soothe his throat. He regarded her with a mixture of respect and fear, and obediently drank, holding the mug in both hands like a child. The bitterness made him cough.

He never again mentioned his lady friend, or his debts, or the other silly things he had spoken of at our first dinner.

We made wedding plans. I dreamed of a white cake decorated with flowers, a dress like a wedding cake, a bouquet of roses like silk and spun sugar.

Joe prepared to move into the apartment with my mother and me. It made sense, after all; there was so much room since my brothers were gone. And I didn't want to leave my mother alone. She would be glad to stay near us. She would help take care of Joe, fix her tea for him every day, since his throat never seemed to mend.

Joe often said in those early days that he couldn't live without me.

Of course he didn't mean that. It was just love-talk.

Ilana

There was something not quite right about it all, though I could not put my finger on what it was.

I told myself it was because I had never had a wedding myself and had never even attended one. I did not know how courting people were supposed to act.

I had followed Anya's instructions, and it all had happened the way she predicted.

And yet there was a feeling of unease, it was like a bad smell hovering in the apartment, like an ugly stain on the back of your skirt that no one will mention.

Sashie was happy, but she seemed happier alone, in front of her mirror trying on the hat with the white veil, than she did when she was with Joe. Her conversations with him were strained and formal.

And Joe himself did not seem quite real to me, he did not give off the living heat that Shmuel had. I sometimes found myself watching Joe closely to make sure he was breathing. I thought that if he were sliced open he would be bloodless and dry; he would be made of mealy translucent layers like an onion.

But Sashie was happy, and that was what mattered, wasn't it? She had never found much happiness with me. I admit this. Now I hoped she would be able to find some kind of happiness away from me. This was my gift to her.

Sashie

The wedding was small, we could not afford much. My mother did not want to waste money on a white dress I would only wear once.

I suppose you're wearing *that* to the wedding? I said.

She was still in her widow's black.

Of course, she said.

Black at a wedding is bad luck, I said, and anyway it's *so* unattractive.

Don't talk to me about bad luck, she said darkly.

She wore her black dress but everything was lovely just the same, as elegant as I could make it. There was a small ceremony in an office at the courthouse, we were in a hurry you see, no time to rent a hall and have music and dancing. It was just us, and my mother, for Joe had no family. But he looked fine and dashing in a dark suit, and he smiled at me so charmingly.

We were married then, it was all official, written indelibly on paper.

There they were, our names, side by side.

Later we came back to the apartment which I had decorated with fresh flowers everywhere, and drapery (what are you doing with my bedsheets, my mother had said), and Tessie and Marianne came in to eat cake. Annabelle had been invited but declined to come, or so my mother said. Joe brought in some of his friends and they stood in a corner slapping each other on the back and laughing loudly, and it was good to hear the rumble of male voices in the room again after all these years.

Right from the start Joe was properly respectful with me in front of other people.

He hardly touched me. Only when absolutely necessary. He seldom even met my eyes.

This was as it should be. We were not like those couples who rubbed and drooled on each other in public. We were better than that. More refined.

When the guests had left the apartment was strangely quiet again.

My mother said softly: Be fruitful and multiply.

She swept the floor clean of crumbs.

Joe drank a last cup of wine. And then another, because the bottle was nearly empty anyway.

We went into my bedroom. *Our* bedroom now; he brought over two suitcases full of his belongings earlier in the day. I had pushed together the two beds that had once been my brothers'.

Joe smiled at me and began to remove his clothes. When the jacket came off I was slightly disturbed to see the yellow sweat stains at the underarms of his white shirt. I'll need some bleach, I thought.

He removed his shoes and I saw that his socks were full of holes, his toes protruded obscenely. This I did not like, but I told myself: he needs a woman to look after him, that's all.

The socks came off. His feet frankly repulsed me.

He looked up and noticed me watching then, and I quickly rearranged my face, I did not want him to know what I was thinking.

He seemed to misinterpret my expression, mistaking it for an amorous one, because he unfastened his trousers, and let them fall to the floor, and then began dancing, waltzing around me in wide circles with his shirttails flapping.

His hair which had been so carefully slicked back now flopped forward in sticky strands.

I turned and turned to keep my eyes on him. He looked narrower somehow, less impressive without his jacket and with the beard growth that had begun on his jaw. And his legs, it was the first time I had seen his legs.

There was a *great* deal of hair on them.

Joe would require some polish, I realized.

He stopped his spinning and came close and began to tug at my clothes.

Oh stop it Joe, I said, that's so uncouth.

Without stopping it, he said: What on earth do you mean? This is what married people do.

Oh, I knew this, of course.

I knew what marriage meant. I had thought about it.

It was just that it seemed so very different now that I was facing the ugly bald fact of it. Now that I was staring down the barrel, so to speak.

It seemed very *unsanitary*, this thing we were going to do.

And undignified.

I thought of my parents standing together, my mother with her hands on my father's chest. I did the same to Joe.

That's right, he said with wine on his breath.

I looked up at him and wondered where he had spent his childhood, and what his mother's name was, and whether he was left or right-handed. I hardly knew this man.

All that was not so important. It could come later.

We went and lay in the bed then, and I felt better once we were between the clean white sheets. He lay against me and I asked him to turn out the lights because I did not like to see him so terrifyingly close, with his amazing profusion of pores and tiny hairs in odd places. He did, and I liked that much better.

Joe did his duty then, he consummated the marriage and it was slightly uncomfortable but not too bad, though he frightened me terribly by gasping and groaning as if he were in pain.

And his hair pomade left a mess on the pillow, I discovered the next morning.

As we spent more nights together I learned to accommodate him better, and I even looked forward to the times in bed with him. He worked long days, and these nights in bed were the only time I had alone with him, the only chance I had to discuss private matters.

As time went on I discovered that the best time to voice my request and demands was early on in the proceedings. He was alert and impatient then and gave in quickly. And *after* the act was the best time to tell him less pressing news, when he was relaxed and purged and half (or wholly) asleep. He would agree to almost anything then.

Joe?

Hmmm?

Joe, do you find me attractive?

Of course I do. How many times do I have to tell you?

I know, but . . . Joe?

What?

Do you think I look like my mother?

Could you lift your head a minute? My arm's falling asleep. There. Do you?

Do I what? Oh, I don't know. A little bit. There's a resemblance.

Do you think I'll turn into her when I get older? *Much* older, I mean.

God, I hope not.

Why not? Joe? Do you not like my mother?

Oh, I like her fine, I guess. It's just the way she looks at me sometimes, makes my skin crawl.

How does she look at you?

And the way she talks to herself at night. Haven't you heard her?

Yes, but *how* does she look at you?

It's that look widows have, I guess. Dried up and lonely, thinking about what they're not getting anymore.

Don't talk about my mother like that.

Gives me the creeps.

Joe?

Joe?

The two beds often drifted apart in the night, and we had to push them back together.

In the mornings he was bleary-eyed, bloated, I hardly recognized him. But once he had washed and shaved and dressed for work, Joe looked as handsome as ever. This was the Joe I adored.

At night we kept the lights off and when he touched me in the dark I pictured the daytime Joe in my head, in his hat and gloves and fresh-shined shoes. That helped.

The apartment seemed much smaller than it ever had before. I could not help noticing the way my mother and Joe brushed against each other in the tiny kitchen, squeezed past each other in the narrow hallway. In the mornings, as Joe tramped back and forth between bedroom and bathroom in various states of undress, I noticed my mother watching him. I'd previously thought she was frowning at the puddles of water he tracked on the floor. Now I wondered if she were looking at something else.

One night a bit of paper slipped from Joe's pocket and as he bent over to retrieve it I saw my mother's eyes linger on him much longer than the situation demanded.

I knew I was being ridiculous. My mother was an old woman, after all.

Yet she climbed the stairs faster than I; and from behind, with her skinny arms and her hair in two long braids, she looked like a little girl.

I tried to spend as much time alone with Joe as possible. I found myself forever shutting doors, sliding my chair closer. I wondered if my mother noticed, if she felt neglected.

But she seemed quite happy with her new privacy. Of course, my mother has her own version of happiness, it is not like other people's.

I intended to redecorate the apartment but I was soon distracted.

I discovered I was pregnant.

When I told my mother her face softened as it had not in years.

I told Joe and he was overjoyed, he picked me up and spun me around. He had never done that before, and it made me want to vomit, but I was glad that he was glad.

He was *so* happy for me that he went out with some of his friends to celebrate and did not return until dawn, rumpled and smelling of wine.

I do not need to tell you about the pregnancy, about the birth.

That's a process my mother loves to talk about, she is fascinated by it. I am not.

It's a story that has been told a thousand times.

It's always the same, it does not bear repeating.

Jonathan was a beautiful baby, it was an easy birth though my mother was horrified that I had gone to a hospital and actually enlisted the aid of a doctor.

He'll be cursed, she said, you'll bring evil luck down on us all.

My mother. After all these years she still clung to those peasant superstitions.

She conceded to come to the hospital afterward, where she cradled the baby and crooned wordlessly. Jonathan was perfectly healthy, with dark hair like his father's and startling blue eyes like his grandfather.

Joe was red faced and bursting with pride. He took the baby in his arms once, and looked terrified, and never picked him up again.

I might hurt him, he said.

He went out to celebrate and I did not see him till I came home.

Jonathan was a beautiful baby, as I kept telling myself and everyone kept telling me. But I was tired and listless in the weeks following and the grayness of the apartment oppressed me. His screams, the odor of him, his needs, they oppressed me.

My mother cared for Jonathan during that time. My milk stopped and I tried to explain to her about formulas and sterilization, but she brushed me away.

I never knew how she fed him, but Jonathan was plump and happy. I saw no bottles, no boxes of powder in the kitchen; it was as if she were nursing him herself.

I lay in bed and heard them talking in the kitchen, her voice and Joe's rising and falling, too close together. Talking about me, I knew, conspiring together. I heard laughter, the baby crying. Wailing, without pause for breath, like a teakettle. What were they doing to make him scream like that?

The screaming went on and on, and I was no longer sure if I was awake or dreaming. I could not stand it, I rose and went to the door and peered down the hallway to the lit kitchen which glowed orange like a furnace. I saw Joe sitting in a chair and my mother bending close over him and I was somehow not surprised to see them like that, their mouths so close. I had expected it. My devious mother.

Then my mother shifted, and I saw her hand working and there was the flash of a steel blade dangerously close to his face. She's going to cut his eyes out, I thought, and this did not surprise me either. My mother was capable of anything.

I ran into the kitchen to grab her arm, and I saw the scissors in her hand. I realized she was trimming Joe's hair, the way she used to trim my brothers', with newspapers spread over the floor to catch the trimmings. She and Joe both stared at me, surprised.

Only a haircut, their innocent eyes seemed to say.

But they looked guilty, I thought.

Oh good, you're up, my mother said.

It was unbearably hot in the kitchen so I went back to bed without a word.

Later my mother's face hovered over me. She put a glass of water in my hand.

Joe left me alone all this time. He was considerate that way.

My mother was not. She kept trying to rouse me.

It's not my place. A child needs his mother, she said to me one day.

Was she referring to my son or my husband?

I lay in bed, a wet cloth on my forehead. I dreamt of cool things: lace curtains, bone china, crystal goblets, the tinkling of the glass doodads on chandeliers.

It is not natural, my mother said from the doorway, balancing Jonathan on her hip. I am glad to do this, but it is not natural. Your child needs you.

I can't, I said.

She sat on the edge of the bed, the baby against her shoulder. She touched my face.

We had never been especially close, and were not now.

Never been close, yet at the same time *too* close, I was suffocating, the room was squeezing me like a girdle. Her hip touched me and through the sheets it felt burning hot.

I had no idea what she was thinking.

And as she sat near me, studying my face, I realized for the first time that she found me as incomprehensible as I found her.

Whatever is the problem? she said.

I'm unhappy, I said.

But why?

I hate this apartment, I whispered.

I had wanted to say that for years but knew it was futile.

Perhaps you should move then, she said and abruptly rose and left the room.

I knew she would never want to leave this apartment. She had lived here since she came to this country, it was practically a member of the family by now. She would never leave it, and I could not leave her.

So I was surprised that, when Joe came home one evening announcing he had been given a promotion, my mother said: It's time to move to a new place.

Joe said he would look for another apartment.

I did not entirely trust his taste but it did not matter, we would be leaving this dark apartment with its dingy memories, leaving this neighborhood of narrow streets, loud radio music, stray cats, undergarments strung on clotheslines above the street, gutters clogged with unnamable things.

I got out of bed. I curled my hair for the first time in months.

I took my son in my arms.

And in a matter of days Joe said he had found an apartment he knew I would love.

Ilana

I did not want to go with them.

This apartment was crammed with memories, stains, the musty clothes of people long absent. I could not imagine leaving. The new place was so far away that people spoke differently, dressed differently. Even the light fell differently, it was paler and colder. It would be like traveling to a new country. Where would I buy my cabbages and cinnamon? Who would sell me the leather scraps to mend my shoes?

And how would Shmuel find his way to bed?

I had hoped they would move without me. Sashie needed to learn to care for her own child. She did not need me. She and her husband needed privacy, they needed to get acquainted. After a year of marriage they hardly knew each other.

And I admit that after a lifetime of tending to other people, I was looking forward to taking care of no one but myself.

Sashie had never enjoyed my company. Yet she insisted I move with them.

She said it was her daughterly duty, but I think it was something more.

I think she was afraid to be alone with Joe. I had brought their marriage into being, and she seemed to think it would fall apart without me.

And I also think she was suspicious of me. She was forever peering over my shoulder, bursting into my room unannounced. She wanted me to stay where she could keep an eye on me.

So I went with them. Partly because Sashie insisted. But mainly for Jonathan. He squeezed my finger in his strong little fist and gave me hope.

Sashie

We moved into the new apartment when Jonathan was still a tiny baby.

I was so excited.

I was so glad to move, not just for myself but for Jonathan. The old neighborhood had gotten so bad, drunks asleep on the doorsteps who didn't wake up even when you stepped on them to get out, little girls barely out of pigtails prostituting themselves on street corners. I was sure the place would have a bad influence on him.

Suddenly Jonathan seemed more important than anything.

Everything seemed new to me. Shining and different.

A fresh start.

I resolved to clear my head, think of nothing but the future.

Six rooms! For just Joe and Jonathan and me. And my mother of course. We couldn't leave her behind.

It was an exclusive building. Joe had to go through an interview just to apply for the apartment. Of course I hadn't been worried about *that*, Joe was the sort of man people liked immediately. He knew how to talk to people. I told you what a big, fine-looking man he was; such shoulders, such a chin, such wavy hair. Such a shine on his shoes, the handkerchief in his pocket, folded just so. He had impeccable manners. But he was not effeminate, not a bit. Whenever he met men he would give them a crushing handshake, and a little nod, and a look that meant: you know and I know that I could beat you to a pulp if I wanted, but why don't we act civilized instead?

He was such a fine figure of a man. I wanted Jonathan to grow up to be just like him.

So we moved in, and our old furniture didn't half fill up the place. I couldn't wait to fix everything up. My mother settled into her room and kept to herself there. I didn't mind. She still embarrassed me; in this fine place I was more aware than before of her accent, and the thick rolled stockings she wore, and her hair which she dyed pitch-black with something that looked like shoe polish. But I was glad to have her with me.

I met our next-door neighbor, Mrs. Fishbein, who seemed a respectable sort. She came to the door in pearls and white gloves, lacquered gray curls and spectacles on a chain; she invited me to take tea with her sometime. And our neighbor across the hall, Mr. Mizzer, *he* looked just like Abraham Lincoln, and he was a retired banker, so of course he was all right.

Mrs. Fishbein was the first to tell me about the street cleaners. Our building was in a particularly exclusive neighborhood; there was a private street-cleaning service that came once a week. There were strict rules governing the placement and sorting of garbage. The cleaners came on Tuesday nights and cleared away everything that did not belong.

It sounded too wonderful to be true.

I lay awake far into the night the following Tuesday. Finally I heard them: a mechanical, scuttling, buzzing sound down in the street, like a hundred brushes and dustpans, or thousands of little forks and knives scraping up the last of dinner. A soothing, restful sound.

The next morning the streets were spotless. They sparkled. I put Jonathan in the perambulator and took him for a walk. Look Jonathan, I said, look at the nice clean streets. But he seemed more interested in the toy my mother had given him: a carved wooden figure, with blunt features and what looked like real hair. The thing was unsanitary.

The cleaners do a wonderful job, I told Mrs. Fishbein.

Yes, she said, it's taken a great deal of effort, but the streets are finally in a decent condition.

Mrs. Fishbein, I discovered, owned a young pug dog that liked to bark in the wee hours of the morning. The dog irritated me to no end, but after her kindness to me I felt I couldn't mention it. Besides I knew better than to antagonize the neighbors right from the start.

Joe came home from work tired in the evenings. I met him at the door with a drink and a kiss. Isn't it *wonderful*, Joe? I must have said this to him a hundred times. I loved pattering to meet him over the handsome hardwood floors. I loved the pure clean light that came in through the tall windows.

Wonderful, he always said with little conviction. He had to work harder and longer than before; the maintenance fees for the apartment were more than he had anticipated.

I thought the *incompleteness* of the apartment disturbed him. I knew that once I decorated the place thoroughly he would see how wonderful it was.

Every Tuesday night I lay awake to listen to the street cleaners. The streets on Wednesday mornings were marvelous. They looked polished.

The streets beyond our neighborhood seemed so dull and dirty by comparison. People sitting on stoops half dressed, garbage bags, tin cans and broken bottles, scratchy radio music, dilapidated cars, children dashing through an open fire hydrant—isn't that illegal? I did not like to leave our neighborhood even to shop. And I certainly never took Jonathan.

Then I discovered catalogs. I ordered curtains, slipcovers, lamps, rugs, end tables. The convenience! I told them all the measurements and colors over the phone, I told them my name in a clear, slow voice, and then ten days later the things arrived in nice clean cardboard boxes.

The deliverymen assembled some of the furniture for me. I did not like the look of them, their black fingernails, but I could not do it myself, and I did not want to ask Joe. I wanted to surprise him.

The white gauzy curtains, the new crystal in the cabinets—everything looked wonderful. I picked up the phone and ordered more.

But when Joe came home he hardly noticed. He seemed tired, not at all his usual cheerful self. When I gave him a kiss hello he grabbed me and buried his face in my neck as if he needed comfort. I could smell wilted cologne and a sweaty kind of weariness on his collar. I could feel him nuzzling and smacking against my fresh clean dress, and he began to tug me toward the bedroom.

Oh Joe, not now, I said.

It's not that I *mind* acting like silly newlyweds. Not a bit. I don't mind at all, *now and then*. But Joe wanted to do it so *often*, and always at the most inconvenient times. And he messed up the bed so, he wrinkled the sheets, practically pulled them off the bed sometimes. I was hours straightening up afterward. Not to mention what he did to my clothes. The way he tore them up—as if he'd never seen a button before, or a hook-and-eye fastener!

Besides I was afraid of the influence it might have on Jonathan; I was sure overhearing such a thing could have an unhealthy effect on a child.

So Joe let me go, and my mother and I fixed the dinner, and we ate and then sat for a time with drinks and magazines. We spoke little. In fact I don't think Joe said two words. It was a lovely domestic evening. So peaceful and serene. The living room looked marvelous.

That night the street cleaners sounded smooth and graceful, as if they were ballet dancers pirouetting down the street catching dust on their tutus.

The next morning Mrs. Fishbein told me that one of the children who lived upstairs left his bicycle on the stoop overnight. Now it was gone. We could hear him bawling above our heads.

It was unfortunate, perhaps, but it was the child's own fault. He should have followed the rules. Everyone else in the building did. Everyone came home early Tuesday evenings, stayed inside, drew their curtains, locked their doors.

A few nights later Joe came home looking brisk and determined. Let's go out tonight! Come on! he said. He grabbed my arms and swung me around.

Where? I said.

Anywhere you want, he said.

I looked at him. He appeared handsome as usual, but looking closer I saw one tiny hair protruding from his nostril. Once I noticed it, I could not *stop* seeing it. I looked around the room. I had ordered new throw pillows for the sofa with tassels on the corners. I had hung new drapes that hid the windows completely. I had polished every surface with a toothbrush and a special abrasive powder.

I want to stay here, I said.

He threw up his hands.

After that he came home later in the evenings. He said he had to discuss business with clients over dinner. He said he had to meet old friends.

I did not mind. I was generous with him, let him spend his time as he wanted. I was not a domineering housewife. Besides, I had so much work to do.

My mother kept to herself. She had her own life, she came and went as she pleased. I stayed away from her room; the sight distressed me. I reminded myself that she was born in a country where people bathed once a month and kept their chickens in the kitchen in winter. She had come very far, considering. I never questioned her, and I was glad whenever she took charge of Jonathan. Somehow she never seemed to mind changing his diapers.

Tuesday nights were my favorite time. The cleaners had a brisk military sound, like marching troops spearing wastepaper on their bayonets.

Late at night after they had finished I always felt clean and purged and luxuriously peaceful. Sometimes I felt so good I woke Joe and let him have a little fun with me. But he had to promise not to thrash much or disorder the bedclothes.

Several weeks later on a sunny Wednesday I came upon Mrs. Fishbein sobbing in the hallway. She said her pug had disappeared; she felt sure he had wandered down to the street the night before. I tried to comfort her, but the dog never reappeared and I cannot say that I was sorry.

We received notices in our mailboxes stating that the street cleaners were upgrading their services at no extra charge. They would now come on both Tuesdays and Thursdays.

I was thrilled. Now I lay awake two nights a week listening to the cleaners, like low-rumbling clouds rolling through, or a crackling forest fire.

Mrs. Fishbein mourned her pug. The days were uncommonly bright. Jonathan grew and thrived. One Thursday I forgot to bring the perambulator up from the street and the next day it was gone. It was a small loss. But Jonathan raged for hours, screaming for the little wooden doll that had been left inside it, under the blanket.

Joe came home early on Tuesdays and Thursdays like everyone else, but on the other nights, on Wednesdays and Fridays and weekends, he stayed out later and later and came stumbling home in the wee hours.

And then a rather odd thing happened.

On the first floor of our building there lived an elderly woman who kept two dozen cats in her apartment. She had moved in long ago, before the screening process was established; she'd lived in the building for years, in spite of people's polite attempts to dislodge her, and the cats. It was unsanitary; the smell; the very *idea* of two dozen cats! Not to mention inhumane to the cats themselves. Not to mention what people might think when they walked past our building.

What happened was simply: one Thursday, around twilight, it seems the cat woman stepped outside to empty some litter trays. She apparently locked herself out of her apartment. Now she had disappeared.

I discussed it with Mrs. Fishbein in the hallway. I'm sure she just wandered off, went into the wrong building, she was senile, that's all, I told her. But Mrs. Fishbein shook her head with frightened eyes.

What would you do if it had been your mother? she said.

She closed the door between us.

I had hardly been listening, yet her words stuck in my head for days.

What *would* I do? The thought of my mother neatly, silently swept away. No one's fault, no guilt, no one to blame. An extra room. No longer being reminded of what she did to my brothers, or how she felt about Joe.

A clean and empty space.

Terrible thought.

I pushed it away. Though it returned unbidden from time to time.

I loved my mother, after all.

But the thought lingered sometimes in the night as I lay listening for the street cleaners. The mind has a way of fixing on thoughts of dropping babies from windows or jumping from bridges or pulling triggers—possibilities, accidents you imagine in detail but hope *never* actually happen.

The cat woman did not return. Her apartment was cleaned out, the cats were taken away, and a nice-looking young couple with a grand piano moved in.

Our neighbors began coming home earlier and earlier on Tuesdays and Thursdays. I still loved the sounds on those nights: a crisp clean scuttling, like those amazon ants in tropical countries that sweep through villages devouring everything in their path.

Mrs. Fishbein clutched at my arm and whispered that one of the children from upstairs had gone for a bike ride near sundown on a cleaning day and had not returned.

It's like the angel of death passing over, she whispered.

I told her not to be silly. Children like to run away from home sometimes, I said, but they always come back.

She shook her head and retreated into her apartment.

It was nothing, only talk. Those children were too noisy anyway.

Mrs. Fishbein began leaving strange things out in the street on cleaning days. A lamp, a quilt, a boxed cake, new gloves, bottles of pills. Little offerings for the cleaners, as if she wanted to appease them. As time went on the gifts grew more elaborate: she set up little shrines with lighted candles, incense, handwritten poems, a stuffed turkey, an umbrella, her own dresses and corsets neatly folded and tied with ribbon.

All of it gone, swallowed up the next day.

I mentioned her to Mr. Mizzer once, tried to get him to laugh about it. He frowned and shook his head and said: The cleaners can't go on like this. It has to stop. We have to do something.

I was furious, but I managed to keep my voice level as I said: How can we ask them to stop? We *need* them. If they stop coming then everything will go back to the way it was, trash piling up, the drunks and prostitutes, the strangers on our doorsteps, crime and disease and horribleness everywhere. We *can't* go back to that.

He retreated into his own apartment, which was full of musty books. Dust catchers, I called them.

The apartment building was so quiet now. I loved to wander the empty halls, peer out the windows at the sparkling streets.

One day Mrs. Fishbein tapped at my door. I don't wish to upset you, she said, but on a recent evening I saw your husband walking with another woman.

I'm sure it was nothing, I told her.

They were *extremely* close, she said.

It must have been his sister, I said quickly.

They were embracing, she said. *Kissing, I'm afraid*, she added in a whisper.

His sister's Canadian, and you know what *they're* like, I told Mrs. Fishbein.

Of course I did not believe her for a second. Joe would never do such a thing; I knew him too well. He would never do such a thing to our family. I resolved not to say anything about it to him; I did not even want him to see that I was upset; it would worry him. So I concealed the whole incident from him which was easy enough to do since we seldom spoke anymore.

But somehow I could no longer sleep at night, and not even the cleaners could soothe me. And there was the matter of the matchbooks I found in his trouser pockets, taken from various nearby bars.

I finally decided to see for myself. I would do it for Joe's sake. I would prove that Mrs. Fishbein was blind, and insane, and a babbling fool. I dressed myself carefully, gloves and a hat with a veil, and special galoshes to keep my shoes clean; and I set out that night to find him.

I had not been outside the neighborhood for so, so long. The streets were strange and frightening. So *dark*, and there were *puddles* everywhere, and people lounging against walls doing nothing in particular. I walked as quickly as I could; even the air seemed filthy, clammy, it clung damply in my lungs. And the *noise*: cars screeching, people calling out, the radios—is that what they call *music*?

I brought the matchbooks in my purse, and strained my mind to find the proper streets. My side was aching, but I was determined.

I found him at the third bar I checked. A dark, smoky place, men and women pressed close together, talking too loud and laughing, and dirty sawdust on the floor. I saw him sitting in a corner with a woman. He had his arm around her, they were both smoking with their faces inches apart, talking and blowing smoke at each other. She had dyed hair, a tired sagging face. And yet they were smiling. Joe smiling! I saw him touch her breast in that public place.

I fled. Street-corner men called after me, hooting. I ran home as fast as I could. Oh, the relief of the clean bare streets. Oh, the lovely clean hallways, gray and antiseptic as a hospital. And finally the heavenly apartment with the sealed windows, the pure air, sheets crisp as new paper.

I was distraught for days. I did not know what to do. I did not want anyone to know. Our domestic life was so perfect, I could not understand how he could do such a thing. Our lovely marriage, our lovely home, our lovely child. Joe would surely have a detrimental effect on his development. A broken family would traumatize Jonathan at this stage. I had to protect my child at all costs. I had to preserve our family's reputation, if only for him.

I said nothing to Joe. I waited.

And then, in this time of strife, I discovered I was pregnant.

I was furious. I did not want another child. I wanted to concentrate all my energies on raising Jonathan, I wanted him to become a fine handsome man like his father, but I needed to carefully cultivate in him Joe's good qualities and weed out the bad ones. I had no *time* for a second child.

I could not eat or sleep. I spent hours soaking in scented bathwater.

Mrs. Fishbein came tapping at my door again. How many sisters does your husband *have?* she asked.

I closed the door in her face.

I could not bear it anymore. I told my mother everything. She patted my arm, gave me a sharp look, and told me not to worry. I listened to her. I saw a strength, a certainty in her eyes.

The next day, a Tuesday, we again received notices in our mailboxes. The street cleaners were again upgrading their services: they would now come every night.

I meant to bring the notice up to our apartment, with the other mail, but somehow or other I lost it. That night I lay awake beside Joe's dead and distant weight. The street cleaners shrilled like locusts.

The following day I lay in bed as usual long after Joe left for work. Then I bathed. I scrubbed the grouting between the tiles in the bathroom, then I bathed a second time. I took a dusting cloth and wandered through the apartment. I could not for the life of me find a speck of dirt.

I went into the nursery and lifted Jonathan. He was clean and powdered, his big eyes pure and innocent. He looked so like Joe, he really did. I promised myself that I would work hard to make Jonathan into the kind of man Joe *used* to be. The man Joe *could* have been if only he had tried a little harder. It would require a great deal of attention to keep Jonathan on the proper path. A great deal of cold baths and toothpaste, rules and tight-fitting shoes and bleach. But it would be worth it.

I thought of the child inside me, and it occurred to me that it might be a boy, and he might look like Joe, and in that case I would have to raise him perfectly as well. If it was a girl, I wouldn't bother.

I laid Jonathan back down, covered him carefully, and dimmed the lights.

I came upon my mother crocheting quietly in the living room. I said: By the way, did you happen to tell Joe, the street cleaners will be coming every night from now on, they will be coming tonight, so he should come home early.

I didn't tell him, she said calmly. I must have forgotten.

I said: I must have forgotten, too.

That night the street cleaners dipped and swooped like birds of prey, they circled like scavengers, they bored in like maggots, and I slept deep and sound.

Ilana

I had only wanted the best for her. I only wanted her to be happy.

I should have known better. I should not have trusted Anya.

It was mostly my mistake.

But I thought my daughter was somewhat to blame as well, though I could not have said why. She had handled her husband wrongly, there was something lacking, a coldness between them like a glass wall.

Perhaps it had something to do with that place we lived in, all cold smooth surfaces and high ceilings that made me anxious, too much space all around. We were rabbits in an open field.

There was no way to send down roots in such a place; it resisted me like a waxed surface repelling water.

I was glad to go back to the old neighborhood, where things made sense and I could find work to do with my hands.

There were the children, at least.

She could thank him for that.

She had gotten something out of the bargain.

Sashie

Back we went, to the old neighborhood, my mother and Jonathan and I.

We found an apartment in a different building on the same street as our old one. It felt just like the old place, same smells of cabbage and onions, same dripping faucets, same shouts in the stairwell.

The previous tenant had left behind broken-backed furniture, lamps that did not work. We did not bother to remove it before bringing in our own, so that the rooms were crammed with furniture, barely room to walk.

My pregnancy made it doubly difficult to squeeze between the sharp edges of bureaus and davenports and great hulking lumps of furniture I could not even identify. Everything festooned with ugly carved woodworking, carved gargoyles and leaves and enormous bulbous wooden fruit.

I knew I deserved better. I did not belong there. I had more refined tastes, I had hopes and aspirations. I needed gentler conditions, more delicate company.

My mother retreated and I didn't care. She folded herself inward, hid her heart away.

I tried to keep the place clean, but dust seemed to spring up on surfaces overnight. Even just-washed dishes, drying in the rack, wore films of gray dust in the mornings.

I concentrated on myself, on maintaining my clothes, curling my hair, containing the mess and leakages and blooming stains and general untidiness of pregnancy.

My daughter was born. The details are not worth mentioning.

Even with the two small children squalling at all hours, the apartment seemed dull, barren, quiet.

By now I knew to attribute this to the absence of any men. Men bring life into a place. Without them there is only working and waiting. There is no story worth telling.

It was a pity Joe had not worked out as I'd hoped.

Luckily there was Jonathan. I had high hopes for him. I watched him grow and become bright and strong and handsome, and my mother watched him too with a kind of hungry anticipation. I knew she was thinking of Wolf and Eli, hearing their voices when Jonathan went running and laughing round and round and deep in the labyrinth of furniture, oblivious to our expectations.

It seemed he went into that forest of furniture a boy and came out a man, so fast do children grow.

I dreamt of a butcher shop on a poorly lit street.

It looked familiar, though I could not think where I had seen it before. My mother did all our shopping.

The fat butcher behind the counter wiped his hands on his apron, leaving red handprints. On the wall before him hung photographs of thick-bodied blond girls trussed in too-tight white dresses. I opened the door of the shop and entered and a bell tinkled above my head. The mat beneath my feet read WELCOME.

The photographs began to move and shift, the girls in the pictures grew until they filled the frames, they pressed their faces up close, as if the pictures' surfaces were windows they were trapped behind. They pressed so close their breaths fogged the glass and I could see pimples, and shreds of dinner caught in their teeth.

The girls drew pictures with their fingers on the clouded glass.

Tallies, words, messages. To me?

What would you like, the butcher asked me. He spoke rudely and impatiently though the shop was empty. I looked outside at the vague dark street. I could not tell if it was late night or early morning, the light was indecisive, and I did not know what to order.

I looked in the glass case before me. Laid out alongside the cuts of meat and chicken parts on the ice I saw clothes neatly folded, gloves, worn shoes, tarnished jewelry, false teeth, watches, candlesticks, and trinkets as in a pawnshop.

Well? the butcher said and pulled at his mustache, drawing his upper lip away from his teeth and letting it slap back. You haven't got all day, missy, he said.

I watched his lip being pulled again and again.

You've got a narrow window, he said, a narrow window of opportunity here, you see what I'm saying? And your window's just about shut. This is your last chance, lady.

He leaned closer and I looked past him at the great slabs of meat hanging on hooks behind him, pink and red and larger than men. They dripped into the sawdust on the floor. White joints and long bones and shiny gristle.

And as I looked, the carcasses began to writhe on their hooks. They twisted, thrashed, as if trying to free themselves. A long rack of ribs curled up on itself like a caterpillar, like a trapeze artist! A length of tongue flopped obscenely, spraying drops of blood. The more they moved, the more the hooks dug in and tore the flesh.

The butcher, oblivious to the activity behind him, sighed impatiently and waited for my order. Flecks of blood rained down on his bald head.

The lengths of entrails on the floor behind him began to untangle themselves; they raised their heads like cobras and tried to crawl back into the cavities they had been torn from.

A chunk of heart muscle behind the glass began to beat.

The butcher gave a grunt of disgust and reached behind him, pulling a live chicken from a crate. He held it down on the counter in front of me and I saw its eyes, enormous sad eyes like a man's, with long lashes. Those eyes rolled here and there in a panic, then they looked straight at me and began leaking tears from their corners.

Halved, or quartered, or cut in parts? the butcher said.

But the cleaver came down before I could answer. Again and again.

The eyes continued to look at me.

Too late. Too late to say I had wanted it whole.

I told my mother about the dream the next morning.

Can you *imagine*? I said.

My mother took my hand and held it tightly. Don't cry, she said.
I hadn't realized I was crying.

It must be because that shopkeeper was so *rude* to me, I said. So impatient, so pushy. I can't bear it when people are rude to me, even in dreams. People are so uncivil these days, don't you think?

I'm sorry, she said and held my hand.

Ilana

Afterward I regretted what we had done. I regretted the whole business.

I wished I had not meddled in her life in the first place. I was too eager to get her neatly matched up and settled and sent off. I should have let her find her own bumbling way.

I had placed this man in her hands, and then when he offended us we had thrown him away.

We had brushed him out of our lives like a speck of dust. It was the first time Sashie and I had united our efforts in anything.

Sharing the guilt certainly did not bring us any closer together.

I had hardly known Joe. That had made it easier to get rid of him. Yet the thought of him kept me up at night.

Sashie was troubled too though she did not admit it. Her remorse came out in her dreams; the consequences of what we had done sprung upon her then. The ugly loss, the gaping holes, the lost opportunities.

We never spoke of it. But it bound us together.

It nagged at us like stitches in flesh that itch and tug and long to be torn out no matter how much it might hurt.

Mara

Watch this, Jonathan said.

We were in the back bedroom where the curtains were always drawn and wallpaper peeled from the walls in strips like scales. Our mother lay on the bed, asleep. She slept a lot.

Come closer, Jonathan said, already on his toes beside the high bed, leaning over it.

I could see her breasts rising and falling, the black vents of her nostrils. Her breath faintly squeaked somewhere deep in her throat. She slept fully dressed, with her shoes still on, wearing all of her jewelry: a ring on every finger, earrings, strings of beads around her neck, brooches pinned to the front of her dress. She slept with one hand at her throat, as if expecting some disaster.

She had always warned me to be sure to wear clean underwear without any tears. You never know when you might get run over by a bus, or fall in the river or something, she said. If the people at the hospital or the morgue discovered torn underpants, it would bring shame down upon the family for generations.

Now she lay on her back, head in the exact center of the pillow. The room smelled sharply of ammonia, though I could see dust in the corners. The sheets on the bed were starched stiff as paper, and the wall beyond was plastered with photographs of women with strange dreamy smiles and men with smug grins and hair sculpted in waves.

My mother occasionally called me into this room to bring her a glass of water or a magazine. I never came here on my own.

Watch this, Jonathan said and bent close to her and blew softly in her ear.

My mother's legs kicked and churned the sheets, her head rocked from side to side and one hand flew up and swatted in Jonathan's direction. Then she subsided, the hand fell down. Jonathan watched her, his dark hair covering one eye.

She does the same thing every time, he whispered. He blew in her ear again, and again she went through the same motions like a windup doll. Her skirt rose above her knees. She seemed much bigger lying down than she did standing up. Jonathan was watching her, smiling.

He breathed into her a third time, and she mumbled some words deep in her throat.

We ran back to the kitchen.

You act just like her when you're asleep, he informed me. I've done it to you.

You have not, I said.

I have, he said, you just don't know it 'cause you were asleep.

I could not dispute that.

He seemed so wise to me, he had a way of stating things so you could not argue with them. He had a thin neck I loved, and soft hair that was always falling forward to hide sections of his face so that you never saw all of it at once. And his ears stuck out at the tops like the handles on the sugar bowl.

I've seen you when you're dreaming, he said.

You have not, I said. Though it was true I always felt as if *someone* were watching me, at all times, checking my behavior. When I was alone, when I was in bed, when I was in the bathroom. But that someone couldn't be Jonathan.

Now you do it, he said. Go blow in her ear. It'll be funny.

No, I said, I might wake her and then she'll get mad.

Not if you do it right, he said.

No, I said. We were not supposed to disturb my mother. When she was roused, her anger took the form of vigorous mothering. This meant enforcing ice-cold baths, then digging the teeth of a comb into my scalp as she pulled out tangles, then a week of wearing old-fashioned woolen underwear that itched and chafed, especially in summer. During those times of punishing attention, she would cook greenish, lumpy dinners and give us sudden, ambushing kisses that pinched, that left us sticky and sore.

I preferred it when she ignored us.

It's your turn, Jonathan said. If you won't do it to her then do it to grandmother.

Our grandmother was more accessible, not as distant and aloof as our mother. She was closer to our size, she had tiny hands. She could do anything: remove splinters from fingers and eyelashes from eyes, pluck out loose teeth, untangle knots, fix stomachaches, cure hiccoughs. Her touch felt natural, not like my mother's awkward jabs. My grandmother could pick me up, carry me cradled against her hip as if I were a baby, even though I was so big my feet nearly dragged on the floor.

But she was more frightening than my mother somehow. She said things that made no sense, she muttered a language that was more like a hacking cough, she spoke to people who were not there. She knew things without needing to be told.

She was the one I thought was watching me, all the time, even when I slept.

We went into the sitting room where my grandmother sat napping in a chair shaped like a throne. Her hands clutched the pile of knitting in her lap. The window to her left let in a narrow band of light that fell across her like a seat belt.

Go on, Jonathan said and nudged me.

Her breathing was soft and even, her head tipped back. Her lids were half open and I could see the wet whites of her eyes, like hard-boiled eggs. Was she really asleep? I could feel her breath against my forehead. I looked into the dark chambers of her ear and half expected something horrible and furry to crawl out. I pursed my lips to blow as Jonathan had, but then decided to check once more that she was asleep. I looked close at her blank, lidded eyes and as I did they twitched and swung around. Her pupils met mine and her hand gripped my arm.

I jumped. To keep from screaming I bit my tongue so hard I saw sparks.

What do you think you're doing? she said. I could hear Jonathan laughing somewhere behind me.

I thought you were asleep, I said.

You should always sleep with one eye open, she said. Preferably two. It's best to be prepared.

Yes, I said. My tongue was sore.

And don't be sneaking around, you might find out things you'd rather not know, she added.

Oh.

Here, I'm making this for you, she said and held up her knitting. Try it on, she said, to see if it's long enough.

She tugged the sweater over my head. It was scratchy and hot inside, dark with pinpricks of light shining through between stitches. Where were the sleeves? I could not find the armholes and the yarn kept snagging on my fingernails. I wanted to get my head out in the open but I could not find the collar. It must have gotten twisted around somehow; I turned and tugged and it was getting hotter and hotter. I thought I found a sleeve and pushed my hand farther and farther, but there was no end to it. I turned around and bumped into a chair. Jonathan was laughing, out there, somewhere, and I thought my grandmother was laughing too but I could not be sure because I had never heard her laugh before.

The sweater was my own little world, an entire universe with a hot woolly sky and dots of light like stars, and I thought I would never get out of it. I tried to take it off and start over, but it got caught somehow underneath my armpits and would not budge. I had my arms above my head, bent at odd angles, and my fingers found something loose and tugged and tugged at it, but it was only my own hair. The sweater was growing heavier and heavier.

Now I felt something sharp, jabbing at my cheeks and ears every time I moved. Her knitting needles? Were they still stuck in the sweater somewhere? I tried to call to them but my voice was trapped inside the sweater with me. I will be here forever, I thought, in this hot tight place all alone, with everyone else on the outside laughing at me. I'll get old. I'll die in here.

The sweater was pressed tight against my face now, sucking in and out with my breath.

I had been inside there for hours, it seemed. Weeks. I could feel that summer was ending, there was a cold autumn wind against my legs. I heard dry leaves scraping against the window, the street vendors folding up their tables and the homeless violinist on the corner blowing on his fingers.

The sweater was like a live thing, clinging to me, a parasite, and I had the idea that if I rammed myself against the wall I would kill it. So I ran, helter-skelter, caroming off corners, sliding on the floor. I heard something crash, and then I fell. I felt hands peeling the sweater off me.

I took a deep breath. The cool air was nice on my face. I looked around the familiar room, its piles of furniture like a junk shop.

Jonathan and my grandmother held the sweater between them.

Stop laughing at me, I said.

We weren't laughing, my grandmother said.

What a baby, Jonathan said. Can't even dress yourself yet?

Leave her alone, my grandmother said. She inspected the sweater, which hung limp and inconsequential in her hands.

It's a bit too small, she said. I guess you've grown.

My grandmother told me stories sometimes.

Usually when I annoyed her.

I annoyed her by asking too many questions.

I pestered her because she would not give me satisfactory answers. I was sure it wasn't because she didn't know, but because she wanted to keep the answer from me, for some reason.

People were always keeping things from me, it seemed.

Hoarding their secrets.

One time, when I had asked *Why?* once too often, she said: Did you know that before a baby is born she knows everything there is to know? An unborn baby knows everything that has happened, and all that will happen, and all the whys and wherefores.

All babies? I said. Even me?

Even you. But then what happens is, just before a baby is born into the world, an angel strikes her on the mouth, and it makes her forget everything.

That's why babies cry when they are born, she added. They're mourning all the knowledge they've lost. They're crying because they'll have to try to learn it all over again. And they know they won't be able to, a lifetime isn't long enough.

She touched the indentation above her upper lip and said: That's why you have this mark, here, between your nose and mouth. That's where the angel struck you.

Really?

Of course. How else would that mark get there?

I did not have an answer for that.

I looked at my face in the mirror, fingering the little groove. I thought I could almost remember the wonderful things I had known before I was born, they teased at the corners of my mind.

Mirror-gazing again? Jonathan said. He came up behind me, saying: Mirror, mirror on the wall, who's the fairest one of all? Not you, that's for sure.

He leaned against me and dug his pointed chin into the top of my head. It hurt. This was his way of being affectionate. I looked at our two faces, one above the other in the mirror.

I gasped then, and choked a little. It was not because Jonathan had flipped his eyelids inside out, spread his nostrils, and stuck out his tongue.

It was because above his mouth there was no indentation at all.

The angel must have missed him.

I did not like school much.

Once I had learned to read, I decided school had served its purpose and I did not want to go anymore. I wanted to be left alone with my library books.

But I had to go.

Do you want to grow up ignorant like your grandmother? my mother always said (after making sure my grandmother was out of earshot).

No, I said.

Of course I did not want to be like my grandmother.

My mother was wrong, though. My grandmother was illiterate, but she was hardly ignorant. Just the opposite, in fact. She knew too much.

Still, I did not want to be like her, for her mind was always far away, rooted in a foreign country that seemed to exist only in her head.

I wanted to belong *here*.

And I wanted to recover all that lost knowledge that angel had knocked out of me when I was born. I wanted to know everything so I would not have to ask questions of anyone ever again.

So I went to school.

The students in my classes seemed like such children, I suppose because I was accustomed to being only with older people: my mother, grandmother, older brother.

My school was several blocks from my neighborhood. It had tall windows, clocks with balky hands, that smell of sweat and mildew and sour milk that only schools have. The classrooms were decorated with pictures of Washington, Lincoln, and Roosevelt, with maps of the world, with color posters of vegetables and meat that proclaimed YOU ARE WHAT YOU EAT! In the back of the room was a dank corner where you hung your coat and a boy named Freddie waited to twist your arm until you gave up your milk money.

There was a girl in my class with long yellow hair, and plaid skirts and sweaters of the kind I begged my mother to buy me but she never did. This girl looked at me sometimes, across the room, her eyes wide. As if she were interested in me. Curious.

I thought I would not mind, much, if she wanted to be my friend.

One afternoon I was heading home from school when she walked up beside me. I smiled at her, a mysterious smile, a smile I had been practicing in the mirror for a moment like this.

We walked for a bit.

I held my books in front of my chest, like she did.

I tried to think of things to say. I would open my mouth and start to say something, then change my mind and hum a little instead. I don't think she noticed.

God, those shoes, where did you get them? she said.

My grandmother made them, I said. She cut up an old pair of my mother's.

Nobody else has shoes like that, she said.

Oh really, I said as if I hadn't noticed and agonized over it already.

She said: Your grandmother's a witch. She eats little children. She drinks their blood.

No she's not, I said. She does not.

She does too, the girl said. My mother told me.

That's a lie, I said.

It's true and you know it. Just look at her.

I know what she looks like, I said.

The girl said: She eats children, that's why she's so little herself. You are what you eat, right?

No.

That's why she has such long black hair. Nobody else that old has hair like that. Long and dark like a little girl's.

She dyes it, I said.

No she doesn't, the girl said. The only reason she hasn't eaten *you* yet is because you're so ugly.

She ran off then, and joined her friends who were waiting for her. They all laughed and leaned close together.

I walked home alone.

She had a scar on her knee, that girl, from where a birthmark had been removed. A big purple mark, with a deep root like a turnip. And she had a mole, raised and brown on her thigh. She was a spotted freak in a short skirt. People said birthmarks weren't catching, but who wanted to find out?

My brother played stickball in the street with his friends after school. I did not see him till the evenings.

Don't you hate school? I asked him.

It's not so bad, he said.

Of course things were easier for him because he knew everything already. He had all that knowledge in his head, but he was too lazy to put it to use. My grades were better than his. But he had the better clothes, and the straighter teeth, and could run fast. He knew how to talk to people.

That night my grandmother made her beet soup. It was bright red, murky. Amorphous shreds of things settled to the bottom. I pushed the bowl away.

Eat it, my grandmother said. It will make you strong.

I looked at her, at the black hair and dark eyebrows. There was something wrong with her, there were not enough lines on her face, I thought. She and my mother looked nearly the same age.

Eat it, she said sternly.

I saw what she was up to, what she was planning. She wanted me to become like her. She wanted someone to tell all her horrible secrets to.

I would not do it. I would not let her.

Ilana

I had high hopes for Mara.

I saw something familiar in the stubborn jaw, in her secretive eyes.

I realized I had neglected her mother, and I resolved not to do the same to her.

But she did not appreciate the attentions. Every story I told her, she managed to twist around until it became a personal affront. She pushed away my offerings, the soup, the tea, the honey pastry. Everything she touched turned sour. The sweaters I knit for her grew thorns, they became hair shirts even before they left my hands.

She cried when I combed her hair, she said I pulled too hard.

She always thought I wanted to hurt her.

But I wanted to teach her to be strong. Not like her mother.

I tried, don't you see?

But she can be so difficult, you know how she is.

How do you reach a girl like that?

It is like tossing a ball to someone who refuses to catch it, who stubbornly holds her arms at her sides and waits for the ball to strike her in the face. Over and over, until it is not a game anymore.

Sashie

I had dreams about fires, so I wore my jewelry to bed in case the dreams came true and I had to flee the apartment suddenly. I did not want to be caught unawares.

The dreams were pleasant, they were warm and slow and orange-lit, and a fireman broke down the door and then carried me down a ladder as the smoke rolled all around us. I could never understand how he could climb down the ladder without the use of his hands, and I could never clearly see his face, but it did not matter. I could see the hair that curled behind his ear, and his Adam's apple, and his hands and rubber boots.

My jewelry melted from the heat, and I felt a burning in my chest that might have been the underwire in my brassiere turning to liquid.

We went down and down, the fireman descending the ladder as easily as walking down stairs, and we never reached the bottom before I woke up.

My children seemed to take care of themselves. I did not notice them much. Sometimes I forgot I *had* children. I would hear Jonathan clattering down the hall and think it was one of my brothers. I would see Mara's face floating above a book in a dark corner and wonder if she was the little sister I had sometimes imagined but never really wanted.

I felt like a girl still. After all, here was my mother, unchanged, in the dress she had worn for the past twenty years, still holding conversations with my father that I could not quite catch. Here I was in this apartment where the light fell just as it did when I was a child. Here was a girl who slammed doors and kept to herself, here was a boy who stood on his head in the kitchen with his heels knocking against the wall.

I dreamed of a line of women walking in the snow, each one stepping in the footprints of the one before. All around them lay vast stretches of smooth snow, unmarked, unexplored.

This life of mine was like a loop of film, no beginning or ending, just the same figures going through the same motions in endless repetition.

It seemed inevitable that Jonathan would leave us and never return, that Mara would be with us forever.

I wanted to avert this somehow.

I watched Mara in the bathroom studying her own face in the mirror.

You should wash your face more carefully, you'll be getting to the pimples age soon, I told her. She whirled around, startled. Here, let me show you, I said. No, not like *that,* like *this.*

She was all knees and elbows suddenly, flailing past me out of the bathroom.

She looked ancient, that girl. She was born old. Did not take care of herself.

Every afternoon she slipped away, all alone. One time I decided to follow her. I thought perhaps she was meeting boys. If she was, I would put a stop to it. She was too young for that.

I trailed her to the public library, which seemed harmless enough. But perhaps there was someone waiting for her deep within the bookcases, someone waiting with groping hands and a pink tongue.

I watched as she returned some books and then drifted up and down the aisles, now and then taking a book from a shelf and flipping through it. I grew bored. Books have never interested me.

I went to the reading room so I could sit and rest my feet. The shoes I was wearing were my favorite pair, they still looked impeccable, but they had grown a bit tight. It must have been because of the weather, I've heard the humidity makes the leather contract.

I noticed the man at the table next to mine assiduously taking notes. Books were spread around him in neat stacks. He was wearing a *bowler*. And a *cravat*. I had not seen such a well-turned-out person in years. The handkerchief protruded in a perfect point from the breast pocket.

Subtly I glanced beneath the table and noted his cuffs, socks, well-shined shoes.

His eyes met mine for a long pleasant moment.

I went home then, for a lady does not linger in public places.

I returned the next day and remembered to wear my gloves. He was at the same table, deep in his research. I picked up the nearest book at hand and sat near him. I opened it and tried to read, but the words on the page were so shocking and vulgar that I was embarrassed to read them in this public place.

I noticed the gentleman was wearing the exact same clothes as he had the day before. This displeased me somewhat, but he seemed so clean and well groomed that I did not want to give up hope right away.

So I sat, and I waited, and I tried not to read the book in front of me (is *this* the kind of thing people are reading nowadays?). Finally the man closed his books, gathered his papers, and prepared to leave.

I followed him to the door, and he held it open so I could pass through after him. A gentleman, through and through.

It was easier than I thought it would be to speak to him, and he became quite voluble when I asked about his research. And though he was wider in the middle than I would have liked, and though his fingers were ink stained, and though I reflected that the bowler hat was quite out of fashion, even a bit ridiculous, in spite of these things I felt my heart begin to pound in a way it had not in years.

He asked if he might walk me home, and I saw his eyes settle on my ring finger. I was glad of the gloves. I took his arm and the masses of people on the sidewalk parted for us in a way they did not when I was alone.

My companion was going on at length about something but I admit I was not really listening, I was enjoying the sound of four feet stepping in unison, the rumble of a low voice directed at me. From time to time I said: Do you think? and Yes, exactly.

Things have *changed* so, don't you think? he said. Nothing is like it used to be. Especially women. Women seem so *brittle* now, they're not as *pliant* as they used to be, don't you think?

Ahead of us I saw a girl weaving slowly along, her head bent over a book. My escort had his eyes on me and plowed into her. The book fell from her hands.

My God, he said, lock where you're going. You shouldn't be walking around with your nose stuck in a book.

The girl crouched over the fallen book as if it had been shot. She squinted up at us.

You ought to apologize, the man said. You know, you'd be a pretty girl if you'd wipe that ugly expression off your face.

The girl glared more fiercely. Then she looked at me and her eyes widened. *Mother,* she said.

The man glanced from her to me. Something changed in his face.

Mother, Mara said again.

Is she yours? the man said but I was already walking ahead.

The man hesitated, then followed.

Do you know that girl? he said.

I took his arm and said: I must have reminded her of someone.

He walked me home, but the rhythm was gone; he looked at me suspiciously the whole time and refused my offer of tea. He never told me his name, and his coat sleeve left a musty smell on my fingertips. He vanished up the street, walking so rapidly I thought he might split his pants.

Mara came home much later.

Why did you do that? she said hoarsely.

Do what? I said.

You know what, she said.

I don't know what you mean. You must have me confused with someone else.

She said: I know it was you. With some strange man. You pretended you didn't know me.

I didn't see—that is—I wasn't wearing my glasses—

You don't *have* glasses, she said. And if you want to know, that man comes to the library every single day, I've seen him, and he stacks up books all around him so that no one can see that all he's doing is drawing dirty pictures on little scraps of paper!

She went to her room.

I did not go back to the library.

I saw the man once more. Much later. It was pouring down rain, and he was dressed in the exact same clothes as before: suit, cravat, wing tips, bowler hat. He was strolling in the park, sheltering beneath an enormous umbrella and sprinkling the trees with a silver-plated watering can.

Mara

It was summer. I had a game of solitaire spread out across the stoop.

I did not like being outside, with children running past and screaming. But the air in the apartment was unbearable.

Down the block children jumped in and out of the water gushing from an open hydrant. They stood in the gutter in their soaked shorts and T-shirts, barefoot in the trash and bottles. Soon someone would step on broken glass.

Sweat dripped off my forehead and dotted the steps.

One of the boys straddled the hydrant so that the water spewed from between his legs. The others hooted and shrieked with laughter.

The streets baked. Everything gave up its smell to the air. I could smell garbage, gasoline, exhaust. But I also thought I could smell bricks, asphalt, the bright metallic scent of cars that have sat in the sun until they are too hot to touch.

My brother shot from the door, trampling through my game and scattering the cards. He began racing up the street.

I chased after him, my eyes on the faded patch on the seat of his trousers. Where are you going? I called.

Can't you hear it? he shouted over his shoulder.

Up and down the street children were pouring from doorways,

tumbling down the stoops, dropping down from fires escapes. They all ran in the same direction.

What is it? I said, catching up to Jonathan.

Don't you hear it? he panted. That music, there it is again—da da, dum da da. Hear it?

No, I said. I searched his face carefully to see if he was teasing.

Come on then, he said. Come see.

He took my arm and pulled me along. He never invited me anywhere anymore, so I went. I could see one of my solitaire cards still stuck to his shoe.

We rounded a corner and there it was—a white van, a clown's face painted on the side.

That's all? I said, disgusted. The ice cream truck?

But children were streaming past us, and Jonathan broke away from me and elbowed his way to the front of the wave.

I saw a panel sliding back and a pair of hands emerged, collecting coins, distributing Popsicles and shaved ice in paper cones already gone soggy. The children came, little ones and older ones my brother's age, all of them oddly bright-eyed and eager, their mouths half open.

Those hands were large, a man's hands, but carefully manicured, the nails polished and square. The nail on the left pinky finger was nearly an inch long. I thought the backs of the hands were covered in dark curly hair, until I came closer and saw that it was really swirls of dark tattoos.

Isn't it great? my brother said. He had a green Popsicle jammed halfway down his throat, a second one melting in the pocket of his shirt just over his heart. The clamor around us had died down; all I heard now were sucking sounds. The crowd of children, fifty or more, stood rooted to the spot. Licking and swallowing. The ice cream truck pulled away from the curb.

The sun beat down but no one moved toward shade.

Can I try some? I asked, my voice loud in the silence.

No, my brother said and took a step back. Get your own, he said.

The last bit of ice was about to slide from the stick; he caught it and licked his palm.

Come on, I said and reached for him. All around me children cupped their hands protectively over their cones. Half of them had vanilla or chocolate smeared across their faces.

He'll be back, my brother said reassuringly. The other children nodded, glassy-eyed. The little boy next to me had vanilla ice cream plugging one nostril, and red juice in his hair, and he smiled blissfully.

Ice cream's for little kids, I told my brother, but he would not be provoked.

You're missing out, he said.

The next afternoon I saw my brother dashing down the stairs. Can't you hear it? he cried.

I followed him again though I heard nothing. Again we joined the stream of children that filled the street. I had money in my pocket this time. I pushed and wormed my way toward the window of the white van, where the hands dipped in and out. I drew closer and closer, holding the dollar bill above my head but just as I thought I might be noticed, the hands retreated and the van pulled away.

The bald black-toothed clown painted on the side seemed to be jeering at me.

The sun baked my hair.

I looked around, at wide eyes and Popsicles sliding in and out of mouths. The ices were of colors I had never seen before, vibrant unnatural colors like neon tubes. Inedible colors. Like the colors of certain poisonous fish and insects. The children's mouths were stained with them.

Isn't it the best? my brother said.

I didn't get any, I said but he did not seem to hear.

In the stifling hot nights I crept into his room and watched him sleep. A milky drool leaked from his mouth.

The heat wave did not seem to bother my grandmother. She did not sweat, and wrapped herself in more layers of clothes than she did in winter. It was as if her layers could keep the heat out, just as they could keep the cold out.

If you can't sleep, she said, you and Jonathan should sleep on the fire escape, there might be some breeze.

So we did that. The sky never really got dark at night, it never turned black, it stayed a deep twilight blue til dawn. It reflected the glow of the city's lights. I never saw a single star.

I lay on my side and watched my brother sleep. He slept with his head flung back and his mouth open as if he were surprised. I tried the trick of blowing in his ear but he did not stir. He was a deep sleeper, oblivious to the sirens and garbage trucks in the street.

One night, however, his eyes popped open. There it is! he whispered. I saw his teeth shining.

There *what* is? I said though I could guess.

He stood against the sky in his pajamas, skinny chest thrust out. Then he clattered down the steps of the fire escape, down four floors and then swung from the last landing and dropped to the street.

I fell asleep waiting for him to come back.

Early in the morning I found him asleep and peaceful beside me with a cool minty smell drifting from his nose and mouth.

Night after night he heard the music and disappeared.

Stay here, I told him one night as he was getting up to leave.

I can't, he said, it's so loud. That music. I have to. Can't you hear it?

Don't go, I said. I'll tell mother.

She won't care, he said.

I'll tell grandmother then, I said.

That made him pause a moment. Then he clattered away and I saw his dark figure darting up the street.

At dawn I woke and found him sleeping with a smile on his face and something sweet and sticky smeared on his mouth. I wanted to know what it was. I bent over him and tasted it. It was cherry flavored at first but bitter underneath, like cough syrup. I tasted it again.

His eyes opened then. What are you doing? he said.

Nothing.

God, you look scary this close up, he said. Get away, he said and gave me a push. But it was a gentle push, he was laughing.

The next night I went to bed in my clothes and shoes, like my mother. When my brother got up to leave, I followed him down the fire escape. The drop to the street was much farther than I had thought. My shoes smacked on the pavement and I fell over with a grunt.

Mara, what are you *doing*? he said.

I hear it now, I said. I swear I do.

He gazed at me, smiling. Isn't it beautiful? he said.

I said: Yes.

Beautiful, he said, his head lifted and alert like a deer's. It's like bells, isn't it? he said.

Exactly, I said. He turned and ran and I followed.

The streets were quiet, deserted. We ran down the center of the streets and the traffic lights clicked through their colors above our heads. The shops were covered with iron grills, and the windows of the apartments above were all dark. The only sound was the patter of our feet.

And soon we heard the patter of other feet, slowly building and increasing like raindrops. Children joined us from all sides, in pajamas and underpants and their fathers' cast-off undershirts.

We ran, and everyone seemed to know the way except me. We ran down toward the river and I could not understand why, I could not see the white van anywhere. The others ran tirelessly, like a dream, they seemed to float above the ground. But I felt very much awake, and very tired, my breath was raw in my throat and I had a stitch in my side.

It's louder then ever, isn't it? my brother said breathlessly.

Yes, I said though I was falling behind. They were all running like characters in a cartoon, their legs an indiscernible blur. I'm coming, I said as they passed me, all of them in a pack, and soon outdistanced me.

Wait up, I said but they were gone, I could just barely see their pale shapes.

I followed at a slow trot. Soon I could see the river, the water shining. It looked solid enough to walk on. Lights twinkled faintly on the far side. There was a sweet, burnt smell in the air from the sugar factory on the opposite shore. And then I saw the ladder.

It touched the ground and reached high into the night sky. It hung there, taller than the tallest skyscraper. I could not see where it ended, it vanished in the clouds. The rungs glowed faintly and I could see children steadily climbing upward. Some sucked their thumbs as they climbed, some slipped and missed rungs but did not seem to care. The older ones helped the smaller ones along, shielding them from falling.

I looked up, craning my neck, and I thought for a moment I saw a white van, floating in the sky. I was not sure. But I swear I heard something, the faintest musical whine that came close and then receded like a mosquito buzzing past my ear.

I heard that music, I did!

And I started toward the ladder. But as I gripped the lowest rung it seemed such a far way to go, and looked so high, and I was so tired. I did not trust it; how could I be sure of what was at the top?

Anyway I have never liked heights.

So I turned and walked homeward. I did not look back.

I did not want to know what I was missing.

It was dawn by the time I reached home. I knocked on my mother's bedroom door, and my grandmother's, and told them Jonathan had disappeared.

You're imagining things again, aren't you, Mara? said my mother.

Where did he go? my grandmother said. She seemed to have shrunk; her nightgown pooled around her ankles and her hair trailed behind her on the floor. She looked like a child playing dress-up.

I pointed toward the river.

My grandmother dressed and bustled down the stairs. She came back several hours later with my brother stumbling and dozing against her shoulder. She said she had found him sleeping beneath the bridge, surrounded by crumpled paper cones and splintered Popsicle sticks. He still wore a sticky brown beard.

You'll sleep inside from now on, she said. The both of you.

So we did, and my grandmother made sure the windows were tightly closed before she went to bed, though the heat was stifling.

My brother had trouble sleeping in the weeks that followed. He often came and woke me up in the middle of the night.

How did it go? he said. The music? How did it go? I'm forgetting it. Sing a little of it for me, will you?

I can't, I said.

Just hum it then.

No, I said.

You never really heard it, did you? he said.

I did.

You didn't. You're lying.

What was at the top, Jonathan? What did you see up there?

You wouldn't understand, he said. His forehead was sweaty, his hair sticking up in spikes.

He never would tell me, and soon the heat broke, and then it was autumn and he began high school. He grew a soft mustache on his lip, seemingly overnight. I searched his bed for evidence of further night excursions, and I found a dried stain on his sheets but it did not seem to be ice cream. When I asked him about the ladder he said he could not remember it anymore. At first he was just saying it, but soon I knew he meant it. His memory had always been poor and now he really had forgotten it all.

It was one more thing that I had missed out on, one more thing I would wonder about forever afterward. One more thing that was kept from me.

Ilana

I told Sashie: I don't like what is happening to your children.

They're doing just fine, she said. Jonathan is getting to be so handsome, don't you think?

Mara is very strange now, I don't like it.

Sashie said: She has always been a little sulky. She just does it for attention. She'll stop if we ignore it.

I told her: You're wrong. Watch her. She walks as if the floor is thin ice. She checks beneath the cushion of a chair before sitting down. She looks behind doors. Yesterday I made her an egg and she would not eat it unless I tasted it first. Then I found her counting the knives in the silverware drawer.

Sashie said: There is nothing wrong with being fastidious.

I said: Looking at me out of the corners of her eyes. I don't like it.

She would look nice if she would only take better care of herself.

She is all contrary, all twisted around the wrong way like an ingrown hair.

Mother, *please*, Sashie said. You're more paranoid than she is.

I said: She is too much like me, I think. We repel each other like magnets.

Jonathan is fine, though, don't you think? she said.

He is too flimsy, too loose in the joints, or something. He needs a father, he needs a man in the house.

He *is* the man of the house now. You leave my son alone. He has turned out just fine.

I said: I should do something. There must be something I could do.

Haven't you meddled enough? These are my children, not yours. You had your chance.

I had nothing more to say, then. I went to my room and shut the door and sat on the bed. I felt the bed creak and settle as Shmuel sat down on the other side, with his back to me. I did not turn around to look because if I did he would hurry away too quickly to be seen. It was better to sit like this, and sense him over my shoulder, and know he was there. To know that I *could* turn and catch a glimpse of him was enough. I did not have to actually do it.

I should have known this would happen. My granddaughter is too like me. My daughter too. Sometimes holding something too tightly, trying to guide it too closely will only make it turn against you. Like a river bursting through the dikes and dams and flooding over the fields.

My daughter did not seem to hear me anymore. She could blot

out my voice with her own. I did not know when it had happened, it was a gradual thing, her voice rising and rising up to drown out mine. And soon Mara would add her voice too, soon the sound would rise up on all sides and wash over me and I would not even be able to hear myself anymore.

Mara

Listen to this.

This is the story of my brother and the woman he wanted to marry.

I love my brother dearly, and I admire him and respect his judgment, but I will say that this woman was not one of his wiser decisions.

My brother and I were very close when we were growing up. For years we shared the same room. My mother and grandmother adored Jonathan. He was the spitting image of our dead father, everyone noticed this and told him so. When my mother was watching, he walked slowly and sat quietly at a time when other boys his age were jumping off furniture and making tommy-gun noises. At the time he explained to me that his brains were soft and runny like applesauce, and if he fell down they would all spill out.

I was younger than he was, but I always felt the urge to take care of him. In my earliest games I cooked imaginary dinners for him, poured imaginary coffee, washed and ironed his imaginary shirts.

Then he grew up and began to make something of himself. He started medical school, he wanted to become a doctor. My mother was thrilled, she thought this would be just the thing for him. My brother was so fine and bright and handsome, he would heal people and cure diseases and bring babies into the world. He would be famous, everyone would love him, he would have a magic touch. It made my mother almost weep just to think about it: this shining future of his. She also talked about how much money he would make, how rich and successful he would be. He will support us all in our old age, she liked to say.

But the truth of the matter was: I was the one expected to take care of them in their old age. I had thought about leaving home when I turned eighteen, I planned to travel somewhere and learn how to fly airplanes, to hunt elephants on the African plains, to dance in a chorus line; oh, any number of things. But eighteen came and went, and I was still at home, making tea for my grandmother in the fashion of the old country: strong, in a glass, with sugar cube on the side. Years passed and I was still preparing the Epsom salts for my mother to soak her feet in, still taking meat out of the icebox so it could defrost overnight.

And my brother still lived at home while he went to medical school, to save money, so I got to make his dinner and coffee and iron his shirts in reality, as I had once played. I suppose this should have made me happy. My mother and grandmother were glad to have him near, they were delighted when he showed them his white doctor's coat, his stethoscope. He brought home his instruments, he examined their eyes and ears and throats and told them how healthy they were. They laughed and admired his beautiful hands. And even when he didn't notice them at all, when he was studying or shaving before the mirror, they would watch him proudly. As if it were an accomplishment, to shave his own face.

As I said, I loved my brother dearly, but we were not as close as we had been as children. Now he was hardly home, and seldom alone, and my mother constantly fawned over him because each passing day made him resemble more closely our dead father. At least that is what my mother said. I knew my father only from pictures. When I looked at my brother all I could see was his resemblance to me, I could see myself in him, I could see what I could have been if circumstances had been different.

Because, you see, I had always been the cleverer one; though he was two years older I had always made up our games. I learned to tie my shoes first, how to count and how to read. I was jumping off the roof of the shed in the courtyard while he was still sitting in a flowered armchair with his chin in his hands trying to keep his brains from spilling on the floor.

Not that I was jealous. Not in the least. They needed me, they were my family. My grandmother would not admit it but she would soon grow frail, she would need my help more and more. And my brother, the great medical student, he could hardly take care of himself. He would come home from the hospital in the evenings, fling himself onto his bed, and groan. So I would bring him coffee, read to him from his textbooks, remind him of exams.

I did not like to look at myself in the mirror. I had become so tall, my face was a stranger's, and I had a red rash on my hands and arms from working. In my thoughts, I pictured myself as a child still. I saw that bold-faced girl, saw her jumping from roofs and fire escapes, and then marching home dry-eyed, defiant, with her knees full of gravel and broken glass. The day's experiment had been successful: I had discovered that if I didn't look at the wounds and didn't think about them, I wouldn't feel them. They did not exist.

But I did not feel jealous of my brother. I only felt a bit—fatigued, I suppose, it was only natural. There was a touch of claustrophobia, which is to be expected when four full-grown adults share an apartment built for two. And there was the relentless tugging of my grandmother's crochet hook as she spun out afghans and scarves and bulky socks in her corner of the living room—it's a small thing, I suppose. But, although you might not guess it, I am a sensitive person. Imagine the dim light of evening, early winter. My grandmother's eyes are half-closed, she's barely breathing, and the metal hook is twitching and jerking its way through the mounds of hairy wool with a rasping sound, the hook catches the light like a beetle, it moves insistently all by itself like some horrible insect burrowing into some poor creature's hide, I look at her sitting there and it's like a large hairy dead animal crawling with maggots.

It's a small thing, but it affected me.

So I kept my eyes on the work in front of me, and looked forward to the day when my brother would complete his studies and become a famous surgeon. I imagined him sewing up people's insides with a golden needle, as easily as darning up socks, everything bloodless and smooth, and the patients would leap from the tables and embrace him and bring him sacks of money. Yes, I knew it would not be so simple. But still I envisioned money, great amounts of money, our mother and grandmother taken care of, and my brother and me free to fly to a distant place and begin our real lives.

And then my brother met the woman he wanted to marry.

Her name was Chloe and he met her at the hospital swimming pool.

You see, the hospital where he worked was one of these new, progressive hospitals where they liked to try out the latest therapies and experiments. The pool had been built very recently, in a big frosted-glass room added on to the back of the hospital, and it was for patients who were paralyzed or otherwise injured, so they could get in the water and float about like children and learn to use their bodies all over again.

My brother was not terribly strong, but he was proud of his body and liked to exercise. He got permission to use the pool and he began to swim often. He described it all to me one evening. He said the water was heated, and also the air so that it felt tropical and strange, like a greenhouse; the water was an improbable blue color and the winter light that filtered through the frosted windows was violet-tinged and mysterious, and people's voices echoed about weirdly, they sounded round and melodious and hardly human, and when you sank underwater there was no sound at all, only a square blue room made of tiles, silent.

The patients clung to the edge of the pool, they cried out or paddled feebly at first; they did not trust themselves. But my brother liked to dive deep and look up at their dangling feet, their bellies, and the wavering light on the surface. He also swam laps across the pool, back and forth, very fast with a lot of splash and style, and all the patients and nurses and doctors admired him. Not because he was particularly good, I think, but because he is the sort of person who is always admired.

He told me about the pool, his voice drifting in and out of focus. His eyes and nostrils were pink, his hair wet and sleek, he reeked of the chlorine. My mother touched him and said: Oh you're soaking, oh you'll catch your death of cold coming home wet in this weather. My brother brushed her away.

They were using the hospital pool for other therapies as well. The doctors had invited pregnant women to come and swim in the pool. The doctors wanted to see how the unborn babies would react, they wanted to see if the babies would remember, and not be afraid of water, after birth.

The day my brother met Chloe the pool was full of pregnant women. Full of their pale, bulbous bodies, bobbing and gliding about in a graceful, languorous way. My brother sank to the bottom of the pool and watched them rising and falling. They seemed translucent against the light; he thought he could see the babies somersaulting around inside them. They trailed veils of bubbles behind them, they floated in close groups like whales. Light fell in sparkling shafts through the water. And then suddenly a sleek dark shape darted among them, dispersed them, and then dove down next to him.

This was Chloe. They hit it off immediately, my brother told me later. She was a much faster swimmer than he, and very smart, he said. He smiled at me with all his teeth. I told him he looked feverish, told him he ought to give up the swimming for a few days, as a doctor he should think of the risks.

He had been seeing her for three months before he brought her home.

He had invited her to dinner with us. I tried to fix up the apartment. But what could I do? The furniture had not been moved in years. The table legs had sunk into the carpets and taken root. The doilies on the chairs and sofa had yellowed and stiffened; I could not scrape them off with my fingernails. The tabletops and cabinets were filled with my mother's fussy figurines and the strange dark things my grandmother collected. Dried herbs and thick liquids in jars. My grandmother would not let me touch them, even to dust them.

I did what I could, covered the kitchen table with the sheet from my bed, dimmed the lights and lit candles. We waited; my mother wrung her hands, while my grandmother worked her hook, frowning. I searched through cabinets and found a bottle of wine. I opened it. It had gone sour, it stank like old cheese. Then my brother walked in the door with the girl on his arm and the room was full of noise and uproar though no one had said a word.

Now, I am an ordinary person. I am not superstitious, I am not religious. I only believe what I can see and hear and understand. But I tell you—the moment I saw her I knew something was not right about that girl. Something about her was wrong, *off*, like the wine. I can't explain how I knew. But with one look at her pointed little face I knew she could bring only grief and disgrace.

What kind of name is Chloe? A silly frivolous name. She had a small, fine-boned face, masses of hair lying over her shoulders, painted nails. A cheap little thing. She had a high, nasal voice like the neighing of a pony. A gap between her teeth.

She was talking to my mother, explaining how she worked at the hospital, like Jonathan; no, she was not a nurse, only a nurse's aide, mainly her work was to keep the patients comfortable, give them sponge baths and so forth. Jonathan jumped in, saying: The patients love her, she's very gentle. My brother was smiling strangely. I had never seen him like this before, he looked ill.

I looked at her suspiciously. To me the words *sponge bath* were like *massage*: a euphemism for something lurid and tasteless. I looked at her more closely and noted her dark veiled look. Then I saw her eyes distinctly and they were dark and light all at once, iridescent and lifeless as fish eyes. I saw her for what she was, a deep knowing creature with designs on my brother. I knew, and she looked at me and saw that I knew, and she stepped more closely into the lee of my brother's body, protected in his shadow.

And I saw that she had gained some kind of hold on my brother, some unnatural bond, for why else would he speak so frenetically, smile so wildly while avoiding my eyes? He was sweating, he made the whole room feel warm.

So we had the dinner but I cannot recall a minute of it, I was conscious only of her small hand clutching my brother's sleeve, and the look in her eyes which was old and ancient and evil and had nothing to do with her high whinnying voice as she and Jonathan laughed and talked about their swims in the pool and the patients in the hospital, ill people miraculously cured, brain surgery that gave people new personalities, drugs and microbes and invisible rays that were going to change the world.

Afterward my brother took her home, returned to us, and told us he planned to marry her. As soon as possible, he announced, and then they would live together in some new place.

My mother wept; she was sorry to think of losing him. But she was not overly upset; she had not seen what I saw. My mother was happy in my brother's happiness and could see nothing else. Even my grandmother, usually so perceptive, uncannily so, voiced no objections.

I did not want to see my brother sucked down into some dark place with this strange girl. I wanted to warn him. But he would not give me a chance; he did his hospital work, took swims, spent his evenings with her, came home at odd hours bright-eyed and distracted. She smoked cigarettes, so whenever he had been with her I could smell it. This disgusted me more than anything else. The smell of her, so blatant.

Finally one evening I trapped him, forced him to listen, asked him, begged him: How can you do this? Don't you see how wrong it is?

He laughed as if I had made a joke. He reeked of her.

How can you go away and leave me like this? I said.

Oh, come now, he said, I'll never leave you.

I am serious, I told him. You can't do this.

I'm serious too, he said.

I could tell he was hardly listening. I told him: You need me.

Of course I do, he said smiling. You're my sister.

No, I said, you really need me.

And then I reminded him of the thing we never spoke of, and he finally stopped smiling.

You see, years earlier I had taken his entrance examinations for him for medical school. The examinations then were not regulated as strictly as they are now. It was a simple thing for me to take the exams and sign our last name. He could never have passed them himself. I love my brother dearly, but his mind is like a sieve.

Since that time I had helped him with his classes whenever I could, prepared him for exams. Occasionally, in a show of pride, he would reject my help. But I was certain he would never be able to finish medical school without me. I reminded him of this.

I thought he would give in when I delivered this blow. But he only looked at me strangely, as if he were seeing me for the first time.

He wanted to marry her immediately, but then he was invited to spend a month training with a famous doctor in another city. He decided to seize the opportunity, and he would marry Chloe as soon as he returned. He set about preparing for his departure; he was very excited; it was the first time he had ever left home.

The day before his departure he came to our mother and asked if Chloe could stay with us while he was gone. She could use his room.

Apparently she had been turned out of her apartment suddenly and had nowhere to go. Apparently she had no family close by.

It will give you a chance to get to know her, my brother explained.

The whole situation seemed suspicious to me, but no one else seemed to notice.

My mother agreed enthusiastically, my grandmother crocheted and said nothing.

My brother left. And the strange girl Chloe moved in.

Now I had no peace. She seemed to fill the apartment. My initial impression of her was not disproved, no, it was heightened by the close quarters. My mother enjoyed her company, she suspected nothing. The girl was crafty that way.

Her smell, the cigarettes, a nauseating lilac perfume—she permeated the apartment. And her eyes never lost their cold amphibious stare. Even while chattering to my mother or arranging her hair before the bathroom mirror, I would see in her eyes a deviousness, a secret intelligence.

I knew why she had come. She wanted my brother, she wanted to wrest him from me. She knew I was the only one who understood what was happening and would stand in her way. She was plotting and planning, trying to catch me unawares.

I could not eat. I could not sleep, I feared she would come and smother me in the night with a pillow. She was like a cat, a cat who rubs against your legs, purring, in the day, and then lies on your face as you sleep to drown you in the night. I would not meet her eyes, I knew if I did she would hypnotize me without a word, lead me to jump from a window or swallow my tongue.

You see, I understood who she was. I had found her out. She was one of those dark sea creatures who lure men to their deaths for sport, like the mermaids that call out to sailors in the moonlight and then drag them to the ocean floor trapped in their long scaly hair; like the sirens with their irresistible yammering.

I knew she was one of these underwater beings, with their strange bodies and cold blood. I knew because of the way she took long baths, every night she stayed with us. I watched her through the keyhole, luxuriating in the water, smoking a cigarette. I could not see all that she did; there were strange sounds, strange smells, I knew she was metamorphosing behind the door, growing fins and scales. I saw her hair floating in the steamy air, undulating like seaweed moving with the current.

I knew.

I knew because of her teeth: rows and rows, needle sharp, like a carp's.

I knew because of the way she first came to my brother: through the water, silent, unsuspected, darting like a snake past the pale innocent pregnant women wallowing on the surface like cows in deep grass.

I had to save my brother, but I did not know how to get rid of her. I wanted to ask my grandmother, she was considered an authority on these matters. But she would know nothing about a sea creature like Chloe; my grandmother knew only the imps and goblins of the old country. She claimed she knew how to drive out the household spirits that extinguished cookstove fires and soured the milk, said she once brought a stillborn baby to life by blowing in one ear, causing the angel of death to flee out the other. Her little rituals involved candles, hair, whispered words. I had never truly believed in her stories, but it did seem that whenever I displeased her in some way I would later find myself afflicted with indigestion, chancre sores, hangnails, sties, dreams of falling, menstrual cramps like a crochet hook in the belly.

So I spoke to no one, I watched and waited, I listened at night as Chloe splashed in the bathtub, I knew she was thinking of my brother, my brother swimming, perhaps she was imagining his head suddenly appearing, rising up dripping and disembodied from the bathwater between her legs, his head held between her hands like John the Baptist's on a plate. She churned the water about, gurgled; steam crept beneath the door and drifted through the cold apartment, advancing and touching and recoiling like a live thing.

The days passed, soon my brother would return. Soon they would be married, out of reach. I heard Chloe tell my mother: a small wedding, I'm an orphan you see, I have no family, so just a ceremony for us, and afterward we'll take a trip to the seaside.

I knew I had to act. I thought of my brother, my poor brother, his body lying on the ocean floor plastered with starfish and sea urchins sucking out his juices, hermit crabs creeping in and out of his eye sockets, eels gliding in and out of the secret grottoes of his body.

There came an afternoon when I heard an incredible sound: silence. My grandmother's relentless hook had stilled; it slipped from her grip and clattered to the floor. She was asleep, enveloped in her latest creation: an afghan, white and blue, large enough for a double bed. She was nearly finished with it, nearly buried by it. All I could see of her were her crabbed fingers, and a hank of her hair, greasy jet-black: she dyed it herself with her own secret concoction.

I watched her sleep; her breath hissed in and out with a regular ticking in the throat, like the click of a valve, as if she were made of machinery inside. Softly, softly, how the floorboards moaned, I reached past her, opened the door of the glass-front cabinet and took one of her forbidden bottles.

It was a square bottle, heavy, the dust on it an inch thick. It was filled with a dark, viscous liquid, dense and shiny. I knew Chloe would like it. You know how fish are so oily. She could use it on her scales. I put a ribbon on the bottle, presented it to her that night.

It's for your bath, I said.

She took it and thanked me, but I did not dare look at her, for fear my eyes would give me away. We stood in the narrow hall together for a moment, toe to toe. I was aware more than ever before of her smell, a rank fish-market smell. My brother would be coming home the next day.

She said she was sorry we had not become better friends. She said she knew we had one thing in common: we both loved Jonathan very much. She thanked me again.

Her voice sounded perfectly natural, but I knew it was a ruse and she was growing more and more monstrous even as she spoke. I would not meet her gaze, it would turn me to stone. I said good night, walked down the hall, waited until I heard her start her bath, and then turned back to watch her through the keyhole.

I watched her pour the black liquid into the bathwater, saw it froth up. The bathroom was already filled with steam. I watched her step into the tub, one foot then the other, then she lowered herself into the water. I saw her face, damp with sweat, cigarette between her lips, eyes closed. I held my breath.

I thought my gift would drag her down the way oil spills can smother seals and fish and waterbirds. I thought she might thrash around and slowly sink down like the weary dinosaurs in tar pits. But she did not.

I waited, blood pounding in my ears and the doorknob pressing into my forehead. I saw the speck of ash linger at the end of her cigarette, quiver, fall. A spark. The bathwater burst into flame. A roar of air, and the fire shot up; the shock of light and a blast of air made me fall back and lean against the wall. It was so beautiful. I couldn't see anything for a moment; then I saw beautiful green flowers blooming against the backs of my eyelids. I warmed my hands.

Later, later I stood on the sidewalk in front of the building, hugging my mother and grandmother to me as we stood among sirens and flashing lights, and handsome firemen offered us blankets and hot chocolate. Our neighbors huddled around us in their nightshirts. They all clutched their valuables: jewel boxes, insurance policies, tiny yipping dogs with bows in their hair.

Afterward everyone said the worst thing about it was the scream—the piercing, keening shriek of agony and despair that woke them all from sleep. They all agreed it was the most horrible thing they had ever heard, like fingernails on a chalkboard the size of the sky, yet a human sound, the sound of a child being dragged under the wheels of a train, a sound that made their hearts shrivel up and die inside them.

Of course they were exaggerating. The sound was not as bad as they said. It was a sound you may have heard yourself, if you are familiar with seafood. If you have ever cooked a lobster.

Ilana

I should have known this would happen.

Mara. It was inevitable.

I had watched her view of the world narrow and skew like a funhouse mirror over the years. I'd seen her crash into corners of furniture, and try to place her foot on a phantom stair as if she lived in a house invisible to the rest of us. I had watched her feelings for her brother sharpen and bloom into jealousy.

But I did not think it would come to this.

I never thought she would act.

I feel it is my fault. I should not have left my things where she could get at them.

You see, I had grown careless. I thought she was not interested in my work, so I had not guarded it carefully. She had always laughed at it, called it quackery and superstition.

But apparently she believed in it enough to use it for her own purposes.

I had found the bottle, uncorked and empty in the smoky apartment. I knew what she had done.

There's a streak of violence in her. I see it now. Sometimes she can barely contain it.

Where did she get it, I wonder?

Mara

My brother returned from the distant city; he went to see Chloe in the hospital; he came home speechless and heartbroken.

I tried to comfort him. I knew it was upsetting for him to finally see the true Chloe, as I had seen her all along. I had glimpsed her myself in the clean white hospital bed, her hair singed off, her eyelids and ears gone, her body covered in stiff, shiny scales. The webbing between her fingers and toes. I thought she looked beautiful, so pure and natural.

My brother would not be comforted.

Our apartment was intact, though damp and smoky. No one could understand how the fire started, and everyone praised me for helping my mother and grandmother to safety.

My brother moved back into his room. I thought everything would return to normal. I had never been so happy.

But my brother abandoned his medical studies. He visited the hospital but spent most of his time in the apartment. All the starch had gone out of him. Slumped shoulders and a bruised face like a defeated boxer. He did not speak to us, or wash himself. He shuffled around the rooms in bedroom slippers, staring out of windows, jingling the change in his pockets.

He sat for long afternoons with our grandmother. Close together in her dark corner. I cannot imagine what they had to say to each other.

He wandered the apartment at all hours, oblivious to the weather outside. He brushed past me in the hallways without a word.

I knew what he was feeling. I have always known, without him needing to tell me. I knew he would come to me. In time.

One day I found him at the living-room window, holding the drape back with one hand.

It's raining, Jonathan, I said.

What?

It's raining, I said.

Yes, he said, sunlight reflecting on his glasses.

The next day he ran away to sea.

My mother and grandmother and I, we all missed him dreadfully. We waited, days and weeks, for some word from him. I was certain he would come for us, any day now he would come, with a pirate ship and a chest full of treasure.

My grandmother's afghan, the double-sized one she had nearly finished, was destroyed in the fire. She was very agitated about it, glaring and silent for days. Then she took up her hook and began something new.

What is it going to be? I asked her the other day.

This one, she said, is for you.

She looked at me, her eyes were very clear and measuring. The hook wormed its way into the wool.

Sasha.

That was my mother's name. All her life she'd wanted an American-sounding name; as a child she'd chosen Shirley. I can imagine her then, pinning her hair in curling papers, prissing up her mouth in front of the mirror, begging: Shirley, call me Shirley, mother.

For years my grandmother ignored her, played deaf; nights she whispered *Sashie* in my sleeping mother's ear; days she wrote *Sasha* with salt in the bread before she baked it.

Eventually my mother gave up.

When I was born (or so I am told, and I have no reason to doubt it) my mother was determined to give me an American name. The most American-sounding name she could think of.

Mary. That was what she wanted to call me.

Blond curls, little lambs.

My grandmother went livid at the news: You can't name the child that! You can't name her after the mother of the Christian god. We'll be cursed forever. You've already cursed the child by giving birth with all those men watching. Why do you want to make it worse?

I can picture them in the hospital room after my birth: my mother lying tense and furious under the sheets (she had wanted a boy anyway), her back ramrod-straight, as if the bed were some kind of torture device and any minute she expected a pendulum to swing, a blade to fall; my grandmother hovering near, nimble and birdlike in her black clothes, flapping and croaking like a raven; and the nurse, white-capped and befuddled, offering the birth certificate to first one and then the other, waiting for them to answer her question about the baby's name; and the baby herself, a forgotten lump in the corner, swaddled and screaming at the top of her lungs.

They argued. This I know.

A gentile name, she'll be cursed all her life!

I want her to fit in, an American girl!

I wonder if they slapped and spit like schoolgirls.

I wonder if my grandmother hiked up her skirts, climbed right up on the bed, pinned down my mother, knelt on her chest and twisted her hair, smothered her with pillows, demanding *holler 'nuff!* like a bullying street boy while my mother kicked and screeched, churning the bedclothes.

I can picture this so clearly that I don't think I'm imagining it; it *must* have happened this way.

Eventually they compromised.

Mara, my mother wrote on the birth certificate (with my grandmother's hand on her wrist, I imagine).

Mara. It means bitterness.

I kept his room clean for him. I knew he would be coming back.

Tucked the sheets smooth and tight. Wiped the dust off the windowsills. I bought him new pencils, sharpened them, put them in the mug on his desk. Every few days I tested them, sharpened them again.

The weather was warm, damp, and strange; there was a wet film on everything. The heat settled in starting early in the morning and hovered over the city all day. My scalp pricked, my palms were slick. My hair smelled of mildew.

Mara, wash your hair for God's sake, my mother said.

You see, I did not like to go into the bathroom. I did not like the thought of water falling on my head.

My grandmother stayed in her dark corner, her fingers working and lips drawn tight. Whenever I came near she tried to hide her work, shielding it with her arms, burying it in her lap, with furtive glances.

As if she could hide anything from me.

As if it weren't obvious she was beginning her umpteenth afghan, or scarf, or wretched sock.

As if I cared.

My mother went often to visit Chloe in the hospital. She felt it was her duty, she said, the girl had no family, no one at all. So several days a week she put on a lace collar and a hat and gloves and went to sit by the bedside of a crisp hollow shell of a girl, whose eyes were sealed with scar tissue, whose mouth was a round hole outlined with charcoal. Why did she bother?

I went with her once. Chloe's skin looked shiny, hard, burnished, like a shell; in places it had cracked and split; you could see a wet dark jelly inside. No longer the Chloe I knew; not even a person, just a messy little smear on the white sheets of the hospital bed, like the congealed remains of someone's lunch left on a napkin.

She never stirred, hardly breathed. She was hooked by the arm to a bag of fluid above her bed; a saline solution dripping into her veins, to remind her of the ocean, no doubt.

Chloe's doctor stopped in and spoke to my mother for a few minutes. He was very tall, with a red pompous face and wavy silver hair. My mother sat up straighter and raised her chin and smiled, and I knew the reason for the lace collar and hat. They spoke softly, confidentially, with many solemn nods.

I decided not to go to the hospital again.

I spent much of my time in Jonathan's room.

There was a photograph on his dresser, taken the day he graduated high school. In the picture he smiles with his mortarboard tilted at a rakish angle, he pushes his lower lip out with his tongue in an odd grimace, his brown hair glows auburn in the sun. I am standing closer to the camera, hulking in the foreground, half my body cut off by the edge of the picture. I'm frowning, a deep furrow between my brows, my mouth open; my hands clutch my program in a fussy, frantic gesture, I look like a lost tourist. The outline of my brassiere is clearly visible through my dress. It was a modest dress, I bought it because it was on sale, I had no idea it became transparent in direct sunlight until that graduation.

Jonathan is flanked by his best friend, Martin, and his girl of the moment. One of a long series of insubstantial girls, her name was Amy but she insisted on spelling it Aimee, and dotted the i with a little heart.

Jonathan has his arms around their shoulders, all three appear to be laughing at something that may or may not be me.

I had always hated that picture, but it was the most recent one with the two of us together.

We had played under his bed together as children. We used to inch along on our stomachs beneath the low box spring, until we reached the far wall. Our mother had once been a fanatical cleaner but gave up when she moved to this apartment that seemed to cultivate dust like a crop. The forgotten space beneath the bed was thick with dust. It was our own private world, a musty gray kingdom. We breathed and sent the dust balls rolling; we could pretend they were tumbleweeds blowing across the main street of a Western town like the ones Jonathan read books about. The dust was pixie dust, it would make us fly. It was moondust, the Sahara, the surface of Mars. We were kings of it, the entire realm; and I used to think, as we lay belly-down in that small coffinlike space, with nothing but our faces close together and the miniature landscape taking shape, I used to think that it was all I wanted in the world, I wanted to stay there forever.

Jonathan with his chin on the floor, dust on his eyelashes, eyes bright in the dimness, his hand nudging mine. How beautiful he was back then.

Mara, what on earth are you doing? my mother said.

I was on my hands and knees, my head beneath the bedspread. Checking for dust, I said.

I have some news, she said. She sounded as if she were strangling. I sat back on my heels and looked up. Her face was all knotted with suppressed emotion.

I followed her into the living room. My grandmother looked up expectantly.

The doctors say Chloe is pregnant, my mother announced.

My grandmother said: Ah.

I said: Whose?

My mother said: That's the thing. You don't think *Jonathan* would—they weren't married yet, Jonathan would *never*—he was a man of honor, he respected her, I'm sure he was waiting—saving himself for marriage—

I said: Then the baby must be someone else's.

Another man? But how *could* Chloe?—they were going to get married—they still might—when Jonathan comes home—

I said: It would not surprise me. She was a tramp, a floozy.

You really think—another man?

I said: I'm positive.

My grandmother finished her tea, smacked her lips, and studied the dregs.

Thank God Jonathan *didn't* marry her then, my mother said. This would have broken his heart, to find this out. Thank God things worked out this way. I'm not saying I'm glad about the fire—certainly not, the poor girl—but I must say, every cloud has a silver lining—

Yes, I said.

I'm glad we've found out the truth. Before it was too late. Now, when Jonathan comes home, he can start fresh, finish medical school, find a nice new girl—

Yes, I said. My face hurt; the muscles were straining in an unaccustomed way. I realized I was smiling.

My grandmother looked up from her tea leaves. She said: Sashie, when that child is born you must bring it home.

Haven't you been listening? my mother said. It's not—

It *is*, my grandmother said firmly. Your grandchild, my great-grandchild. When it is born, you must bring it home.

How can you be sure?

I'm sure, said my grandmother and fixed her with a stare.

My mother hesitated, torn.

It's impossible, I said.

Don't you want a grandchild, Sashie? my grandmother said softly. You won't get another chance. Your son's not coming back. And *that* one won't be giving you any grandchildren, not unless she mends her ways.

She jabbed her finger at me.

My mother's face softened.

Jonathan's child, my grandmother said. It will look just like him, you wait and see. A beautiful child.

My mother was nodding, nodding.

Don't you see, she's a tramp, Chloe's a tramp, the child can't possibly be Jonathan's, I said desperately. I thought I'd gotten rid of Chloe, for good, and now here she was, creeping back into our lives, stretching out her tentacles. The thought of Chloe's brat growing up in our home made me ill. Just imagine: we would have to buy it a fishbowl, later an aquarium, plastic seaweed and a fake diver blowing bubbles.

Since Chloe was unconscious, unable to give birth, the doctors had to cut the baby from her prematurely by cesarean section.

A girl.

I was not there, but I imagine it was like gutting a fish, a nice clean cut and a scooping out of the wet sloppy stuff.

They said that when she was plucked from her mother's waters the baby opened her mouth and a stream of bubbles flew from her lips; they drifted around the room, hovered around the lights like moths before popping.

The baby was kept at the hospital for weeks, inside a glass meat case, hooked up to wires and rubber plumbing. She was shriveled and sickly, with a cross expression. Perhaps that had to do with the tubes up her nose. The nurses had put a tiny knitted hat on her head, which, together with her wrinkled face, made her look like the caretaker of our building, a bald toothless old man who wore ribbed watch caps winter and summer.

She's beautiful, my mother breathed. She spent hours in the nursery touching the tiny hand with a rubber-gloved finger.

She's a tough old bird, my grandmother said. She had actually left the neighborhood, for the first time in months, to see the baby. For some reason she did not squawk this time about men in the delivery room.

The baby did in fact look like a pale boiled chicken, skimpy meat sliding from the bones.

She looks just like Jonathan did. Except Jonathan was much bigger. But the same eyes, my mother said.

I looked at the infant and my worst fears were confirmed. I could see the marks on her neck, where the gills had only recently closed up. She kicked her legs as if swimming. And there was the look on her face, when she opened her mouth, as if she could not understand this strange new element, air, that she suddenly found herself in.

My grandmother put aside her secret project, stuffed it between the sofa cushions. She bought soft angora yarn and set to making baby blankets, baby sweaters. And ridiculous booties and tufted bonnets.

How do you like your niece? she asked me. She looked happier than she had in years; she had loosened her hair from the severe braid, it was still oily black but looked softer and gentler hanging around her shoulders.

She's *not* my niece, I said. I don't like the mother, I can't imagine who the father is, and she's just a pathetic stunted little thing.

My grandmother's hand darted out. I thought she was going to slap me; instead she held my chin and studied my face carefully. You're jealous, she said.

Me! Of what?

Of Chloe, she said. This girl, Chloe, burned up, half alive, gives birth to a beautiful child. And what have you done? Nothing.

I'll have children, wonderful children, someday. I'm stronger than her, smarter than her, my children will be tall and healthy and clever, not scrawny like hers. Mine will grow up to change the world. And I'll have them when I'm good and ready, not before.

You can't make them by yourself, you know. Not even in this day and age, my grandmother said.

I know.

How do you plan to find a father for those babies?

I will find someone. Someday.

You're jealous of Chloe because she made a child with your precious Jonathan, my grandmother said.

No, I said. No, I'm not. No, she didn't. No. No.

Apparently Chloe had no family, no close friends, no one who knew anything about her. After some discussion with doctors and social workers, my mother was given permission to bring the baby home.

She and my grandmother prepared Jonathan's room for the baby.

Jonathan's room!

But what if he comes back? I protested weakly.

Then he'll find his daughter right here waiting for him, my mother replied.

Fortunately they changed little in the room, simply brought in a cradle and set up the desk to use as a changing table. I could not help smiling to think of soft baby skin lying right where I had kept Jonathan's carefully sharpened pencils.

Now for privacy I kept to my own little closet of a room. At night I thought of what my grandmother had said. I removed my clothes and stood before the mirror. My own body was like a stranger to me, I so seldom thought of it. Most days I felt like merely a pair of eyes floating through the world, a pair of eyes and a mouth that occasionally spat out remarks, and a tightly knotted brain that constantly twisted in and in on itself like two mating slugs. The rest of my body felt like something I used but that did not really belong to me, like the clothes I put on in the morning. It was all so much machinery, puppet limbs attached with strings.

Now I looked at my body as I had not for years. There was so much of it. I stroked my skin, soft and alive, not like Chloe's insect shell. I touched my belly, where children would be made. I imagined tiny workmen inside, shouting orders, assembling babies from the food I had eaten. I thought of the amazing potential lurking in my body, the countless perfect children waiting to be born. I would not have to do a thing, my body would be able to produce these wonders unbidden.

Once I performed the initial step, of course.

My mother brought the baby home from the hospital one rainy evening. She carried the small sulking bundle through the apartment, cooing and burbling. My grandmother hovered nearby. I kept in corners, did not want to get too close. That smell babies have, so frank, so demanding, it filled our home in minutes. They brought her into Jonathan's room, laid her in the cradle. She was whimpering.

Perhaps babies were desirable assets, and perhaps I was beginning to want one for myself; but this particular one I did *not* like, she was too much like Chloe, it turned my stomach to look at her.

My grandmother hushed her, rocked and rocked her, dimmed the lights and rocked the cradle like the rocking rise and fall of ocean waves.

The chores began: the cries in the middle of the night, the diapers, the formula to be heated and the bottles sterilized, the attentive baths, the burping, the descent into baby talk, the murmured discussions about reflexes, fontanels, sleeping positions.

My mother and grandmother shared the duties, did not ask for my help.

How is the navel healing? they asked each other. How does her breathing sound to you?

As she did on all significant occasions, my grandmother busied herself with her herbs, crushed and brewed them, made us all drink the bitter tea, even a sip for the baby, who squalled. She snipped bits of the downy baby hair for some private ceremony, and tied a red string around the little wrist.

It was impossible to ignore the baby. She dominated the apartment. I hated her cries, and her bleary, half-closed eyes; she seemed to be watching me slyly, as if she knew all about me.

At night as I lay in bed I thought of Jonathan, wondered where he was, when he would return. I remembered our games. One night I could not sleep for hours. I rose quietly and went to his room.

A night-light cast an orange glow. I sat softly on the bed. Then I lay, sniffed the pillow and the coverlet for traces of him. Of course I smelled only soap and cleanness. He had been gone for so long. The cradle rocked softly all by itself.

I knelt by the cradle and studied her. She lay on her back, head to one side, hands curled in little fists. She heaved a sigh, a sigh as deep and world-weary as an old woman's. The brows puckered in a frown, then smoothed themselves. I touched one of her balled-up fists, and she immediately clutched my finger. So tightly, a monkey grip. My heart twisted. Yes, I knew it was only a reflex. I knew. And yet.

I looked at her, and with a start I saw Jonathan there. Unmistakably, I saw my beautiful brother in that round baby face. I saw, and I knew that she was his daughter. I knew. Without a doubt.

I lifted her and held her, I expected her to scream out since I had never held a baby in my life, but she didn't, merely settled herself against my shoulder and lapsed back into sleep. How comforting and right her weight felt against my chest, her breath in my ear. She fit so perfectly in my arms, as if she were made for them. I supported her head with one hand, her padded bottom with the other; I stroked and joggled and rocked; I found myself humming under my breath a tune I'd never heard before.

The moon drifted free of the clouds just then and the room was flooded with silver light. I pressed my cheek against the downy head and then I knew, as abruptly as I had realized that this was Jonathan's child, I now knew that she was also mine.

I knew. Any fool would be able to tell, from the way the baby settled into my arms, that I was this child's mother. She belonged to me.

I would tell her so. As soon as she was old enough to understand. And she would have no reason to believe anything different.

Chloe died in the hospital, her burnt-out shell crumbling to dust.

Finally.

I felt my grandmother's eyes on me when we heard the news. I struggled not to smile.

My grandmother mourned for the girl, but then she had never stopped her mourning; as long as I had known her she had worn black and thought more about the dead than the living.

Ilana

There was a new baby in the house.

Sometimes when her crying woke me in the night, I started up from sleep thinking: Eli? Wolf?

So many babies had passed through my arms that I could not always distinguish among them. I thought of other girl babies I had held, tiny girls just like this one with the heavy brows marring the soft baby features.

I remembered Sashie struggling discontentedly in my arms, Mara spitting up on my shoulder. I forgot, sometimes, which came first. It did not matter.

In spite of all that had come before, this new baby gave me hope. I wanted to mold the soft plates of her skull, rub her gums as the teeth burst forth, tell her all the things I had never been able to articulate before.

Mara

It became more and more clear to me as time went on.

This daughter was mine. Perhaps not in flesh but in spirit.

She was the child we might have had, Jonathan and I, if circumstances had been different.

I held her in my arms hour after hour. The small mouth sought out my breast, came away disappointed. That gave me a peculiar feeling.

Her face always puckered up when I held her.

Maybe I gripped her a bit too tightly. Perhaps.

But I had to.

Those other two were always trying to snatch her away.

My mother and grandmother were battling me for the baby. Couldn't they see that she was mine?

It was a constant, subtle thing. A silent war the three of us waged. One would sterilize and prepare a bottle, and then another would pluck it from her hand and run to the nursery. We all hovered over the cradle as she slept, all wanting to be the first face she saw when she awoke. We elbowed each other aside at the changing table. Even my mother, usually so fastidious, dipped her hand in.

We all wanted her.

It was not fair. My grandmother had given birth to a daughter she hadn't wanted, my mother borne a daughter she hadn't wanted. Now it was my turn. Why did they want to take this one from me?

This was my last chance.

It was the last chance for all of us.

The last chance for what?

To make a connection, perhaps.

To fill these empty arms.

We named her Naomi. I chose it and the other two consented. We all thought of the old story: Ruth and Orpah and Naomi standing on the open road, Orpah the coward going home weak and sniveling, and then Ruth turning to Naomi and promising her devotion with words like a song: *Entreat me not to leave thee . . . for where thou goest I will go, and there will I be buried.*

A promise to lay down one's life for another, and to do it gladly.

That was exactly what we offered this child. That kind of devotion was what we felt for her, though we could not articulate it.

None of us I admit are particularly eloquent.

We all held her, we passed her from hand to hand, each of us crooning in her ear: Know that I will never leave you. Know that I am here forever. I will teach you everything.

We passed her along, from hand to hand. It made me think of disasters, of long lines of men passing buckets of water from hand to hand at a fire, or men heaving along sacks of sand during a flood.

Naomi soon became Nomie on our lazy tongues.

Nomie, we called her.

She brightened the apartment. We watched her grow. All three of us tried to mother her.

I thought, surely once she starts to walk and talk, she will point out her rightful mother, she will call my name, run to me, and those two will be forced to retreat.

But she did not. She was a grave, quiet child and she treated us all equally, held us all at a distance. As she grew older she withdrew even more. Her hair grew long, she would not let us cut it, she hid behind it like a veil.

I knew she favored me over the others but did not want to hurt the feelings of the other two. She was a considerate child.

She liked to play in the dark maze of furniture in the front room, just as her father and I had once played there.

That had to mean something.

Sometimes she vanished in the jumble for hours; I would plow through the cobwebs and stacked chairs looking for her but I could never find her until she wanted to be found. Sometimes she vanished for hours. I did not like that.

Her looks developed into a familiar pattern, the long black hair and dark eyes and lips a shade too wide for her face. Just like me. Just like all of us, in fact, though my mother's hair was now touched with gray, and my grandmother's was an unnatural metallic black.

My mother and grandmother noted that Nomie did not have her father's blue eyes, blue like the remarkable eyes of my grandfather.

I was sick of hearing about those eyes.

I thought Nomie was beautiful. She could not be improved.

But then mothers always want to think their children are perfect.

There! You see what I said, without even thinking? This was further proof that Nomie was my child.

I thought that once she was old enough she would declare her loyalties. I would wait until she was ready. I dreamt sometimes of taking her away from the other two, leaving this apartment where I had spent my entire life, leaving this city. But I could not think how, or where to go.

And then of course I had to wait for Jonathan. I couldn't leave. He would be coming back here sometime. I needed to be here when he did.

When he came I would bring Nomie to him and say: Isn't she beautiful? Haven't I done a fine job with her? Can't you see how there is not a trace of Chloe in her? Haven't I suffered long enough for you? And he would agree, and we would go away together, with Nomie, and build our castles in the dust.

So I would wait.

Until then there was so much to do. I had to choke out any hint of Chloe that bubbled to the surface of Nomie's skin. I had to shield her from my grandmother's grisly incoherent tales, my mother's delusions of grandeur. I needed to keep her on the true path.

She grew so quickly.

It seemed to happen in an afternoon.

She staggered into the furniture maze as a babe in training pants, and then an hour later out came this long-legged scowling girl asking about the blood in her underwear.

I swear it seemed to happen that fast.

I needed to hold her tightly, tightly.

Ilana

They have followed me here, those three.

I left them behind long ago and they have found me again.

No one else seems to notice them, they have disguised themselves so cleverly. But I can see through their little ruse.

I tried to tell my daughter and my granddaughter: Look. Them. You see. There.

I used the simplest terms so they would be sure to understand. I tried to keep the panic out of my voice. They only patted my hands, nodded and smiled like idiots.

I am living in a madhouse.

At least the sky knows something is amiss. It is gray, overcast, sagging down low to be propped up by the tips of buildings like a water-soaked tent. The city is full of sour pockets of air that you walk into unsuspecting and suddenly find yourself choking and vaguely embarrassed as if you had somehow caused it.

There is dust everywhere in this room. I sweep it into little piles with the side of my hand, then leave them there for someone else to deal with. Such a tangle of hair there is in the dust: black and brown and gray. A stranger would wonder what kind of piebald molting creature lived here.

This girl sits near me sometimes, her face looks so familiar it might be my own. I looked like that once; I still do when I close my eyes. Mirrors are a cruel trick, they show you only one point in time when the truth lies elsewhere.

Talking to her is like talking to myself.

She crouches near me, this girl with my face which she twists into bitter shapes around the gum she chews. Never speaks. Sometimes she has the portable radio and sits with the earpieces burrowed deep in her ears and her eyes far away. Other times she looks at me in such a knowing way that it frightens me. She reminds me of babies born in the village where I grew up, babies whom people said were born old, babies who did not cry and watched us all with world-weary eyes and died within days.

This girl is like that. She looks as if she might understand if I tried to warn her, tried to explain, tried to tell her about the three of them.

Those three.

You see, I traveled so far to escape them. I traveled to this place, where their kind do not exist, where the world obeys different rules. Here where the future is uncertain and the past is far away and you can make both up as you go along if you want.

I thought I had left them far behind. I stopped hearing them in my head, I had not even dreamt about them for years.

But now suddenly after all this time they have found me. I have begun seeing them again.

They have changed, certainly. They are crafty. But I can see through their disguises, I recognize their voices. The trouble is that this city is so full of noise I cannot hear their words clearly.

I saw them first in the Laundromat. Three women, gossiping non-stop, sorting socks. They had smooth black skin and lush hair; one had three gold teeth, one had gold earrings, one had a gold loop in her nose. I watched them through the window, between the letters painted on the glass, and I heard their voices drifting through the open door on clouds of sweet detergent.

I could not understand most of what they said; their voices were soft and thick, velvety and low. But I heard a few words that made me start, words in a language I had not heard in years; and one of them turned and looked at me, a sly unblinking stare, so that I knew, beyond a doubt.

I saw them a second time; three women, waiting for the bus, shopping bags at their feet. The bags reeked of fish, wetness leaked from them and crept into the pavement making ancient designs. Their mouths, constantly talking. Their hands never still. The roar of the bus drowned out their words. But I knew it was them; they did not board the bus when it came, they were waiting there for something else. They held their bench and watched the oblivious people passing by.

I wanted to be sure. I edged close to the back of their bench, I bent low, I sniffed softly and caught their smell, that distinctive smell, the sweetness and rot. No one else in the world had that smell.

Their ears twitched; I knew they had sensed me. I turned, I wanted to run, to fly away as I had long ago, but now I could not, I was earthbound, I could only put one foot in front of the other, with nightmarish slowness, fearing their breath on my neck at every step. With the clarity of vision that comes with panic I watched a golden beetle scuttle past my feet on the pavement, traveling faster than I. I saw my shadow change with the incremental movement of the sun, cringing in anticipation of a blow.

All this I saw in that moment of longing to run, sandbagged by flesh, waiting to feel their fingers. But just then another bus arrived, and the gush of people that burst from the gates rushed between me and them; it broke their hold, hid me from their view. The traffic light changed; the press of people carried me across the street to the opposite shore.

The air was full of the hum of autos, moving shoulders. An elaborate baby carriage, two children riding inside like royalty, rolled over my foot. A man in heavy boots plowed past, a long loaf of bread held against his shoulder like a rifle. A boy stumbled and fell against me, his head was close shaven, the shape of the skull clear and vulnerable beneath the skin. His hands moved over me swiftly, expertly, delving into pockets and cuffs and coming up empty. I felt his fingers on my wrist, his body pressing close then shouldering on.

For a long time I watched the back of his head bobbing and weaving in the currents of the crowd, a head delicate as eggshell, shining with the secrets it held.

Did you know that if you hold an egg up to the light you will be able to see the merest faintest shadow of the creature curled up inside?

I turned and looked back at the bus stop. I thought I saw three figures still sitting on the bench, I thought it was the same three, but I could not be sure.

I have trouble seeing lately.

The trouble is not in my eyes; my vision is as sharp as ever. It is the world that has become more blurred.

It is the air here, they talk of pollution, ions, electricity, ozone, something. The air is limp, greasy, it blunts the senses. No one sees clearly anymore.

So I got away from the three messengers that time.

But soon I was seeing them everywhere.

On the buses, on the steps of churches and hospitals, sitting on park benches. Always three women, similar enough to be sisters, always talking, always casting conspiratorial sly glances all around. I spied them in the market, waiting on corners for the light to change, standing together flagging a taxi, sitting together all sharing the same newspaper, and once for a brief fantastic moment on the public basketball courts engaged in a game of three-on-three with some tall black youths.

When they appeared in the alley behind our building I tried to tell Sashie.

She nodded and patted my hand then placed a cup of tea in it.

I looked down at them from the window. They lingered in the alley, pretending to be occupied. They had slipped into the alley, all three of them, under the pretense of placing a single scrap of paper in the trash can. But I knew why they were there.

They rattled the lids, chattered casually. They knew I was watching.

I had been silent so long.

I had shut myself off in a small dark place, away from the stream of events. Safe in this apartment, impervious as a tomb. I had shut myself away just as my grandmother had a lifetime ago, walling herself in with bricks of stale bread. I had watched the city rise up around me, watched my daughter and then my grandchildren from a distance so that they seemed tiny, nothing more than ants in an anthill.

Now suddenly I felt alive again; the arrival of those three had given me a vicious jolt. Suddenly I was thrust again into the world.

Where had these enormous buildings come from? These fantastic lights? What is this music? Everything was beautifully, terrifyingly vivid, and enormous, and much too loud. Cars passed in a blur. I had never seen such colors, they dazzled my eyes. These people of all different colors, their thick muscles and beautiful skin. Where had these magnificent people come from? Where were their wings?

I felt alive again, and all was beautiful, and all was fraught with danger.

Those three women would find me sooner or later, I knew, and they would tell me the things I did not want to hear. Their ugly gossip, their dire predictions.

They would bring me back to that place I had fled so many years ago. They would take away everything I had done and been until I was only a hollow shell in the center of a vast barren plain.

If I go away from this place and leave nothing behind, then it will be as if I had never existed at all.

The only way to stave them off was to tell someone.

I needed to beat them at their own game, drown out their story with mine.

I thought suddenly of that girl who listens, that girl with my face, the only one who listens to me now.

I was afraid for you. I feared they would notice you, recognize my features on your face. They will drag you back with them and force you to repeat it all, go through the motions over and over, a treadmill life.

The only way to protect you is to warn you. That is what I am trying to do.

Please listen. Please do not pat my hand or offer me tea.

If I tell you what I know then perhaps you will be able to evade them. Mara and Sashie have already failed without knowing it, they have fallen into the ruts long ago; they are treading in circles in their in-looking lives, circles within circles, getting smaller and smaller until soon they will be spinning in place. But you, I want to teach you to break away.

It is a paradox, isn't it? To make you learn about history and its patterns in the hope that you will rebel against the lesson, escape those patterns and go your own way.

Will you listen? Or will you cover your ears, run from the room, drown me out with your own voice?

You are listening, aren't you?

Mara

I came home today and found them at it again.

My grandmother telling tales with silent Nomie curled beside her, rapt, chin on knee. Worse than a neighborhood gossip, my grandmother is.

With gossip, at least, you know to take it with a grain of salt.

My grandmother tells stories as if they are the gospel truth.

I stood quiet in the doorway a minute, listening to that voice that seems more familiar than my own, it is the voice my conscience takes on these days, she echoes my own inner chiding.

This can't go on.

I listened, and then broke in: *That* story? Again? If you've told that story once, you've told it a thousand times.

She looked up at me. Well then, this time will make it a thousand and one, she said calmly.

Nomie said nothing, played with the fringe on my grandmother's shawl, counting the strands, knotting, braiding.

The stories are what keep us alive, my grandmother said in her significant way that brooked no argument; she bowed her head and resumed her story in tones only Nomie could hear.

A thousand and one of her rotten tales; how could Nomie stand it?

My grandmother seems determined to talk herself to death.

It is taking quite a while.

Oh, I have long ceased to be intimidated by those knowing looks of hers, her way of divining people's thoughts from their eyes or the nape of their necks, her air of holding a dark mysterious knowledge the rest of us are too imbecile to grasp. I have begun to see those things for what they really are: the false grandiosity of old age.

Yes, I have ceased to be afraid of her. I left the room, quickly, when she glared at me—but only because I did not want to hear any more of the story.

Those stories of hers, I do not want Nomie listening to them. They are not fit things for an impressionable young girl to hear. They are not fit for anyone, really, neither scholars nor madmen nor insomniac Arabian kings.

What bothers me most about her stories are not the naked and bloody details; it is that she calls them the truth, gives them the stamp of history. She dresses up her lies like kings in rags, or wolves in sheep's clothing. No one in their right mind would be fooled. Seeing Nomie at her knee I had wanted to say: What great eyes you have, grandmother, what big teeth.

When I was Nomie's age I too wanted to believe in certain things, and when I discovered they were false it felt like the worst kind of betrayal.

I want to spare Nomie that feeling.

I have never listened carefully to my grandmother's stories, but I don't need to; those stories from the old country are all the same.

The truth is, her stories are lies. Every one.

Oh, this can't go on.

Ilana

These days I think about Ari.

I wonder if he is still alive.

If he is, I wonder how he has satisfied his appetite all these years. How many hundreds of thick-necked officers?

He must be an old man now. The hair on his shoulders must be silver.

I wonder if he is angry at me for leaving him behind.

That splash in the water. I would not look at it, did not turn around.

Don't you see, it wasn't you I wanted to leave behind, it was everything else about that place.

And now it has turned out to be futile, I have left nothing behind, it all has followed me here. I thought I could raise my children differently here. But I look at my daughter, and her daughter, and I see in them the same fierceness and singleness of purpose that people had over there.

Do you remember our mother and father?

Perhaps one day long ago, by chance, walking in the forest, you might have met my dear ones, my sons. Perhaps one day as you glided along the ocean floor you might have seen my grandson. He loved to swim.

One of these days I know I will step outside the door and find myself again in a city of dust, crumbling and empty, clocks broken and silent in the gutters, and ships like the carcasses of great fallen birds lying on the floor of a vast dry seabed.

Sashie

Lately my mother has been babbling about three old women she has seen, women who have been following her everywhere. They have come for her, she says.

Now every time she comes home she darts into the apartment, slams the door, leans against it and locks it. Out of breath, her head scarf askew, hair wild.

What will people think of me, letting my mother wander the streets looking like this?

She's stubborn. I can't do a thing with her.

She keeps insisting that these old women are plaguing her.

She doesn't seem to realize that she is an old woman herself, and that the sight of her probably frightens people.

Lately she has been taking Nomie aside and telling her things, I don't know what exactly but I can guess. I know her mind is full of darkness, nastiness, things best forgotten or left unmentioned. She is giving Nomie strange ideas about her heritage, about *us*.

These days when I look for Nomie I always find her with her great-grandmother, sitting together in a corner of the dark room among the old furniture, both wrapped in my mother's moldy shawl. Nomie, usually so sulky (that is natural: she is fourteen) now sits gazing at my mother as if she is in love (*that* is not at all natural).

It is unhealthy. It will taint her young mind.

I've read newspaper articles about things like this.

I don't know where my mother gets her grotesque stories. Mara and I have wondered if she's picked them up from something she has read, or seen on television. But we've never seen her open a book, and she treats the television set like an unwanted guest: when one of us switches it on in the evenings she turns her back to it and lets out affronted little sniffs.

Of course we've suspected senility; she must be well into her nineties, after all. She does not know exactly how old she is, she does not know the exact date and year of her birth. It's not that she's forgotten it—she never knew. No one kept track, in that backward place where she was born. Can you imagine? How can someone not know her own birthday?

But her mind seems as sharp as ever. She has the bus schedules memorized, for instance. Any time of day or night, when she hears the rumble beneath the window, she'll say something like: There's the three-thirty-seven express, or: That's the one-seventy-six, Arthur's driving, he's always a little late.

I worry that she will fall down, break a hip, get knocked down and robbed in the street. She doesn't seem to realize she is an old woman, she continues to work like a horse, wanders the city on her mysterious errands.

Maybe it is that, after a lifetime of hard labor, her body does not know how to stop.

I cannot even call her an old woman, exactly. She is at the next stage, something *beyond* an old woman. Whatever that might be.

For *I* am an old woman now. I admit this.

The idea that we are colleagues is a frightening thought.

Whenever she starts in with the stories, I tell her (gently, of course): That's impossible, mother. It never happened like that.

And she says: Yes it did. How do you know about it, I don't remember *you* being there.

And I tell her: Of course I wasn't there, I wasn't born yet.

Then how can you know, she says triumphantly. I was there, I saw it all, I remember exactly what happened.

I would like to ask her for proof, for photographs, newspaper clippings, love letters. But I know she has no such thing, only these pictures in her head. And anyway, I know better than to press her. She is an old woman at the end of her life, trying to dress up a drab past in shocking colors, in sequins and armor.

And she is my mother. So I try to let her be. It is only for the sake of Nomie that I question her at all. I think Nomie should know the truth.

When I get the chance I will take Nomie aside and tell her *my* version of things. I will explain to her about my mother, how she twists things. I think I will tell Nomie to continue to humor my mother, pretend to swallow her stories. For her sake.

That would be the kindest thing to do, I think.

So now when I see them, see my mother's tongue wagging, I try to keep my mouth still. My mother clings fiercely to her stories. She is childishly stubborn. I will leave her to these castles made of dust and barnyards and enchanted forests, this ramshackle past she has built with her hands and hovers over like a sandbox king.

But I could not stop puzzling over where she got these stories. And why she told them, what pride or shame drove her to it.

I suspected she was hiding something. The stories were her way of disguising something she did not want to face.

I wanted to know what was hidden behind her shabbily fantastical peasant past.

And finally one day I couldn't bear it any longer.

I waited till she left the house on one of her scavenging strolls through the neighborhood. (I have seen her digging through trash cans, seen her pulling people's wet clothes off laundry lines, casually palming lemons and apples off grocery stands and strolling away. She lives by her own laws, my mother.) I went into her room and unearthed the truth, and proof.

Quite literally unearthed: I had to dig down under the spreading debris in her room, under old molding blankets, cardboard boxes, pots of tired-looking plants, the spent matches and rolling papers and plastic bags of marijuana she buys from the boy in the hooded sweatshirt on the corner (she calls it a medicinal herb and says it is good for her cough. I simply look the other way). The curtains at the windows, yellow with age, gave the light an antique sepia evening color, though it was barely midday.

I know it was wrong to do, invade her privacy. But look what I found.

A Fabergé egg, the genuine article, just like the ones you see in museums. It was covered with jewels on the outside; I tested them against my teeth, scratched them against the window. There was a cunning little diorama inside, impossibly detailed. I did not have time to look carefully, I was too excited. And anyway, the outside of the egg, the jeweled surface, captivated me more. The thing was priceless.

And to think she had it buried beneath the bed, like trash. How could she have gotten it?

Right then I realized the truth, after all this time, the mystery of her family. They hadn't been peasants at all, they must have been very wealthy. Part of the aristocracy, even. One of the old noble families. Here was the proof, right here in my hands.

Funny, how in a way I had always known. Or at least suspected. I had sensed that I was something special; noble blood cannot be denied.

I wondered: did they have an estate? A country home? Servants, horses, elaborate many-syllabled names? Why had she given all that up? Had they been forced to flee the revolution?

And then I found something more. In the fourth cardboard box I looked through, filled with crumbling yellow papers and small brown spiders scurrying from the light, I found the documents, bluntly scrawled in a foreign language. I was able to translate, roughly, and I saw that they were identification papers. My mother's and father's, folded together.

I gasped then, inhaled dust and choked.

My parents were brother and sister.

My own parents? Living in incest all these years?

I squatted there, squinting in the dust studying the two papers so brittle with age they seemed on the verge of cracking rather than tearing.

Brother and sister? Perhaps it was a mistake, a deception born out of confusion or convenience or simple ignorance. But the more I studied on it, the more it seemed to make sense.

Brother and sister. A forbidden love. No wonder they had fled their home, moved to a new country where no one knew them. No wonder they had to leave the family estate, the servants and carriages and elaborate balls (I had already begun imagining my lost birthright). They had come here with their sinful love, to live secretly.

My mother? I asked myself. Living in sin with her brother? Incest?

Look at those eyes. She's capable of anything.

I *was* looking, for there she stood above me, her head still wrapped in a scarf, staring as I squatted on my heels beside the bed. Those eyes. She snatched the papers from my hands, gave me a nudge with her foot so that I fell sprawling backward. I looked past her then, at the dust motes hanging in the sunlight, glinting, floating in the air, never settling, like those Bible-era wasps you see in museums, frozen for centuries, suspended in amber.

Her eyes were frozen like that.

I scrambled from the room like a chastised child.

But satisfied. I had found out the truth, her royal family, her incestuous desires.

No wonder she wanted to disguise it all in fairy tales and magic.

I stood in the bathroom studying my face. I thought of velvet gowns, jewels in my hair, painted portraits. I turned to see the profile. I definitely saw traces of nobility, a Hapsburg chin, it belonged on a cameo pin.

Yes, it did occur to me that my brothers and I were the products of incest.

But the realization did not trouble me overmuch. It's historical fact, you know, that royal families often married within themselves to keep the blood pure. It had been done for centuries. My parents' union was not such a tawdry illicit thing; to me it was the height of refinement.

I had uncovered her secret. And there was proof, incontestable proof that you could hold in your hands. Tangible evidence, that was the only way to be sure of anything. Tangible evidence that you could wave in someone's face.

I felt I understood her better than I ever had before.

I would not tell her I knew her secret. I would let her continue to hide her past in shadows, in poverty and death and fairy tales.

But Nomie, I thought, Nomie should hear the truth. Nomie should be allowed to know.

I went to the museums quite often now. Almost every day. I would put on my gloves, and my pearls (faux, but you could not tell), and the small violet hat, and I would go to the museums and wander the endless huge rooms full of antique furniture and paintings in thick elaborate frames.

I looked at the bed where a king had strangled his seventh wife. I looked at the portraits of sickly angelic heirs, propped up stiffly like dolls, who would die before they inherited their thrones. Paintings of ladies in bejeweled gowns, men in stiff ruffled collars or brocade waistcoats.

Mostly I went to the rooms of the Fabergé-style eggs. I basked in their glow, I could dream there.

I was happier than I had been in years.

Joe? He had been a weak man, a common man. I had intimidated him. He had not been worthy.

The museum rooms were vast and echoing, like churches, like ballrooms.

The line would continue, I thought. An indelible line continuing into the future.

I thought of certain sections of the Bible, the endless dull passages of who begot whom, and who then begot whom, down and down through the generations.

It seemed important, now. Having children had never seemed such a lofty thing to me before. Now it did.

Then I saw the portrait and nearly fainted.

Truly, I did, I wavered on my feet and a kind museum guard leaped forward and grabbed my arm.

A portrait of my mother.

I *swear* to you. Hanging in a museum.

In the portrait she was much younger than I had ever known her, she must have been close to Nomie's age. But I recognized her immediately, it was unmistakable.

The features. It had to be her. The girl in the portrait had my mother's birthmark next to her mouth, a pink smear like misapplied lipstick. That mark had a very peculiar shape, very distinctive, I had been staring at that mark on my mother's mouth for all my life, and now here it was on the face in the painting.

There were other distinguishing marks too, bumps and scars. My mother had many. As a child I'd once asked her to tell me about them; she'd said only that she'd had a rough childhood. From looking at her face you'd think a rough childhood meant tumbling down stairs several times a day.

But the most decisive thing was the eyes staring out of the paint.

Those were her eyes, there were none other like them.

Frozen in time, a wasp in amber.

Those eyes, fierce and fearless, capable of anything.

In the portrait she wore a dress like I had never seen before, embroidered and jeweled all over the bodice, long full sleeves. Her hair—there had been so much of it then—had been arranged in loops and ringlets and flounces, an elaborate dark mass atop her small head.

I hardly need to add that the girl in the portrait had her jaw clenched, her hands curled into fists. Both were habitual, unconscious gestures of my mother's.

Don't you see, it *had* to be her? Women in brocade dresses simply do not pose for portraits with their fists clenched. There was not a single other portrait, in that entire museum filled with hundreds, with hands like that.

I wandered for hours, seeing nothing, my head floating.

I went home that evening and there was my mother, peeling potatoes in the kitchen with Nomie beside her. There it was, the same mark on her mouth. The same crooked scar at the corner of her eyebrow. Those hands, so tight around knife and potato, as if the potato needed to be subdued.

I did not know what to say to her. I felt a kind of awe, different from the kind I had felt for her before. I had always sensed that she had some kind of power hidden away, but I had always assumed it was dark and conniving rather than a tragic noble sort.

Watching her I had an ugly feeling then. I was jealous of her, I admit, jealous of the shining elegant past she had had, the kind of elegance I had always longed for and never found. And I was angry, too, that she had not shared it, had not shared the treasures of her past with me. Not just the tangible things, but the wonderful memories she must have had of that time. She'd kept them all to herself, selfish woman. She'd been silent so long.

And now when she opened her mouth it was to spew rubbish.

She put on this charade of peasants and poverty just to taunt me.

I was not angry for myself. Oh no. I was angry for Nomie's sake.

Nomie who sat there fingering potato peelings as my mother withheld the truth, the magnificent shining truth, and fed her up on unwholesome make-believe and lies.

Ilana

Today I was telling about my parents' courtship. I was remembering how my mother's face looked when she was possessed by the dybbuk, so weirdly slack and empty. I remembered the hoarse foreign voice forcing its way out of her throat, and the way everyone in the village drew away from her and even my father with his scarred cheeks looked afraid.

I was remembering how the chickens followed her, and the worms sprang up from the ground.

Later, on their wedding day, she wore a blue dress and flowers in her hair and I had never seen anyone so beautiful. She and my father fed each other wedding cake, and his mouth was so wide she could place her entire hand inside with ease.

And I remembered Shmuel's parents, how their faces lit up when their daughter married the baker. The daughter had a wall-eye, and prematurely graying hair, so she felt blessed to be getting married at all. The baker was painfully shy and stuttered when he spoke, so he felt equally blessed. I remembered how happy we were for them, how we all joined hands and danced the minute he crushed the glass with his heel. I remembered how their children came so quickly, one after the other. Seven children all smeared with flour.

I remembered how they died, their bodies stacked with others high as a haystack. The sight was familiar. My family had been piled up the same way.

Today I was telling the story of my grandmother's wedding night. She was still a child then, my grandmother. She still wore her hair in braids and had nothing sticking out of her chest but ribs the night she knelt before my grandfather's chair and washed his feet for the first time in a bowl of milk. She kept her head bowed and shivered when he drew one finger slowly along the shining white part in her hair.

I could see it so vividly, as if it had happened the night before. My grandfather's chair, his emptied boots, the shutters drawn against the cold, the red blanket on the wide low bed that waited ominously in the shadows.

I finished telling these stories, and others, and then went to bed feeling content.

It was not until hours later that I started awake and realized I could not possibly have witnessed these things.

But I could picture them all so clearly! As if I had been there!

It frightens me that I can no longer tell which tales have been told to me by others and which I have witnessed myself.

They all have the ring of truth.

Nomie

I have been having these dreams lately.

In the dreams there is a ladder that reaches from the ground to the stars, with children climbing up and down and the smell of burnt sugar.

I dream of a dress shop where all the salesgirls wear large oval mirrors attached to their hats. They stand in a circle as I try on the dresses, so that every direction I turn I see myself, framed above their fawning faces.

In the dreams there are men raining from the sky and crumpling to the ground, cursing their commanders and the war and the manufacturers of their faulty parachutes.

I dream of a ship at sea, of sheets piled up like snowbanks, of a black-haired man whose shoulders are so broad he cannot fit through the doorway.

I dream about things I have never seen, only heard about, but they are more real to me than anything.

People say you should believe none of what you hear and half of what you see.

To live by that you would end up with nothing to believe in, and what would be the use of that? You might as well lie down and die, because that will be the only sure thing left you.

I can believe anything. For a little while.

I have no mother, or three, depending on your point of view.

There's Mara, who when I was younger would hold me too tightly, press my face against her bony hip. She used to say: You can call me mama, if you want. It's almost the same word.

She told me endless stories about my father and showed me postcards he had sent her from various port cities: Lisbon, Sidney, Miami. In her stories my father was sometimes a sailor, sometimes a doctor, and always on his way back to us.

Later I looked at those postcards, saw that they were blank on the back.

She was dark and angular, her eyes so deep-set they were always in shadow. Her hair was coarse and long and she left bits of it everywhere: black hairs in the sink, on the seats of chairs, clinging to her clothes, stuck between the pages of books.

Then there's Sashie who always told me to behave, to walk with my spine straight and ignore the boys on the street. You're special, she told me, you're not like them, they're rabble. Different blood runs in you. Hold your head up, for God's sake.

She touched me sometimes but in an awkward way, as if she was not sure how to do it.

She had gray in her hair and arranged it in an upswept stiff way. She wore collars like doilies and always lipstick, lipstick that bled into the lines around her mouth.

Then there's Ilana, whom I could not bear to call my great-grandmother because saying that word is like trying to shout across a canyon, across endless distance. And she did not seem far away at all, she gave me conspiratorial glances and told me secrets, and our hands when we pressed them together to measure were exactly the same size.

When I was small she made me a cape and a hood all in red, and I wore it for years whenever I went outside; and she told me a story about a girl who wore a hood made of a wolf's hide.

She was reserved, not pushy like the other two. I had to seek her out.

I had to walk into the dark room that terrified me when I was younger, walk into the mess of dark ramshackle furniture, precariously stacked so it seemed it might fall any moment and crush you. There were spiders, and an unidentifiable scuttling that might have been mice, and a strange sickening dust that was soft and sticky as pollen. But if I braved the forest, I would find the treasure in the center of it: Ilana, with her knitting and her hands that were hard and at the same time soft like clothes laundered a thousand times.

I did not think it unusual, when I was younger, to have three mothers. I assumed everyone did.

Mara used to have a job in a hospital. She was not supposed to bring me but sometimes she did.

She was not a doctor, or even a nurse, though I think she would have liked to be.

She did a lot of cleaning: making up beds and mopping and wheeling carts around.

I liked to knock on doors and pay visits to strangers while she worked. I met a man with tubes in his nostrils and a blue cast to his face. He had a large beaky nose and the strong sunlight from the window shone through it, making it pinkly translucent, I could see the veins threading through it. He gave me the most beautiful smile when I came in, though his teeth were in a glass by the bed. We played cards all afternoon.

I saw the room where babies lay in rows, in glass cases, like meat at a butcher shop or expensive jewelry arrayed on velvet.

I met a woman who ate pills like candy, all different colors, and she offered me some. Her face was kind though her eyes moved loosely in two different directions.

I talked to a woman with very little hair. It was soft and downy like a baby chick's. She told me she had had her breasts removed. I did not understand what she meant (I was much younger then). Removed? Removed to where? Where were they now?

I saw a dead person for the first time. I did not know he was dead at the time. I thought he was very shy and did not want to talk.

One time I was sitting in a waiting room with a man who was waiting for something. His eyes were leaking, and he was wiping his face with wadded tissues. First he was telling me about his wife, and what had happened to her and what the doctors said and what they were doing to her and about every asshole he was going to sue for malpractice if anything went wrong. Then he was snuffling into the tissues some more and drinking from a small bottle and sweating out of every pore in his face. And then he was sitting beside me and then he was wiping his face on my shirt and I sat very still and told myself he was only doing it because he had used up all his tissues. No other reason. Later on the bus ride home Mara asked me what I had gotten all over myself. I did not tell her. I did not want to touch it with my hands.

Mara left the hospital job not long after that. She told me she had quit.

But Sashie told me she had been fired for breaking the rules. She had been caught in the nursery, cradling other people's babies.

At mealtimes all three of them would try to slip the choicest bits from their plates to mine. Take this, Ilana would say, it will make your blood strong. This will clear up your skin, Sashie would say, directing a forkful toward my mouth. Mara would say little, would simply transfer most of her meal to my plate with an expression of stern martyrdom.

Eat it, they all said. Eat it, I didn't want it anyway. Really.

I don't need it, I don't matter anymore, they seemed to say. *You're the one who needs to grow up big and strong.*

Looking at my loaded plate and their bare ones was usually enough to make me lose my appetite.

Mother, I said sometimes, just to see the way all three raised their heads expectantly.

I was always pulled in three directions as I was growing up.

I was used to it.

But the spring I was fourteen it got much worse, so that I thought they would tear me to pieces.

It started when something happened to Ilana.

She came home one day with a wild light in her eye. Her hands shook as they stroked my hair. Hours after she had returned she was still out of breath.

Please tell me, I said, please tell me, whatever it is.

She told me then, about the three women whom she had left behind long ago, who had crossed oceans and years to find her again. She repeated her stories of how they cackled and scratched themselves and picked the fleas from each others' hair, and how they spoke of things she did not want to hear but could not shut out.

How they unspooled the thread and measured it and cut it. How some lengths of thread were short and others long; and once the thread had been cut it could not be changed, neither the short threads made longer nor the long threads made shorter. No matter how much people might want the pieces to be different.

The threads had been cut. There was no hope of it being any other way.

She said: I have told you once and I will tell you again—I came to this country from a land far away because I thought here I might be able to cut my own thread as I chose.

She said that at one time she thought she had succeeded, but now she was not so sure. She was no longer sure if she was cutting her own thread, or if it was being cut for her.

These things sound strange. But I understood with one part of my brain.

She began telling me other things that she had kept inside a long time.

Sometimes she spoke a language I had never heard, and seemed surprised that I did not understand.

When Ilana began her telling, Sashie and Mara noticed and began their own. Theirs consisted of drawing me aside, whispering in my ear with their eyes rolling suspiciously all around. Mara even came in my room at night to mutter words over me when she thought I was sleeping.

They accused and denied, each told me she was telling me the truth and everyone else was lying.

I felt as if I were being courted, as if they were all trying to gain favor. As if I were some kind of sleepless king, and they were telling stories, desperately telling stories as if it was their last chance, as if they would die in the morning.

Their voices all sounded the same. Sometimes when they were telling their stories I closed my eyes and could not tell who was speaking. The same voice, in varying degrees of brittleness. The same inflections, same gestures of speech.

My mother, all three said, with a mixture of love and fear.

My brother, they said with adoration.

My daughter, they said, their voices fearful and uncertain.

Mother. Brother. Daughter.

If you did not look you would think it was the same person every time.

That is heredity, I suppose: passing along the same eyes and hair, the same tenacity, same style of speaking. The same voices.

My voice, I suppose, sounds like theirs.

And perhaps we all sound alike because Ilana taught Sashie to speak, Sashie taught Mara, and they all taught me. So that people tell me I have a touch of a foreign accent, something they can't place, though I have never been out of this city. It is Ilana's voice, passed down and diluted.

Our conversations must sound like a person arguing with herself.

Their faces looming over me, the features were all the same. Same but different. Sashie's neck looked strained from constantly lifting her chin, her eyes tired from always looking down her nose. Mara's face looked bloated, congested with secrecy, with suppressed thoughts and mucus and yearnings she could barely hold in.

And Ilana. Her face was covered with lines, not deep, the thinnest of lines like threads lying on the surface of her skin. And she had the mark I loved, a smear of red next to her mouth, that drew your eyes to her lips.

Sashie woke me in the middle of the night to tell me the things she had forgotten to mention during the day. Mara offered to braid my hair, and when I sat before her she wrapped her hands in my hair and held tight for hours, telling me more stories about my father, how fine-looking he was and how he loved her and how much she had done for him, with her breath hot and wet in my ear. Sashie came to my school one day, took me out of class and brought me to a museum where she showed me jeweled eggs and gloomy paintings. Once when Ilana was out, Sashie took my hand and drew me into Ilana's room, showed me crumbling documents and told me about blood and nobility and a lost fortune. Her eyes shone, her spit flew. She dabbed at her mouth with a lace handkerchief.

Ilana's tales were the only ones I wanted to hear.

How can you stand to listen to her? Mara said to me. It's all lies and foolishness. Do you really believe all that? She probably told you she walked across the Atlantic in a pair of magic boots.

No, I said.

She can't prove anything, Sashie said. She has no proof, all she has are these words and pictures in her head. How can you trust that?

I just do.

. . .

Ilana lived in the largest room in the apartment, and she kept it so dim you could hardly see its boundaries. Sashie's room was smaller, the walls entirely covered with yellowed pictures of starlets from generations ago. Mara's room was smaller still, it was the room that had once been my father's and she slept there among outdated medical textbooks and pencils she allowed no one to use. My room was the smallest of all, it was encircled by the others, a windowless closet in the heart of the apartment.

The rooms were like a series of nesting boxes. Each could fit inside the next. They were like those hollow wooden dolls that can be opened to reveal smaller ones, which can be opened to reveal another. And so on and so on forever.

Rooms within rooms and stories within stories.

I did not have many friends at school.

I did not have any, in fact.

I did not mind, I had too much company already, with Sashie and Mara constantly hovering like vultures. It was a relief to go to school, push my way through the crowded hallways, read books, and ignore everyone around me. People spoke to me and I did not know what to say to them.

I stayed indoors most of the time, which kept my skin very white. And my hair was as black as Ilana's. I wore black clothes all the time, just as she did.

When I was in elementary school the other girls had called me a witch, scratched me with their nails, giggled behind their notebooks. But now I was in high school and suddenly everyone wore black and had pale skin and cultivated a disheveled haunted look. Now I blended in.

Still I had nothing to say to anyone. They were like a strange foreign tribe, with their own catchphrases and rituals. I let my hair flop forward to cover my face. I felt safe in there, a black forest.

I met Vito by nearly stepping on him one day on my way home from school.

He was sprawled out across the front stoop of my building, blocking the way. He had his head tipped back, hands clutching his chest. I did not know if he was hurt or asleep or dead. I thought I should check his throat for a pulse. Then I thought I should pull down his T-shirt where it had ridden up to expose his belly. Then I thought I would just step around him.

He looked too young to be a homeless person. His clothes were too clean.

I raised my foot to step over him when he suddenly opened his eyes, sat up, and grabbed my ankle. Finally, he said.

I tried to pull away. Finally what? I said.

I've been waiting for you all afternoon.

Why?

I've seen you at school, he said. Come sit here a minute, he said and patted the stoop beside him.

I shifted from foot to foot. I wanted to dash inside and up the stairs. But I could not stop looking at him, at the metal studs that pierced both his cheeks.

You go to my school? I said.

Yeah.

I've never seen you before, I said.

Well, you're missing out, baby, he said and I saw the flash of a stud in his tongue.

What do you want?

Want to get to know you, he said. You're one of those quiet types I bet, he said, look like you've got something going on. And I want to know what it is.

He put out a hand and tugged at my skirt. Sit down a minute and talk to me, he said. Little ol' Vito isn't going to hurt you.

I sat.

No one had ever expressed an interest in what I had to say before. People were always too busy making me listen.

He put his hand on my thigh. The nails were close-bitten. His hair was bleached a harsh, unnatural color and he wore a string of tiny red beads around his neck. I could see that he was just a little older than me, but his face already had the beginnings of creases around the eyes and mouth. Tired skin. His eyes were strange and dilated, but they fixed on me and stayed there and waited. I liked that.

I could not stop staring at the metal in his cheeks, on his tongue, piercing his eyebrow. I ached for him, the kind of pity you feel for a run-over animal in the street. I had the urge to protect him from whatever it was that had abused him like this, worn him down and punched him full of holes like a sieve.

Then I remembered he had *chosen* these things, he had inflicted them on himself.

Are you sure you go to my school?

Yeah, yeah, he said. Do you want a cigarette?

I took one and held it and did what he did. I sucked in and blew. My lungs hurt. I watched him, hoping to see smoke leak out of the holes in his face.

Nomie! someone gasped.

I looked up to see Mara at the bottom of the steps with her raincoat wrapped tightly around her though it was spring. Her forehead was shiny with sweat.

What are you *doing*? she said.

The smoke drifted out of my mouth, floated in front of my face like a veil.

Oh my God, Vito said, who the hell is *that*?

Nomie, get upstairs right now, Mara said.

I stood. Vito leaned back against the step behind him. His shirt had ridden up again; I could see a patch of skin, a stripe of hair, a strip of underwear. Is that your mother? he asked.

I looked at Mara, who was waiting for my answer. I looked at him.

God no. *That's* not my mother, I said and clattered up the stairs.

I thought of what Ilana had told me once, that Mara had something twisted and bitter in her, something that had started out right but then doubled back on itself and gone wrong like an ingrown hair.

I thought of that hair, growing rampant within her, spreading all through her body, twining around her bones like vines, branching and climbing around her heart and liver, weakening the structure from within.

I stood in the bathroom and looked at my face in the mirror, at my birthright hair, this hair that had been passed down from generation to generation, binding us all together. Suddenly I did not want to be like them anymore. I took the scissors and cut. And cut again. Like severing an umbilical cord. I cut it in big heavy handfuls that fell to the bathroom tiles and lay there like dead animals. I kept at it, liking the crisp sound, until there was nothing left to cut.

My skull had such an interesting shape. A part of myself I had never seen before.

Sashie let out a shriek when she saw me. Oh, Nomie, your beautiful hair!

I hoped Mara would cry out too. I wanted her to be angry.

But she wasn't.

I like it, you look so much more like your father now, she said and smiled.

Ilana looked at me and her lips trembled and she said: You look like that girl from downstairs, the one who escaped the camps. The one who hung herself.

No she doesn't, Sashie said quickly.

What are you talking about? Mara said.

Ilana had her hands over her ears.

I could not stand the pain in her face. It will grow back, just like before, I swear it will, I told Ilana over and over but she would not meet my eyes and closed the door to her bedroom.

It's cool, Vito said, running his hand over and over my scalp.

We were sitting on the roof of my building, in a forest of television antennas. The tar was melting, sticking to the seat of my pants, the palms of my hands. The traffic on the street sounded far away and the sky was patched with bruised spots that might have been clouds or pollution.

It felt like the building was swaying, very slightly, with the wind.

The roof was flat and had no walls or railings enclosing it. Pigeons landed and watched us.

We sat as close to the edge as possible, to prove we were not afraid.

Vito gave me a cigarette he had made himself. It tasted different from the regular ones.

This kind is much better, he said.

Fortified with vitamins. New and improved, he added and laughed.

Have you always lived here? I said.

Nah, he said. My mom and me, we move around a lot. Lots of one-year leases. She's cool. She doesn't care what I do.

She doesn't care? That sounds so nice, I said. I couldn't even imagine that.

Then I said: What about your father?

Poppa was a rolling stone, he said and laughed shortly. He took the cigarette from me and sucked in the sweet smoke. The smell made me think of Ilana.

What about your folks? he said.

I don't know. I don't know where they are. I never met them.

Oh . . . I get it. You're adopted.

No . . . my mother's dead. It's complicated. You see, she was this kind of mermaid-woman that couldn't live out of water, and my father was a doctor but never finished school, and he's busy traveling around the world and hasn't had time to make it home yet but he will.

Oh. . . . So who was that crazy-lookin' lady we saw the other day?

That's my aunt. But she thinks she's my mother. Although the one who's more like my mother than anyone is my great-grandmother. But I don't like to call her my great-grandmother. And she doesn't even know who I am, exactly.

Whoa, he said admiringly. You're living with a bunch of freaks.

And for all I know I'm not even related to them! Maybe there was a mistake, a mix-up, and my real parents are out there looking for me right now! I said.

I blurted this out without thinking. But then I thought about it and the idea appealed to me. Maybe I was not their daughter at all. They told me I was, but why should I believe them? Why should I believe their far-fetched stories about people I had never seen? Where was their proof?

I could be anyone, I thought. Anyone. I was a person of mystery and possibilities. My life, which had always seemed so narrow, now burst open and scattered all around. The sky seemed so bright, and I smoked more of the cigarette and looked at Vito and he seemed to have three arms, then four, then six and all of them were beautiful.

I liked to feel his metal stud in my mouth when we kissed, liked to feel it clicking against my teeth. Getting our bodies to line up was more difficult. I kept landing a knee in his stomach, my chin in his mouth.

Do you want to do it? he said, his hands at the waistband of my pants.

No, I said.

Why not?

I don't know.

Everybody does it. *Everybody.*

I'm too young.

Oh, come on. I bet all your friends have done it already.

I don't know.

Admit it, they have. I bet you can't even name *one* friend who hasn't done it yet.

No.

One name. Give me just one name. See, you can't. They've all done it.

That's not why.

Come on, it's normal. Everybody does it. Don't you know that?

I know, I said because I didn't want to tell him I had no friends and had no idea what other people did. He was like an ambassador from that world, sent to educate me about their customs.

Come on, he said, you'll like it. You'll thank me later.

Okay, I said because I believed him. Or I wanted to believe him. It was ingrained in me. For so long I had been taught to believe what people told me. It was hard to break the habit.

Are you ready?

You want to do it right here?

Why not?

Someone might see us.

Who? The pigeons?

He was moving with quick determination, his eyes hugely dilated.

Wait, I said. And *oh*, I said, and *stop* and *slow* and *not there*. I looked at the sky and felt him rubbing in that sensitive place and it felt wrong, like when you rub your eye too hard with your knuckles. *No*, I said, and *please* and *are you finished?* and *are you finished?* and *are you finished yet?*

Then I lay back and waited and watched his body rise and fall in an eager desperate way until he said he was done. How do you feel? he said.

I wanted to say: Why didn't anyone tell me it would be like this? Why didn't anyone prepare me?

I had known the facts, but the reality of it was quite different.

I said nothing.

I felt something hot trickle down my leg and I lay back on the hot black tar and wished more than anything that it would snow, I wanted snow to come down and cover everything.

Late that night Mara came into my room. Stood by the bed in her white robe, her hair falling down her back.

You're awake, aren't you? she said.

Closer she came.

Can't sleep? she said. Something bothering you?

She sat down on the edge of the bed. The mattress sagged and I slid toward her.

You can tell me, you know, she said and stroked my head.

I wondered if she knew something, if she had seen us on the roof. I could not make out her face.

I know you're lonely, she said, you don't have to be ashamed to admit it.

The heavy medicinal smell of her hand ointment hung all around.

Oh, all right, she said.

She sighed as if giving in to something and said: All right then, if you want. I'll stay with you until you fall asleep if you want me to, I don't mind.

But I didn't . . . I said softly.

You don't have to be afraid of anything, she went on as if she had not heard me. There's nothing to be afraid of, you're just imagining things. I'll stay here until you fall asleep. So you don't have to lie awake alone. I know how terrible that can be.

Those voices, she said, they're not real, they're in your head.

I tried to move away from her but the bed was too narrow; there was nowhere to go. Her sticky warmth crept under the covers.

I won't ever leave you, she said. Not like *some* people.

I pressed closer to the wall.

I waited.

And waited.

I waited and waited and it did not come.

School had let out so I had plenty of time to concentrate on waiting.

Soon I was checking the blank white crotch of my underpants every hour.

I waited some more and when I was sure I told Vito.

You're *what*? he said. How can that be?

We were sitting together on my stoop. I could not sit still, kept knocking my knees together. I was keeping an eye out for Mara, Sashie, Ilana—all of them. I was smoking his cigarettes as fast as I could, one after the other, thinking maybe they would kill it.

Sorry, man, he said, I thought you were on the pill.

You did not, I screamed. Why would you think *that*?

I did, I swear. I guess I got you mixed up with someone else.

I looked at him and wanted to run a string around all the studs in his face and then pull it tight suddenly to make his face shut up like a drawstring bag.

Who? I said.

I mean . . . I didn't mean it like that, he said and tried to kiss me. I bit his neck as hard as I could.

Leave me alone, I screamed, but all that came out was a whisper.

The apartment was suffocating. I was sure all three of them could tell. Surely they could smell it, even see it. Wasn't it obvious? My body was reeking, it was transparent, blatantly proclaiming its condition to the world. Surely Ilana could tell?

But she said nothing, ran her fingers over my face.

I could never tell her my secret. I knew how she felt about children, they were a blessing, she would never understand if I said I wanted to get rid of it.

I couldn't have a baby. Could I? Now? It was impossible.

I could not bring a baby into this apartment. This series of boxes, these rooms nesting within one another. Where would we put a baby? In a box small enough to fit inside the smallest room, so that we could all surround it, enclose it, smother it with attentions?

I thought of the pictures I had seen of fetuses, showing the progression. The thing that started as a tiny dot and progressed in stages until it swelled into a newborn. Those embryos of different sizes, they reminded me of wooden nesting dolls. Unborn babies were like the smallest of dolls, the very innermost ones, the thing that lay inside the belly of each of them, the heart of them all.

I knew what would happen if the baby were born. I could see that Sashie and Mara were already beginning to give up on me; I was not the model daughter they had hoped for. I knew they would pounce on the child and try to start over, begin anew. Pull her this way and that, try to mold her in their hands. No child deserved that.

The pattern repeating. An endless procession of women following a single set of footprints in the snow.

What were the alternatives? Vito was no help. It was to be expected; all men died or disappeared and left you alone. That was something I had learned.

Why had I listened to him?

Why hadn't anyone warned me?

Why hadn't they told me what might happen?

I felt so angry at all of them: Mara, Sashie, Ilana.

Why hadn't they prepared me for this?

I thought of how Sashie's stories always seemed to avoid any mention of intercourse and conception; she did not think these things worth dwelling on, they were not suitable for a lady's lips or my ears, they were best skimmed over.

And Mara had nothing to say about the matter. She only muttered words too low to hear, glared out of the corners of her eyes, pressed her knees tight together.

Then I thought of Ilana.

All at once I remembered Ilana telling me about Baba's twisted wire and her nighttime visitors, not the men but the frightened women who came to the back door; and about the army officer with the thick neck and shiny boots; and about my great-grandfather placing his hands on her belly and imploring her to be fruitful and multiply. Ilana *had* warned me, I realized. But I had not been paying attention in the right way. I had thought her stories were only about *her*; I had not thought they had anything to do with *me*.

It was too late to ask her for advice now. But the thought of her stories had given me an idea.

I pressed the doorbell and heard a muffled chime deep within the apartment.

I heard the slow shuffle of footsteps, the rusty scrape of locks.

She was much smaller than I expected, hobbling on two canes and her back so bent that her chin rested on her bosom. But she still wore heavy jewelry: ropes and ropes of pearls, and earrings that dragged down her earlobes, and rings on every finger. And like Ilana she kept her hair dyed its once-upon-a-time original color: a fiery orange with yellow streaks like false gold.

I didn't think you'd still be here! I blurted out when she came to the door. I could not stop staring at her feet, those stiff unnatural carved things in high-heeled red mules.

Were you hoping I was dead? she said sharply.

No . . . I . . .

She lifted her glasses to her nose and peered at me. Then she lifted a second pair of glasses and placed them over the first and looked again. She placed a third set on the tip of her nose before the other two and studied me through the triple lenses. Her eyes widened.

Ah, I know who you are, she said. I mean, not *exactly*, but I'd know that face anywhere.

I explained: I found your address in among Sashie's things. It was written on an invitation. An invitation to her wedding party. I guess she forgot to send it.

She laughed at that; I saw the shiny white of her teeth, the bright pink of perfect plastic gums. She said: That was Ilana's doing, I'm sure. I'm sure Ilana was supposed to give it to me and never did. She did not want me there, didn't want me near her family, she thought I was bad luck. Always did.

You remember, then? I said, surprised.

Of course, she said. And you are—what? Ilana's granddaughter?

Great-granddaughter, I said. And you're . . . *Annabelle*, I said carefully.

Anya, she said. It's back to Anya now. I've realized I can't ever get away from it, so why pretend? Come in, come in, don't stand in the hallway like a salesman.

I followed her through a room so layered with dust it looked like an archaeological excavation, and then we stood in her kitchen, which looked lived-in and tidy. All the cans and pots stood on the lower shelves where she could reach them.

Let me heat up some beet soup for you, she said.

No, that's all right, I said, my great-grandmother makes it for me all the time.

Her face stiffened. Well, *I* don't have anyone to make it for, she said stubbornly and shifted a pot to the stove.

I don't want to bother you, I said, I just wanted to ask you something.

I told her my problem.

I thought . . . you might . . . do that sort of thing. Or know someone who would, I said.

What? she said. Just because it was done to me, once, that makes me an expert?

No, that's not what I meant. I just thought you would know . . . how I would go about having it done, I said.

She was pressing close to me, peering in my face.

If you want to know, it's true that I have helped women in trouble. When they had no choice. Many women. Right here in this kitchen! she said.

I could pay you, I said. Not a lot, but—

No! No more! she cried and her spit landed on my face. No more! There are doctors and hospitals for that sort of thing. They can do it right. I may look like an ignorant old woman to you, but I know that much.

You won't help me, then? I said, looking at the floor.

I would only hurt you, you foolish child, she said. These things are dangerous. Don't you think there's a reason I never had any children? It was not by choice, I tell you. I went to that old herb woman for help and she damaged me forever, and I was only a little girl then. About your age. Are you listening?

Yes, I said.

Sometimes I wish I had never gone to her at all, I wish I had stayed at home and had the child. My life would have been completely different. I was always so jealous of Ilana. She had everything I didn't. Everything I wanted and would never have. And no, I'm not talking about feet! she said.

I looked up from her wooden nubs. She put her thumb beneath my chin.

She has children, grandchildren, great-grandchildren. Now maybe great-*great*-grandchildren even! And me, what do I have? Nothing. Other people's children plaguing me, soup that no one eats. Little girl, you should think carefully about what you do next. Don't make the mistake I did. Do you want to end up like me?

I said nothing. She had backed me into a corner.

She laughed. You look just like Ilana, trying to plot your escape, she said. She reached up and stroked my head. She said: Your eyes are like hers. But your hair! How did this happen? Was it an accident?

I like it this way, I said. It's different.

Did Ilana ever tell you how she cut off my hair? At the time we were both desperate to leave, and she said it was holding us back. But I think she secretly wanted to do it all along. She enjoyed chopping it off. She was jealous of me, I think. We were jealous of each other, what a pair. We might have been friends if things were different. . . .

Anya poured a bowl of the beet soup and tried to make me eat it, but the deep redness of it turned my stomach. She grasped my arm with sharp fingers and pulled herself closer. Her false teeth suddenly frightened me, they were too white and much too large for her face. And there was nothing more for us to say to each other (though she did not think so: she had plenty she still wanted to tell me) so I left.

I went to the hospital. I tried to keep my mind white and blank. I did not want to think about what I was doing, I just wanted to get it over with.

Vito came with me but he was no help at all. We wandered the white halls, sat waiting on blue plastic chairs, got chased out of forbidden areas by nurses in ugly white shoes.

I did not know what to do, where to go, whom to ask.

I just want to get it over with, I said and held my stomach.

The lights buzzed above our heads. We heard footsteps, endless footsteps tapping along the hallways. Approaching, receding, approaching again. Never appearing. There was a brown puddle spreading on the floor.

I don't think they can do it right away, anyway, Vito said cheerfully. I think they make you sign stuff and come back in a few days.

I don't care.

And I think you have to get parental permission too, he said.

I looked at him. The harsh light had drained all color from his face, his nostrils were rimmed with pink and his pupils gaped. He looked worse than I felt.

Don't cry, he said. Man, don't do that. Listen, I have an idea. I know a place, a clinic, I have this friend whose girlfriend works there. We could go there, they would take us, they wouldn't give you any shit. The only problem is it's kind of far away.

No, I said. No, I'm not leaving this place until they take it out of me. I'm not leaving. I'll sleep here.

He scratched his head, dry skin snowfalling on the shoulders of his black T-shirt.

And I might have sat there forever if I had not seen something at the end of the hall. Something that set my teeth on edge, that sent me flying.

Hey, Nomie, wait up, Vito panted. Hey, where are you going?

Hush, I breathed as we skidded around corners and slid on newly mopped floors.

Nomie! What's the rush?

Shut up, I hissed and suddenly we were in the emergency room dodging around mobs of people in red-spattered blue scrubs and doctors shouting out medical terms that sounded lewd and obscene. And then a whole fleet of stretchers rolled in, people strapped to boards and wrapped in blankets and raising their hands up to the sky calling out to their gods and their mothers.

Nomie, Vito called and I said: Quit screaming my name! and then we were back out on the street.

The sunlight felt good and calming and I stopped running.

What happened? What did you see? he asked.

Someone I thought I knew, I said.

It had been Mara, in a pink uniform and rubber gloves, her dark brows slicing across her face. Had she seen us?

Mara. Somehow she had gotten her job back.

Mara

Oh, I knew this would happen.

Nomie has disappeared.

My mother is beside herself.

My grandmother says nothing. I'm sure she knows, she knows where Nomie is but she won't tell us.

After all the yapping she's been doing lately, now she won't open her mouth.

This is all her fault, I know it. She's been telling those stories, giving Nomie ideas.

Outside the snow tumbles down. A freak flurry in the middle of July.

My grandmother won't tell us a thing, just sits there muttering about three old women following her. She doesn't care about what could happen to Nomie at all.

How could she just vanish like this? my mother said.

She didn't just vanish; she ran away. She's at that age, I told her. I did not want to worry her unduly.

It's mother, my mother whispered. Mother made her do this, I know it.

So you see I was not imagining things. My mother had come to the same conclusion about my grandmother.

We should put her in a nursing home, I said as casually as I could. For her own good, I said, her own safety. She's blind as a bat, one of these days she'll be hit by a car. Her room, it's a fire hazard. This can't go on.

Yes, my mother said.

I could see she liked the idea.

We really aren't able to take care of all her needs you know. Much as we love her, I said. Much as we'd like to. And this place, so many sharp edges, those steep stairs.

My mother was nodding.

How I hated her then, her pursed-up mouth, her sucked-in cheeks as if she were constantly posing for a picture. But I needed her as an ally.

We need to put her where she can't do any more harm, I said.

We leaned together, whispering. We did not want my grandmother to overhear us. It would upset her unnecessarily to hear what we were planning. She would not want us to waste money on such a thing, that's what she might say.

I had saved some money over the years from my hospital jobs, it lay in a drawer beneath piles of dull sensible underclothes. I had been saving it for when Jonathan came back, for when we went away together.

But the nursing home was much more important. For my grandmother's own good.

I thought of the apartment without her.

She was the cause of the oppressive, claustrophobic feel of the place.

Without her it would be so much pleasanter. Only me and Nomie, together. Nomie would be sure to listen to me without my grandmother distracting her every minute.

Just me and Nomie. Nomie and I.

And my mother, of course.

I would worry about that later.

For now I wanted only to remove my grandmother. To a better place.

I loved her, I was willing to make sacrifices for her. I was giving up my entire future, my chance to leave this apartment and go elsewhere—all so that her last days would be more comfortable.

My mother, as it turned out, also had a bundle of money hidden away.

From your father, she explained.

My father? She never, ever spoke of my father who had died before I was born. She had never even told me how he died. I assumed it had been something pedestrian, hit by a streetcar maybe, or a sudden heart attack while crossing the road.

We had long whispered discussions, made inquiries. My mother and I were closer than we had ever been, we were united in a common purpose. We heard of a place that sounded promising, I went to visit it. It was not beautiful, a tall stark building, but it seemed very secure. The residents were not allowed to wander about unattended. And when residents became too excited or too loud, they were gently sedated, gently restrained. There was a small cement yard—no messy flowers, harmful insects. I particularly liked the high iron fence.

It seemed perfect, and I wanted to move my grandmother there right away, but I was told that the place was full, and we would have to wait for an opening.

The secretary I spoke with did not say it, but I understood we would have to wait for someone to die.

This seemed inconvenient. I wondered if there were any way to remove this obstacle, hurry the process along.

I wanted to move my grandmother out of the apartment before Nomie came back. I did not want the two of them to have any more time together. It had occurred to me that my grandmother might be telling her all sorts of lies about Chloe, and my brother, and me.

I did not want that.

I told my mother all about the home and we were both satisfied. We needed only to wait.

We sat together companionably hunched over our cups of tea in the kitchen. In the dark front room in the middle of her labyrinth my grandmother sat knitting sweaters. Knitting her brow, knitting her fingers together. I don't know how she found her way among the jungle of furniture; I wondered if she unrolled a ball of yarn as she went in, to help her on the way back. Perhaps she left a trail behind her, the breakfast crumbs dribbling from her dress.

I stared out the window and let my mother drone on and on about country estates, inheritances, precious jewels, royal blood, secret journeys, forbidden love, incest.

I was not listening carefully. What was she babbling about, I wondered. She knew nothing about love. Or incest, for that matter. She had never loved her brothers as I had loved mine.

All this time, of course, we were waiting for Nomie to return. The strange snow kept falling and the city seemed grimier than usual. Darkness gathered at four o'clock, the buildings swayed and leaned threateningly as if they were about to topple over and bury us all.

We had informed the police, of course. There did not seem to be much else we could do.

Just like her father, she was. Going off like that. Impetuous.

When she came back I would make sure she never went away like that again.

Where could she go? She had never lived away from the apartment, she knew no one. Only that boy with little bits of metal embedded in his face like shrapnel. And I had forbidden her to see him anymore.

When she got cold enough out there she would come back. And when she came back I would be waiting.

I will be waiting for you, Nomie.

I will be waiting, sweet one.

Just inside the door.

Nomie

Where did you get this car?

I borrowed it, Vito said.

From who?

I don't know.

You stole it, you mean.

No, he said, it's not stealing. I'm not going to keep it, so it's not stealing. We're just borrowing it for this trip.

The car was wide and slow and dignified. Foam oozed out of the tears in the seat and the floor was littered with newspapers and coffee cups. It was the first car I had ever been in aside from cabs. That made it seem luxurious.

Dawn was just breaking when we left, a baby-pink light in the sky. We drove through parts of the city I had never seen before, that I had not known existed. Buildings rose up with points and curved spires, and gargoyles leaned from the eaves sticking out their tongues. The streets were deserted, metal grills covered the store-fronts. The sun rose bright orange, a ball of fire.

I should have been excited to be leaving the city for the first time. I was setting out just as Ilana had at my age. I would get to see the world firsthand, instead of hearing about it filtered through the stories of other people.

But I did not care, I was cold, I sat with my knees pulled to my chest and stared at the little snow globe stuck to the dashboard of the car, watched the little white bits swirl around in the water. It hovered straight in front of me, as if it were a mirage we were driving toward.

Oh man, I don't believe it, it's snowing, Vito said.

I did not bother to look up.

I can't believe it. In the middle of summer.

I kept my eyes on the snow inside the globe.

Hey, it'll cover our tracks, he said and forced out a laugh.

He was enjoying himself, his eyes still crusted with sleep and a big bottle of soda nestled up against his crotch. I did not ask him how he learned to drive, when he learned to steal cars. I did not care.

We drove over bridges and along dull gray highways. My body felt numb and heavy, a sackful of ball bearings. I watched the snow swirling around in the oval of glass. Inside was a forest, and a tiny Santa, and a little house all cozy and safe.

Are you sure you want to do this? Vito said. Are you sure you want to kill it?

I'm trying to save it, I said.

Save it? he said.

I said nothing.

How could I explain?

I looked at the people in the other cars around us. People sealed in behind glass, like tropical fish in aquariums. As if they would die if the outside air touched them. People seemed so fragile to me suddenly, so easily broken. Not just those people in the cars. All people. Vito, me, the child inside me. Any of us could be snuffed out in an instant. Arbitrarily. Or on a whim. A sudden tug on the steering wheel to send the car flying. A decision made on the spur of the moment.

I wanted to crawl inside that tiny house within the globe and hide, and listen to the waves and white snow beat against the windows.

The town was on the coast; there were neon-lit bars and long low strips of motels. It was like an enchanted city, so quiet, utterly asleep. It was a summer place, and when the sudden snow had come down it had muffled everything.

We walked along the empty beach. Snow covered the sand and the waves were slate-colored and rough. There was an amusement park, deserted, spread out along the boardwalk. We passed by the stalls and shooting galleries, all shuttered. Dingy tents sagged beneath loads of snow. The wooden horses on the calliope wore mantles of white. The rickety framework of a roller coaster loomed above us like a dinosaur skeleton. I was wearing Vito's jacket over my own and still I was cold.

There were faded posters of freaks: Siamese twins joined at the head, a man in a tiger skin and a necklace of skulls, a woman with gills, a man with a long furry tail. An enormous painted clown leered at us from a billboard. Red hair, enormous teeth. I thought of Anya.

We got back in the car and drove to the bar where Vito was supposed to meet his friend. Wait here, he said as he got out of the car.

But I'm coming in, I said.

I'll just be a minute, he said. You can't come, you look too young. You'll get kicked out.

No, I said.

I just have to talk about something with him, real quick. Here, keep the heat on, I'll be right back, I promise, he said and tossed me the keys.

I waited ten minutes for him, then twenty, and then I went in.

It was dark inside, lit by orange-and-blue beer signs and the glow of cigarettes. I could feel the noise from the jukebox pulsing through the floor. Heavyset men sat hunched over tables and the bar, their heads hanging low as if they were too heavy to hold up. I did not see Vito. I sat on a stool and waited.

What you doing here, anyway? the man sitting next to me said as if he were continuing an old conversation. He had a bleary face, three empty glasses before him, a big red porous nose.

Nothing, I said.

You must be doing something, he said.

I can't stand this, I said. People keep telling me things, making up stories and lying, and I don't know what to believe anymore.

Oh yeah? he said, interested, his tongue lolling out of his mouth. I think I can help you.

Really? I said.

He said: You say you're looking for the truth? I'll tell you where to find it.

The music was giving me a headache. Where was Vito?

He said: You're looking for the truth? The truth is in my pants.

He laughed loudly then, and the man beside him laughed, and the laughter was wet and sloppy, it spilled all over the counter and onto the floor.

The friend leaned over toward me, his eyes were little five-pointed stars, spinning, and he said: Maybe it's something you can't quite *put your finger on*. Right?

The first man said: The answer's right there, just reach in and grab it.

They laughed and laughed and though I didn't want to, my eyes kept falling on their pants, coarse ill-fitting pants that were tight in the thighs and lumpy over their crotches.

I heard catcalls, wolf whistles—a whole menagerie.

Then Vito came up out of the dark and I turned to him in relief but he was glaring, his teeth clenched, and he spat out: *I thought I told you to wait in the car.*

We spent the night curled up on the peeling vinyl of the backseat.

I could hear the waves pounding.

Do you want to do it? Vito said, his hands on my shoulder blades. We might as well, he said, you won't have to worry about getting pregnant this time, right?

His breath was sour as old cheese.

Get away from me, I said.

I fell asleep shivering and woke up sweating.

Most of the snow had melted in the night.

He drove me to the clinic. It was a small square white building with shrubs along the front and a crowd of people by the door.

I'll come pick you up in a few hours, he said.

You're not coming with me?

I've got to talk to Russell some more. Just business. He wants me to bring some stuff back to the city for him. Just go in there, ask for Stephanie, she'll help you out.

What? You want me to go in there alone?

The people by the door screamed at us. They held up enormous bloody photographs and spat at the car.

Why are they screaming at me? They don't even know me, I said.

Their faces pressed up close to the window. It was the same face, over and over, men and women, old and young, but the same chanting mouths, same frenzied eyes.

I can't do this, I said.

They're just protesters, he said. Just a bunch of stupid people. Don't listen to them.

I know, I said and looked at them and they were just a mass of movement, an ignorant mob, hardly human at all. I could ignore that.

But then I saw that one of them held a baby and everything stopped. She balanced the baby on one hip, carelessly. She was swept up in the chanting like the rest and bouncing up and down, her fist in the air. But the baby looked at me, he met my eyes with a wide curious gaze. He rode calmly up and down on his mother's hip as if she were a horse on a merry-go-round, his hair ruffled up all over his head. Those eyes held me. He was beautiful. He was shaking his head.

How could I do this?

I can't, I said.

You can, Vito said. It's for the best. And we came all this way.

No, I said. But in one quick motion he reached past me, opened the door, and pushed me out of the car.

They were all around me, shouting in my face. They pressed up against me and held their horrible pictures in front of my eyes, pictures of tiny hands and feet and eyes sealed closed and mouths open in terror. And as the shouting went on and on and hands tugged at my clothes everything blended together til I could not tell the difference between the red sweating faces of the protesters and the hideously enlarged bloody faces in their obscene photographs.

I closed my eyes and someone took my arm and led me firmly and insistently through the red sea. I opened my eyes when it was quiet again and I took a deep breath thinking I was far away from it all but then I realized I was inside the building.

I did not see who had brought me in. I could hear the chanting, very faintly, outside the doors. I could not go back out there just yet.

I would wait a little while. And then go.

In here everything was clean and brisk and efficient. Green tile covered the floors.

I sat in an orange plastic chair with uneven legs.

Who are you here to see? a nurse asked me.

Stephanie, I said automatically.

She's busy right now, the nurse told me.

I sat and waited. And waited. Women came and sat in the other chairs. Some came with men, some came with their mothers. Some looked frightened, but most looked as if they were shut completely within themselves, struggling with a private puzzle that no one could help them with. None of them looked pregnant, I thought.

Most of them were holding their bellies.

I realized I was holding mine and quickly sat on my hands.

I was not like them, I thought. I was different.

The women came and went, but there was one man who sat and waited as long as I did. He had long legs stretched out before him, a windbreaker with the hood pulled up over his head. I could see the cross hanging around his neck, but I could not see his face.

I wondered how he felt, sitting here waiting for his wife or girlfriend or sister or mother.

I wished Ilana were with me. If Sashie were here she would pretend it was not happening, that was her way of coping with things. She would talk brightly about the decor, the artificial plants. The weather. And Mara, Mara would see it all as a plot, a conspiracy directed at her. I think she has always had secret plans of her own, and that is what makes her so suspicious of everyone else. Her paranoia taints her view of everything. One day she will grow suspicious of herself, and she will drive herself mad chasing herself in circles.

Only Ilana saw things clearly. I realized this now. She did not even know my name, but she was the only person who knew me as I really was.

Here's Stephanie, someone said and I looked up to see a woman in white walking down the hallway at the side of a gray-haired man in a white coat with a folder in his hand. I stood up and the man in the windbreaker rose too and his hand came up.

I turned and looked at him, thinking: what is he doing? Who is he greeting? What kind of handshake is that? And everyone else in the room was looking at him too but for a different reason.

There was a sort of spark in the vicinity of his hand, and I did not hear the noise, only the echo which went on and on as the gray-haired man fell toward me, the folder falling from his hands. For a long moment I looked at the ugly red splotches blooming on his coat, like beet soup on a white tablecloth when you spill it by mistake, and I saw the look in his eyes which was not frightened or pained but only surprised.

Then he was collapsed on the floor with blood pooling around him, it pulsed out of him rhythmically, like the rhythm of waves, it bubbled out of his mouth, and I was thinking idiotically: get this man to a hospital! And then: he's in one already, how lucky! There were screams, a flurry of motion as nurses ran to him and the gunman had already disappeared somehow, like a magic trick and I did not know what to do so I ran. Not the way I had come, but down a hallway and through door after door until I found one marked *emergency exit*, and I burst through it to the screaming of sirens thinking: yes, that's exactly what this is.

The sand was wet and the waves rolled in.

The amusement park had shed its coat of snow and now looked more ramshackle than before. You could see the nails and paste and strings that held it all together. Families in small clusters drifted here and there. No one seemed to be controlling the rides, they ran by themselves, their old clockwork grinding away.

The scaffolding shuddered ominously every time the roller coaster made its rounds. The passengers screamed as they flew downhill—not because they were frightened, but because they thought they were supposed to be.

You could see now how chipped and faded the calliope horses were. The music that poured out was painfully off-key. But the children who rode them did not care. They rode shouting, rearing, bucking, rocking back and forth, stroking the wooden manes. In their eyes it all was beautiful.

And so it *was* beautiful.

I walked by the ocean and watched the waves rise up closer and closer. I looked at that dark line where the ocean met the sky, and Ilana was right, it was like nothing I had ever seen before in my life. The meeting of water and air. Like a long thread drawn tight.

It divided but it also joined.

I thought of the man's blood pushing out of him and spreading on the floor. Drops of it had dried on my hands, on my shirt. Dark little dots, almost black. And as I thought of him I began bleeding, as if the sight of him made my own blood want to jump out of my body and join his. I bled and bled, soaking my underpants, first a trickle and then a stream, as if my insides were weeping.

It's my period, I said to a seagull. My period is just late, that's all.

That's all it is.

All this fuss and worry just because my period was a little late, I chided myself.

This blood, it couldn't be anything else but that. Could it?

It could not be the other thing. It couldn't be.

I did not even want to think the word.

Somehow I would not be able to bear it if it was.

Later I saw Vito and some newfound friends traipsing along the beach.

Here you are, he said, we've been looking for you. Is it all done? Are you all taken care of?

No, I said.

Why not?

A man got killed, I said, right in front of me.

No way, he said.

I tried to tell them what had happened. The man with the gun and the blood spreading.

Oh come on, Vito said. You're kidding, right?

Look at the blood on my shirt, I said.

Well, sure, he said, of course, you were in a hospital, there's hurt people and blood and stuff all over the place in a hospital. That's the whole damn point, right?

The men he was with all laughed in an ugly way but I did not look at them, not once, I looked only at Vito.

Come on, he said, admit it. You chickened out. You don't have to make up a crazy story like that to cover it up.

But I saw it all. I was there. It was horrible.

I told them over and over what I had seen but it did not help, no one believed it. They told me I watched too much television. They told me to shut up and grow up and quit crying wolf.

Vito, I said, you believe me, don't you?

He smiled, looked away, dug his toe in the sand.

Get away from me, I said, don't touch me, don't ever speak to me again.

I ran, and he called after me: Aw, come back, Nomie, come have a good time with us.

I kept running, and heard his friends laughing and him, and he called out: That's right, you big baby, go crying home to mama.

Yes, I thought, I will, I will, but not before I'm good and ready.

I ran and my footprints followed behind me in curving and dancing lines, helter-skelter in branching patterns all over the beach.

Something washed up on the shore one day. A dark slumped shape as large as a horse. Seaweed clung to it in great soggy skeins, barnacles clutched at its sides. The waves touched its edges and slid away. Touched and slid. Touched and slid.

I walked closer and saw black hair, an outflung arm. I saw the edge of a face bloated with seawater. The skin was white, mottled, stretched tight. In spots it was scaly, iridescent.

I saw an eye, a brow that I thought I knew. But before I could be sure the waves drove up and pulled him back into the sea.

I had money that I had borrowed (no, stolen) from Mara's drawer. I walked and I ran and I rode buses next to old women who fell asleep with their heads on my shoulder. I went a long way, and I looked all about me, and I saw ugliness and wonders that you would not believe if I told you.

I walked through snow and I sailed on water, and I went down below to the dark incredible colonies where people made their homes in deserted subway tunnels, and I went to another hospital and saw a baby the size of a jumbo shrimp living and breathing with the aid of machines, and I met a woman who had cut off her own foot because she heard voices that told her to do it and she was much at peace afterward, and I saw a child with the eyes of a saint and a head the size of a beach ball, and I saw another man shot and killed, this time for a tiny bit of white powder that everyone wanted because it could give them magical visions and the power to forget everything.

Ilana

I am trying to remember how I met Shmuel. I remember him falling out of a tree and lying in the snow, frozen and cold, his eyes like chipped blue glass and red beads at his throat where it had been torn open.

My son was a beautiful boy. He hung from the fire escape to impress me and could finish off a gallon of milk all by himself. Sometimes we called him Wolf and sometimes Eli, but I cannot remember why we gave him two names.

Yesterday I saw a harpy in the kitchen, a wild-haired harpy just like the ones we used to see back home, circling above the forest. This one was perched at the table, sipping from a glass and tipping her head back to let it slide down her throat. Tearing at the hunk of bread she gripped in her claws. She paused in her chewing to glare at me, and I saw that she wore my granddaughter's face.

But how can that be? The harpies steal faces only from the dead, not the living. And Mara is not dead. Is she?

Perhaps she is dead, and I have forgotten about it.

I have not seen a harpy for so long. They do not come here, I think it is because they have no room to fly with these tall buildings all around. All these shiny, reflective surfaces would drive them mad.

What is my mother's name? Did I ever know it?

There are so many things I cannot see clearly anymore, only catch glimpses of out of the corner of my eye.

I feel frightened these days. I am not sure why. It is not a thing that frightens me, but the absence of a thing. A sense of things spilling, rolling away from me, out of my grasp like beads of mercury skittering across the floor.

I know something is missing, though I cannot place what it is. What could be missing? Everything is right here where I put it: the bed, the chair, the candles, the pot of herbs on the windowsill.

Shmuel still comes and sits by the bed. He tells me not to worry.

But I'm afraid to look at him, afraid I will not recognize his face anymore.

It weighs on me sometimes, this burden of remembering everyone's name. When I misplace a name I feel such panic, as if I had killed someone.

But there are so many names, they are crushing me.

Sometimes I think that if I could share the load it would not be so bad.

Or have I already found someone to share it? Sometimes I think I have.

Other times I suspect it is only wishful thinking.

Sashie

Nomie has come home, thank heaven.

We had been out of our minds with worry.

She had been gone almost three weeks.

She seems fine, perfectly healthy and fine except for her clothes and shoes which were unspeakably filthy.

That was easily mended, I threw them out, bought her some new clothes, but she refused to wear them.

And she refused to speak.

When she came home she said not a word, ran straight to my mother and took her hands, buried her face in my mother's lap. My mother said nothing either, just bent over her and stroked her head, the short bristly hairs.

Nomie will not tell us where she has been, what she has been doing, why on earth she wanted to run away from us like that.

I tried to put my arms around her but I miscalculated and struck her in the face instead. She must have grown, or shrunk, in the weeks she was gone.

Mara and I suspected that she talked to my mother when they were alone, though we were not able to catch them at it.

We did not tell her about our plans for my mother, we did not want to spoil her homecoming.

The nursing home was good news, of course, but perhaps Nomie would not see it that way. She is contrary sometimes.

The other night I cornered my mother alone and told her about the nursing home.

Isn't it wonderful? I said.

It's the luckiest thing, I added, the secretary there just called and said that someone had died! So you can move in right away!

She cried out as if I had struck her.

It's a wonderful place, I told her, all nicely heated, and you'll have a pretty little room with a nice roommate to keep you company, and the nurses will keep their eye on you and you'll never have to go outside. Won't that be wonderful?

Never, she said.

It's what you need, I told her. You don't realize it, but you can't manage on your own anymore, and Mara and I aren't able to do it all for you.

You can't shut me in, she said.

It's for your own good, I told her.

Barbed wire, she said.

I told her she was being stubborn. I told her she was acting like a child.

I know that place, she said. It has no doors.

What are you saying? Of course it does, I told her, they are automatic, you don't even need to touch them, they fly open by themselves, and there are nice ramps for the wheelchairs.

There are no doors, she insisted, I have seen it. And the roof is covered with sticky tar so that when the pigeons land on it they stick fast. They starve to death, the roof is covered with bones.

All this time I was careful not to meet her eyes.

Not even the pigeons escape, she said.

Later I saw her clinging to Nomie and Nomie clung to her. It seemed more urgent than ever that we get her out of the apartment as soon as possible.

When Nomie heard about our plans she broke her silence to scream at us: You can't do this. You can't take her away.

We have to, I told her.

And Mara pulled Nomie aside and said softly: She doesn't know it yet, but she's sick, very sick. She's losing her mind, she has no idea what she's saying anymore. It's obvious. Surely you can tell. It's obvious to everyone but her.

Nomie glared at us.

Mara said: The best thing you can do for her, the best way to help her, is to help us take her to a place where they can take care of her.

I said: It's not like she'll be gone forever. You can visit her there.

No she can't, Mara blurted and then flushed darkly.

Nomie stared at both of us. You can't do this, she said again and fled the room.

After witnessing such behavior from Nomie, Mara and I were more convinced than ever that my mother had to go.

The sooner the better.

I have become more and more convinced that it is the right thing to do.

I know it is. It is for her own good.

And I know that she wants this too.

You see, after all these years I have finally learned how to listen to her, how to hear the truth behind her words. She *wants* help but her pride won't let her admit it. She does not want to admit how weak and helpless she has become, doesn't want to admit she needs the home. So she puts up this vigorous protest, this false swagger. It is all an act.

She says she doesn't want this but I know she does.

Inside she is begging for help.

It's obvious to me now.

And there is another reason why she should go.

I think that moving away will bring her peace, it will help her escape those women she keeps talking about who plague her so.

She keeps talking hysterically about three women who follow her everywhere and oppress her. I thought at first she was imagining them. Now I have finally realized who those three women must be.

Mara. And Nomie. And me.

Nomie

When I came home Mara and Sashie picked and tugged at me but all I wanted was to see Ilana and look in her eyes. I wanted to say that I believed it all. I wanted to ask her to tell me more.

But when I saw her I did not need to say a thing.

She understood.

She reached into her skirt, then, and in her cupped hands she showed me the egg that she had told me about. It was jeweled on the outside, like the ones Sashie had showed me in a museum once. But it had gone all rotten and neglected; the stones were dull, with dirt caught between them, long hairs and bits of lint clinging.

Look inside, she said.

So I looked.

There it was.

Do you see? she said.

Oh yes.

Good, she said and took it from me, hid it away in her dress.

We put our hands together, as we always did, and for the first time mine seemed a bit larger, my fingertips edging over hers, I must have grown. She took her hands away, smoothed them over my hair, again and again. I heard a strange sound.

They're coming for me soon, those three, coming to take me away, she said. I can tell. Each time I see them they come a little closer.

Then she told me about the nursing home.

But I can't go there, she said. I can't be boxed in, those three will corner me for sure.

You can't go in there, I said. I won't let them do it, shut you up like that.

Ilana held my hand so tightly it hurt. I have to go away, she whispered, somewhere they will never find me.

Far away, she said, over the canyons and across the seas. To the very edge of the sky.

And then what? I said.

Then I will pierce right through it, she said, it's only a painted paper backdrop after all.

Are you sure? I said.

More than anything.

Sashie

It's the strangest thing. Yesterday I found a notice that had been slipped beneath our door. The logo at the top and the type were familiar though I could not remember where I had seen them before.

The notice stated that the building management had decided to engage a cleaning service to improve all apartments, at no cost to the tenants. The cleaners would come once a month and in addition to ordinary tasks they would shampoo carpets, repaint walls, and wash windows.

I am thrilled. And this is an especially convenient time for them to come. With my mother moving out, there will be an entire room to be cleared and redone.

I am so excited.

This news makes me forget all our petty little troubles.

Perhaps I will buy some new curtains.

We need to start living in a way more befitting our station, after all. We are not ordinary people like our neighbors; we are of nobler blood.

Some of this furniture might actually be quite pretty, once it's dusted off and arranged properly.

It does seem a *little* strange, though, when I stop to think about it. The management has never taken much of an interest in us before. Our kitchen faucet has dripped for years, and the superintendent repeatedly brushes off my complaints about a rat in the wall.

And it is strange that the notice did not mention *when*, exactly, the cleaners will be coming. I want to know. I want to be ready for them, I do not want them to catch me unawares.

As the day wore on I began listening for them, several times I thought I heard their brisk steps in the street. The rattle of their cleaning machines.

Several times I heard the scrape of a broom in the hall, and swung the door open to look.

Nothing.

Last night I lay awake, eagerly listening to their scuttling, scratching. I heard them coming closer.

Closer and closer.

Too close, perhaps. It seemed they were scrubbing and rasping just on the other side of the wall.

But is it possible to get *too* clean? I don't think so.

They are coming. They are coming.

They do not like slovenliness. I must get up early, set my hair, polish my shoes.

I must be ready for them when they come.

Nomie

Where is she? says Mara.

What have you done with her? cries Sashie.

She can't just disappear like this, Mara says.

You know, don't you Nomie? I know you do, says Sashie.

You helped her, didn't you? Mara says.

Why won't you tell us anything? Don't you want to help? Don't you know your mother could be out there freezing to death in the snow right this second? squawks Sashie, not noticing her slip.

Your mother could be lying under a bus right now, Mara says to me.

They discovered her absence this morning. Her bed made, the room neat. The window open, curtains flapping, snow already piling up on the floor. It is the second freak snowfall of the summer.

They both leaned out the window. She couldn't have made it down the fire escape, not at her age, Mara had said.

The apartment feels different without her. Unmoored. All of us feel it.

I go into the front room and look at the mass of furniture and it is just that, furniture. Nothing more. Chairs and tables and hassocks, a breakfront with its glass broken.

My hair keeps making this funny sound when I shake it, I say.

Mara shouts: Wash your hair, for God's sake. And tell us where she is, you filthy girl.

Sashie says: Don't speak to her like that. It's not her fault mother's gone.

She pauses, glances from Mara to me, and says: Is it?

They pace and mutter in the kitchen, their voices a disturbed cooing like anxious pigeons.

If she does not turn up soon they will have to forfeit her spot at the nursing home, allow someone else to take it.

They keep asking me where she is. They seem to think I helped her, perhaps arranged for a journey.

Could Nomie have done that, they wonder.

It is true that I spent time on the docks, among the sailors and coils of rope as thick as your arm. I have seen those great ships. I have seen deals being made. I have a bundle of money. I know the way.

But I won't say anything one way or the other.

It doesn't matter.

I know she is not coming back.

Mara

Nomie refuses to give up any information. But we will find my grandmother sooner or later. I know it.

We will find her and put her in a safe place.

My mother is useless, fluttering and fussing and pausing every few moments to listen at the window or the door.

Hush Mara, she says with one finger uplifted in her idiotic way.

Do you hear that? she says.

Just the usual noise, I tell her. I say: Actually it seems much quieter around here, now that *she's* gone.

But my mother's face is strained and tense, she is not hearing me at all, she is listening for something else.

I give up on her and go to my room. Here I find a sweater, neatly folded on my bed. How did I not notice this before? It is my grandmother's work, I can tell. I shake it out, hold it up.

Foolish woman. Does she think this one little gift will appease me now, after I've had to endure a lifetime of her selfishness?

It *is* rather nice, though, beautifully soft, the yarn a mixture of black and gray with tiny threads of red and brown running through it.

And it *is* strangely cold today, what will all the snow. I will put it on, not because I forgive her, oh no, only because it is cold and all my other sweaters are packed in the bottom of the drawer.

I pull it over my head but cannot find the neck hole right off. I try to find the sleeves but they must have gotten twisted or tucked under in some way. I pull harder, waiting for my head to pop through the collar but it doesn't happen and the sleeves have gotten turned inside out. The sweater is very warm, a little *too* warm and it traps my own stale breath next to my face.

I decide to start over, but now I can't seem to pull it off. I turn around and the sweater shrinks tighter, pulls in closer.

I suddenly remember the sweater I put on years ago, and how I barely escaped from it with my life.

But I was a silly hysterical girl then. I was imagining it.

I turn about and turn about. The room is full of sharp corners I never noticed before. And the sweater has become so scratchy inside, like a pricker bush, it has little pointed teeth.

It's getting damp now with my sweat. It is too warm in here. Not enough air.

It hugs me so closely now, as if it is a part of my own body.

I think I will lie down on the bed for a minute and collect my thoughts.

I can feel my heart pounding a quick panicky beat.

As if I were actually foolish enough to think I will never get out of here.

Nomie

A little while ago I went into Ilana's room. It was cold, the snow was covering everything because no one had bothered to shut the window. I sat on her bed and was surprised to find her jeweled egg nestled beneath her pillow. I wondered why she had not taken it with her.

I held it in my hands. I thought: it should not be whole, it should have shattered when she left, it should have broken open to let all the wonders inside come flying out.

Then I held it up to my eye and looked inside at the castle and the lake and the darkly sparkling city, and I thought I saw, in among the crowds of finely dressed people, a girl with hair to the floor and a fiddler with his bow raised, and two young men leaning recklessly from windows, and a man the size of a horse rolling over like a dog, and a dozen children clinging to the skirts of a woman who in turn clung to a black-bearded man.

Then I looked again and saw that the egg was empty, the inside surface was all reflective, a curved mirror, and I was looking at my own pupil and inside it a thousand tiny points of light.

She is not coming back.

I remember something she said before she left. I had asked her where she wanted to go, what she would like to do.

She said that more than anything she wanted to lie down in the snow next to her husband, two black marks on a white page.

Acknowledgments

I would like to express my thanks to Reagan Arthur, Leigh Feldman, the Fine Arts Work Center in Provincetown, the Corporation of Yaddo, my teachers at Harvard and New York University, and to all the friends and family who gave their support along the way.

Judy Budnitz

Flying Leap

'I don't know what planet Budnitz comes from, but I'm happy to have her. *Flying Leap* is a tremendous debut – funny, dark, weird, adventurous, slanted and enchanted.'   *Newsweek*

The twenty-three stories in this debut collection provide short, sharp shocks – jolts of recognition, surprise or delight. In her tales of ordinary people in extraordinary situations, Judy Budnitz plays with the boundaries of time and reality, from the young man persuaded to donate his heart to his dying mother, to the girl in post-apocalyptic suburbia whose only friend is a man in a dog suit, to a short history of women contained within the pages of a fall fashion catalogue. Laced with wit and imagination, these stories announce the arrival of a uniquely talented new voice in fiction, a young writer leaping boldly into the next generation of American writers.

'Amazingly original . . . These unsettling stories leave you wanting more.'   *17*

'Stunningly visual . . . Judy Budnitz is terrifically talented. It will be interesting to see how far her own flying leaps take her.'   *Boston Globe*

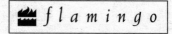